THE THREADS OF THESEUS

MATT LARKIN

The Threads of Theseus
Tapestry of Fate Book 5
MATT LARKIN
Editors: Sarah Chorn, Regina Dowling
Cover: Felix Ortiz, Shawn T. King
Map: Francesca Baerald

Incandescent Phoenix Books
mattlarkinbooks.com

TITAN ERA
OKEANUS
THULE
HYPERBOREA
KELTIA
ILLYRIS
SALON
RASSENIA
MNEMOSYNIA
THRINAKIA
OLMECATL
TARTESSOS
KARKHEDON
KARTH
KEMET
MEMPHIS
TIWANAKU
TIWANAKU
INUMIDEN
OSIRION
THE GREAT VELDT
KUSH
KONGO JUNGLE
HY-BRASIL
KGALAGADI DESERT
AZANIA

KER-YS
XIRONG
ISSEDONIA
NYXLANDS
YAN
WAKOKU
FLAMING MOUNTAINS
JINYANG
ARIMASPIA
APE MOUNTAINS
YINDAI
HYLEAN WOODS
XIANYANG
YAMATO
KIMMERIA
YING
XIAO
PHLEGRA
THENISKYRA
GEBI DESERT
XIANG
KOLCHIS
BO
WANGGEON
THEBES
KOLCHIS
AXEINOS SEA
DANGUN
OLYMPIAN MOUNTAINS
KUNLUN MOUNTAINS
ELLADOS
IOLKOS
PHRYGIA
PHAEAKIA
ILIUM
YUESHANG
DELPHI
THEBES
ARAD MOUNTAINS
BYBLOS
ITHAKA
LESVOS
VYADHAPURA
NUSANTARA ISLES
ARGOS
KORINTH
SKYROS
PHOEBA
KROKYLEA
KRONION
PHOENIKIA
NERITUM
NAXOS
RHIOS
LYDIA
TYROS
HAWAIKI
AEOLIA
HELION
ATLANTIS
KNOSOS
NUSANTARA
ATLANTIS
THALASSA
ALAIA
OGYG
UGART
MUGEDANG
NESHIA
BADIAN STEPPES
NINEVEH
DREAMING DESERT
ASUR
BABILIM
DREAMING LANDS
BULU
BABILIM
KISSATU
RAPAI
DURANKI MOUNTAINS
MU
NYSA
SHALMALI
HUKAG MOUNTAINS
SUMERU MOUNTAINS
TAKHKHASILA
BARBARIKON
PATALIPUTRA
HINDUSH
DHANYAKATAKA
KUMARI KANDAM

THE WHISPER

It starts with a whisper, a haunting intimation of a World askew. That we are, in the end, caught in a death spiral, time nearly played out, whilst entropy tugs ever harder upon the Wheel of Fate.

Looking now into the dying embers, we at last apprehend Truth, and in it the revelation that the vaunted tales of old were not what we thought ... And neither, in fact, were we.

For if we have lived before, might not all we've dreamt be but our souls' memories of Worlds become dust ...

A QUICK NOTE

For full colour, higher-res maps, character lists, location overviews,
and glossaries, check out the bonus resources here:
https://tinyurl.com/hw52dzss

And if you liked this book, be sure to check out my offer for a free
novella at the end.

PROLOGUE

Gloaming Era, Dark Age

*A*s Amirani had feared, Vulgeth had become a nexus of darkness, with Naamah's dark power uncontained. The Archon stirred, and the even the fragile protection of Erlik's Veil could not hold her back forever.

In the twisted woods beyond the city, Amirani stalked among the ruins of an ancient temple dating to better days. Now, vampires ran rampant over the countryside while the Forgotten dug away at the foundations of the World. Everything had skewed and, almost, he longed for the days of Dark Faerie.

This Era, too, was ending, and he needed to both ensure it ended and ensure some remnant of Man could endure. He needed a means of combating the spreading Dark, and he could think of no better option than one he oft mused upon but never allowed himself to pursue.

A risk, to fold into his greater gambit.

They came to him in ones and twos, those few last heirs of the

Adityas, though they had long forgotten their heritage and were now known, instead, as the uriaşi. Men who carried Aditi's blood and, in his pyromantic visions, would one day rise and claim the Mortal Realm as their due once more. They would call themselves Titans.

Vorsanos escorted Kersnik, the last of those to arrive, and the pair of them sat around the pit at the temple's heart where Amirani had kindled a low flame. Great swathes of the roof had fallen in, leaving the place less enclosed than Amirani might have preferred, but it held import and he had no desire to conduct this initiation within the bounds of the accursed city of Vulgeth.

When eight men and women had gathered round the flame, Amirani drifted over to occupy the vacant space Vorsanos had left for him. Reaching towards the pit, he fed a bit of his Prana into the embers. They leapt to life, erupting into a roaring bonfire. A collective gasp escaped from those gathered, and Amirani suppressed a smile.

Even these jaded, battered warriors might find something of awe left in the World. It was a blessing, he supposed.

"In days long gone, I walked beyond the bounds of this world," Amirani said. "I trod in ash-choked wastes and found the source of Fire and claimed it, took it into my breast." He stretched a hand towards the pit, and tendrils of flame leapt from it in spiralling arcs, coiling about his hand and forearm.

Now, two of the onlookers scooted away, one tracing a Zalmoxic sign of warding in the air.

Amirani ignored him. "I stole the First Flame from the Elder Gods, and now, I give it to the uriaşi, that they might break the hold of night that creeps upon the world."

"How?" Kersnik asked.

A wise question indeed, and within his mind Surtr cackled, a sound like ash grating over ash. "It is alive, drawn from the spirits of the burning world. You must learn to walk with such infernos raging inside your breast, as well. To hold their power and not allow it to consume you, though ever will it try. Every breath you take shall be sucked down like scorching winds. Every time you rest, it will writhe against you and seek to become master rather than servant." He looked at each of them in turn, satisfied to see them squirm, for they ought to fear the power he offered them. "Become a Firewalker, and you shall struggle to remain yourself for the rest of your days."

As he looked back across the gathered uriași, the flames caught his gaze. They pulled him, taunting him with the flicker of images. A tower, in the future, where he taught the same skills not to divine-blooded uriași but to *Men*. A swirling miasma of history paraded through his mind, a premonition that he would become this teacher, the one forever bringing Fire to Man, down through the ages of Era after Era.

The import of the moment had him frozen in its grasp and all he could do was stare at the crackling flame. How many Eras would he do this? How many Eras would there be? He couldn't decide whether to take comfort in the thought the cycle endured longer than he'd imagined, or to look upon the unending stream of death in abject horror. What had he begun?

Vorsanos's hand upon his shoulder shook him from the pyromantic trance, and Amirani blinked.

"Holding the Flame within your breast may also serve to ignite the Sight in some of you. It will draw you toward pyromancy as a means of divination, for better or worse. If you pass through this fire, it will change you, body and soul, forever."

"Pass through?" a woman asked.

"Oh," Amirani said, "yes. To become a Firewalker, one walks through fire."

She paled, and others began to whisper.

Kersnik rose, any hint of fear well concealed behind his grimace. "Then shall we begin, Firebringer?"

Ah. That name was going to stick, wasn't it? Amirani looked to Vorsanos, who nodded.

Amirani would use a piece of the First Flame within his breast to draw forth the Fire spirits, pull them close to the Veil, where his students could touch them. His visions had shown him the way, vibrant and painful.

He reached out, letting the Flame deepen. Letting it reach out into Phlegethon, where the caorthannach built the Brass City. They would come, so eager for the chance to take hosts here. He shifted his vision to peer through the Veil and see into the Penumbra. They drew nigh, their cackles carried upon nether winds, felt rather than heard. They were, in a sense, children of Agni, and he had stolen their brother.

A vibration built inside his chest. "You must form a pact with the spirit that comes to you. As you burn, you will feel it press upon your soul. Allow it in, but with reservation. You must retain yourself." And how easy it would be for them to lose it. "I shall lend my own will against the spirit, but you and you alone must bear the brunt of it."

Kersnik looked to him, not backing down. So be it.

Amirani nodded.

And Kersnik stepped into the fire, becoming the first Firewalker of his Era.

PART I

Accepting then that we all exist within a cave and cannot perceive the Ontos—certainly not in its entirety—we may assume our world is but shadows. One must then ask: shadows of what? What is the deeper reality we cannot see? Beyond the physical, there must exist a realm of perfection, the source of the shadows. Here, though we cannot see them, are the unchanging Eide, the Ideals—whence, in fact we derive the term "eidolon"—of all that is or might be. Abstractions with greater reality than the paltry physical shapes.

    — Urania, Analects of the Muses

1

PANDORA

725 Bronze Age

The rolling woods of Kalydon soon gave way to brush-covered highlands of central Elládos. Rugged escarpments and rocky cliffs broke the landscape beneath the cloudless blue sky. The beaten road toward Thebes was a long one, and Pandora and Theseus would need to skirt Mount Parnassus and the Minyan lands before they reached the great city.

Though they had found easy rapport, Pandora noted Theseus had spoken little of himself. Rather, the earnest young man pestered her most of the first day for more tales of Herakles, no matter how much she protested she had not accompanied Herakles on the famed labours that so enthralled the boy. Indeed, Theseus knew more of Herakles's accomplishments than Pandora, even if she knew better than most the demigod's reasons for undertaking such impossible tasks. She had set him upon that path, in offering the hope of redemption through heroic deeds.

Around noon, they paused beneath a fig tree, claiming a few of the succulent fruits from the branches. After savouring the juice from one, Pandora looked to her companion. "How did a young man such as yourself become embroiled in King Oeneus's boar hunt?"

From the way a fool grin spread over his face, Theseus had awaited just such a question. "Want to know my story, then? Ha! Well, I cannot as yet measure up to the deeds of Herakles or legendary Perseus. But give me time, and I swear my name will join theirs when bard songs ring through the marble halls of kings and queens."

For a moment, Pandora considered mentioning she had known Perseus as well. Theseus knew her as Nike, thinking her a Titan, and thus could have accepted she had known a man who lived a century back. But it pained her to think Perseus gone now, and she found herself little inclined to speak on the topic. It had proved hard enough to accept it when she had learnt Herakles was, in fact, Perseus's great-grandson.

Regardless, Theseus ploughed on, unaware of her brief melancholy.

"My mother is named Aethra, the daughter of King Pittheus of Troezen. Were you to say to me you had never heard of it, I would not take offence. It's a small polis upon the Strait of Korinth, founded by my grandfather and named for his fallen brother. It's home to something like nine grandmothers and a seagull, or so I thought as a young child.

"I was bastard born, you see, and—stories claimed—the son of Poseidon, though I later learnt this was, in fact, a tale spread by my grandfather Pittheus. The rumour that my mother had borne a child to an Olympian somewhat obviated the shame she had for bearing a child out of wedlock. But as is wont to happen, the people of Troezen whispered behind her back. How could it not be her fault, they would say, for having drawn a Titan's eye to herself in the first place? Such run the thoughts of the masses. My mother was considered oft to blame for each ill turn of the wind or poor catch at sea. The shameful princess who got herself seduced—or raped, which was all the same in their eyes—by an Olympian and had not the good sense to flee from her home as had Europa or Io or any of the others."

Pandora bit her lip to stop herself from objecting that both women had been abducted and never given the chance to return home. From his bitter tone, Theseus knew all too well the malicious absurdity inherent in blaming the women for plights beyond their choosing.

By unspoken accord, they resumed their trek.

"Well, Pittheus was a descendant of Pelops, the once-great king whose many sons had tamed southern Elládos in days of old." Pelops? Pandora had known a son of Tantalus by that name, a boy dying of a wasting disease. His father had made sacrifices to the gods, and the boy managed a miraculous recovery. The memory of Tantalus further soured her mood. Knowing what she did now, perhaps Tantalus had, in fact, treated Pelops with Nectar. Not that it absolved Tantalus of all he'd done to Pandora.

"So, I was raised by my grandfather and my mother and rarely saw other children. They fled from me, having heard I was a bastard, and that they would taint themselves by my mere society. I played alone, racing through the halls of Pittheus's palace, darting between the marble columns and pretending to hunt monsters in the darkened wine cellars beneath our home. Amid encompassing shadows, I would stalk, silent as a ghost, eager to slay the drakon Python struck down by Apollon or the famed chimera brought low by Bellerophon. Or running, swift as my bare feet could carry me, sand squelching betwixt my toes, I would cast myself as Perseus skewering Ketus, ready to rescue Andromeda."

Rather than look at Theseus, Pandora kept her eyes on the road, the fig dangling from her fingers almost forgotten. It was more than passing odd to hear someone speak of a distant past with such reverence, but regarding events she had witnessed and people she had known. A wistfulness tickled her, and she could feel tears threatening at the reminder of another price of her sojourns through time.

"One day, about a year ago, word came of the return of Herakles, the warrior who had once broken the Minyan king at the head of Thebes's army. The stories told how he rose from disgrace to slay an invincible lion in Nemea, saving a town from its ravages. I was enraptured, not only at having a new hero to emulate, but at the thought that this man, his name hated and tainted, was earning the respect of the masses across Elládos. Surely, I thought, were I to accomplish such deeds, I would escape the scorn of those who named me bastard.

"My mother, Aethra, saw me on the seashore, testing my limits as a son of Poseidon. Convinced I ought to be able to hold my breath for longer than any Man or swim the whole of the Strait and reach Athenai. Mayhap she feared I would drown myself like the misguided fool I was.

"'It's time you had the truth of your birth, Theseus,' she said and bid me walk alongside her. Up the rocky slope we climbed. Until we came to a flat stone shelf, and upon this she sat, her gaze sweeping across the waters. She was looking to Athenai, I think, and imagining what events must have unfolded there. On a smaller rock, I perched beside her, sensing that she would speak when she was ready.

"Time dragged on. I took to watching distant gulls, her promise of a tale of my past almost forgotten by the time she spoke. 'It was sixteen years ago when King Aegeus came to call upon my father, an old friend of his. In his cups, he confided that he feared his brother, Pallas, who had fifteen sons, whilst Aegeus remained childless. Both were of the line of great Pandion, and Pallas's sons had a worthy claim to the throne, should Aegeus fail to produce an heir. So desperate had Aegeus become, he told your grandfather that he believed he must marry again, in secret, unbeknownst to his wife.'

"Mother had my rapt attention then and looked me deep in the eye. I remember ... her hazel eyes seemed almost aflame with the orange flecks sometimes found in the Kreiad genos. 'My father had recently received a prophecy from an Oracle,' Mother said. 'The Oracle told him that I would not marry well, at least not before the eyes of Man, but that my son would earn fame enough his name would echo among the immortals.' You can imagine, of course, Goddess, how much pride swelled at hearing such a prophecy hung over me. 'So,' Mother said, 'my father told me I was to marry Aegeus in secret.' I imagine that my mother was not overly pleased to learn she could never reveal the truth of her marriage and would thus live in infamy the rest of her life. But if she resented it, she never told me nor let on.

"She fell silent a moment more, then rose from the slab upon which she had rested. 'After we had spent a few days and nights together, Aegeus brought me to this very spot and told me he must leave, return to Athenai, and see to his throne. With strength I could not fathom, he hefted this stone and beneath laid his burnished sword and his fine sandals, and said to me that, should I bear a strong son, when he is old enough to retrieve these items, I should tell him the truth of his heritage. Aegeus claimed that by this sword alone would he know his heir. So, Theseus, you are not the son of Poseidon but of the king of great Athenai. And if you can prove yourself worthy, perhaps you can save your father and his line. This is the duty he laid upon you before your birth.'

"I cannot say whence came the strength to heft such an enormous slab of rock, but somehow I found it within myself. Heaving, drenched in sweat and muscles protesting, I raised it enough I could slide it over my shoulders, snatch up the items, and get clear before it came crashing down once more. My mother never needed to ask whether I would go to Athenai, for she knew the glory offered there was all I had ever sought.

"Given what she had said of Pallas and his sons, though, I knew I would need more than mere birthright to save my father's claim to the throne. I would need to arrive having first forged my own legend. Like Herakles, I swore to undertake labours that would spread my fame across Elládos, such that my arrival would forestall any treachery the sons of Pallas might intend."

The road had dragged on, and Pandora could not quite say when Theseus had fallen silent. His tale had left her entranced, walking whilst scarce realising time passed. Theseus was a son of the king of Athenai. He was thus a descendant of Athene, Pandora's own granddaughter. After quick calculations in her head, she judged Theseus was probably some twenty or twenty-five generations removed from herself. The Moirai's frightful Tapestry seemed woven of such hopelessly entangled threads, she could scarce fathom the scope of it.

"Thus, you joined the hunt?" she asked.

"Oh," Theseus said with a grunt. He cracked his neck. "Not right away. There was more between here and there. I first would imbrue my father's sword with the blood of murderers and thieves."

ONCE THEY HAD GATHERED FIREWOOD, with the setting sun drenching the hills in honeyed gold, Theseus resumed his tale. "Leaving Troezen, I took to wandering the less trodden roads that cut through Elládos. I passed through villages and towns, seeking tales of bandits and beasts, intent to make my name. I heard first of a supposed descendant of Hephaistos himself—I do not know if the rumour held truth—who was said to waylay travellers who sought to trek between Thebes and Korinth. This man, one Periphetes, carried with him a great club of iron which, according to the villagers, he would use to pummel to dust all who came before him.

"I admit to a *small* twinge of doubt at the thought of facing a possible demigod in combat, having never before slain a man. But Ananke had thrown such an opportunity before me, and thus I could scarce spurn it. With somewhat hesitant steps, I followed the road, taking my time and making every effort to seem carefree. I had not the finery to seem wealthy, and certainly no chariot or horse to carry forth such a facade, but it seemed such mattered little to Periphetes.

"One moment, I was walking along, eyeing some ominous dark clouds rolling in over the horizon. The next, a slavering madman was racing at me from the woods beside the road. As the villagers had warned me, he bore a club with a head of spiked iron, the dried blood upon it giving the metal an almost black look. No words did my attacker speak, and I scarce had time to draw my father's sword before he was upon me.

"All my play at heroism amounted to naught then, staring down at death approaching. Countless afternoons in the fields, training with a wooden sword, it availed me little. I remember … The teeth in his open, shrieking maw were brown and splintered, his gums black. Why that detail should stick in my mind when so much else became a blur, I cannot say. I dodged away from his wild overhead swing, and his club smacked into the dirt where I had stood a moment before.

"Heart pounding, I danced aside, suddenly finding my xiphos, however fine, became paltry in light of the superior reach Periphetes's oversized weapon gave him. His next swing came whooshing at my head, a vicious horizontal swipe. Had I moved a single breath slower, it would have splattered my skull. But I dropped to my knees and the club sailed overhead. On instinct alone, I rammed my xiphos into his gut.

"Hot blood gushed from the wound, coating my arm, slicking my fingers. There was a stench of copper and shit that cut through even my own terror and shock at what I had done. The sword was so wet, it slipped from my trembling hand, and Periphetes stumbled backwards several steps before slumping onto his arse. He dropped his club as he did so, his hands clenching around my blade still wedged in his bowels.

"His eyes …" Theseus paused and swallowed. He grunted something incomprehensible.

Pandora gave him time, turning her attention to skinning the rabbit Theseus had caught that afternoon.

The young man glowered and cracked his neck. "I think he was even more shocked than than I was. Like he couldn't believe someone had actually challenged him, much less slain him. And I could see such agony wracking him. My heart was still hammering with such fervour it had become the only sound I could hear. But somehow, it seemed fitting to end him with his own blood-darked club. So, I took it up in both hands and drew nigh, and he made no effort to flee. Maybe he knew all he could hope for now was a swift death. With an overhead blow, I crushed his skull as he had done to so many others.

"I didn't sleep that night. Kept seeing his face. Those vile, rotting teeth. That awful, reeking wound. Most of all, the pain and fear and surprise in his eyes. Killing him wasn't quite as it sounded in the songs."

Pandora frowned in sympathy before spitting the rabbit and setting it to roast. "Few things are. Bards make it sound so glorious, deeds of valour and battle. They never mention that you spend most of the time ready to piss yourself. They don't tell you what it feels like to see a soul slip from its mortal sheath and know you have done that from which there can be no return."

Theseus steadied himself. He poked at the fire, probably for something to keep busy. "I was, uh … was caked filthy with his blood. All I could think was to wash the stain of it from me. Dazed, I wandered. Don't know how long. But I was walking toward to Strait of Korinth, thinking to wade into the sea. Hoping to cleanse it all from me.

"When I drew nigh, though, I heard a man screaming, begging for mercy. I darted toward the sound. Was that bravery? Or was I still too befuddled by the violence I'd just committed to even know what I was about? I crested a low hill and beheld a man, his arms bound to the top of a pine tree bent almost double, his legs chained to a stone. A rope had pulled the tree into an untenable shape, and another man was beside it, sniggering as he sawed through that rope with baleful relish. One slow, shallow pass of his knife at a time.

"Once that rope snapped, the tree would spring back into position, tearing the man's victim in half. I could not have imagined a more painful—or terrifying—end. Something came over me. A desperation to deny such atrocities by any means. I snatched a stone from the escarpment and, without another thought, hurled it at the villain. I don't recall yelling, but in my fury, I must have, for the bandit turned toward me an instant before the rock would have connected with the back of his skull. Instead, he took the blow between the eyes, staggered a single step, and pitched over backward.

"With all the speed I had ever managed, I raced toward the victim, certain the fraying rope would snap on its own before I reached him. It held, however, and with my father's sword, I cut the bindings that held him to the tree. 'Zeus Almighty!' he cried, tears of relief and lingering terror slurring his words. I moved to check the bandit and found my blow had slain him already.

"Thus, in the space of a day, I had killed two men. Was this not the very aim with which I had set out? Was this not the glory I had sought after with such fervour? The bandit—I later learnt his name was Sinis, called the Pine Bender—had on him keys to the fetters that bound his victim to the rock. Even as I unchained him, the tether upon the tree snapped. The pine lurched upward with a creaking roar, showering the pair of us in its needles. We both sat there, gaping, looking at it as it swayed back and forth before settling. I could not help but imagine the effect such power would have had upon a man. I'm sure the one I rescued felt the same.

"When he embraced me, weeping openly by then, and promised to offer sacrifices to the gods in my name every year for so long as he should live, only then did I feel my resolve once more quicken. In his broken, shuddering gratitude, I knew that, in taking the life of those two monsters, I had saved many others. I still wanted fame, yes, for my own sake and for my father's. More than that, I began to understand what I think must be the true reason behind Herakles's labours.

"So, I gave him my name, and I left him. Washed the blood from body and clothes. Travelled on. Later, I met a woman, Phaea, who told me of an enormous pig rampaging in Kalydon. By this time, I had heard tale of Herakles having slain the hydra, as well, and I knew a calling had come upon me. And there, hunting that boar, I met the man himself. And you, Goddess."

"Stop calling me that," Pandora insisted. "Titans are not gods." Nor was she even a Titan, though a Heliad, and thus surely descended from Titans.

"As you say, Lady Nike."

Pandora sighed and removed the rabbit from the spit. "And you will continue down this path? Seeking out conflict?"

He nodded and accepted a chunk of meat she tore off. "Until such time as my name is joined to Herakles and Perseus and the others, I shall. When I've claimed the fame I need, I will return to Athenai and come to my father's aid."

He was so very young, she thought. But it was clear Theseus would not be swayed. Was it his will and nature that guided him? Perhaps. But Pandora could not help but wonder if the Moirai had not wrapt their threads around his neck, as well. They were, all of them, caught within the weave of the Tapestry.

2

ARTEMIS

725 Bronze Age

From the tree line, leaning against an oak, Artemis saw when Prince Meleager sliced his sword across the throat of her beloved Orion. Or across the neck of what remained of Orion, his flesh now transformed into the obscene, glorious hybrid of Man and boar, his soul squelched by the cyclopean will of the ancient Boar God. She knew, in seeing her lover choke on his own blood in his final moments, she ought to have been wracked with utter horror. Disbelief and defiance ought to have warred within her soul, and she should have raced forwards and used the staff she bore—the very same that had first bound the Boar to Orion—to stave in Meleager's offending skull.

Yet Dionysus's soothing caresses thrummed inside her, a whisper of assurance. It promised that all transpired as it must. There was sadness, for certain, and anger at what this Man had done. But the God had promised her that his was a long game, one still playing out upon the very face of the World. Dionysus wove with the loom of the

Fates themselves, and one such as Artemis could not but bend to his awesome will.

"Atalanta shall have the hide," she heard the prince proclaim. "For she drew first blood."

Not even Dionysus's tendrils of power within her soul were enough to quite suppress the shudder that tore through her. To think that her adopted daughter would unwittingly claim the skin of her foster father as a prize evoked such disgust she took a step forwards to put a stop to the blasphemous turns of Ananke.

Not yet.

Dionysus's command came not in words so much as a compulsion, one crawling up from the base of her own mind. She was meant to let play out these events, and she could not act against the will of God.

So, she watched as Meleager argued with his uncle, the fool man insisting upon denying any prize to a woman. The pair of them scuffled, and Artemis was little grieved to see Meleager's uncle impale himself upon the prince's sword during the struggle. The prince rose, dropping his sword, aghast at his own actions. As though his victim had not well deserved his fate.

It's coming.

Once more, it was not Dionysus's *voice* in her mind. Rather a foreign intuition that crept upon her and bestowed certainty unlike she had ever known before. Meleager toppled over sideways.

"Meleager!" Atalanta yelled, Artemis's daughter racing to the side of the prince so clearly besotted by her.

With the instinct bestowed upon her by the God, Artemis knew what transpired. The entity that had previously taken Orion now crept inside the flesh of Orion's murderer. The Boar God was not a being of flesh and blood but of Ether, given form in the Mortal Realm only when it *stole* such a form from unwilling hosts. The spirit had preserved Orion's body for a short time, before Meleager had ruined that flesh a second time.

She knew, with intuition granted through her bond with Dionysus, that the Boar God would rise once more, wearing the flesh of

Meleager. That its rage would never end. It would tear through the gathered hunters with the force of a tornado. Should they slay it once more, it would take another of them. Maybe, given time, someone would overcome the Boar God, but she imagined half of Elládos would be charnel before that happened.

But such was not the will of Dionysus, and hers was not to question why he had let the creature rampage for a time and now sought to curtail further slaughter. She wanted to ask, if he thought to bring down the Olympians, why not use the Boar God to carve a path all the way to those lofty slopes? She wanted to push the God for clarity.

But Maenads were meant to serve. The plans of God lay beyond the scope of the minds of Men or Titans.

She felt the tendrils of his will guiding her forwards, the butt of her staff clacking upon the rocky ground as she moved. The hunters saw her and parted around her passing. Whilst Nike and Herakles tended to the stricken prince, Artemis's daughter fretted.

The girl's distress cut through even the sense of destiny that gripped Artemis. How could she bear the suffering of one she named her own child?

"Atalanta," Artemis whispered, laying a hand upon the girl's shoulder.

Nike looked up, met her gaze.

Sunder the Boar God's connection with this Realm.

Artemis hefted the spiralling staff over her head and flooded Pneuma into her limbs for Potency. Even so, it took a momentous effort before the wood snapped. As it broke, vestiges of Otherworldly power trickled unseen over her fingers, fine as tickling dust. At once, Meleager ceased his convulsions.

Vertigo swelled over Artemis, and she swayed, kept on her feet only when Nike rose and caught her arm. Once, long ago, she had called Nike a friend. Her mind felt clouded with haze, but she remembered that. That had been when Nike fought for Zeus, the foe of the great God. Did that make her an enemy now? Artemis desperately hoped otherwise. Breathless, she mouthed the other woman's name.

Her daughter flung her arms around Artemis, offering her weeping gratitude for saving the prince. The man Artemis would have rather liked to have slain himself for what he'd done to Orion. She turned to gaze back at the corpse of her beloved. Surely he would willingly have given his life in service to glorious Dionysus, had he known of the God. The Boar God was gone from Orion now, and only his broken body remained.

She wanted to weep for him but found herself unable to do so. Perhaps that tendril of God's power in her soul kept such indulgent emotions from overflowing. So she told herself.

Nike grabbed her arm and pulled her away before Artemis had managed to gather her thoughts, much less her strength. Breaking that staff had taken something out of her, that was certain. When they stood alone in a glade, Nike forced Artemis to meet her gaze. And she saw the accusation there and could not look for long.

"You called this thing here in the first place."

Unable to deny the accusation, Artemis offered a single, slight nod. She had wanted to punish the whole of Elládos for taking Orion from her. She knew she had felt that wrath, at some point. And Dionysus had come ... and ...

A fog was in her mind. She needed more of her God's soothing Bacchic wine to ease her worries and still her churning thoughts.

Cruel, petty Eurystheus had forced Herakles to go for the hind in service to his own vanity. As if Herakles was better than his father. As if any of the Men of this land deserved aught save her wrath.

Abruptly, Nike stroked her cheek. The warmth of such a touch shattered Artemis's dark musing and cleared a patch of the haze drifting within her mind. The Men of Elládos worshipped the Olympians, true, and Artemis had her grievances with both them and their gods. But was not unleashing something like the Boar God sheer madness? She had participated in rampant slaughter for the sake of chaos.

"I'm sorry for ..." Nike began, then paused when a tremble shook her. It was hard to cling to anger when the other woman so plainly understood her. Cared for her. "For all the iniquities of Fate and the World."

It almost broke her. Only the return of Dionysus's touch cut through her growing confusion and returned the clarity of purpose she had almost lost. Nike was Zeus's ally. Such precluded her being Artemis's friend.

"I need to find Hekate," Nike said. How could it be the woman would not know Hekate was gone? Lost for centuries and, mostlike, never coming back. "Do you know where she is?"

"I have not seen her in long years." But the God, too, sought after Artemis's former friend. Hekate was too great an ally to Zeus, and she too would have to fall for the Olympian order to crumble and the World to be set right.

Nike nodded, her disappointment plain. "We ... have to make the future we want." The woman seemed almost stricken by her frustration, like it stole the breath from her.

Artemis could have laughed at Nike's statement, did it not so sting. "We can speak such words with practiced ease, Nike." No, Zeus's ally, all his allies, remained oblivious to the truth, of both God and Ananke. "The World is not so accommodating."

"Then make it accommodate." A slight pause. "But not like this. You are better than this."

Was she? Nike had once more cut through the comforting connection Artemis held to her God. She could have hated her for that. Could have loved her for it. Artemis fell back and bit her lip. She let her face fall into her hands. She needed Dionysus's strength. Oh, Thoth, she needed to flee from this hold he had upon her! "Find Hekate, then. There is a ... danger pursuing her, I think. A force that means her ill."

"What force?"

Artemis shook her head. Even now, her God would not permit her to name him to Nike. Her tongue refused to answer such a question with aught more than obliqueness. "Something Primordial, I think."

Nike nodded as though Artemis's useless warning might have offered the least aid to her. "Go with care, my friend."

But staggering, weakened, and lost, Artemis was left to wander.

NIKE and many of the other hunters had gone, making their way to the roads that called to them. Prince Meleager returned to his home, taking Atalanta with him, and his mother the queen held a feast in his honour. Oh, how that rankled, to see the wretch hoisted high after his slaying of Orion.

The haze in her brain had Artemis lurking on the fringes of town, slumping in alleys to snatch desperate bouts of fitful sleep. Her God crept ever into her mind. Each time she closed her eyes, his fingers brushed her temples. His invisible lips kissed her neck, her back, her breasts, teasing forth an aching need in her.

She must return to him. She must drink from his sacred wine once more and thus restore her flagging confidence in her deity.

No, she told herself. First, she must attend to Orion.

Atalanta had not seen the corpse of her foster father, so intent was she upon making her way to her paramour's bed. Artemis alone had buried her beloved. So how could she abide the happiness of his killer?

The World convulsed, unsteady beneath her feet, as she wended through the halls of King Oeneus. Despite her condition, it proved little challenge to conceal herself from the slaves and servants who bustled about in preparation for the hero's feast Queen Althaea now hosted. Some saw her and dared not question the presence of a Titan. Others she slipped around, clinging to the shadows, though she needed to brace herself against the walls to keep steady.

Return to your God ...

The summons thrummed through her flesh, calling forth an answer from her body. Artemis pressed a hand to her brow in hopes of pushing down the rising pressure betwixt her eyes. Without the quenching grace of Bacchic wine, her tongue felt parched by desert sands. Without the touch of God upon her body, her every breath ravaged her tortured soul.

In moments, the doors would be thrown wide, the guests welcomed into Oeneus's hall, and hateful Meleager heaped with praise and glory for Orion's death.

Slaughtered like a pig before the butcher.

Did the thought come from Dionysus or from her own anguish?

Artemis slapped a hand against a marble column. Why in Tartarus could she not weep? How she longed for that release. What a palliative it might prove if the dam within her could break. But no matter how she beat against the walls of her heart, they refused to crack. Her traitorous sentiments did not permit her true grief, only anguish.

Thus, dizzy and dripping with chill sweat, looking not the least like an Olympian, did she come to Queen Althaea's chambers. Had the servants seen her, hunched as she'd walked, they might have taken her for a drunken aristos rather than a Titan. But when the queen looked to her, Artemis summoned the last reserves of her will to stand tall. Artemis was a Phoebid. A daughter of Helios, yes, but it was her descent from Phoebe that shone through, and which Men might recognise in her.

Return to the prurient embrace of God's arms ...

For a moment, the queen's eyes widened, and she opened her mouth as if to call for guards at the intrusion. Recognition dawned though, and Althaea dropped to her knees. "Goddess Artemis."

"Your brother fought against the Boar of Kalydon."

Artemis had the sense that, had Dionysus wished, he could have tightened his leash about her and tugged her back to him at any time. He permitted her this vengeance. Even God understood the need to avenge wrongs done to one's loved ones.

"He died there." Strain thickened Althaea's voice. The feast would honour the fallen almost as much as it did her victorious son.

"Yes," Artemis agreed. "But not by the tusk of any boar. Rather, upon an iron blade he fell."

"W-what?" Her obeisance forgotten, Althaea was on her feet at once.

Artemis's legs threatened to give out from beneath her. She needed to return to Dionysus. She needed the Bacchic wine before she collapsed in upon herself, reduced to a simpering heap of useless flesh. "Your brother was struck down by your own son over a petty quarrel about the spoils of victory. Whilst you honour Meleager, your brother's unquiet shade squirms at the edge of the Underworld."

Artemis suspected such was even true. How could the man not begrudge his nephew for his death, even if it had been an accident?

Blanching, Althaea staggered backwards, bumped into the hearth, and slapped a hand over her mouth.

Artemis allowed herself a sigh of relief. It would not be a happy feast for Meleager.

3

HEKATE

1576 Silver Age

Stone grated, dust spilling upon Hekate's face even as the pale candlelight cast blinding flashes into eyes that knew only darkness. When her vision returned, a grey, desiccated face greeted her, the red gleam of its eyes making plain its wretched nature. The flesh-eating creature that the Kumari Kandamians called a preta or ghul. A revenant, though not in possession of any corpse, Hekate had to assume.

The ghost backed away, allowing Hekate to sit, gasping down reflexive gulps of air. Beyond the preta, holding a second candle, stood Persephone.

Painful hope lanced through the resigned, maddening horror that had gripped her, and Hekate turned about, searching every dancing shadow for Hades's wraiths.

"I couldn't leave you here," Persephone whispered. The wan light cast her face in ominous chiaroscuro, but Hekate would always recognise the girl she had considered a third daughter. Denied Ambrosia, age had begun to work its cruelties upon her. A wonder, in fact, now that Hekate considered it, that Persephone had aged so little in the two centuries since her abduction.

Hekate tried to climb from the sarcophagus, but her legs gave out. Though she had no physical flesh, it seemed even her soul expected cramps after being so long confined. The preta caught her arm, keeping her from slumping to the ground.

"This is Melinoë," Persephone said. Demeter's daughter stepped in to wrap her arms around Hekate, the ghost falling back in silence. Hekate returned the embrace, her relief at escaping that box so great she could not force out words.

Melinoë had fallen back to the threshold, peering into the gloom, and Hekate, too, found her gaze continuously darting about, searching for ambush.

"Melinoë is my daughter by Hades," Persephone admitted when she at last released Hekate.

Mind reeling from imprisonment, Hekate didn't know how to begin to process that. Ghosts, being dead, had no capacity to seed or carry life. Her grimoire indicated some ghosts could transmogrify into living spirits, though. Had Hades managed this? Or had he conceived through some more profane exercise of his momentous power?

"I came to get you out," Hekate rasped, forcing herself back to the more pressing situation. "I can get us back across the river."

Persephone's mouth quirked in a sad smile. "He always believed you would try." Wait, was this a trap? Hades had known she would attempt this? "Only his arrogance in thinking you beaten allowed us to reach you now. Hekate ..." Persephone's weak smile could have broken her heart. "I am dead. Once I had borne him Melinoë, I ... I took my own life in a vain hope of escaping this place. Of course, I should have known better. He had always planned to kill me before my beauty vanished entirely."

Her words bludgeoned Hekate. Beat her to a bloody pulp, left her gasping for air, unable to find her voice.

"And even could I have left," Persephone continued, "both of my children are ghosts."

Both. "Zagreus," Hekate fair growled that name.

"Hades has corrupted his mind, but still, he remains my son and I cannot turn my back upon him anymore than you could abandon your children."

Hekate had thought she *had* come here for one of her children. "How is it that Zeus's son serves Hades, while Hades's daughter is willing to betray him?"

It was Melinoë who answered, her voice hollow and echoing with disdainful mockery. "Whence comes Hades? From a world where even a dead cock places man above woman."

Even in death? Of course. Why would Hades become more magnanimous in such a place than he'd been as a prince with all the world's bounty dropped in his lap? It took but a moment to apprehend the whole of Melinoë's plight. Hades had gone to some lengths to sire a child and rejected that child on seeing it female.

Another question loomed, however. One Hekate had never been sure how to ask, but one that demanded an answer. "How could … how could Zeus father a child on his own daughter?"

Persephone's face held oceans of shame and answers beyond words. "He really wanted … said it would be nice, just once, to bond us closer."

Aghast, gut churning in disgust, Hekate held up her hand lest the girl continue. Another word might have broken her. She could not hear this. Not *this.*

"He has some plan for Zagreus," Persephone said, "though I know not what. He's been hoarding souls toward some momentous undertaking. Some means of revenging himself upon my father." And Hekate almost wanted to see Hades succeed now. Even the King of the Dead seemed less vile than the King of the Living. "Maybe vengeance upon you as well."

Yes, well, that sounded somewhat less pleasant. Hekate had earned Hades's ire, many times over.

The desperate compulsion to condemn Persephone for allowing

herself to be seduced almost overwhelmed Hekate. Only, Hekate too had made her share of mistakes, and many had paid the price for them. "I won't leave here without you."

"You have to. There's naught you can do for me, Hekate. My body turned to dust more than a century ago." Resignation painted her face and strained her voice. "Melinoë can help you escape Kek."

No, no, no. She had come so far, endured so very much. Had sought for centuries to find a way to save Persephone from this fate.

"I will remain here," the girl said, as if Hekate's thoughts were writ plain upon her face. "I have my children. I endure."

Hekate wanted to scream. To beat her fists against the walls in denial of her utter failure. Most of all, to destroy Hades for the suffering he had wrought. The agonies he had visited upon Persephone. Anguish that, in the end, came back to Hekate and Zeus.

Had she come here ... to *fail?*

But another thought swirled up. A hope that had before seemed impossible, but maybe, here in this place ... "Hades has dominated his wraiths with his will."

"Yes," Persephone said.

"If I could wrest their wills free, they might turn on him."

Already, the other woman was shaking her head. "He has gorged himself upon souls for centuries. You cannot overcome him thus, Hekate. Mostlike, he intends to kill you, let you become a wraith, and bind you as well." She allowed herself a mirthless smile at the thought. Wouldn't it be amusing, when Aeshma showed up to claim its due? "Your only chance lies in escape before he realises you are free. Flee, and never return to the Underworld."

Was it petty vengeance against Hades that forced her to refuse? She wanted to believe it loyalty to reclaim her lost friend. "Perhaps I cannot overcome his will and free them all. But I will strip him of one in particular. I will find Keuthonymos. I owe him as much."

"You didn't come here for him," Persephone protested.

"I *should* have. I should have long back, and I aim to rectify it now."

Melinoë took a step toward her. "I can help you find the wraith.

But I cannot reveal my perfidy in front of it. If you fail, my actions would be reported to Hades. Father would see me suffer without end for daring to thwart his will."

Hekate offered a grim nod. "Just get me to Keuthos."

MUCH THOUGH SHE strove to keep her gaze upon the gloomy halls ahead—faintly illuminated by pale candles set into periodic alcoves—Hekate could not stop herself from casting surreptitious glances at Melinoë. Persephone's daughter had endured in death having never known life. The ruination of her Etheric body came not from deterioration of flesh, for if she had ever possessed any, surely it had withered soon after her birth. How she had managed to evolve into this semblance of a grown woman, Hekate could not fathom. Most ghosts, so far as she knew, did not age past their deaths, maintaining such an image of themselves as last they perceived.

Perhaps the answer lay in the bitter truth that Melinoë had not lived long enough to *have* a self-image.

"Do you judge me?" the ghost rasped.

Hekate managed a bitter snort at that. Who was she to judge anyone, living or dead? "I am a sorceress. I have traded my own soul, piece by piece, for ephemeral powers. When at last I perish, I shall *envy* you the existence you now endure."

A rock-hard grip seized her bicep and twisted her around, forcing her to meet that incarnadine gaze. "Envy the misbegotten reject enslaved to her father's schemes and yet still seen as naught but a shadow of her brother?"

The ghost's pain wriggled beneath the surface of that glowering dead face. A veritable sea of torments, the greatest of which came in the rejection of one who ought to have treasured her. Who had bent the laws of reality to sire her, then cast her aside when she did not fit the image of the son he sought.

Why was it, no matter how broken one's parents, one forever sought their approval?

"I will see you freed of this." The words slipped out, unplanned, and no doubt ill-spoken. How could Hekate hope to keep such a promise? In Hades she had created a monster she could no longer hope to control. Cosmic hubris had prompted her to think she might create a king of ghosts bound to her power. That she might murder a man in the most horrific way imaginable and not transform him into a blight upon the cosmos.

All the evil wrought in the name of Hades's madness, of his vengeance, fell upon *her*.

And thus, she refused to withdraw her claim. That promise hung in the air between herself and the ghost, Melinoë's rubescent eyes searching for hint of deception. She would find none, though. However long it took, Hekate resolved, she would see Persephone and her daughter freed from Hades's grasp.

With a grunt, Melinoë released her, then plodded down the corridor. At last, she paused before a wide subterranean chamber supported by stalagmites carved into skull-covered pillars. Candles set within the columns cast wavering green light, teasing out the shape of this place. Rents in the floor, some ten or more feet long, opened into black voids that might well have pitched into the limitless depths of the Roil. Fell, howling winds whispered up from those chasms, carrying with them the scent of a decaying bog.

Melinoë pointed toward an opening on the far side of the chamber. "There, it feeds."

With each step this way, the terror of the wraith had tightened her chest further. Anticipation of reclaiming her friend failed to cover the dread of what this creature could do to her. Sorcerers sacrificed so much of their human emotions. Not fear, though. There was always fear. The worry that all those spirits casually enslaved would come for vengeance. The dread of impending damnation. The unease inherent in touching the Realms beyond, knowing one ventured into predator-filled waters. Unless she missed her guess, even the maddest of sorcerers, those who had perceived darker truths of the World and lost themselves in revelations—quivered in the depths of their broken souls.

In the end, maybe, sorcerers were the only ones who realised just how much there *was* to fear in the dark.

Whimpers greeted her as she threaded a narrow path between rents. The fraying final gasps of a soul being devoured within the alcove had her clenching her jaw. Did spirits utterly destroy the souls they consumed? No mortal could ever be certain, but deep down, she feared not even that fate would spare her from the demonic reckoning ahead.

Though she tried to keep silent, could not hear her own sandals upon stone over the dwindling sounds of screams, a sudden hiss from the wraith announced it—he—had sensed her presence. Like a fog spilling from an icy peak, Keuthos wafted into the chamber, the fraying ends of his shroud billowing about him, vanishing into the darkness.

Hekate had not attempted a contest of wills with a wraith, much less with one controlled by ... whatever Hades had become. Most necromancers would have named vying against such a ghost suicidal madness. Perhaps it was. Much too late to turn back now.

The wraith drifted close until Hekate's flesh prickled at the presence of the turbulent Dark nigh brushing against her. "Hekate ..." Keuthos cooed, the sound a mind-flensing caress. A promise of unspeakable agonies wrapt in seductive allure.

At the same instant the wraith launched itself at her, shroud flying up to encircle her like wings, Hekate punched her hand into its chest. Her necromantic abilities pierced Etheric flesh, fingers wrapping around the still heart that yet served as the core of Keuthos's abraded soul. Even so, his impact drove her down, spilling her onto her back. Skeletal claws dug into the left side of her cheek, her flesh desiccating and weeping as bits of her essence bled away.

Screaming. Shrieking at the unnameable agonies of having her life sucked out, even as that shrouded face leaned close, allowing the chaotic void to scrape over her.

With the sum of all her will, Hekate grasped Keuthos's heart. She remembered the Hyperborean boy she had met in Byblos, in the Lodge of Whispers. Young and fair, and so innocently lusting for her.

She remembered the long days and long nights in the Empty Desert. A thousand, thousand conversations, the best of which led nowhere and amounted to naught. Or perhaps those nights led in slow spirals to the very hearts of the two young sorcerers, before they had lost themselves.

She remembered bitter words in Helion.

"You do not know the path you follow ... I would help you if I could ..."

How right he had been back then. How right about everything.

Even his death at Kratos's hands fell upon her, for he, the loyal fool, had tried to shelter them from the Ouranid League.

"I'll keep you by my side from this moment forth," she had promised, only to have him snatched away, throat crunched beneath a Titan sandal.

"Come back to me," she pled.

More of herself, of vestiges of her humanity still lingering, began to fray. Intangible pieces of her core bled into the air, sucked down by the wraith. Agonised convulsions wracked her.

"Keuthos!" she wept, fingers digging into the ashen mass of his heart. Within, she could *feel* the seething Dark, the moil of Khaos that had so warped her friend. "Come back to me."

There, a gossamer fetter had encircled that heart. A manifestation of Hades's hold over Keuthos. Or, at least, her perception of that manifestation, her mind projecting it as a chain. All she had left in her she poured into tugging upon that chain. Along the tether, Hades's sudden awareness shot through her like a current, desperate to hold taut his necromantic bindings. The so-called God of the Dead was not fast enough though, not against one who knew Keuthos so well, who had spent so much time with him as a man she could reach those last, threadbare fragments of his soul.

A snap lashed against her as the chain broke. An instant of blinding pain that drowned out all sensation. When sight and hearing returned, she blinked and found Keuthos now standing over her, his shroud wrapt tight about his head and torso, though still billowing about the ground.

"Impossible ..." he hissed.

"I wasn't going to leave you," she said. Speaking felt like crawling face-first over shattered ostraka.

"I cannot believe it worked," Melinoë said, now trudging into the chamber.

At least Hekate could take comfort in the abundance of confidence the pair of them held in her.

She spared a glance for Persephone's daughter. "Come with us."

A single shake of her head. "I will not leave my mother."

Which Hekate had known already.

"We must ... move ..." Keuthos rasped. "He will be ... coming to reclaim ... his servant ..."

Hekate's knees threatened to give out beneath her as she tried to rise, forcing her to catch herself on her hands. Nyx, that had taken all she had! But Keuthos was right. If Hades reached them, he'd kill her and reassert his claim over her friend.

Teeth gritted against pain and exhaustion, Hekate managed her feet. "Lead the way."

THE UNDULANT LANDSCAPE of the Roil flowed before them, a path leading down to the River Styx and, she dared to hope, their egress from this nightmare. With Keuthos's guidance, Hekate had found a secret route out of Kek, one that had deposited them in the mountains.

The wraith's words now, though, had her twisting about to gape at the silent billowing of his tattered shroud, imagining what his visage —if such still existed—must have looked like beneath it.

"I would *never* bind you to my will," she insisted, "neither inside my body nor through evocation."

"And yet ... you will not ... provide a body ..."

"My body is on Sarpedon, Keuthos. I don't exactly have a fresh corpse lying around."

"Because ... you never ... intended to ... come for me ..." Though the wraith's voice susurrated like the wind, somehow he had instilled it with the crack of a whip. A well-deserved rebuke, for she had failed him these long centuries, without doubt.

"I didn't know how to reach this necropolis," she protested. "I didn't even know *which* necropolis to find you in until I met Zagreus." Her excuses sounded weak, even to her own ears.

Her only answer was an irate hiss. Rage and pain made him impatient, she knew. After an age of torment, the wraith scarce dared to image even the small reprieve he'd find in returning to the Mortal Realm.

But she'd spoken the truth—she would need to arrange a dead body for him to claim. Doing so might allow him to return as a revenant.

Careful of her footing, Hekate resumed her descent toward the river. Hades would be seeking them, of course, so they could afford no further delay. She'd made it only a dozen paces when her sandal skidded over obsidian that turned slick beneath her heel. An icy grip on her flailing wrist kept her from tumbling face-first down the incline.

"Thank you," she mumbled.

When she had her footing once more, Keuthos released her.

As they drew nigh to the river, she glanced at him. "Can we afford to wait on the ferry? Won't he know we must come this way?"

"Mostlike ... he does not yet realise ... we have escaped the city walls."

The wraith's supposition did not offer so much reassurance as Hekate might have wished.

Perhaps he realised it. Perhaps he saw the danger. "Along the shore ... lies another dock ..."

Hekate peered along the tenebrous bank of the river. Onyx protrusions rose from an amorphous, malevolent landscape that would make passage along it treacherous and slow. Even if Hades had not learnt they had left Kek, he soon would, and his remaining wraiths would come for their souls.

Yet down the river, she saw no sign of Kharon's ferry. Indeed, might the creature know they had betrayed its master? Too many questions, and she just didn't know—

A burbling in the waters drew her eye an instant before water spilled down a rising form, lithe and naked. Matted dark hair seemed to merge with the black waters as the feminine shape arose, her skin tinged grey-blue and, beneath her ribs, broken by hints of ebony scales.

"Styx?" Hekate gasped.

Opalescent eyes met her own, nictitating, hinting at alien thoughts swirling beneath the surface.

Baring sharklike teeth, Styx lurched upward, a waterspout flinging her from the river to land upon the dock. As she flew, Hekate thought that, within the dark waters, she saw a hint of a fish tail, though when Styx landed, it was on legs. Albeit legs marred by more dark scales.

Somehow dead Styx had become a mer. "Submit," Tethys's daughter cooed, voice deep as the river whence she'd emerged. Her words thrummed through Hekate's skull, making her knees wobble and her head bow. The request seemed so reasonable, after all. Why should she not prostrate herself before this river goddess and offer due obeisance? Why should she not cease her struggles ...

She did not see Keuthos move, but she heard the wraith's sibilant hiss and the mer's answering growl.

As if a veil had fallen away from her eyes, Hekate could see once more, could think and behold. And wonder at how Styx had managed to affect her mind with the Voice. Could she attribute it to her exhaustion, or did the mer truly hold such power that her enchantment would work even upon Hekate?

Either way, Styx fell back now, the mer dodging swipes of Keuthos's skeletal claws. The wraith moved fast, shroud flapping, disguising his strikes. Styx hissed as Keuthos connected, fingers lacerating her abdomen. Even so, the mer managed to get a hand upon the wraith. Her blow sent him stumbling toward the river. Black waters surged to meet him like a rising fist. They smacked into Hekate's companion, and Keuthos vanished beneath the turbulent dark.

With a growl, Hekate launched herself at Styx, drawing upon Potency. The mer spun, baring teeth, but Hekate's punch collided with the same spot in her stomach that Keuthos had rent open. Her hand punched through scale and flesh. Her fingers wrapt around guts. A savage yank pulled Styx's entrails out.

Sparing a glance at the waters, she caught sight of Keuthos splashing ashore, his shroud now plastered against an emaciated form. One lacking substance beneath the ribs, so far as she could tell.

Desperately clutching her insides, Styx crawled toward the refuge of her river. Hekate stepped around her, positioning herself betwixt the mer and her escape, and knelt. "You know," she said, meeting the mer's gaze, "I never liked you. Your taunts and jibes tormented a young girl who might have seen you as an older sister, had you been less of a bitch. But the wheel turns, and those who tyrannise oft get their due." It was hard to make out emotion within those pupilless eyes, but Hekate fancied she saw the delicious flicker of fear within. "Still. I might have forgiven, might have let go ... Had you not raised a brood even more spiteful and depraved than yourself."

Those eyes widened.

Hekate seized Styx's slimy hair and dragged the wretched mer toward where Keuthos now knelt, caught in tremors that left his form flickering as if it might break apart and be drawn into the Dark of this place. Something she'd not allow.

"Did you know it was your own brutal child, Kratos, who murdered Keuthonymos?" Hekate asked. She flung the mer before the wraith. "Crushed his throat beneath his sandal." She kicked Styx in the neck, allowing herself a malicious grin at the sound of crunching vertebrae. Flapping gills seemed to gasp for water from which to draw more air. "Take her soul," she said to Keuthos. "Restore yourself."

The way he skittered over the prone mermaid evoked images of Kemetian scarabs swarming a carcass. A sodden shroud concealed whatever macabre display might accompany the devouring of a soul, but even beneath it, Hekate saw a thrashing that abated all too soon. When the wraith rose—flowed upward more than stood—all that remained of Styx was a desiccated husk that had already begun to sink into the land.

"The ferry ... comes ..." Keuthos said, facing Hekate and making no comment on what they had done to the mer.

Maybe there was naught to be said. Either way, it was past time to quit the Underworld.

4

ATHENE

716 Bronze Age

$\mathcal{H}$erakles had vanished. Athene had searched the breadth of Elládos for him and found little trace. He had not returned to Thebes nor to his ancestors' territory of Mykenai, though Alkmena and Iphikles had gone there for shelter. Her son had not visited Korinth or Argos or Delphi. Athene had sought for him in the waters, desperate for even a fleeting glimpse that would tell her that, somewhere, her boy yet lived.

And she had found only the emptiness of her unquiet mind.

He'd slain his children, and then he'd disappeared from Gaia.

In the end, she had resolved to make for Aiaíā. She had smelt Nectar in Herakles's home, though she had believed that Kirke had given over creating that poison after her exile. Some three years back, she'd called upon her sister, and though she could not deny the sorry loneliness that had claimed Kirke, Athene had thought perhaps the isolation might do Kirke good. Her sister was always the type to need time to herself, and her perverse alchemical pursuits had wrought so much harm. When Kirke had seen her upon Aiaíā, she had devoted herself instead to her gardens and her pets—strange as keeping a pack of wolves as pets might be, Athene could not judge—and her reading and meditation. She had sworn she was done with Nectar, and Athene had believed her.

It was a quiet life, but Athene dared hope Kirke might flourish in it until, one day, Helios relented and released her.

But then Herakles had clearly been poisoned with Nectar. Had he taken it with intent? Had someone dosed him with it? Either way, for the brew to be in his home meant Kirke was still making it. It meant she'd lied to Athene about abandoning such pursuits. And Athene would have an answer of her sister for that. Her poisons had burnt away Herakles's children—Athene's grandchildren—and stolen futures.

In Athenai, as she bartered passage to Helion, her father came to her. Athene most oft travelled in disguise, relying upon the glamour Prometheus had taught her to avoid drawing attention. Zeus revelled in attention, drinking the fear and worship his passage engendered like honeyed wine. Men and women cast themselves from his way and dropped prone in obeisance and the hope the King of Olympus would not take offence if they had not moved with sufficient haste.

Arms folded over her chest, Athene watched his approach. How had he found her? Her glamour, which presently cast her as an ageing merchant's wife, disguised her even from Titans, and Father lacked the Sight to have predicted her presence. But Zeus made straight for her, removing any doubt that he knew her when he looked upon her.

He towered over her on the cobbled walkway before the harbour, looking down at her eyes with a sneer on his face. "Dispense with this charade, Daughter. I'll not have my stomach turned by staring at the pock-marked visage of a peasant whilst we speak."

Of course, half of Athenai now watched them. Most had never looked upon the King of Olympus in the flesh, but statues to him bedecked the whole of Elládos. Even had they not recognised his face, his Titan height and imperious khiton would have made plain his status.

Athene grimaced, but he'd not left her much choice in the matter, and so she allowed the glamour to fall from her in a sheen. Onlookers gasped at the sudden change, her full height revealed, her attire no longer that of a merchant's wife, but rather a traveller's khiton that left bare her arms. Her one affectation was a spiralling golden armlet, a gift her father had bestowed upon her years back, one which she'd not been able to bring herself to cast aside.

His gaze alighted on the object a moment. "Well, at least you bought something of worth for yourself."

Bought? Athene worked to keep her face impassive. He did not recognise the armlet? It had been a prize he'd granted her after she'd won a battle against some Phrygian Titans who'd challenged Olympian supremacy in Athene's youth. Whilst she'd hardly worn it every day since, he must have seen her with it a thousand times in the centuries that followed. Clearly, the gift of his favour had meant far more to her than it had to him.

"Now," he said, dismissing further pleasantries. Father grabbed her by the elbow and dragged her close. "Long years you've languished in the cold mortal wastes, Daughter. Long enough to have, one might dare to hope, learnt the graveness of your past mistakes."

Keeping any expression from her face took effort. "That would be fair to say, Father." Though she would not have called her time wandering the Thalassa World languishing. Away from the influences of Olympus, she had, if aught, flourished, able to bloom without the stifling politics and self-indulgent whims of her brethren to hold her back. Freed from the influences of her youth, she liked to think she had found her way to her true self and her true calling in helping mortals to elevate themselves.

"Sufficiently chastened, then," her father said, giving not the least impression of having followed her line of thought. He waved his hand as if to dismiss the whole of the past seven centuries. "Consider then your banishment henceforth abrogated. Get yourself to Olympus." His eyes opened a hair too wide, as though a ghost had blandly strolled the harbour, yet when she looked, all she saw was the gathered throng watching them. "We have much to speak on ..." He leant close in a conspiratorial whisper. "The gossamer threads of Ananke wrap round our necks."

Some twenty years back, when Herakles was still a babe, she'd encountered her father, and he'd demanded answers about what her Sight had shown her. Though he'd misliked it, she'd had no good answers for him. Time, it seemed, had not alleviated his desire for insight as to the shape of Fate. Athene did not look forward to whatever conversation Zeus thought to have with her on the subject, though she was glad he'd not deigned to discuss such weighty matters here, amid gawkers and shouting fishmongers and squawking seagulls.

"I've something to tend to first, Father."

His face darkened, a storm forming inside the depths of his ice-blue eyes. "Then be quick about it. I have a pegasus with me. Once it has taken you to attend to your business, present yourself at Olympus. Do not keep me waiting long."

Such a command left little room for argument.

ON BACK OF the pegasus Father had granted her, a speckled brown mare with grey-tipped pinions, Athene flew to Helion. She rested the mount and took her own repast in the hall of Helios, dodging his questions about why she had not come calling in centuries. She might have told him that the same gilded palaces that had once thrilled her now struck as opulent to the point of obscenity. She might have accused him of sitting upon a throne of gold whilst much of the population of his poleis struggled to earn enough drachmae to buy bread. Athene had not held society with him, or any Titan lords, in an age, and would not have done so now, either, had time not felt so pressing.

Such things she might have said.

But she held her peace. Men called her a goddess of mysteries now, she knew. Was that, in part, because she had learnt when not to speak, whilst so many Titans spewed forth every excremental thought that crossed their sybaritic minds? Maybe such was the source of Prometheus's reputation as one so unfathomable even to other Titans. Her grandfather knew too well how to ward his thoughts and keep his own counsel.

After she had rested, she came to reclaim her steed. When she had asked, Father had claimed the mount had no name. Athene assumed, rather, he did not care enough to know what the Olympian stable hands had called the animal. Neither did Athene have a means to find out that name at the moment.

She stood in Helion's stables, watching the Heliad king's stableboy brush the pegasus with frantic urgency. "Be at ease," she said, moving to the animal's side and stroking her wings.

"Sorry, my lady. Didn't know you'd be back so soon, is all. I just finished watering her and she was hungry, like she hadn't eaten in a fortnight." The boy abruptly stiffened, like he'd just realised his words might be construed as criticism toward a Titan.

In truth, Athene couldn't be certain that her father had cared for the pegasus. She recalled many a time when Hera, who considered herself head of all beasts upon Olympus, had chided him for acting like pegasi were disposable. But Father saw his own intentions, whatever they may have been at the time, as far more pressing than any earthly need an animal might have for water or rest. Had Athene herself once acted with such callous disregard? She was fair certain she had, and it brought a flush of shame to her cheeks.

"Take your time," she told the stableboy. "It's no fault of yours." She continued to stroke the animal's silky feathers. The grey in those reminded her of gathering clouds threatening an afternoon drizzle. "Nephos," she said to the horse. "I shall call you Nephos."

The pegasus whinnied and shook her head in what Athene decided to take for approval.

When Nephos was cleaned and saddled, Athene gave the stable hand a drachma, mounted the mare, and rode her out onto the field beyond the Helion acropolis. A gentle press of her knees, and the pegasus intuited her intent. She broke into a trot, picking up speed before her wings lifted them airborne.

THE TEARS CAME AGAIN, unbidden, as she flew, and Athene scrubbed them away, telling herself it was but the chill wind stinging her eyes.

Why had she even bothered heading to Aiaíā? What did she hope to gain by confronting her sister over Herakles's affliction? The Nectar he'd taken had forced him to his action, of that she was certain. Like so many of Kirke's workings, the drug was a blight upon Gaia. A curse upon Athene's son.

She landed Nephos alongside the Pithkias River and left her to graze and take water. Athene's first time here, she'd come into the port village and needed to call on Eos to learn the details of where Kirke's estate was located. Helios's sister had sent a messenger to show Athene to the river and told her to follow it inland, toward her old palace. She had claimed then that she did not like to look upon her former home, though she had not said why.

The estate in which Kirke now lived had once belonged to Eos, as governess of this island, and to her husband. But they had let it fall into decline, and when they gave it to Kirke, they had left her no servants to help with the manse's upkeep. Now, its weathered walls had become a mirror of Kirke's own withered soul.

Oh, Athene had felt such sympathy for Kirke, banished here. She'd had papyrus scrolls sent from Athenai when she could, had visited as time allowed, though the voyage by ship took weeks. She had ... cared for Kirke, had embraced her as a sister. And Kirke's wretched alchemy had destroyed the child Athene loved with all her heart.

Why, then, should she not sweep in here in a rage and scream her wrath at this woman? Why should she not kick in the door and shatter the amphorae Kirke no doubt kept well stocked with too much wine? Let her sister feel a taste of Athene's agony?

Yes, she wanted to do it. But she was not that person any longer, and she would not let Kirke drive her to such engulfing rage. No, let Kirke justify herself, if she could.

Kirke's wolf pack snarled at Athene's approach, forming around her and yet keeping a wary distance. Perhaps they sensed the rage that simmered beneath her surface.

Having no doubt heard the growls of her pack, Kirke appeared from within her manse, face concerned. "What happened?"

Athene paced up to the portico's edge. The house beyond her sister was dark. But then, that mostlike meant Kirke had been working in some secret workshop, brewing her illicit creations. Athene could not stand to even look at the woman. "I thought you had stopped making Nectar."

"Yeah, I was banished here for it, but I just couldn't give over. These days, I sell only to salmon and deer. They don't pay so well, but if they balk, I can always eat them. Which, you know, I never did with my other clients. I mean, because I'm not a Gígas." When Athene at last looked to Kirke, her sister had steepled her fingers as if she could push away her guilt. "Yeah ... I'm not. Which you already know."

Even now, Kirke jested? Even *now*?

"Do I seem amused to you?" Athene imagined her fist breaking the other woman's jaw. Just because one did not intend to act on a violent impulse did not mean indulging in the fantasy held no satisfaction.

"You know, sometimes it's hard to tell with you." Kirke's voice had lost its humour.

But she had not the right to anger. No, this day, that right belonged to Athene alone.

At last, Athene lifted her gaze to look into Kirke's golden eyes. "My son choked on your poisons, Kirke. It stripped him of his mind, and you cannot begin to imagine the horrors his madness wrought."

"I ... I haven't left the island in fifteen years, Athene. I don't make aught like that, I have not for so long ... I cannot imagine how Herakles—"

Athene held up a hand. She could not stand to hear more from

Kirke. What had Athene possibly hoped to gain in coming to this island? Something fled from her then, like a great wind had swept away all her wrath and left only an empty hollow. "You should have stopped doing this long before now."

"Aught I made would have lost its potency years back. I swear, sister, I did not—"

"Don't call me that. A woman whose works destroyed the life of my son has no right to name me sister." Because the wind had stolen that too. It had whipped and whirled. And it had smothered the warmth that had arisen between her and Kirke.

There was no more familial comfort here.

There was no more rage.

There was just ... emptiness.

"I ..." Kirke began.

But naught she had to say mattered anymore. Athene turned from her, the woman she had called sister. Fresh tears stung her eyes. Grief for what had been betwixt them, Athene thought. For surely that bond was dead.

It was buried in the dirt of Thebes, alongside her grandchildren.

Athene walked away and left a stranger behind her.

5

PANDORA

725 Bronze Age

The road toward Thebes had presented Theseus with further bandits upon which to test his mettle, and Pandora had deigned to allow him the chance, playing at the helpless damsel, though her Phoenix abilities could have overcome most threats. The self-proclaimed King Kerykon challenged Theseus to a pankration match, and, upon learning the so-called king strangled those he defeated, Theseus decided to repay him in kind.

As they neared the cliffs of Thebes, they met a man with a reputation for kicking passersby off the precipice. Pandora winced at his screams as Theseus hurled him toward the same fate into which he had cast so many others. However much these men deserved their deaths, still, the violence left her feeling tainted, as though she had waded through a mire and could not wash the filth from her limbs.

More, she mused in silence on how many of such men had seemed to crop up in this Bronze Age. Bandits and pirates had always plagued trade routes, yes, but considering Theseus's stories and all she'd seen, it felt as though the chaos had amplified. Men grew quicker to prey upon one another, slowly filling whatever void was left as the Olympians dwelt longer and longer upon their isolated mountain.

Had the predations of Titans alone served to curb the darker inclinations of Man?

Such were her thoughts when, at last, Thebes drew into view.

Given the time she had lived in the Theban palace with Prometheus and Pyrrha, Pandora's return carried the flavour of a long-awaited homecoming. The city had changed, of course, with passage of time. And yet, she knew well the six gates that led within the great defensive wall. She knew the twin rivers flanking the polis and the mesmerising falls that pitched from the northern river over the seven-hundred-foot cliff on which Thebes sat.

"Zeus's majesty ..." Theseus swore as they made their way along the path into the West Gate, its dust packed hard by the passing of innumerable sandals over the years. "It is a glory, is it not? Here, Herakles served in the army of old King Kreon, thwarting the Minyans. And before the South Gate, Oedipus—now king himself— he overcame the Sphinx in a contest of riddles." Contest of riddles? That was the first she had heard of it. A reminder of how much history continued to unfold around her, even as she leapt through it in great bounds. At times, the Moirai's Tapestry seemed infinitely complex.

"I don't suppose you know how to reach Kolchis?" Pandora asked as they passed into the city proper.

"No, Godd—" Theseus cut himself off. "No, but I've resolved I shall accompany you there once we find the way."

"Wait, what?" Pandora drew to a stop in the middle of the street and spun upon her companion, heedless of the grumbles of those forced to wend their way around her. "Why in Hades's dark domain would you want to do that?"

Theseus shrugged. "A worthy way to build my legend? Besides, it seems clear you could use the aid. Kolchis is a land of legend—and, some say, sorcery—scarce known to mortals, and if even you, Lady

Nike, cannot say how to reach it, then all the more reason you should have my aid."

Pandora had told him little of her reason for venturing to the fabled land of Kolchis. Certainly not that her daughter had, in a dream, called her there, much less that her daughter was the feared Titan goddess of sorcery herself.

In truth, whether she agreed with his reasoning or no, having a companion along on the trek did appeal. "In tales, Kolchis lies somewhere beyond the Axeinos Sea," Pandora said. "Some say it was founded by Koios in the Golden Age, possibly after some spat with his wife Phoebe."

Theseus motioned for her to follow, and they passed from the main breezeway—where standing still was beginning to earn them glares from the foot traffic—into an alley beside a cobbler's workshop. "That's as it may be. Bards' tales as I heard them say that, for centuries now, the Titan Aeëtes has ruled there. The songs claim he and the whole of his brood are steeped in foul sorcery. None may approach his lands save with his blessing, for the Axeinos Sea is plagued by man-eating birds."

"Birds?"

"With talons like iron and beaks like bronze. They say the monsters can hurl razor-sharp feathers at their prey before they swoop down upon the unwary."

Pandora huffed. "I'm not going to be able to find a captain to sail me there, am I?"

That drew a snicker from Theseus. "If you did, he would have to be cut from a cloth of legend."

As THESEUS HAD PREDICTED, Pandora found no one willing to barter for passage to Kolchis, nor even a single sailor who claimed to have laid eyes upon the fabled land, at least none whom time had not greyed and wearied. Only a whisper, a rumour that, without a charm of blessing from King Aeëtes, there was no means of surviving a crossing of the Axeinos Sea.

They could trek the wilds of Phlegra and Kimmeria to skirt the sea's edge, but tales claimed such spaces were home to Gigantes and chimeras and Gaia alone knew what else. Too, came the tales of man-slaying Amazons that, if true, would mean travelling with Theseus would prove problematic. Or they could sail to Ilium in Phrygia and make way over the vast trackless steppes and wastelands.

How had Hekate even reached the legendary polis? Pandora's sorceress daughter must have known secret ways, even if Aeëtes had not provided her some token of blessing.

"I say we make for Iolkos," Theseus said. "It lies almost upon the Axeinos itself, and perhaps from there we can find one brave enough to chance the voyage."

And Pandora had little better option before her.

PANDORA FOUND passage aboard a Theban vessel bound not for Iolkos but Ilium. It was almost enough to have her considering the overland trek through Phrygia, hazardous though it seemed. Either way, Ilium would put her close to the Axeinos Sea and thus nearer to her daughter.

Whilst the crew prepared the ship to get underway, Pandora leant upon the gunwale on the trireme's upper deck, watching the city, though in truth she paid Thebes little mind. Her thoughts buzzed like a swarm of bees, flying from one suspicion to the next. The shadow of an unnameable dread flitted along her periphery, tightening her chest and forcing her to focus upon one breath after another.

Pyrrha had invited her to Kolchis, yes, but not with the warmth Pandora had always sought from her daughter. Along the route to Thebes, she had rehearsed and discarded oh so many arguments to try to sway Pyrrha from her path into unleashing the nightmare future Pandora had beheld. But Pandora knew better than anyone that the ouroboros of Ananke was slippery, worming its way where it willed, both in spite of and because of the attempts to sway its course. She had not yet, in all her frenzied flights through time, succeeded in altering the Moirai's frightful Tapestry.

History is merciless, Prometheus would say.

But there was ever so much at stake now.

"Herakles!" Theseus abruptly shouted, hopping up and down and waving his hands in the air.

Pandora followed his gaze to spot the demigod, along with his nephew, scrambling to make the ship before it shoved off the pier's end. Behind them, too, came others from the Kalydonian hunt: the Tethids Kastor and Pollux and the one Atalanta had called an Oracle, Amphiaraos. And two more men besides. One was the Kroniad—Telamon, she thought—the other she did not know.

What strange weave of Ananke should have brought them all together once more, and so soon?

Herakles and his company boarded—the captain glowered at the delay but was scarce going to leave them behind—and soon, Herakles himself spotted her and climbed to the upper deck. After clasping arms and exchanging pleasantries with the demigod, Theseus departed to attend to the others still below.

That left Pandora alone—as alone as one could be on a ship—with Herakles, and the hulking demigod leant on the gunwale beside her with a great huff. That lion pelt still dangled behind him now, not worn because of the day's heat. "I'd not thought to cross our paths again so soon," he said. "Everywhere I turn, though, I find you waiting, Nike."

"The Moirai weave all our threads with little regard for our intents." The ouroboros ever tightened its coils.

Another snort. "You, I think, they have special intent for."

Special intent or special torment, Pandora could not say. "How come you to Thebes, Herakles?"

The big man grimaced, not answering at once. The ship's crew shoved off the pier, and Pandora watched as three rows of oars splashed down into the azure waters of the Aegean Sea. "Kreon no longer reigns in Thebes." The demigod left unspoken that, if his former father-in-law had yet ruled here, he'd have not dared show his face in the polis. "Catching a ship here was a matter of some expedience. I am tasked with new labours, Nike." His voice still carried that haunted timbre, and she could not help but think he spoke also to someone besides her, someone she could not see.

Was there some hint of madness in him? Once, Pandora had disdained Herakles for his crimes. Now she had spent too much time in his company to despise him. Pity, though, she would have offered him in heaps and piles, would he have accepted it.

His great, rolling shoulders shook with a tremendous sigh. "Eurystheus has heard tale of vicious birds that prey upon voyagers over the Axeinos Sea. He tasked me with slaying as many as needed to make passage upon these waters safe for Men once more." Grimacing, Herakles now looked to her. "And when his daughter, the Princess Admete, heard I would venture nigh to the lands of the Amazons, she demanded I retrieve the legendary golden girdle of Queen Hippolyta. Some say it was a present to her from her father, Ares himself."

So, he had been assigned two labours at once. Both nigh to impossible, and one impossibly vain and petty. Clearing the sea of monsters might have appealed to Herakles's desire for redemption. Pandora doubted he much appreciated being sent to steal a belt.

Pandora tapped a finger upon her lips. "Did you not tell me Eurystheus had forbidden you to take aid on your labours without his permission?"

"Iolaus and the others?" Herakles glanced in the direction of his nephew. "Do you recall the Kroniad hunter, Jason?"

Pandora nodded. She had not caught the name of every member of the hunt, but she never forgot anyone she did meet.

"It seems he had his own tale to tell. After we departed, he announced himself as the lost prince of Iolkos, a descendant of Aiolos." Herakles managed a hint of a grin at her raised brow, though he could not have guessed she had known Aiolos in the days of Perseus. "He came to the hunt seeking out worthy companions for an even more treacherous undertaking than the slaying of that boar, if you can believe it. To claim his throne, the sitting king, Pelias, has demanded he venture to far Kolchis and claim the fabled Golden Fleece, the great treasure of King Aeëtes. He calls upon all those seeking to make a name for themselves in what he named the greatest undertaking of heroes in our age."

Kolchis, again. Did the Moirai dangle this opportunity before her?

It was hard to miss the ironic bite of Herakles's tone. For him, who took every action in the name of assuaging guilt for his crimes, it no doubt sounded a fool's errand. But then, if Jason was indeed denied his home, perhaps he was justified in taking any steps before him to reclaim it. Few things mattered more than home and family. For her daughter, Pandora would cross the perilous sea. For her loved ones, she would continue to cross the vast expanses of time.

"So Kastor and Pollux wished to recruit myself, and the seer Amphiaraos—he's of their polis—informed them where to find me and Iolaus. Thus, we make first for Ilium, and on to Iolkos. Jason and the others made sail out of Argos and no doubt will reach Iolkos first. If he can indeed give us a ship to reach Kolchis, I suppose I must be on it, since I can trek from there to Themiskyra."

"I am also bound for Kolchis," Pandora said slowly. "And I suppose that means both of us must be on that ship when it sails."

6

HERAKLES

725 Bronze Age

$\mathcal{A}$s their trireme made for Ilium, Herakles stood on the deck beside Amphiaraos and his father, Oekles. The young Tethid seer seemed lost in thought, gaze locked upon the clouds as they drifted across the cerulean sky. Or perhaps he looked to the far distance, where hints of grey smeared the firmament, presaging rougher weather ahead.

"... A young man needs a wife to tether him," Oekles was saying, though Herakles had only half listened to his prattle. "Beyond the need for heirs, I mean. Talaus is kin to the princes, Kastor and Pollux there"—he pointed to the princes of Argos where they lingered talking to the captain—"and thus, his daughter Eriphyle ought to make a fine bride for my boy. Don't you think?"

Herakles grunted. "Do they fancy one another?"

Oekles turned to look askance at him. "What matters that? No, they've never even spoken, though she's fair enough to look at if that's your worry."

It was not, but Herakles doubted Oekles would have understood the point he strove for, no matter how long they belaboured it. In the shadows around the ladder to the lower decks, the shades of Herakles's children watched him, judging. Always judging.

"Eriphyle is a proper princess," Oekles continued. "Refined and well-manner—"

"Oh, fuck Poseidon's scaly arse!" Nike blurted.

Oekles seemed to choke on something, flushing and averting his eyes.

The goddess rushed up to the gunwale where Herakles stood, grabbed him, and pointed into the distance. There, beneath the cliffs forming the shore of Phrygia, a woman stood, naked and fettered to the rocks, such that the waves lapped at her shins. From this distance, Herakles could not make out her screams over the noise of the sea, but terror was writ plain upon her face.

"Poseidon?" he asked, not looking away from the woman and her plight.

"One of his favourite forms of sacrifice, I think. He tried it with Andromeda and, unless I miss my guess, has now demanded a similar sacrifice of some other hapless woman. Why does it always have to be girls, and why naked?"

Did Nike imply lecherousness in the sea god? Did Poseidon derive some perverse pleasure from the commingling of their terror and humiliation?

"If it's like last time," Nike said, "some form of sea monster is inbound already."

"It is for Herakles alone," Amphiaraos mumbled, though the Oracle still watched the skies rather than the seas like the rest of them.

Even before the seer spoke, Herakles had resolved to let no one die to sate Poseidon's vanity. But Amphiaraos claimed he must face this alone. Another labour? Whether Eurystheus acknowledged this or no, he would honour his children by saving the woman.

"Keep the ship well clear," Herakles said.

"What are you going to—" Nike began.

Herakles vaulted the gunwale and dove beneath the sea. The waters, though warm here in the early summer, still jolted, and it took a moment to orient himself. Then, surging Pneuma into Potency, he swam for the woman with great strokes. Even before he made it, he saw the disturbance in the waters out at sea. A churning of the deep as some enormity approached, surging toward its victim just as Nike had warned.

Bursting to the surface, Herakles gasped for breath and pulled himself onto the rocks where the woman was bound. Now, her shrieks cut even over the crashing of the waves as they battered the rock wall.

"Help me!"

Herakles glanced seaward. A mass rose in the depths, like a rolling hill of water closing in upon him. He had precious little time. Flooding yet more Pneuma into his muscles, he grabbed the chains close to where the spoke had been pounded into the rock and, placing one foot upon the wall, heaved. Dust rained and metal groaned. Stones began to crack.

Behind him, a bellow ripped out of the sea, splitting the sky, and sending trembles racing through the cliffside. The sound shook his very bones, clattered his teeth, and left his ears ringing. With a final grunt, Herakles tore free the chains—though he could not hear that final rasp—and the woman stumbled forwards but caught herself.

He spun and beheld the doom closing in.

The creature's saurian head and neck had breached the surface, and now it fixed him with an incandescent gaze. Tendrils like fibrous whiskers sprouted in a dozen strands trailing from its head, while spines jutted backwards, joined by frills and fins. This beast, this sea drakon, he could feel its wrath at his temerity in trying to steal away its prize.

The surge of incoming water rose up then as it drew to a stop, blocking his view the instant before the wave crashed down over him and the woman. Herakles flung his body overtop her and caught the fetters, shielding her from the brunt of the impact. The force of the wave slammed the both of them against the cliff an instant before it swept them back out to sea.

Swirling dark claimed him, saltwater shooting up his nose. Blinding. *Searing.*

A sputtering gasp as he reached air once more, one hand still gripping the fetters, though he did not know even if the woman retained consciousness. Potency-fuelled strokes carried him to the rocks, and he draped the chains over one that jutted high from the waters.

Another roar cut through the ringing in his ears.

And that gaping saurian maw swooped down toward them. Kicking off the rocks, Herakles leapt up to meet it. Jaws closed around him, but his momentum carried him past the teeth. He snared the tongue, even as darkness descended. The putrid reek of this cavern, its extreme heat, it suffocated. He would not have long.

Calling upon all the Pneuma he could, he punched a tooth. It cracked beneath his blow, and the monster rocked and heaved. Its bellow allowed daylight to stream back in—and with it, precious air. The tongue tried to hurl him into the creature's gullet. Herakles punched another fist into the drakon's gums, ripping them away until he could find purchase. His next blow shattered the cracked tooth.

Convulsions of agony wracked the monster, but Herakles was not finished. Again and again, his blows rained, tearing out the inside of its mouth. The drakon dove beneath the waves, swallowing a torrent of seawater in an attempt to wash him down. Its flesh shredded, but he refused to release his hold.

Until, at last, gagging and thrashing, it opened its maw enough for him to kick off and escape. Maybe he ought to have swum for the surface. Instead, as he slipped out betwixt broken teeth, Herakles snared one of those whisker-tendrils. His lungs already ached. Soon they would scream for air.

But if he let the drakon go, Poseidon might send it against Ilium once more, and Herakles's attempt to save the sacrifice would have only made things worse. So, he climbed the whisker to mount the drakon's face.

His ancestor Perseus had managed this.

So would he.

He climbed, fighting the current, until he could pull himself level with the well of incandescence that was a draconic eye. In its fervid depths, he saw wrath, yes. And fear, too. This eye was bigger than his whole body, but it knew his intent. The drakon flailed and twisted in a desperate attempt to dislodge Herakles.

But it would not work. He would not give up. One more beast dedicated to the memory of the boys he had betrayed.

He rammed his fist into the drakon's eye.

DRACONIC BLOOD SCALDED LIKE ACID. Herakles suspected only being underwater had spared him yet worse burns, and still, his arms were raw, weeping blood and stinging with a pain that had him gritting his teeth with each step up the long path to the city.

Great cyclopean walls surrounded the polis of Ilium, higher and thicker than any Herakles had yet beheld. Lofty towers rose up at irregular intervals, giving the Ilians a commanding view of the land. The city lay upon a hill, well beyond its port, the sole point of weakness in otherwise adamantine defences.

Most of his party trailed behind him, caught up in idle chatter Herakles chose to ignore.

Now clad in an ill-fitted khiton and walking beside him was Hesione, the woman he had rescued. She was the daughter of Laomedon, the Ilian king. As Nike had predicted, her sacrifice had been offered up to Poseidon after Laomedon had earned the wrath of the King of the Seas by failing to uphold agreed-upon tribute. What had possessed her father to refuse the Olympian god, Hesione had not known, and Herakles had thought better of pressing for answers.

Mayhap she ought to thave fled Ilium after such a betrayal. Laomedon had exposed her to save his polis from the wrath of the sea drakon, true. Yet in his place ... No, Herakles would not have sacrificed one of his children on any account. Indeed, he'd have torn asunder Gaia and plumbed once more the depths of Tartarus to steal back from Fate a single moment more with one of those boys. To hear their ringing laughter, to comfort their fears, to sit quietly and watch their open-mouthed slumbering.

Herakles could not excuse King Laomedon, whatever his reasons. If he had not the strength to challenge Poseidon, he ought not have broken faith in the first place. In fact, little was worse than a faithless king. Though he had never met Laomedon, already that pile of donkey shit reminded him rather of Eurystheus.

Nike, Iolaus, and Theseus had consented to remain with the ships and ensure both their safety and that the captain did not try to depart without Herakles and the others. Amphiaraos, too, had lingered, seeming lost in some stupor induced by whatever patterns he saw in the approaching storm.

Before they reached the city gates, Telamon jogged up to meet Herakles. It was his spare khiton Hesione wore now, and, from the way his gaze lingered upon her, Herakles thought he might have fancied the Ilian princess. Telamon and his brother Peleus hailed from Aegina, a tiny island off the coast of Kronion, just past Salamis. After a hunting quarrel left their third brother dead, they'd fled in exile and found shelter with Eurytion. Given that Peleus had then accidentally slain Eurytion while hunting the Kalydonian boar, Herakles had resolved never to hunt beside either brother again.

Still, he empathised with demigods beset by perpetual ill turns of Ananke, and he and Telamon had fallen into many a deep conversation on the trek to Thebes and the voyage to Ilium. "Why return her to her father at all?" Telamon had pitched his voice low enough that Hesione, on Herakles's other side, might not have caught his words.

Herakles shrugged, not bothering to admit he had pondered that very question. "Is your concern for her—or because you seek a royal wife?"

"You were granted one for your deeds," Telamon grumbled, and Herakles stiffened at the reminder of Megara.

"How very well that turned out for all concerned," he snapped.

Ahead, in the sprawling shadow cast by those cyclopean walls, the shades of three murdered boys watched his progress.

THE CITY GATES were thrown wide at their approach, and they were welcomed as heroes, the gathered throngs cheering for their returned princess. Face blank, Herakles wondered at their temerity. Not one of these men or women had raised a hand to rescue Hesione from her plight, and now they acted as though she had meant so very much to them.

A royal envoy met them just beyond the gates, and Hesione rushed forwards to embrace a young man in the lead, whom Herakles took for a prince.

"Priam!" She threw her arms around him, and he held her close, looking over her shoulder to Herakles and the others.

After a moment, Priam gripped his sister's arms and eased her aside. "Be welcome in Ilium. My father promised a pegasus to any who could slay that abomination. I can't even ..." The young man sputtered, overcome with emotion. He had only the barest wisps of a beard. Though he had brought four guards with him, Herakles began to doubt Laomedon had actually sent him. Why would the king send such a small envoy to meet the warriors who saved his daughter?

Priam and Hesione fell into whispers, and a suppressed sob wracked her shoulders before he wrapt an arm about them. Still holding his sister, Priam guided them back to the palace, the guards flanking them, though the rear pair cast frequent glances back at Herakles and his group.

Silent, Herakles trailed behind them, walking beside his allies.

Oekles clapt his bicep. "A pegasus! Usually, only Titans can ever claim such a mount, eh? Oh, but the greatest demigod heroes have ridden one for a time. Perseus and Bellerophon. And now your name will join with theirs for all time."

Perseus was already Herakles's great-grandfather, though he had to admit, the idea of having his own pegasus did bring a hint of a smile to his face. With such a mount, he could fly to Themiskyra and accomplish the labour with much greater ease. Nor, if he was honest, would he mind such enhancement to his fame, even if it was not his primary aim.

"Shame he doesn't have one for all of us," Telamon said with an overwrought pout, drawing chuckles from his brother.

Kastor clucked his tongue. "Me, I'd settle for some gold and jewels. That, and the supplies we need. Better to be well provisioned before attempting the voyage ahead of us."

Herakles held his peace, all the way to the palace, listening to their chatter, but not joining in. Something sat ill about Priam coming by himself. Perhaps he had been out and about in the city and thus was the first to hear of what had transpired. But why had Laomedon not sent others to greet them in the time it had taken them to climb first the hill and now to the peak, where sat the royal citadel?

They were ushered into the throne room, a great chamber with vaulted ceilings supported by painted columns. A fresco depicting the glory of Tros covered the back wall, while two sides remained open to the air, leading out onto a vast terrace from which the royals could survey the whole of their lands. If Herakles remembered his lessons with Athene, Tros had been a descendant of Dardanus, one of Zeus's other bastards.

Two dozen spearmen stood at attention, rimming either side of the throne. Laomedon sat there, chin upon his palm, his greying beard spilling through his splayed fingers as he watched them. Herakles and his party formed a line, waiting as Priam led his sister up to their father and exchanged a few words. With a sniff, the king sat upright and spread his hands. Herakles could not make out whatever he said to his children, but he waved them off to the side, where they met with other finely clad men. More princes? One of them bestowed upon Hesione a golden veil, which she donned.

At last, Laomedon beckoned Herakles forwards, his face drawn into a tight smile. "My daughter tells me you are Herakles. And who are these others?"

Herakles looked at each of his companions in turn. "Princes Kastor and Pollux of Argos. Their cousin Oekles, also out of Argos. Princes Telamon and Peleus of Aegina."

They each offered a nod as Herakles introduced them. It was Telamon who spoke. "We are told you promised a pegasus to any who slew that monster and saved Princess Hesione. As Herakles has performed that feat, we have come to collect the prize."

Now Laomedon's smile grew even thinner. "Oh, yes." He cleared his throat. "Bring me the statuette," he said to one of the other princes. "The one from the atrium."

"Statuette?" Telamon asked.

Herakles felt his muscles clenching. A feeling he could not name —a sensation so atavistic as to defy categories imposed by civilisation —crept upon him.

"Yes, yes," Laomedon said. "Indeed, a fine carving of a pegasus, wrought in elegant marble by a famed sculptor. A worthy prize for—"

Just like godsdamned Eurystheus. A pompous prick who sat and ruled over a population without honour or care for anyone save himself. Herakles clenched his fists at his sides. How dare this slug betray him? How dare he betray his own child with such perfidy? Was her life not worth at least upholding his own word?

"Father?" Priam asked. "That's not—"

A sharp look from Laomedon silenced him. Not Hesione though, who scoffed and rolled her eyes.

"No," Telamon said, taking a threatening step toward the throne. "No, you attempt to swindle us."

More than a score of spearpoints dropped, all pointed toward Telamon.

Herakles continued to clench and unclench his fists. In his mind's eye, Eurystheus's loathsome aspect now sat upon Laomedon's shoulder. Sneering, deriding.

The prince returned, bearing a statue the size of a cat between his palms. Herakles scarcely saw it.

"The reward was a *live* pegasus," Telamon protested. "A prize worthy of a demigod who fought such a monster."

Laomedon sneered. "I'm afraid you are mistaken, Elládosi. I never offered anyone—"

"Liar!" Herakles roared, though he had not thought to speak at all. One moment, he'd intended to storm from the hall, and the next, he erupted like a long-dormant volcano grown suddenly wakeful. The laughter of Eurystheus filled the air, mocking him. The shades of his boys glared at the Ilians in open wrath. Herakles strode toward Laomedon, overcome with fury. A haze of red tinged his vision, and he could see naught save his hands around the king's throat.

He was more than himself. Those voices inside grew into a murmuring chorus, filling his head. *This*, this was the unnameable emotion that had begun to claim him. A hundred men in him, all crying out to become the cleansing conflagration of destruction. They promised him that, for death alone did he live.

One of those spears was thrust at him, aimed at his chest. A swipe of his hand splintered the wooden haft and sent the spearman reeling. Chaos erupted.

They came for him, and all Herakles could see was Eurystheus, cackling and insouciant, lapping up misery like a parched beast come at last to a burbling stream. There he sat, a feckless cur grinding others beneath his dusty sandals.

Herakles caught the haft of another spear and shoved, sending a guardsman staggering into his fellows, such that his own people skewered him even as they toppled into a gangly mass. In a dim corner of his mind, he knew the other Elládosi had surged into motion, engaging the remaining spearmen or barring other means of entry to the throne room.

But Herakles saw only Eurystheus.

He saw burning, blazing red, all the World tinted by the hue of royal sadism. His foot was upon Laomedon's throne. His fist crashed into that aureate crown. Once. Twice. Gold was bent, driven through the mess of a pulverised skull and into the splintered wood of the throne behind it.

Herakles was roaring, raging. Something deep in his soul, pulled taut for so long, at last snapped. There must be recompense for the ruination Ananke had made of his life and the sick pleasure Eurystheus had taken in such horror. There must be revenge upon all who made mockery of his suffering.

Become death. Become destruction.

He had the throne in his hands now, smashing it down to pulverise what remained of Laomedon's corpse. The king's sons, the princes, they came at him, swords bared, screaming.

Everyone was screaming.

Herakles caught an attacker's wrist and snapped it like kindling, even as his fist flattened the prince's windpipe.

Hesione was screaming. "Klytius!"

In an instant, that riven shriek cut through the haze of wrath, and Herakles saw the charnel house he and the others had made of this grand throne room. Four demigods had annihilated the soldiers and princes. The king lay splattered and strewn across his once majestic hall. Overturned braziers sent snakes of fire hissing through the palace. Tapestries and plush carpets burnt, choking those vaulted ceilings with tendrils of black smoke.

"Oekles is dead," Kastor cried, kneeling beside his cousin's corpse. A crimson puddle seeped from a spear wound in the man's chest.

The tide of death from which Herakles had almost dragged himself free caught him once more, pulling him under. A fresh paroxysm seized Herakles and he stalked toward the next prince. He did not remember dodging a sword strike. But now he held the man's sword. And it was driven through the prince's chin until the point burst from the top of his skull.

"Lampus …" Hesione sobbed, and Herakles heard, so far away, so distant.

And another, once more, Herakles closing in upon the last of Laomedon's hateful, perfidious brood.

"Not Priam!" Hesione flung herself at him then. He might have cast her aside like a child. He could have stepped around her and crushed the skull of the trembling prince in the palm of his hand.

But the tremor within her voice, it called up a phantasm of Megara, imploring him to have mercy, though he had shown none to his own sons. Hesione thrust her veil at him. "Take it! Take it as his ransom. This is the purest of gold, worked into silken threads."

A hand fell upon Herakles, and he looked to Telamon. "We must go." The Aeginian's gaze darted to Hesione. "I will have the princess as my war prize and hostage." Herakles frowned at his friend, but Telamon pushed on. "Besides it being my right to claim the spoils of such conquest, without a hostage, we shan't make it out of this city. So, I will have her and make her my wife."

"The gate is going to give way!" Pollux shouted, and Herakles saw the demigod was straining to hold a portal that shuddered under repeated blows.

"Take her then," Herakles said, all the wind suddenly blown out of him. His wrath now fled, he felt empty, ready to collapse into a heap and lament the carnage he had wrought. It was in him. It had always been in him, even as a child.

"Be a better king than your father," Telamon said to Priam, one hand upon the prince's sister's shoulder. "A man lives by his word, or not at all. And for Zeus's sake, call off the guards before anyone else dies."

7

THESEUS

725 Bronze Age

"You did *what!*" Nike bellowed at Herakles, seizing the demigod by his blood-splattered tunic as though she meant to throttle him.

Goddess though she was, Theseus had never imagined he would see anyone manhandle the hulking demigod thus. Herakles was many times her size and no doubt could have cast Nike aside with one hand. Instead, the Tethid hung his head and refused to meet her gaze.

"We went for supplies, and you set fire to the palace!" Nike's golden eyes flashed in the light of the afternoon sun, and for a moment, Theseus could have sworn he saw a flicker of flames within those irises. "You murdered the king and his sons!"

They had returned with half the city following, whipped into a frenzy yet not quite willing to strike whilst Telamon held the princess hostage. The moment Theseus had spied the simmering violence, he'd ordered the ship made ready. The captain had misliked leaving his intended destination, but what choice did the man have? Remain and pay the price for his passengers' folly?

"We left one alive ..." Telamon protested with all the vigour of a mollusc.

"And *you*." Releasing Herakles, Nike whirled on the demigod fool enough to interpose himself on Herakles's behalf. "You kidnapped this woman!" Shrieking now, she thrust a finger at Hesione.

Even bold Telamon fell back a step at the goddess's wrath. And small wonder, given legend held she aided in the winning of both of the Titanomachy and Gigantomachy. "It is a man's right to claim slaves as spoils. And I intend to marry her."

"Marriage by abduction is still rape, you ignominious cretin!" Now, Theseus was certain he saw embers sparking to life in her half-clenched palm. Flitting tendrils of smoke wormed skyward from the flames threatening to ignite with Nike's growing wrath. "Did you stop to wonder, to *ask*, whether the woman would wish to marry a man who slaughtered her kin and abducted her from her home? Do you think, should you ask now, she will feel free to speak against it?"

"But, Goddess—" Peleus interrupted, perhaps hoping to spare his brother.

With a single furious glare his way as well, Nike abruptly clenched her fist, extinguishing the smouldering that had nigh erupted there. Instead of engaging further with the recently returned raiders, Nike took hold of Hesione's hand and led her away. Already, the trireme had left the Ilian harbour too far behind to send the princess back. Would Nike demand they come about and drop her ashore once more? No, Theseus thought not. Despite all Nike's words, Hesione had been saved from the monster by the same men who abducted her and murdered the king. The princess would not find a warm welcome at home, he suspected.

"What in Hades's dark crotch was that about?" Peleus demanded. "As if spoils do not go to the victors. Those bastards broke faith with us, then slew Oekles, and she thinks we should walk away without claiming slaves?"

They had not seen it, then. So intent had they been on defending themselves against her words, they had not noticed the burning inside Nike. "You've no idea how close you came to death, this day."

Peleus huffed at Theseus's remonstration. "Titan she may be, but that gives her no right to dictate the terms of war or where we can or cannot stick our cocks. Such is the domain of men."

Pollux snickered. "And I tell you true, I would not mind ..." The jiggle of his eyebrows made plain the Tethid's meaning.

Frowning, Theseus shook his head and walked away from the bunch. It was not as though, on the long road by her side, he had never dreamt of sweet nights with Nike. He had pictured it quite oft, in truth, lying awake at night, or in lulls in conversation as they trekked across hills and plains. He imagined her crawling to him in the darkness, her warm hand reaching for his flesh. Such fancies were but natural, he told himself. But Peleus lent a vulgarness to it all that Theseus found left a sour taste in his mouth.

Still, these were the men bound to join Jason on his quest for Kolchis, and Theseus had promised to accompany Nike there. They had best learn to tolerate one another before someone wound up swimming home.

IOLKOS WAS, so far as Theseus knew, the only polis of real power in all of Phlegra. So much of the land remained wild, roamed by beasts, centaurs, and Gigantes, or covered in barren hills so craggy as to make settlement all but impossible. King Pelias—and Peleus of Argos received no end of ribbing and jibes over the similarity of their names—ruled Iolkos and, as a demigod himself, had done so for decades. It was he, apparently, who had demanded his nephew Jason retrieve the Golden Fleece from Kolchis, though Theseus had few details beyond this.

Amphiaraos seemed to know more, but since the death of his father, the Oracle had sunken into inconsolable dolour and spoke to no one.

The city lay beneath the expanse of hills that comprised the bulk of Phlegra, upon the Axeinos Strait which Men no longer braved for fear of the same iron-winged birds Herakles had come to slay. But then, as Theseus had discussed with Nike, one could not reach Kolchis by land either. Not with any great chance of success.

They moored at the harbour and soon found themselves greeted by Jason himself and a cadre of others. The Iolkan prince yet favoured the arm he'd broken hunting the boar, though he'd removed the sling. Many of the others Theseus knew already from the hunt in Kalydon. Including the Lapith, Pirithous, who brightened and waved upon seeing Theseus up on the ship. Theseus had not known for certain whether ...

But the expression on Pirithous's face made plain he thought Theseus still a welcome cohort. Not waiting for the gangplank, Theseus leapt upon the gunwale, then vaulted to the pier to meet his friend.

Laughing, Pirithous clasped his arm before yanking Theseus into a full embrace. "Gods, it's good to see you once more. I'd not known you'd be counted among the Argonauts."

"Argonauts?"

Another chuckle, and Pirithous pointed to the hull of a ship well under construction upon the beach. "Indeed. Jason named her for the architect, one Argus. Uh ..." Pirithous peered at the workers a moment. "That one, with the mop of greying hair. He's got about as much dressing style as a dead chimera, but they say he's inspired as a shipwright, and that's what counts for us." He leant in conspiratorially. "Some claim he's received insight for this design direct from Athene, if you can believe that."

Pirithous guided Theseus away from the port to a tavern in the polis, where he arranged for cabbage soup and wine. When they had settled upon divans and were a cup in, Pirithous asked how Theseus and the others had come to be there, and Theseus related his journey. How he had travelled with Nike for Thebes, only to meet with Herakles, Amphiaraos, and the others.

"We knew Jason sent call for heroes," Pirithous agreed, "and I found myself eager to join this quest of Jason's, though I know precious little of it. Ah, well, what there is to say, I'll tell you, though perhaps beneath the stars with fewer to overhear."

Theseus found himself glancing about at that. The stars ... He leant in so he could whisper. "After what happened between us that last night ... I mean after the hunt ... I didn't know ..."

Pirithous too cast a furtive glance around the tavern but apparently saw no one listening. "It's only natural, right? Spirits run high in times of life and death." Theseus's friend patted his knee, his hand lingering just long enough to make plain that it might not have been *just* something for a single night.

"THE ARGO SHOULD BE ready by the summer solstice," Pirithous said when the two of them sat beneath the stars, on the beach, looking out over the Strait. Somewhere, in the far distance, lay Ilium, where Herakles had wrought such chaos. Theseus's hero had confided, on the voyage here, that he had lost all control. Had felt like the very spirit of death had overtaken him and guided his hand for a moment. The thought left Theseus cold. "So, with the new year," Pirithous continued, "we sail for the Axeinos Sea. Tomorrow, I'll introduce you to the rest of the crew. We've got time."

Theseus took a deep breath of the sea air, pushing thoughts of Herakles from his mind. Much though he admired the demigod, he intended to make his own name. Doing that meant attending to the quest at hand. "How came you to this?"

Pirithous sighed. "Some of us build fame for our own sakes. Some, because we have no choice but to carve our own names, if we do not wish to be saddled with those of our fathers." Pirithous had never before spoken of his family.

"Who is your father?" Theseus asked.

But his friend shook his head, making plain he'd not the least desire to speak on the matter.

After a moment, Theseus thought it best to change the subject. "Tell me of Jason and the Fleece."

Pirithous grunted in acknowledgment but took a moment to answer. "I can tell you the tale as I had it from Jason himself on our voyage here and what the Lapiths knew of such things. King Kretheus ruled Iolkos in Ares's name. His wife, Tyro, bore him three sons, Aeson—Jason's father—the oldest among them. Tyro too caught the eye of Poseidon, and to him she bore twins, Pelias and Neleus."

"She bore …?"

"She could not have done much to stop an Olympian, could she? Tyro was kin to my own line, and thus, it was with the Lapiths she bore those twins, sad to say, though it was all well before my time. Aeson should have succeeded King Kretheus, but with his divine blood, Pelias proved stronger and had Aeson imprisoned and Neleus exiled from Iolkos. By this time, though, Aeson's wife Polymede—the daughter of the Heliad demigod Autolykus who joins us, in fact—was already with child. Polymede rightly feared for her offspring, for should it be a son, his claim upon the throne of Iolkos would forever prove a threat to Pelias.

"Now, according to Jason, Athene herself introduced Polymede to a wise centaur named Kheiron. To him, she entrusted the rearing of her son, in the wilds."

Theseus turned to look at his friend. "Wait, aren't centaurs monsters?"

Pirithous frowned, looking so pensive Theseus feared he had somehow offended, though he could not see how. "Not always …" he said after a painfully drawn-out silence. "We Lapiths have some history with them, you know. It is true, they can be savage, rapacious even. But sometimes they control themselves too. Maybe … maybe they're not so different from Men. There are good ones among them, yes. And some others who are given over entirely to their bestial natures." He shrugged, looking sheepish. "Mostly, we try for peace with them because the alternative would cost us so much more."

While Theseus had not given much thought to hunting centaurs, he had always imagined, that, like Herakles, he would slay any monster he came across. He could scarce imagine conversing with one.

"Well, so Jason says Kheiron taught him all kinds of things. He—"

"What things?" Theseus interrupted.

"I don't know. Just things, all right?"

"Table manners?"

"Probably not."

A grin had begun to spread over Theseus's face. "Dancing?"

Pirithous rolled his eyes. "I doubt it."

"How to sail a ship or row a boat or swim like a man instead of a horse? It strikes me there is a small chance such skills might prove of use to him in the foreseeable future."

"Now look, Theseus, you want to know what went on between Jason and the centaur, you'd best ask him of it. Do you want to hear the rest of the story or no?"

Theseus spread his hands in acquiescence, and Pirithous narrowed his eyes and affected an overly put-out expression.

"Fine. So, Jason lives in the wilds with Kheiron for twenty years, and in that time, others come and go seeking training with Kheiron, among them Peleus and Telamon, and I think Asklepoius, as well. Meanwhile, an Oracle wanders through Iolkos and spouts off a prophecy that Pelias will be overthrown by a man with but one sandal."

"Seriously?"

"Straight from Apollon's own mouth, I swear it. When Jason was grown, Kheiron told him his birthright was to reclaim the throne of Iolkos, so Jason travelled across miles and miles of wilderness all the way from Mount Pelion. Near my lands, yes. Along the way, he met an old woman who begged him aid to cross a river. According to Jason, she was the goddess Hera in disguise." Pirithous shrugged. "Make of that what you will. He carried her in his arms across the river, lost one of his sandals in the mud, and thus, when he at last reached Iolkos, he strolled through town with one foot bare.

"I have no idea what Pelias would have done had he gotten the chance, but Jason announced his parentage in public, forcing Pelias to, likewise, take a public stance. 'As the son of the rightful king,' Jason said, 'all these lands are mine to claim. So, I call upon you to abdicate now and let us remain peaceful kin.' Pelias might have had him thrown in the dungeon along with his father Aeson, save that so many were watching now. Instead, he demanded Jason prove his worthiness for a throne, as many heroes had done before him. To this end, he tasked Jason to cross the Axeinos Sea and recover the Golden Fleece from King Aeëtes. The grove in which it rests, so sing the bards, is guarded by a sleepless drakon under the command of the sorcerous royals of Kolchis.

"Pelias no doubt thinks the task impossible, but Jason resolved to prove him wrong and rise to this challenge. He came to Kalydon when he heard of the gathering of heroes for the hunt, there to recruit those he might win over to his cause. And the shipwright Argus, a friend of Jason's mother, he agreed to build the finest ship in history to sail those treacherous waters."

Theseus was, by now, stifling his yawns. Still, he had to admit, the tale had a certain appeal: a future king proving his merit with an otherwise impossible task. This, he thought, was a voyage into which he could pour his whole heart.

⁂

IN THE COMING DAYS, Theseus mingled among the gathered heroes, getting to know each in turn. Unlike the hunt for the boar of Kalydon, here they had time to idle whilst Argus finished his task. Thus did he pass the hours with copious wine and the tales of all those who had come from the breadth of Elládos to join on this adventure.

Herakles and Iolaus he knew well enough, the descendants of Perseus himself, come from Mykenai. Herakles sought not the Fleece but prizes of his own. Much though Herakles's words—of losing himself in the madness of battle and the spilling of blood—left Theseus uneasy, still, he wished the demigod Tethid all the luck. Not least because slaying those birds would make the Argo's voyage safer by far.

Nike kept her own company, the sole woman among the crew. Theseus would never know what words had passed between Nike and Hesione, but the Ilian princess had indeed wed Telamon, and the Aeginian had seen Hesione settled in Iolkos, to await his return.

Too, there was Peleus, brother to Telamon, brooding over his accidental murder of Eurytion. When he spoke to Theseus at all, it was with guarded words. Still, deep in his cups, once he had confided that he was, in fact, married to Eurytion's own daughter and had not dared to face her since that fateful day in Kalydon. Theseus could little blame him; he could not imagine a blissful marriage bed awaited him once she learnt he had slain her father.

Amphiaraos spent his time in grief over his father, comforted as best they could manage by his kin Kastor and Pollux, the Gemini. Legend claimed Zeus himself had fathered Pollux, and from what little Theseus had seen of his prowess, he did indeed surpass his mortal brother. Talaus, a Tethid whom Theseus did not know, was apparently their kinsman as well. He had been recruited in Argos when Jason made sail from there. Apparently, the late Oekles had meant his son Amphiaraos to marry Talaus's daughter, and though Oekles had perished, Talaus had promised to honour the man's wishes.

Then there was the Heliad, Autolykus, the son of Hermes, famed for his daring as a thief of cattle and jewels. Theseus misliked the idea of working alongside a thief, but he was Jason's grandfather and thus had earned his space on the ship. Still, Theseus kept a careful eye on his drachmae around the demigod and chose to moderate his drinking whenever the man was lurking nigh.

Also among other former hunters was Nestor, the son of Aeson's exiled brother Neleus, and thus cousin to Jason. Nestor struck Theseus as wise and compassionate. On a few occasions, he had caught the prince in deep philosophical debate with Nike. Perhaps it was the wine, but trying to understand the metaphysics over which they argued left Theseus feeling more like a dog pondering the discussions of Men.

Also from the hunt, Euphemos, son of Poseidon, had come along. Jason had chosen the demigod as their helmsman for his unique knowledge of the seas. According to Euphemos himself, there was no finer sailor on the Thalassa, and he could read the currents of the waters or the shifting of the breeze with more ease than the finest scholar could read scrolls. He was also, Theseus thought, the humblest man he had ever met.

Last was Laertes, the prince of Ithaka, an Atlantid called by some of the others King of Goats. He'd also accompanied Jason back from the hunt, eager to win some real fortune as well as glory.

Eighteen of the greatest warriors of Elládos and Phlegra, ready for a quest that, Jason promised, would carve all their names into the bedrock of legends. Theseus found he could scarce wait to be underway.

8

KIRKE

725 Bronze Age

Curled in a ball, agony shooting through her from the blow Zeus had dealt her, Kirke found she could scarce move. Some part of her mind dwelt not upon the predicament he'd placed her in—impossible—but upon the slaughter of her beloved wolf pack. Such grief, overwhelming as it was, was at least something she could parse. As an immortal, she understood animals could not live forever. One day, years away though it should have been, she'd have needed to bury them, regardless.

One day.

Kirke would face Zeus's torments through centuries. She could not let her mind wander such paths.

She heard footsteps as someone entered, but she could not bring herself to look up. Steps too light for Zeus. Had Eos come to check on her? Kirke's aunt would only use this, even *this*, as an excuse to chide, and Kirke had no strength to bear it.

"Kirke, Kirke," her mother's voice cooed. A hand upon her

shoulder rolled her over to see Mother's golden eyes, fiery hair spilling down around her face.

Coughing fits seized Kirke. Before she had recovered, Mother drew her into an embrace.

In a dream, not so long ago, her mother had touched her mind. Kirke had thought her centuries dead and had scarce dared to believe her dream aught save a dream. But now the great Hekate had returned from whatever unknown realms had drawn her away for more than six centuries.

"He hit me," Kirke wheezed. It sounded inane. Painfully obvious. *Very* painfully. Because Kirke, after centuries, was still an idiot who had not learnt how to talk, always babbling with too many words, or too few.

Slowly, her mother eased her to sit and looked at her face with blatant concern. And an undercurrent of indignation that had Kirke wondering what, if aught, Mother would do about her plight. "Why has he done this?"

"He knows about the Nectar, Mother. He wants me to ... give him the Sight."

Mother did not, at first, respond to that. Then she eased Kirke to her feet. "Come, let's get you cleaned up."

WHEN THEY HAD SUPPED upon hearty soup and Kirke had thrown back an amphora's worth of Phoenikian red, Mother had asked her all the sordid details of how she'd come to dwell in this sorry, faltering estate.

Kirke explained her blundered endeavour to help Pasiphaë conceive. That ill-conceived attempt at sorcery had led to the creation of a monster she'd heard Men now called the Minotaur. She had heard no word of her sister, and she did not know whether Pasiphaë had even survived the ordeal. She told how her father had learnt of her brewing of Nectar, and how he'd banished her here, under the scrutiny of Aunt Eos.

From the face Mother pulled, she cared for Helios's sister even less than Kirke herself did.

"Father built this estate for his sister and her husband, ages back," Kirke said. "But their daughter Aura ran away and later died. It poisoned their marriage, and eventually, after enough time, I think Aunt Eos couldn't stand the sight of this place. The echoes of memory were too thick for her."

"They are thick," Mother had admitted, as if she could see those echoes play out before her eyes. Perhaps she could, looking across the Veil to the psychic shadowscape of the Penumbra.

For a time, Mother fell silent, and Kirke contented herself with throwing back another bowl of wine and pretend the events of the day were but a bad dream. "I can speak to your father about having your exile lifted."

Kirke didn't know whether to laugh or weep. "And how do you think Zeus will react if I leave? He'd hunt me to the ends of Gaia, and we both know it. Maybe ... maybe if I can give him what he wants, he'll forget about me."

But she knew better.

From the look upon Mother's face, she knew it as well. "I'll do whatever I can for you, Kirke. But I do need something of you now." Mother reached into her satchel and removed a metal cube set with numerous interlocking panels. "I need to know how this works."

"Huh." Kirke took the object and turned it around in her hands. "What is this, a puzzle box?" Mother looked dumbstruck, as if a child's game meant so very much to her. Well, whatever. "Yeah, I'm sure I can figure this thing out. Heh, I mean, it'll take my mind off Zeus's absurd demands a bit. Any reprieve might help me come at it from a new angle. But why do you care about a toy, Mother?"

Her mother mouthed words that did not quite form. What in Tartarus was wrong with her?

"Mother?"

"This small puzzle is a key to a greater puzzle, a piece I need to understand." She seemed to choke on the words. "Kirke ... I need to know how the Box works, but don't open it."

"Uh, sure, yeah. I can definitely figure out a puzzle box without solving it. I was also thinking of reading a few scrolls without removing them from their cases. You know, after I sip some Phoenikian red before the grapes are plucked from the vine." She put the stupid toy down beside her. "There's something you could do for me in the meantime."

Mother's presence here, whether or not she could save Kirke from this extremity, did grant her the chance to fix one wrong her imprisonment here had created.

"You want me to speak to Zeus on your behalf."

Kirke rolled her eyes. "Sure, and after you convince him to change his mind, I'd like you to convince the land to rise up and make a bridge off this island. That, and maybe talk a pheasant into cooking itself for me. Ahem, no. Rather, I have a niece, which I assume you don't know because you've been wherever you've been, which was not *here*. My half-brother, Aeëtes, his daughter Medea. Before I was banished here, I was training her a bit in alchemy, but she always wanted *more*, and she keeps writing to me, as if I can explain aught about the Art in a letter."

"You'd have me go to this Medea in … Kolchis?" Mother paused. "Teach her sorcery?"

"Sorcery …" Kirke twisted her face into a hideous glower. "Some lesser arcana, perhaps. Surely you know the impotence a woman feels in the courts of men. Even a little knowledge might offer her a semblance of control over her own life."

The request seemed to weigh heavier upon Mother than Kirke had expected, but after a moment, she nodded. "I'll go to Kolchis."

VIOLENT TREMORS WELLED up within Kirke as Zeus glared at her from her portico. He snatched the phial from her shaking hand. That she knew he saw her terror, revelled in it even, did not mean she could suppress it, and the gleam in his pale eyes revealed he knew it too. He had given her the requested year to complete the work, and she prayed she had succeeded.

"If this doesn't work, I'll return for you in the morning." The malevolent cast of his sneer left her uncertain whether he, in fact, preferred her to fail as a pretence for whatever torment he now envisaged for her. He had already warned her that, if her brew wrought something amiss with him, Hermes had instructions to come for her. Not that Kirke would have dared to poison the king by her own hand. Not that she'd have dared to do a damn thing beneath his withering gaze.

At last, her turned and left her. A nascent sob too terrified to even finish forming lay bundled in her throat. When the king vanished into the woods beyond her field, Kirke slumped down against a marble column, whimpering.

Oh, Hyperion, how had she come to this? Could she run? Eos controlled the harbour, though, and she could not slip past her aunt. No, Father had ensured Kirke remain a prisoner here for all time. Whilst his intent may have been to keep her safe from Zeus, in reality, Father had caged Kirke, left her trapped where Zeus would always know where to find her whenever the mood suited him.

Like his daughter, the Nectar—if it worked to give him the Sight at all—would drive Zeus to addiction, both in and of itself and out of need to ever see more. He would return again and again, she knew, and given his nature, his whims would drive him to hurt her. She could see it coming and still ... still could see no way around it.

Moaning, she beat her fist against the column, as impotent to harm it as she was to change her fate.

Maybe, when Mother returned from Kolchis ... maybe Kirke would beg her to help her escape. Maybe spending the rest of her life in hiding was better than this prison.

Mother ... and Kirke had found precious little time in the past year to even look at the Box she had brought.

Well. Kirke managed a few steadying breaths, pushed herself up, and made her way to her work desk. The metal Box set amid phials and bowls and jars of alchemical reagents, pushed aside in her desperation to create the Nectar Zeus had demanded.

Now, Kirke packed all of that up on shelves, brought out some artisan's tools, and set to examining the Box. Mother had asked for a simple service. It was the least Kirke could do.

NEVER IN ALL Kirke's long life had she beheld a creation so complex, so masterful, as this Box. When Mother had first brought it, Kirke had fiddled with it a bit, but her preoccupation with Zeus's Nectar had prevented her from looking as deep as she might have. Now, the eventide had given in to the dark of a moonless night, and Kirke had twice refilled her oil lamp and still she could not imagine how anyone had made such a thing.

Countless interlocking gears, concealed tumblers, sliding panels … A masterpiece without rival, for certain, and far from a child's toy. Mother had claimed it dangerous, that it was tied to the very Tapestry of the Moirai. Given the complexity of the design, Kirke could almost believe such a thing.

Mother had warned her not to open it, but without doing so, Kirke would never unravel the sum of its workings. She needed a little look at the innermost parts and then—

The moment she solved it and popped open the top panel, everything shifted.

She heard something shift inside her house, as if Zeus had already returned.

"What the—?" she started to ask.

The air fizzed, a sudden change in pressure making her ears pop. The room folded inward, and Kirke tumbled off her stool, seized by vertigo, gasping. Darkness edged in around her vision.

DESPITE HER EMPTY BELLY, Kirke set the plate of food down and wandered from the hall, stumbling into another woman, who caught her by her arms.

"You wonder if the unravelling threads of time shall reveal truth or madness," the woman said, and Kirke looked up into the aureate eyes of another Heliad.

"Pandora?"

She was here, grown, and fiercer now, the look of grim determination clear upon her visage.

Involuntarily, Kirke glanced back toward the hall where Europa chased young Pandora.

"Because it seems too much to grasp," Pandora said.

Kirke found herself unable to swallow. "Y-you ..."

She had seen this moment.

Pandora took her by the arm and guided her out into the courtyard, pausing beneath the shade of a cedar. Fortunate, as Kirke found herself needing to lean upon the tree for support.

"Until now, I've not seen you at a loss for words," Pandora said.

WHEN THE HAZE CLEARED, Kirke found herself lying in cold dirt, in the midst of the woods. Colder than it most oft got here, even in winter, and winter had passed. Her breath frosted the night air. With a grunt, Kirke gained her knees, loam and grass staining her khiton.

Her wild dream made not the least bit of sense.

Taking in her surroundings drove any thought of it from her mind.

This wasn't her woods. Kirke had walked the sylvan expanses of her prison a thousand times, until every tree had become a boon companion. She could have walked every path with her eyes closed. She knew the whole of Aiaíā, and this was not the forest beyond her estate.

Still somewhat dizzy, she rose, steadying herself against a foreign tree. The Box remained in her hand and she had no satchel, so she held on to it and began a slow plod in a random direction. If you had no idea where you were—or how you'd gotten there—you couldn't possibly get any more lost.

She'd made it a few dozen steps only when her skin prickled, hair rising along her arms. Something Otherworldly brushed nigh and Kirke drew up short, casting about in case of dryads or aught else that might come to prey on her in the dark woods. An Etheric disturbance thrummed through the night. If she embraced the Sight, she might learn what transpired, though she'd also open herself to aught that lurked beyond the Veil.

But if she refused, she'd remain ignorant and lost.

So.

Kirke blinked until she managed to look into the dark haze, colour bleeding out of the World as her vision shifted into the Penumbra. Vibrations rippled through the Ether, radiating out from one direction. Kirke followed the distortions and, sure enough, Supernal cants came to her. A sorceress invoked or evoked something this night, her voice the source of such disruption.

Maybe she ought to have fled—getting anywhere close to another practitioner of the Art whilst they incanted was madness—but Kirke needed to know where she was. A shadow drifted past, not a foot from her, and she choked on a yelp. The shade had ignored her for the moment, drawn by the incantation. That could change, however. Kirke blinked the Sight away, allowing her soul to move back into the Mortal Realm.

Still, she crept forwards, reaching the edge of a glade. The moon streamed down on it. Which was impossible because this night had had no moon. And there, in the midst of the glade, Kirke *herself* sat, incanting, calling upon spirits.

Had she slipped into Pasiphaë's sleeping mind? Did her sister dream of the moment that had damned Kirke? Or was this Kirke's own dream? She watched herself making the mistake of trying to help Pasiphaë, her traitorous sister who had spilled her secrets and gotten her exiled to Aiaíā.

Kirke ground her teeth. Fuck, she'd done everything for Pasiphaë, for all her damn siblings, and it never amounted to aught save woe for Kirke.

Well, let the bitch suffer. Let her writhe in torment even as Kirke now did, feeling the constant terror of Zeus's attention upon her. Kirke fell back a few steps, then settled on the ground. Wrath burbled and boiled over like a cauldron set too long upon the flame. Her cants spilled from her almost unbidden.

"Sinoe," she called. "Sinoe, I call upon you. Make her suffer. Make Pasiphaë writhe in agony and recoil in horror fitting for all she has done. Reward her perfidy with torment, Sinoe. Lay my curse upon my sister."

Her words—and the Supernal incantation that preceded them—sent the Ether thrumming as well, a second wave through the night. Madness she knew, but then if this was a dream, let her have her vengeance. How oft Kirke had considered attempting to slip into Pasiphaë's dreams, sending her nightmares as punishment, though Kirke could not reach another's dreams at will.

Had the Box helped her to ... Had the Box ...

Kirke glanced down at it, still in her hand. Pasiphaë had not seen this moment at all, and the details were too precise for her sister to have dreamt them. Kirke rose and scrambled back to the edge of the glade, peering inside it.

There, Sinoe had driven the other Kirke to the ground, mounting her.

"Please ..." Kirke heard herself whimper.

"No," Kirke rasped. This wasn't a dream, was it? It didn't quite have the flavour of oneiromancy ...

Sinoe dropped down on all fours and scrambled off the *other* Kirke, skittering into the woods, only to pause before Kirke herself, leering up at her. Oh, fuck. Was this ... real? A purple tongue shot out from Sinoe's mouth, licked her lips.

"Please ..." she heard the other Kirke call out once more.

A gleam in her eye, Sinoe rose and bounded through the woods, vanishing into the dark. To fulfil the will of *both* Kirkes. Conception for Pasiphaë, yes, and damnation too. Damnation Kirke had now wrought for both her sister and *herself*.

Pressed up against a tree, hidden in the dark, Kirke peered back into the glade and saw herself there, bound in the roots Sinoe had called up, weeping in horror and dread, not knowing what had just happened. That night ... hadn't she felt an inexplicable reverberation through the Ether after her cants had finished? Hadn't she felt ... Kirke *now* interfering, turning her blessing into a curse?

Madness ... Mother claimed the Box was tied to the Tapestry of the Moirai. Had it, in fact, sent her back in time?

Lest her other self see her, Kirke slipped back into the dark of the wood, then leant the back of her head against a tree. Utter, complete madness. But if this was truth and not some oneiromantic weaving of her mind, had she not then caused her own failure this night? Had she not wrought her own fate?

The thought strangled all others from her mind.

9

THESEUS

726 Bronze Age

The solstice arrived, and with it, the revels of the new year. To his credit, King Pelias feasted them all, plying them with grapes and olives, with figs and roast boar. There was basted venison and sweet cakes seasoned with spices imported from some far-off land beyond Phoenikia. And there was wine, of course, enough to leave the Argonauts in bouts of mirth or melancholy, as was each of their natures.

When they had slept off the drink and Hyperion pried open their eyes with his insistent rays, they made for the ship. They came singly or in pairs, each bearing satchels laden with further supplies and arms aplenty for the dangers that must impend. When Theseus arrived on the beach, already, men in service to Argus were hauling the ship into the waters. It sat upon rollers, dragged forth by numerous lines bound to work horses, whilst other men shoved from the back. Among those, Herakles leant his tremendous strength.

The Argo rolled faster than Theseus imagined anyone had

expected, and two men wound up sprawling facedown in the sand as the groaning vessel spilt into the surf with creaking wood and the splashing of froth.

"Something uncanny draws nigh," Amphiaraos said behind Theseus, and Theseus fair jumped out of his sandals. In the commotion of the ship's descent, he'd not heard the Oracle approach.

"What do you mean?"

But already, the seer had moved on, his steps aimless, his gaze locked on the gulls screeching across the morning sky.

"HAVE YOU MET THE NEWEST ARRIVAL?" Pirithous asked, approaching Theseus as he watched slaves loading supplies onto the Argo. Theseus's friend—sometimes more than a friend, he supposed— traced a lazy finger along Theseus's forearm, sending a tingle up Theseus's spine. It was just subtle enough, he imagined, no one would have seen it.

Maybe.

"Who?"

"Oh, we're now nineteen." Pirithous grinned, though the smile seemed forced. "A stranger arrived in the night. Whatever he said to Jason, our glorious leader welcomed this Orpheus on board."

"Who is he?"

"A bard, based on his lyre. Something more besides, I'd wager, though I know precious little of the man. I asked about, and Autolykus claims him a Phrygian. From the way he said it, even that wily old bastard seemed to mistrust the poet, and that's saying something."

Theseus sucked air between his teeth. Someone else to watch, then?

Dark-haired and tall enough to have Titan blood, if Theseus had to guess, he'd have named Orpheus an Atlantid, though he did dress in the Phrygian style, down to the floppy cap. The newcomer sat upon a rock, strumming a lyre that glinted in the sunlight as though some god had aurified the instrument.

If this Orpheus was a worry to Pirithous, Theseus would just as soon know as much about him as possible. Affecting his best saunter, Theseus made his way to where Orpheus strummed. The incipient melodies the bard plucked teased at profundity, and yet each he abandoned before Theseus could form a full decision on the matters, leaving the music tantalising like half-remembered dreams. Did Orpheus play thus in a deliberate attempt to discomfit his companions, or did the bard simply have trouble choosing a piece to focus on?

"You seem to have a gift," Theseus said.

Orpheus paused mid-chord and raised his gaze to Theseus, solemn and filled with a depth of such soul-gnawing heartache that Theseus's breath caught. Orpheus's eyes were dark as midnight, and within them lurked depth beyond the measure of words. "Gifts are freely given. Some things we purchase at too high a price."

The disquiet his music engendered was naught compared to the chills his words evoked. "Why are you here?" Theseus's own voice had dropped almost to a whisper, but he could not force himself to speak with confidence. Something about this man flowed, down beyond Gaia, into her deepest recesses. Beyond. "Why join the Argonauts?"

"Kolchis is said to be a land of sorcerers and alchemists. Among them, they have strange herbs and stranger drugs that, for those initiated, might allow one to walk in places where no Man can otherwise tread."

Orpheus all but dared Theseus to ask where such a place might be. And yet ... yet he could not give voice to the question. "I ... hope you find what you seek there."

So much for taking the bard's measure.

ॐ

At last, they made sail, Euphemos at the helm whilst keen-eyed Laertes kept their lookout. Pirithous at his side, Theseus watched the scattered greenery flanking the Strait roll by, the sunlight glinting off the turquoise waters. They had agreed to turns at the oars, and soon Theseus would need to head below decks where the view would not so dazzle. He was determined to bask in the radiance whilst he could, drinking in the cooling breeze ruffling his hair, the briny mist, and the Argo's surging speed. All of it, all a wonder he intended to emblazon into his memory.

On the bridge, Orpheus began strumming a new melody. Unlike his haunting, abortive songs Theseus had heard upon the shore, the notes here leapt with promise, dancing along the waves and, in Theseus's mind, further increasing the ship's pace. The song teased and lilted, drawing a smile to his face, and Pirithous's too.

The sense of threading not just the currents of the Straits but of history itself, it settled ponderously upon his shoulders. Knowledge he could not explain that never again would there be such a ship as this. Never again such a voyage of heroes into the wondrous unknown.

And when Orpheus's ringing voice joined his lyre, Theseus found himself compelled to close his eyes and let it all wash over him.

But the fair weather did not hold, and the next day, the roiling storm clouds upon the horizon hurtled toward the Argo, borne upon winds sweeping out of Phlegra. Sitting at the oar and heaving in time with the others until his muscles burnt from exhaustion, Theseus could make out little through the porthole beyond Pirithous.

"Heave!" Jason bellowed, voice almost swallowed by the crash of waves, the roaring wind, and the sporadic peals of thunder that punctuated the clamour. "Laertes spots harbour ahead! Keep us steady, you—"

Whatever insult the prince had intended to spur them on was swallowed by another crack of thunder. Outside, blinding-white flashes of lightning made it look as though Zeus saw fit to strike down individual fish from the sea.

The Argo listed to one side and then so far to the other Theseus had to hook his ankle around the bench's leg to keep from sliding off his seat.

"Poseidon's wrath!" Pirithous swore.

Theseus had no time to inquire what his friend had seen through the porthole. The Argo pitched and rocked, tossed about as though beaten by sea monsters, until Theseus wondered that the whole of the ship did not crumble into kindling.

Jason was thrown from his perch upon the ladder, crashed into a beam, and lay still in a hold slowly filling with seawater. Theseus couldn't see their leader anymore. Outside, surging waves blocked what little daylight had pierced the storm, rendering the lower decks a blind maze of shadows.

Another sudden drop, and his teeth clanked together as the ship crashed down once more.

"Hold on!" Pirithous shouted.

What else was Theseus going to do?

EVEN THESEUS'S CALLOUSED HANDS, used to hard work and wielding weapons, were rubbed raw by the time the Argo came to rest in whatever harbour Laertes had found. Blisters upon his fingers wept viscous fluids. His palms stung with everything he touched, especially as he scooped buckets of saltwater from the hold and hurled them, over and over, out of the portholes.

"Where on Gaia are we?" Autolykus demanded.

Herakles had brought Jason onto the bridge, where, Theseus thought, Asklepoius tended to a wound on their leader's head. Euphemos had proclaimed himself most fit to command with Jason incapacitated and ordered the remainder of the Argonauts to bail out the ship.

"The island of Kuzikos, I think," Orpheus answered. Theseus had not even realised the bard had descended into the hold. "Off the Phrygian coast."

With a grunt of pain, Theseus looked up at Orpheus. Bands of sunlight now seeped in through the portholes, but the day was dying fast. The bard stood half in one of those sunbeams, the better part of his face drenched in shadow, golden light limning his chin and one cheek. "You've been here before?"

"No," Orpheus answered. "Men do not tread upon these shores, which lie beyond the bounds of even King Laomedon's grasping reach."

It seemed Orpheus had not yet heard of Laomedon's death. Someone would fill him in, sooner or later. Theseus had no energy left for such things now.

Euphemos half-descended the ladder to look over the crew. "Argus says he needs time to check over the ship, and in full daylight. We can't make sail tonight, so we're going ashore. Find food and supplies as you can, but don't wander too far. We've no idea who lives in this land."

If Orpheus had the knowledge, he did not offer it.

WHEN HYPERION'S fiery gaze scorched the sky, Jason trod among the Argonauts taking in his crew, a hint of rubescent stains spreading through the bandage wrapt around his scalp. Their leader glowered as if he sought someone to blame for the inauspicious start to their voyage and yet could not find fault among any of the mortals or demigods who had flocked to his banner. "Argus says it's best we repair the ship and replace the broken oars before heading underway once more."

Theseus had joined the others on the beach that night, and though some of the crew had gone to forage, no one had found more than a few berries. Nestor and Laertes had sat watch whilst the rest of the Argonauts had slept with bellies half full at best and moods as sodden as their storm-drenched threads.

"In the meantime," Jason continued, "we need to scout the area. Nike, Iolaus, and I will hunt for game in the woods. Herakles, Theseus, and Amphiaraos, watch the ship and cut some lumber under Argus's direction. Nestor and Laertes should rest. The remainder of you, get the lay of this land and find out if we are on an island, as Orpheus suspects."

Theseus found it passing strange that Jason, a man yet to earn his claim to royalty, spouted orders to princes and kings without the least hint of modesty. He spoke like one assured that others would follow his instructions, and to Theseus's mild surprise, the whole of the crew did rise to carry out their assigned tasks. Was it that they had sworn to sail under his command and stood by those oaths? Or rather, did Jason's very manner compel unconscious obedience from men who might have otherwise balked at being ordered about?

After retrieving hatchets from the Argo, Theseus joined Herakles and Amphiaraos—the seer's gaze again locked upon the sky as though he might take flight and escape this place thus—and Argus described in exacting detail what sort of lumber they should cut. *This many pieces, just this long, just this type of wood.* Theseus paid him only enough mind to be certain which tree he was meant to fell.

It was tedious work, yes, the hatchet aggravating his raw fingers and palms. Still, he found a certain comfort in the routine of it. Unlike the treacherous waves, which might rise against them with fury beyond his ability to counter, the felling of trees was, in the end, a matter of time and patience. Each swing of his axe took another chip from the trunk until, at last, even the towering cypress tree creaked. The echo of its dying roar resounded over the craggy hills and through the woods before the tree smacked into the moss and underbrush.

Of course, felling the tree was the easier part. After Theseus had hacked away the branches, Herakles helped him drag the trunk back to the beach. As Theseus mopped the sweat from his brow, old Argus appeared as though he'd been lurking beneath the sand like a gods-damned crab, yammering instructions about how to turn the trunk into oars.

When Theseus knelt upon the beach, sawing away—and cursing Jason for not sending him hunting with the others—Amphiaraos came stumbling along, gaze locked upon the skies as ever, mumbling beneath his breath. The seer might spout nonsense, but it offered a convenient excuse to break from the shaping of oars, so Theseus huffed and followed the Argosian's gaze.

"Birds ..." Amphiaraos muttered, watching the flight of circling shapes, dark against the white of the clouds blanketing the morning sky. "Herakles was hunting birds."

Theseus snorted. "True enough, friend. But those are crows, and I have a doubt King Eurystheus sent him on a labour to rid the world of their ilk."

"They anticipate a feast," Amphiaraos said, face ashen as he looked to Theseus.

The next instant, the Tethid tackled Theseus, sending the both of them sprawling into the sand. Even as he did so, a boulder the size of a horse shrieked overhead. It crashed into the fallen trunk where Theseus had been working, splintering wood and sending the lumber jerking upward. A torrent of sand and debris exploded over Theseus and Amphiaraos, stinging their eyes.

Hardly knowing what he was about, he shoved the Oracle off himself, rolled to his side, and pushed onto his elbows.

There, atop the hill, he saw it. A creature, Man-like only in its initial profile. For it stood eight feet high, at least, naked and covered in shaggy hair, misshapen and contorted with bulges of awkward muscles. Two extra pairs of arms jutted from the Gígas's bloated sides. All six hands—*claws*—lifted skyward and the monster bellowed.

Then, another of the horrors crested the hill, a second boulder clutched in its four upper arms. A third came, and a fourth.

Theseus knew his sword rested against a rock, down the beach. He knew he needed to move, to grab the blade. Needed to take the fight to the monsters lest their missiles crack the Argo's hull. He knew he must act now. But staring at the twisted, bent horrors descending upon the shore, he found his limbs refused him. All he could do was gape as death reared over him.

Hands seized his armpits and heaved, yanking him to his unresponsive feet. Amphiaraos dragged him away from the shards of broken lumber, then jerked him fiercely to one side. Another boulder slammed into the sand, a geyser of the stuff raining over the pair of them.

The next shrieking roar that came was one not of fury but of pain. Half-blinded by grit, Theseus turned to see a Gígas stagger, an arrow having sprouted from its chest. A second arrow struck one of its companions.

Down the beach, Herakles had claimed his bow and was forcing the Gigantes back, giving them no chance to rain further destruction upon Theseus and Amphiaraos.

The seer grabbed the back of Theseus's skull, forcing him to look the Tethid in the eyes. "Prove your mettle."

Theseus's heart was hammering so loud it almost swallowed the Oracle's words. His palms were drenched in clammy sweat. Was this not what he had wanted all along? Had not he sought to slay monsters as Herakles had done and thus carve his legend in stone? So, why then did he stand here trembling, thinking more than aught else he needed to piss? Gritting his teeth, Theseus nodded at Amphiaraos, then the two of them broke into a run. Theseus raced to where his sword—the sword of his valiant father—lay scabbarded and leaning upon a rock.

In a single motion, he snatched it up, spun, and took off racing toward the Gigantes. Prove his mettle.

Prove his mettle.

He had fought Men and demigods. Now ... now, he would face true monsters. These creatures feasted upon the flesh of Man. They would not find Theseus an easy meal. More arrows whizzed past him, driving the Gigantes from the hilltop.

Theseus charged upward, dodging between rocks jutting from the hillside and avoiding loose scree. He tossed the scabbard aside as he climbed.

Prove his mettle.

A Gígas rose to meet him, six clawed hands reaching for him, so eager. A black-fletched arrow thwacked into the creature's shoulder, and it staggered back, giving Theseus an opening. On this, he could not hesitate.

His blade darted forwards into the beast's belly. Its skin was hard as worked leather, but still, the point of his xiphos bit deep. Roaring, both hands upon the hilt, Theseus jerked the blade upward. Jets of hot, reeking blood showered him as he opened the Gígas from gut to sternum. The creature flailed, six arms tracing wild, pained circles.

Theseus danced away as it fell, catching itself upon its upper arms. The eyes that rose to meet his gaze were still too Man-like, full of shock and agony, the creature not believing it could end thus for it. Something rose in Theseus's chest and he screamed defiance at the Gígas.

Two more of the creatures lay fallen from Herakles's arrows whilst Amphiaraos had managed to fell the last with a javelin. One of the ones shot by Herakles tried to crawl away, its progress hampered by four different arrows sprouting from its chest and back.

Theseus hefted his xiphos once more and realised his hand was still trembling. It did not stop him from driving the blade through the back of the Gígas's neck.

10

HERAKLES

726 Bronze Age

Given that the island of Kuzikos seemed home to a race of Gigantes, on his return, Jason agreed the Argo must make sail right away and resupply at the closest available landfall. Theseus, clearly shaken by their encounter with the creatures, stood alone at the bow, one hand resting upon the prow, the other upon the hilt of the sword he wore at his waist. It would have been easier, Herakles supposed, to leave the boy be and take his turn at the oars. Would have been, but with a sigh, Herakles found himself climbing to the upper deck and making his way to the bow.

He said naught when he first reached the boy, just leant against the gunwale and let the sea spray cool his cheeks. The first time Herakles had fought Gigantes had been in the Gigantomachy, but he couldn't well offer details on that battle. Not without either claiming to be seven hundred years old or revealing Pandora—Nike—and her Box and all the mind-rending puzzles that sprung from it. The thought of her had him casting about to spot her at the rear deck.

The Titan had offered him little save curt responses, if that, since Ilium. Her silent rebuke hurt worse for the truth inherent in it. He was a monster; death lurked within the very pith of his soul.

But at this moment, Theseus needed someone, and no one else seemed able to offer him comfort.

"The Kalydonian Boar was worse than that," Herakles said. Which wasn't at all the thing to say and probably didn't help Theseus in the least. He'd seen the boy freeze there, for a moment, on the beach. Theseus had killed before this, Herakles knew, so it wasn't that either. But maybe he'd never felt himself facing a monster *alone*. Would it help if Herakles reminded Theseus he had not been alone on the beach this morning? He doubted it. One could feel alone even in the midst of a battle with allies on all sides. "But we were all together on that one, hmm?"

Theseus snorted. "I barely lent aid that day. You and Atalanta did most of the work."

"Ugh." Herakles shook his head. He'd no talent for soothing the shaken. Still, he wrapt a hand around Theseus's shoulder. "Any man who fought *that* boar has faced death, Theseus. That you did not strike the killing blow does not mean your help amounted to naught. It took all of us, more than twenty hunters, to bring low that *thing*."

"Did you fear when you faced the Nemean lion? When you slew the hydra?"

Herakles glanced back toward the hold. Did the shades of his children lurk there now, watching him, awaiting his undertaking of this next labour? Was he to tell Theseus that, when he fought those monsters, a part of him almost hoped they would claim his life and end his misery? "Terror is always there, Theseus. Let it grant your arm the desperation to pull you through rather than sap it of strength."

Maybe he ought to have sent Nike here. She had a way with words and could have soothed the boy's nerves and, too, had befriended him on their trek. But she would not have deigned to hear him. And he deserved no less from her.

"It gets better," he said, though he wondered if that was more platitude than truth.

❧

WHEN NEXT THEY FOUND HARBOUR, it was along the Phrygian coast, when Argus insisted they could not risk being caught in rough waters once more without fresh oars and reinforcements to the hull. Jason had agreed, and Herakles would not have gainsaid either, for roiling clouds darkened the horizon, churning with malice. Men said Zeus could call storms to make seas impassable or inundate farms with unending torrents. Had Herakles's father sent such challenges upon them?

No, mostlike some other cause lay behind storms sighted twice in as many days.

Ashore, Amphiaraos plodded to Herakles's side, mouth a grim line. "They are here."

Herakles need not ask what the Oracle meant. "Eurystheus's birds … the iron-taloned fiends the king sends me to slay or drive off … They are harpies." Herakles had beheld once such foul spirit already, lurking in the storming depths of Tartarus, its feathers crackling with lightning. The creature had preyed upon Prometheus, and Herakles had slain it to save Pandora's beloved.

"They come for us," Amphiaraos said. "I see, in the swirl of the clouds, a meeting of some import. They have trapt someone within ruins upon the far hilltop." Herakles followed the seer's gaze. In the distance, obscured by scraggly trees and shadowed by the rapidly darkening sky, broken columns rose like jagged teeth.

Perhaps, in days long ago, this had been the site of some Phoenikian colony or an outpost of lesser Phrygian kingdoms. Was it because of these harpies that this settlement had dwindled until, at last, Gaia began to swallow it once more?

Herakles clenched his fist at his side. "I must do this alone. Such are the terms of Eurystheus's commands." If a person within those ruins was beset by the harpies, Herakles's coming would serve dual purpose: he would accomplish one of his labours, yes, but too he could save someone from becoming prey to these vile birds.

The young Oracle nodded as if he had known such things before ever beginning this conversation. "I will see to it no others disturb your work, demigod."

BOW AND AN ARROW in one hand, Herakles crept up the escarpment, sandals disturbing more scree than he'd have liked. Still, he imagined the frequent peals of thunder and howling winds would have covered the sounds of his passage. Spears of lightning flashed from above, leaving momentary afterimages dancing before his eyes. He could not afford to tear his gaze from the sky, though, for somewhere among the pitch-black, tumultuous clouds, there must lurk harpies.

On hands and knees, he crested the rise and peered into the ruins. From the remnants of the peristyle around the structure, this place had once been a temple to some god or other. Half the roof had caved in and the pediment had toppled over backwards, leaving the vestibule strewn with giant blocks of rubble. On one side, wiry moss crept over the marble in a stubborn carpet.

Once more, Herakles looked skyward. Lightning continued to crackle amid the clouds, breaking in sporadic lances that would streak toward the hill, some reaching close enough to leave the air singed. The hairs on his arms and legs stood on end. Shadows flashed and shifted, but within the darkness above, Herakles could make out no clear shapes. Was he wrong? Were there no harpies here?

No, no, he did not think himself mistaken, much less did he doubt Amphiaraos.

Well then. If they would not show themselves freely, he must draw the monsters to himself. Nocking the arrow to his bow, Herakles rose to his full height and plodded into the portico.

"Show yourself," he shouted to whoever lurked within. "If you would be free of this place, come out now!"

At first, naught happened, and Herakles again turned his gaze to the rumbling heavens. More lightning coruscated above, the thunder growing so loud it left his ears ringing. Winds strong enough to send a smaller man careening whipped his hair and clothes, and he had to brace himself against the chest-high remains of a column.

Where in Hades's dark domain were the damn harpies?

From the shadowed recesses of the temple, a figure shambled forwards, barefoot and clad in naught save stained rags. A mess of hair hung unruly over the man's clean-shaven face. At first, between the gloom and the man's dishevelled state, Herakles did not recognise him. Only when he lifted his gaze, his face illumined by another spear of lightning that revealed the blindfold over his eyes, did Herakles grasp the person before him.

"Tiresias?" In Herakles's youth, Tiresias had served as advisor to Kreon. He had, in fact, according to the tales espoused by no few bards, served as advisor to the mortal kings of Thebes going all the way back to legendary Kadmus himself. Bardic stories offered more than one explanation for the ancient Oracle's supposed immortality, but Herakles had not credited such wild talk.

It was the same man, only beardless and ... not a man at all. Svelte and well-muscled, when dressed in a formal khiton, none could have recognised Tiresias as a woman. But Herakles was more than passing certain he'd seen breasts through the rents in Tiresias's tattered rags.

If the blind Oracle answered, his—her?—words were swallowed by more thunder. Herakles saw two more forms creeping from the ruins. Before he could focus on them, a shadow overhead drew his eye.

With a growl, Herakles spun, drawing back his bow. The shadow pitched and swooped, its razored pinions crackling with lightning that adumbrated its harsh contours. Its cries seemed born not of Gaia but of some monstrous domain beyond the Earth. Those sounds reached into Herakles's mind, into his very soul, and clawed at it as if the harpy's talons had dug into the very depths of him.

He loosed his arrow, but the gales snatched the missile long before it could reach into the dark cloud within which the harpy had vanished. "Damn it." He looked to Tiresias and the pair of men behind her. "Take shelter!"

Herakles was not certain the blind Oracle would know where she'd be safe from the harpies, but he could not afford to distract himself over it, either. He stuck close to the columns, hoping they might offer some sanctuary from—

The harpy crashed into the courtyard, followed an instant later by a second. The creature, a birdlike woman, looked every bit as profane as Herakles remembered from Tartarus. As if a storm itself was forced to take on a living shape, if only briefly. The harpy shrieked, spreading wide wings that glistened with raindrops. Talons scraped over stone, gouging as if made of bladed iron. Then it whipped those wings at him, pinions hurtling toward Herakles like a dozen flung darts. He threw himself to the side. Knife-like projectiles clattered against the marble column where he'd stood, chipping the stone.

Coming up in a roll, Herakles nocked another arrow and loosed. An ironlike wing batted his poorly aimed missile aside, but it gave him the chance to close the distance and tackle the bird-creature, bearing the both of them to the ground. A beak snapped at his face and he twisted aside. He didn't know what had happened to the second harpy, but it would be on him any moment. Flooding Pneuma into Potency, he slammed his fist into the harpy's face. Its hideous head smacked against the cobbles. Once. Twice, leaving it dazed. Herakles grabbed the sides of its head and squeezed, pushing his thumbs into the creature's eyes even as he slammed it against the ground over and over.

Skull and brains splattered feathers.

Another shriek was his only warning, but he used it to flood Pneuma into his skin for Steadfastness. Those razor wings still sliced through his toughened flesh, sending fiery lances of agony shooting along his arms and back. He turned as talons flashed toward his thighs, barely dancing aside. His uppercut took the harpy in the jaw and he heard vertebrae crunch. With the monster stunned, he grabbed its head and slammed it into a column. The force of the impact shattered both stone and the harpy's head.

The awful thing hung limp in his hand and Herakles let it drop.

Only then did the pain hit him full force. Dozens of cuts lacerated his flesh, some deep enough he was losing blood fast. With a groan, he stumbled, steadying himself on the blood-strewn remnants of that column. When he looked back, the bodies of the harpies were gone. All that remained were the corpses of naked women, both with their heads pulverised.

The sight clenched his gut. Bile scorched his throat, and Herakles looked away lest he retch all over the temple.

"Son of Zeus?"

The voice, shaky but heard clear, made him realise the thunder and winds had died all at once, leaving a sudden, eerie stillness to settle upon the hilltop. Lancets of untrammelled sunlight punched through the clouds that still lurked overhead, serving to cast the ruins in sporadic illumination.

"Herakles?" Tiresias asked. That voice, though tremulous, was deep enough he could see why he always believed Tiresias male. "I ... I knew you would come. I heard it in the birdsong."

Oracles. Always knowing more than anyone ought.

"You're a woman," Herakles managed between breaths.

Behind the seer, two young men had begun to approach, haggard and dishevelled. At his words, the lead young man raised hands in warding.

Though her eyes remained concealed by the blindfold, Herakles could see the muscles around them crease in annoyance. "I'm whatever I damn well choose to be, you simple-minded dolt. I've hardly a need for you to decide it for me. I was advising Men upon thrones long before your birth and will be even when you are but ash fluttering in the wind."

Still reeling, Herakles shook his head to clear it and lifted a hand in surrender. "As you say. It's of no real consequence to me." Finally, he regained his breath and looked to the pair beyond Tiresias. "Who are they?"

"The sons of Phrixus," Tiresias snapped, still cantankerous over

Herakles's incautious outburst. "Trapped here by the same harpies as myself."

Herakles looked back down the hill. With the passing of the storm, he could just make out the Argo's hull. "Come then. I've a ship down in—"

"Yes, yes, Son of Zeus. Do you not think I well know that? Why on your papa's pimpled, self-righteous arse do you think the three of us have been waiting for you, hmm? Certainly not for your stimulating wit." With that she—no, definitely *he*—shambled past Herakles, one of the young men taking his elbow to guide the blind seer's passage. "Addlepate," Tiresias mumbled as he passed.

HERAKLES GUIDED the blind prophet and his companions down to the Argo, where the rest of the crew awaited, some open-mouthed, others nodding with approval. Already, clean winds had begun to disperse the storm clouds that had shadowed these lands, and Herakles knew Men could once more sail the Axeinos Sea without fear of frightful birds or Otherworldly storms.

The Argonauts prepared a feast for Tiresias, for it seemed the ancient Theban Oracle had scarce eaten in the past fortnight. Despite his hunger, Herakles noted the Oracle had managed to shift the rags over his chest to avoid allowing anyone else repeating Herakles's blunder. "I offended Aeëtes," Tiresias explained when Nestor asked how he came to be trapped by harpies in that ruin. "The king of Kolchis has learnt sorcery and calls spirits of Storm and Sea to his aid." The how and why of his exact offence, Tiresias declined to reveal.

The young men with him, as it turned out, had come seeking the Oracle in hopes of learning who had acted against their father, one Phrixus. The elder was named Phrontis, the younger Kytorus. Their father had wed King Aeëtes's daughter and had long dwelt in Kolchis but had died under mysterious circumstances. The brothers promised that, in exchange for Herakles saving them from the harpies, they would show Jason the way to Kolchis.

"With strong eastward winds," Phrontis said, "we might make the voyage in well under a fortnight. Assuming Grandfather sends no further spirits to trouble us, of course."

Herakles had no business in Kolchis itself, but Tiresias had told him the destination would bring him as close as possible to the equally legendary Amazonian polis of Themiskyra. Much though Herakles misliked going there to rob the queen of a godsdamned girdle, neither could he shirk a labour wretched Eurystheus has laid upon him. Given what he had done for the Argonauts, Herakles imagined that once Jason had reached Kolchis, he could prevail on him to see him dropped off in Amazon lands.

So, soon they would see Kolchis for themselves. And now, Jason must prove whether he was indeed worthy of the task set before him.

As if summoned by the gods themselves, a thick brume had risen upon the sea as the Argo drew nigh to Kolchis's harbour. Under direction from Kytorus, Euphemos guided their ship up the Phasis river, the crew straining at the oars against a strong current. Wounded as Herakles was, Jason had insisted he not sit at an oar, and thus he had joined their leader upon the bridge, along with Nike, who had even still held herself at a distance from Herakles. Perhaps she would not ever forgive him for the burst of his temper in Ilium. Perhaps she was right not to do so. Theseus, too, was on rest from rowing and stood pensive, watching the passing landscape.

"I will say only this," Tiresias said when Jason had asked him about the fate of their endeavour. "Any weal that may lie within Kolchis, it will come through the arrows of Eros rather than blades dedicated to Ares." Eros, the invisible God of Love, who some bards said—to the chagrin of the Olympians—was the true source of all goodness in the cosmos. If such a god existed, he paid the Olympians little mind. The blind Oracle looked then directly to Theseus as though he could see him. "The arrows of Eros are cruel ones. The wounds they inflict bleed fiercely and are wont to reopen even long after we think them sealed."

Theseus looked to the Oracle, face ashen. A moment later, the young man descended the ladder, escaping from Tiresias's unnerving presence and even more unnerving prophecies.

"The city lies several miles upriver," Kytorus explained when the silence had stretched long enough Herakles saw everyone on deck growing uneasy. "On the north bank there is a fortified hill. Much of the city rests within a network of caves below this hill. But atop it lies Qulha Palace, home of my grandfather, King Aeëtes. He is a sorcerer, ever watching his growing kingdom with jealous eyes. If the gods be with us, this mist shall cover our entry to the city and you can reach the palace before he has time to conspire against you with his Art. The city has grown over the years, spilling well beyond the caves, like mounds of coral coating the sea floor. It is … a bit of a maze to navigate the alleys, I'm afraid."

The king would use sorcery against them? The thought had Herakles shifting with discomfort, and even Nike paled and turned to stare out into the vapours. How did one defend against an attack that could come at any time and across any distance? The curses of sorcerers were not things warriors could slay with spear or blade.

"If we can reach my mother," Kytorus continued, "she might prevail upon her father to reward you for saving my brother and me. We must await nightfall, though, to increase our chances of going undiscovered."

Phrontis scoffed. "If you think he'll hand over his prized Fleece, you delude yourself, brother."

"Be that as it may," Jason said, "I must attempt diplomacy before we resort to violence."

"Yes," Nike cut in, still not looking their way. "I think we saw enough of that in Ilium." Now she did look back at Herakles, eyes narrowed. "I've no business with King Aeëtes or his treasures. This is where we part company, Argonauts."

Herakles wanted to say something. He wanted to beg her forgiveness. But words failed him, as so oft they did, and all he could offer was a grim nod.

"I'll take only a small party," Jason said. "Myself, the sons of Phrixus, Telamon, and Peleus. The rest of you remain on the ship, but with arms readied in case Aeëtes turns against us."

Herakles folded his arms over his chest. He liked to think, perhaps, Jason could manage all this without the need for weapons. He liked to believe it. Or he wished he could.

INTERLUDE: MEDEA

726 Bronze Age

A stranger, another Heliad, had come seeking the goddess Hekate whilst she and Medea had walked the hillsides gathering hellebore and soaking in the power of a growing twilight. The woman—or Titan, mostlike, whom Hekate named Pandora—had embraced the goddess, making plain she held her dear. And yet, after, when Medea had seen the woman flee Hekate's chambers, the goddess had refused to admit Medea or even to speak with her.

Though she told herself a goddess owed her no explanation, though she ran such reminders through her mind until she had whittled them to stubs, she found the rejection left a stinging ache in her soul. She herself was grand-niece to Hekate, and—Medea had thought—some connection beyond mere student and master had begun to germinate between them.

A thick mist now curled about the courtyard, spilling through the open gables in the wall and obscuring the numerous flowing fountains of the gardens. With a huff, she leant against one of the burnished bull statues that rimmed the main breezeway through the courtyard. According to Father's tales, the great smith Hephaistos had crafted these works as a wedding present, in days long past. Medea did not know whether such was truth, but the bulls did radiate an inner heat, the warmth pleasant through her khiton in contrast to the cool brume moistening her flesh.

Aunt Kirke had offered little explanation for why she no longer came in person. Her letters dripped with empathy Medea had first thought genuine, cased in poetic words that all but screamed of Kirke's thwarted desires to return here. But her aunt had not come in two and half decades, and Medea had found herself doubting the woman's sincerity. At least until Kirke had sent her own mother, and at last the explanation that she herself was exiled to the far isle of Aiaía.

But though Medea had fawned over great Hekate, had *worshipped* her, she had not affected the closeness Kirke had once offered. Still. Still! Medea had thought something akin to friendship blossomed between them. But it was another rejection, and she remained alone here. She traced fingers idly along the grooves of the bull's ribs, the warmest part of whatever furnace lurked within. Father knew more of the Art than he deigned to share, Medea knew, but he would not teach her, claiming such pursuits diminished a woman's worth as a bride. "What man," he'd claimed, "wants a wife who might spew curses when vexed by one thing or another, as women forever seem to be?"

"Perhaps men ought aim to prove less vexing," Aunt Kirke had rejoined when Medea had related the incident in a letter. Kirke understood her, though even her aunt had limited her tutoring to alchemy rather than true sorcery. Father had forbidden Medea from sailing for Aiaía, saying she must not leave the safety of Kolchis. For here, his watchful eye warded his daughters against any threat to their virtue and thus their value to *him*. Medea allowed herself a bitter smile as she stared into the wonderfully curling mists. Hekate had told her that, sometimes, spirits lurked within the glory of nature, invisible and yet guiding the currents of the World. The goddess had pushed Medea to strive for the Sight, though the ability to see into the invisible Realms remained a feat beyond Medea.

Well, Hekate, though a Heliad, was hardly a person who favoured mornings, so perhaps tomorrow afternoon Medea could press her for more details about ...

At first she took them for shadows, but no, figures skulked about the mist, dark spectres creeping like thieves through the courtyard. Lampads? Spirits of Mist? No ... these were earthly Men, their harsh whispers not quite concealed by the burble of the fountains. One of them looked straight at her, and Medea shrieked at the sudden realisation intruders had broken into her father's palace.

What madmen would dare defile this place?

The figure raced toward her, and Medea made a break for the closest wing of the palace, where her brother Absyrtus dwelt. The looming presence behind her grew, the sound of heavy sandals slapping upon the marble floor, and she knew she'd never outdistance her pursuer. Medea drew a sharp breath to scream at the top of her lungs in the hopes of calling whatever defences Father had in place—then crashed headlong not into Absyrtus but Khalkiope, their recently widowed elder sister, who now lived beneath Absyrtus's watchful eye.

Her sister's arms encircled her, strong and defiant, as if the two women might stand against a half dozen armed men.

"Kytorus?" Khalkiope asked, and Medea twisted around in her sister's arms.

She saw, indeed, that her nephews Kytorus and Phrontis stood in the courtyard, ahead of several other men she did not know. Heart still in her throat, Medea found herself utterly at a loss for words. Today was a day of many strangers, it seemed.

Her sister released her and surged forward, sweeping her sons into an embrace. In the gloom, Medea could not make out the details of their faces, but she heard sobs burbling from all three, as though they thought to compete with the fountains to fill the courtyard with water.

Perhaps that was why it took so long for Medea to perceive the shadows had grown too deep now, as if a cloud had passed before the moon and now obscured the light. A darkness thick as cloying honey began to drip from the colonnades. The growing shadows muffled sounds. They swallowed hopes and left the strangers shifting, casting furtive glances about themselves whilst their trembling fists clutched at the pommels of their swords.

So thick was the oppressive silence, Medea had not even noticed the dozen guards now surrounding the intruders. Father's men held back, however, as if they had come more as mere ceremony than to apprehend the trespassers. Or perhaps even they too feared what unfolded within the courtyard, blocking out even Thoth's light. The true threat, it gathered around them, unseen, and yet present, summoned by Medea's father.

King Aeëtes himself drifted forward, his guards parting before him like the receding tide, Medea's mother trailing in his wake and seeming as unnerved by whatever he had unleashed here as the rest of them.

"Who are these men?" Father demanded.

All turned to look to him, Medea as well, their tension drawn so taut she imagined she could have snapped in an instant. She did not know how much of the unnatural presence the strangers felt, but without doubt, everyone there perceived something of it. It raised the hair and curdled the guts. It brushed over the skin, unseen, with violating caresses. Prudence demanded she flee and hide herself within the best-lit chamber in the palace. That she order a thousand oil lamps set to encircle her and banish every last shadow from her presence.

Was this the Dark of which Kirke and Hekate had so warned her?

Khalkiope sniffed. "Father, they have saved your grandchildren and returned them to us. Surely that is enough."

Medea, though, watched her father's face. The darkness welled in circles beneath his eyes, as deep there as even the greatest pools of shadow engulfing the courtyard. Deeper perhaps, obscuring even the golden radiance of the Heliad gaze. Her father was no fool. Yet he did not openly question why rescuing heroes came under cover of darkness, sneaking into the palace, rather than proclaiming themselves with joyous heralds.

"Then we must feast them," the king said, "as honour demands for such service."

The lack of emotion behind his words drew from her a shudder she could not suppress.

THE ARGONAUTS, for so the strangers named themselves, were sent to wash, and meanwhile, Medea's father ordered a great board spread for them. The table was laden with figs and dates, with olives, grapes, and muskmelons. Too, there was succulent roasted fowl, basted with pomegranates and garnished with almonds. Wine flowed through the courtyard as if it spewed from the very fountains, such were the streams of servants bearing amphora after amphora.

Despite the late hour, Father had roused lyrists who plucked at sweet melodies that drifted through the gardens, as if to intimate the presence of old friends. Yet Father sat not before the board but rather secluded beneath an eave overhanging the courtyard. The shadows lay heavy about him and he wore them like armour that might shield him from any threat.

It was not always thus. Medea had never met her aunt Pasiphaë, but Father cherished her, at least in so much as he valued any woman, and certainly more than he seemed to care for Medea. Even across the vastness of the Thalassa and the Axeinos Sea both, word of Pasiphaë's shame had flown to them, borne forth with the swiftness of an eagle's wings. The Nymph who had given birth to a monster, this odious Minotaur that had become the terror of Knosós.

And not only of Knosós, for the spectre of that misshapen beast haunted the king of Kolchis too, half a world away. Whilst Father had never once spoken of it, not to Medea leastwise, a bitter change had come over him. Mother claimed he always had his fierce melancholies, yes, but they deepened into glooms deep as the fathomless sea until waves of that darkness would flow from him, lapping at his surroundings.

It was not long after Pasiphaë's tragedy that the sorceress Damkina had come, rich velvet himation draped over a face ever shrouded. Unseen, she would walk through the palace, more whisper than person, going where she willed, perceived only on occasion by the guards she slipped past. The sorceress took counsel alone with Father, behind closed doors, and he paid no mind when Mother hurled spite—and more than one amphora—in her suspicions of what unfolded there.

Medea knew what Mother thought, and perhaps there was truth in her misgivings. But she felt fair certain that this Damkina had corrupted more than flesh in her secret encounters with Father. The shadows swelled. In the years that followed, though Damkina did not return, Aeëtes himself came to be known as a sorcerer-king.

And still he had refused to teach Medea of the Art.

Medea's brother Absyrtus drifted through the hall and paused by her divan. Like her father, Medea sat not at the table but off to herself, although not in the darkness. She sat just close enough to the brazier to enjoy its warmth, but not so close as to deal with the stinging eyes its smoke would induce.

"Take care with these Elládosi," Absyrtus warned as though Medea was a child. Being male alone was enough to give him authority over his sisters, and he savoured that authority like the finest of wines. Father had, in fact, moved Medea's and Khalkiope's chambers into Absyrtus's wing of the palace with strict instructions he was to watch over his sisters. The withering gaze Medea favoured him with seemed lost upon him. "I find it more than passing odd that foreigners should happen upon our sister's missing children just as we were about to give them up for dead."

"Father warned them not to leave the safety of Kolchis," Medea said. But her nephews were headstrong and foolish. She could not disagree with her brother's assessment, though. Titans and sorcerers could hazard passage across the Axeinos. Hekate had, after all, managed it and gave no indication it had troubled her. But since

Father had summoned his spirits after what happened to Pasiphaë, no mortal nor even demigods had survived passage. But these Elládosi had chanced the dark waters, nonetheless. Men did not take such chances without purpose.

"Hmm. There is something I mislike about all this."

"Brother ..." Dammit. Much though she resented his control—and arrogance—she could not stand the thought of harm befalling him. "If they plan treachery, see yourself well protected."

Her brother offered a perfunctory nod before taking his seat at the head of the table. Under Father's authority, Absyrtus would act as host this night. She doubted Father would deign to speak to the foreigners at all.

The Argonauts came, hair still dripping with water. Where their tunics exposed their chests, Medea could see massage oils glistening upon muscled flesh. Yes, it was more than passing odd that Father should so pamper the intruders.

Alone, watching the strangers feast themselves, she swished crimson wine around in her goblet, drinking its aroma more than its flavour.

Breaking with the others, Phrontis approached her, bearing a plate laden with fruits and nuts. Her nephew settled himself beside Medea, his repast balanced upon his knees, and motioned for her to help herself. Medea plucked a few grapes, toying with them between her fingers rather than popping them in her mouth.

"Tell me of the strangers," Medea said, not removing her gaze from the three of them. Though they made a show of feigning conviviality, tension underlay their postures. Was it fear of Father's reputation, or did they come here with ill intent?

"The youngest, Jason, is their leader," Phrontis said. The one her nephew indicated was sandy-haired and taller than most men, but it was his eyes, blue as a clear day, that truly struck her. More than once, Medea had observed this Jason casting glances her way. His unsubtle gaze traced the lines of her body as if imagining tearing her khiton from her shoulders. It was flattering enough to bring a slight flush to her cheeks, though he'd have not seen it from so far away.

"He comes here on a great ship filled with warriors, though he brought only two men ashore to avoid raising alarm among our people. Those two are brothers—and demigods—the larger of them being Telamon, the smaller Peleus."

Now Medea did chew on a couple of grapes, pondering. Strangers had not come to Kolchis in decades. The Axeinos had become closed to travellers, beset by wild storms and dangers aplenty. And a ship of warriors and demigods had now braved those forbidden waters. She found herself ever more certain they wanted something. "What purpose have they in Kolchis?"

Phrontis sniffed. "That's what we need your help with, Aunt." Oh, it was "we" now? These Argonauts had saved Phrontis and his brother, true, and he supposed that now made him one of them? "Jason is tasked to retrieve Grandfather's prized Fleece and will ask him for it presently. My hope is he will relent and hand it over in repayment for the service the Argonauts rendered in saving myself and Kytorus."

Repayment? Medea almost laughed, stifling her bitter, mirthless impulse only to spare Phrontis's fragile ego. Father was not one given to bouts of generosity. He might have offered up some silver as a token of gratitude, but he would never hand over his prize. Not if Helios himself appeared from the sky in a chariot pulled by flying drakons and demanded it of his son.

"What is it you think I shall do for you, Nephew?" Medea asked, still watching Jason and his men. The Argonaut leader now met her gaze, his cerulean eyes widening. There was a fierce hunger in him, that was certain, and not an unpleasing one at that.

"Convince Grandfather to give them what they need and let them part here as friends."

Oh, poor, deluded Phrontis. Medea considered drawing him into a consoling embrace. Father would sooner see these men fettered in iron and hurled into the depths of the sea to feed the sirens than offer them such a prize. Maybe she ought to have warned him such hopes were in vain, but if he told Jason that, the mortal might attempt something rash.

Better if Medea took steps herself to ensure violence did not ensue here. Even as she rose, Father leapt to his feet, shoving aside Kytorus who had been whispering into his ears.

"Blasphemous mortal wretches!" the king bellowed, his voice filling the expanse of the courtyard and resounding off the marble columns. "You come here for my prize? Should I too hand over my very throne? Give me but one reason not to have your tongues torn from your skulls."

Medea saw Telamon wrap a meaty fist around the pommel of his xiphos.

Jason stood slowly, though, hands raised to mollify her father. "Peace, King Aeëtes. We come here because such a quest was impressed upon me by a vile king before I might reclaim my own rightful throne. The Moirai have woven this, but still, I am no thief. I ask you to grant my request, and I swear, all from here to Elládos will know of your magnanimousness. And you will count myself and all my warriors friends, should you ever have need of strong arms against your enemies."

For a time, Father's face remained expressionless. Then a smirk crept over it, humourless and cruel. "If Ananke has sent you for my Fleece, I think then you, leader of the Argonauts, must be fit to pass a test of your valour."

Jason spared a single glance back at Telamon and Peleus. "I am ready for any test, King."

Medea almost pitied the guileless man that could utter such words.

Father's smirk deepened. "At tomorrow's dusk, one of my brazen bulls shall come to life in this very courtyard. If you can overcome the beast, I shall not stop you from claiming your prize, Argonaut."

Jason, fool that he was, bowed in acquiescence of the mad terms. "So shall it be done."

Medea shuddered.

"Medea!" Her sister's frantic whispers froze Medea even as she ducked out of the courtyard, intent on making for her chambers in Absyrtus's wing. A sense of foreboding settled upon her shoulders, so heavy she found herself leaning against the wall as she turned to take in Khalkiope's imploring face.

As if Medea did not already know the words about to pour forth. As if she did not realise as well as her sister what must soon unfold.

"The bull will slay Jason."

"Yes," Medea agreed, and the thought of the handsome foreigner crushed beneath brazen hooves—sky-blue eyes forever shut—displeased her a good deal more than it ought to have, not that she'd have admitted such.

"And when their leader is gone, Father will see that ship razed in the harbour."

Or worse, perhaps beset by spirits under his command, dragged to the depths by sirens, or snatched away by harpies, though Medea would not give voice to such horrid fancies. "If such is the will of the Moirai." She struggled to keep her voice guarded against her own quickening pulse. All of this felt wrong in some way she could not name or measure. What concern of hers if the king of Kolchis decided to smite those come here to claim his treasure? Should she not take her father's side in all things?

Khalkiope gripped Medea's elbows and edged so close her breath warmed Medea's cheek. "My sons worship the foreigners, and if gratitude for their rescue alone would not prompt them to act, their reverence for Jason and his companions will. They will call it honour when they cast themselves in front of Father's wrath."

Medea hesitated. That her nephews would run headfirst into danger like irate mountain goats came as little surprise. They'd done just that in hunting for Oracular answers about their father's death. Still, Khalkiope would find it easier to control her own offspring than her father. "What has any of this to do with me?"

Now her older sister glared at her. "I know well enough Kirke and Hekate have both instructed you in their dark Art, Medea. I do not know what effects the draughts you throw back produce or what benefit you derive from the acrid smoke that oft wafts beneath your door, but I am not fool enough to think it mere incense. No—I don't want to know, either. All such pursuits only served to turn Aunt Kirke dourer and dourer with the passing years. But if any of that avails you in the least, use it to stave off disaster *now*, Medea. Now is when you must act. Otherwise, we shall be forced to live with regrets for what will happen at tomorrow's dusk."

Medea's face stung as though her elder sister had slapped her. Khalkiope had rarely asked her for aught. But this ... Her sister did not understand the workings of the Art, yet even she knew there were dangers. Medea was no true sorceress, not like Hekate or even Aunt Kirke, but her drugs and learning afforded her certain gifts that might make it possible for her to help resolve this.

Not half so well as the goddess Hekate could have.

Leaving Khalkiope behind, Medea scampered back to Hekate's door. Her steps grew quicker with each pace until they hammered almost as hard as her heart. Until her palm smacking against the wood of the goddess's chamber matched that pounding.

"Goddess Hekate," she pleaded. "Goddess, please, I need you this night."

"Leave me be," came the sullen retort.

WITH HER LEGS CROSSED, Medea sat upon a plush carpet she'd laid out in one corner of her room. She'd opened her lockbox and spread her implements out in a semicircular pattern around her station. First came the candles, a half dozen of them she'd lit. The wavering of their flames was hypnotic and would help her mind fall into the necessary state for such an undertaking.

In front of the candles, in ceramic cups the size of her palm, sat various reagents and entheogens tempting her. Hekate and Kirke both had oft warned her against overreliance upon drugs to achieve her ends. Such things could help open the doors of her mind, yes, but they could also lead to addiction and dependence.

Then there were flasks of compounds she had spent months brewing. One particular draught had required tending, almost nightly, for the better part of a year. Before that, it had taken a fortnight of hunting the mountain slopes for the right ingredients. The Honey of Morpheus, alchemists named it, for the famed oneiromancer said to have developed it, ages back. It was Hekate, a compatriot of Morpheus no less, who had taught her the brew.

She wished the goddess were here with her now. She wished the damn sorceress would have cared as much for her as she did for whoever this Pandora was who had so discomfited her.

Staring at the unmarked ceramic phial, Medea told herself she was not wasting it. That she acted not to save Jason and his crew but her nephews. And her sister, who would die should she lose those boys a second time.

Or she could do naught. She could put all these things back in the chest, lock it up and hide it back within her wardrobe. Nyx, maybe she'd even smoke poppy first, have some wild dreams, and choose not to stick her fingers into someone else's problems.

Medea was not half the oneiromancer her teachers were, but with the right drugs, she had managed, on a few occasions, to push her consciousness into the sleeping mind of another. With a few subtle manipulations, one could thus propel a man in a desired direction. Jason's obvious lust for her could be quickened into something deeper. A love so consuming he would do aught she might ask of him —even return home empty-handed in the middle of the night, just as he had come here.

It was easier than trying to get him to drink a love potion, at least. To pull that off, she'd probably have to involve one of the servants, and tale of it would mostlike reach Father sooner rather than later. He'd demand to know what she had fed his guest and might prove rather ... cross ... once he had the truth of it.

Medea pursed her lips. Damn it. Damn Jason for coming here. Damn him for having a pretty face and shining eyes and a bearing that had somehow swept her nephews into his wake. She uncorked the phial of her most valuable entheogen. Honey of Morpheus, indeed. What was a year's work compared to the dire need of the present? Or more precisely, if such were not the circumstances for which she had brewed this, why then make it at all?

Before she could think herself out of it, she threw back the draught. The cloying stuff was so saccharine she gagged, coughing and sputtering. They called it honey because that was one of the ingredients, used to disguise what would otherwise have been a taste so bitter as to induce retching. Medea thought she might almost have preferred that to the feeling of goop coating her throat.

A shudder ran through her. Too late to turn back now. To open one's mind to the Realms beyond the Mortal Realm was to open one's whole self to the entities that lurked in those sidereal expanses. There were beings out there, hungering for souls and flesh and Nyx alone knew what else. Sometimes, with the right drugs, Medea could reach certain of these eidolons. Some could be bargained with. Other times ... well, she had endured certain encounters, certain *experiences* —some of which went on for hours—which she would never relate to anyone, not even Hekate. Some of those encounters, she had even, despite herself, sought to recreate ...

Already, her mind wandered with the effect of the drugs. Her pulse had slowed to a crawl, a whisper in her ears, as if it struggled to push through the thickness of the Honey. As if the Honey had replaced her blood like some blasphemous ichor. The flames upon the candles now danced in discordance, a non-existent wind in her chambers blowing them in different directions. The fires no longer touched the wicks but rather hovered a few hairs above them, writhing in lurid gyrations.

Waves of vertigo lapped at her senses, begging to drag her onto the carpet and into the embrace of dreams. But if she was to seize control of Jason's sleeping mind, she could not sink into her own fantasies. She needed more.

With shaking fingers, she gripped a candle and used it to ignite the mixture of dried poppy and witch-thistle. Then she leant over the rising tendril of smoke and sucked it in. Breathed deep.

Swirling smoke turned already dark halls hazy. Unseen harpists strummed languid chords. The songs bent and twisted like the fingers of smoke. There were men here, in her father's palace. Faceless. Shadows, hungry, bellies bloated with the vastness of their ambitions, eyes blazing with their unspeakable lusts.

They came to conquer. To lay claim. To seize, by word and deed. The world belonged to them, these men. Their gazes scraped her flesh, flensed away the shell of her modesty. Cracked her pride with their ravenous eyes.

Medea struggled to keep her head high. To remind herself she was a princess of Kolchis. This was her place. But, snakelike, doubt slithered between the chords of those harps. How little her title meant beneath their haughty, smirking visages. Pride was hers only until one of these men—or her father, or whomever he chose for her—took it from her.

Mother and Khalkiope had taught her that lesson, all too well, as though she'd needed such reminders.

No, no, no. Focus.

The nebulous dreamscape warped with her misgivings. Lines blurred between the restless dreams of these foreigners—with their half-formed conceptions of Kolchis as a shadowy bastion of sorcerers —and the products of her own disquieted mind. Was Father's hall so darkened by their perceptions or by her own?

No answers were forthcoming.

Focus.

She was being watched. As her sleep deepened, something within stirred, wakening inversely to the thickening of her dreams. Was the danger here real? She dared not linger to find out.

Jason. Among these foreign men, the leader too would slumber, his mind flailing into these dark expanses. She need but find a thread of it ...

There. Her perceptions tightened, and she strode with feigned confidence through the swirling vapours, between the columns of her phantasmagoric impression of this palace. Until she stood behind him as he turned about, searching the darkness for some escape from whatever haunted him here. Oh yes, he too writhed, beset by fears of the nameless presence stirring within these dream halls. Guileless as he was, his mind was untutored in the arcana behind the world. Still, even he felt the unease such presences must engender.

Focus. She had come here to sway the man's soul, to bind it to her will. Love. So small a word for a thing over which, when kindled hot enough, Men would defy custom, honour, or the gods themselves in pursuit of it.

Focus. Love.

Jason turned, his eyes clouded, his face blank with the childlike innocence of one content to let dreams carry him where they willed rather than seize control and weave from this mercurial landscape what he himself needed. Oh, but there was beauty in such simplicity. An *aching* beauty that those who had lost it must forever yearn to touch once again.

Focus. Love. A love fit to crack the very foundations of ambition and raise from its rubble something else, stronger.

Medea traced slow spirals along Jason's chest. It was bare now, for she willed it bare. The murky look in his eyes cleared, giving way to rising passion. Her palm alighted on his cheek, fingers curling in the tufts of his sandy beard. Her lips met his. Warm, soft. A taste like the salt of sea air.

Her pulse quickened in response to his own. Within him lurked such a powerful need, sparked the moment he'd seen her. She reached for that need. If she could draw it out, weave it into some deeper passion than mere hunger for flesh ... If she could but ...

His tongue caressed her own.

One of his hands tightened upon her arse. She had not willed away her dress—had she?—and yet it was gone, nonetheless. And she was glad of it.

Focus. Focus. Focus.

Love.

She slid her leg up along his, moaning as she pressed herself against his burning skin.

Taste and smell and the overpowering explosion of sensation that was hands upon flesh.

Love.

She had it.

MEDEA FOUND herself forced back into the painful starkness of the waking world. She lay on her back, upon the carpet in the corner of her room, the dwindling light of candles glinting in her half-opened eyes. Too bright.

Jason.

The word tasted of the sweetest honey. It was the perfect chord, struck within a crescendo of feeling. So desperate was her need of him, her fingers gripped the carpet, once more imagining the curls of his sandy hair.

She had failed. That knowledge tickled her awareness. She knew she ought to care, ought to find herself terrified by the realisation of what had unfolded. For she had grasped lust and woven it into love, yes. But in the haze of her dream, it had slipped from her grasp like a wriggling eel incensed that any should have the temerity to name themselves its master. And the eel had bitten not Jason—or at least not only Jason, for she had no certainty about him—but *Medea*.

The worst of it, though, was that she could not bring herself to regret. Even whilst burning within the heart of love's flame, few would turn from the pain. Immersed in such light, no matter how searing, who would choose to return to darkness?

Oh, but she wanted to regret. With flailing hands, she reached inside herself, dug deep in the hopes she could summon even a modicum of contrition. But all she found within was Jason's warmth and the knowledge she would do aught he ever asked of her. For him, she would betray her own family, as she now must do.

That thought alone was enough to curdle her gut and send her rolling over, onto her side. That knowledge held the bitterness to summon a single tear. Lying thus on the carpet, the locker of her alchemy sat within arms' reach. Within rested any number of toxic compounds that could release her. Downing a single draught would shatter her obligations to both her kin and her beloved, for neither could ask aught of the dead.

How easy to muse on ending one's own life. Harder by far to reach across the space and choose the poison she would imbibe. Those lay within reach of her hand, yes, and yet miles upon uncounted miles hence.

Medea pressed a palm to her brow and groaned. The welling tear in her eye dribbled down her cheek. Why, oh why, could she not regret this thing she had done to herself? She'd known attempting to control another's will through his dreams carried risks, and she'd ploughed forwards with mulish obstinacy nonetheless, so convinced of her cause. And when love had sunk its venomous fangs into the meat of her heart, still she found herself shamefully *glad* of it.

With a grunt, she rose upon her forearm. One thing she was certain of: she could not allow Father's bull to destroy Jason. Not that.

And if, too, she could not embrace her own death, then she had no choice but to save him from his.

*

WRACKED though she was by her desperate need for Jason—to feel his fingers press her flesh in life as they had done in the dream, to taste his lips upon her own, to shudder with his caresses—even so, Medea remained not insensible. She could not allow any of Father's servants to see her sneak into the chambers given to Jason. Should he think his daughter despoiled by his guest, Father's impugned honour would lead him to such awful vengeance she dare not imagine it.

And how would he react when he learnt Medea had betrayed him utterly? When he realised his prize was stolen? Medea hoped she'd be so far from Kolchis by then that she would never find out the answer to those questions.

Spectre-like, she crept through the halls of Qulha Palace until she found the rooms given to the foreign guests. Her satchel, laden with her potions and poisons and ointments, was a block of lead upon her shoulder, each draught an impossible weight to bear. Every brew she carried was its own individual, bitter betrayal of her family.

With a last, furtive glance around, Medea eased open the door and slipped into Jason's chamber. Silent though she thought herself, the man lurched awake, snatching up his sword from where it had rested against his divan. He did not, however, spring from his bed, which meant perhaps even in the gloom—the only light coming from the moon seeping in through the open window—he must have recognised an unarmed woman.

Her cheeks flushed, her skin hot with rising need. It would be madness to lie with him here, in the flesh, beneath her father's roof. Nor was that her reason in coming. The weighty darkness outside meant dawn would break before long, and she must be gone from here before anyone in the palace bestirred themselves.

It took will enough to drift to him then. It took will not to throw herself at him to relive the joining of their dreams. "Eyes of gold ..." he breathed. "You are the princess Medea."

Self-conscious, she reached a hand to her braid. This was not why she was here. "You go to your death, this eve."

"I do not think so." Haughty confidence filled his voice.

"My father's bull is a furnace of bronze. When it wakes, when he fills it with some conjured spirits, its flames will roast flesh from bone. Should you survive that, it will gore you with horns behind which lurks the strength of the Otherworld. Few among Titans could hope to overcome such a monstrosity, and for a Man, there is little hope."

Jason grunted. "You've come to persuade me to flee, Princess?" A pause. "I dreamt of you." His voice had grown thick with carnal longings. Almost enough to make her forget her reason for being here.

Grateful for the darkness that meant he'd not see the depths of her flush, Medea refused to respond to that. Let him think it but a dream, for she could not admit it more than that. Could not tell him, ever, that she'd tried to snare him using drugs and oneiromancy, only to fall within her own trap. "You will fail in your quest unless you heed my words. Prince, listen well." She removed a phial from her satchel. "At dawn, rub this oil over every trace of your flesh."

"Perhaps you'd rub it in for me."

The image of doing so flashed through her mind. Oh, so damningly tempting. "The oil ..." Her voice trembled. He'd have noticed it, too. "It will make you impervious to flame or blade, at least until the last rays of Hyperion wink out and night rises proper." She pressed the phial into his palm, then withdrew another. "Before you face the bull, drink this one. It will not last as long, but it will give you strength to match the wildest of beasts, enough perhaps even to wrestle such a creature as you must conquer."

He laid a hand upon her knee, drawing a shuddering breath out of her.

"If you destroy the bull, my father will declare you champions and offer a second feast in your honour. But in the night, he will murder your men and burn your ship. He will never let you claim victory, Jason. Never." Her whole body was trembling now. And she knew it must seem strange to speak of her father betraying his own guests thus, violating guest-right and honour. But she doubted the great sorcerer-king Aeëtes feared the Erinyes, and either way, his pride could have overshadowed mountains. He would not let stand even the faintest smudge upon it.

Jason withdrew his hand, finally seeming to apprehend the awful predicament in which he found himself. "Helping me slay the bull will not avail us in the end. I must send my men to claim the Fleece even as I engage the creature."

"A drakon guards it." She shook her head. "No, I've powers for that, as well. You can trust me to retrieve your prize, Prince, and get it back to you. Then you must make your excuses to leave the banquet and sail from here before my father suspects treachery." Her voice caught in her throat. Was she truly to send him away from her? But how else to spare him? "Just ... promise me that when you reach your homeland, remember me, from time to time. I shan't forget you, of that you may hold certain. Perhaps, if you listen closely, you may hear the wind whispering to you, to remind you how you escaped this land ..."

Now, the foreigner leant forwards to grasp her hand. "Let the wind blow as it wills. But if you come with me, you could be a queen in Iolkos once I reclaim my throne. Men and women will cast honour upon your feet, Princess. They would name you a goddess for saving the heroes of Elládos and Phlegra. Be mine, Medea, and naught save bitter death shall ever sever the bond betwixt our hearts."

She choked on the sudden swell of emotion in her breast. His words, like prophecy, wrapt around the threads she had woven in hopes of kindling lust to love. And as he said, she felt an invisible tether tying him to her as if they were already husband and wife. This was eternal love. This was devotion fit to shake the earth herself.

But ... to leave her home? To abandon her family forever and never again look upon the face of her sister or her mother? And if she went, too, Father would know for certain that she, his own daughter, had betrayed him.

"I ..."

"Come with me," Jason implored, "and we shall have our dreams fulfilled together."

"Yes." Her heart quivered at such a surrender. Would this be the last time she saw the dawn paint these mountains aflame? Had she already enjoyed the final supper she would eat within the palace of her youth? "Yes, I shall accompany you." The words were razors, defining edges of sorrow and joy so sharp they could flense her soul. "Yes."

Ribbons of hope interwove themselves with the strands of despair, forming knots she might never untangle.

"I'm coming with you."

His mouth was on hers. Scarcely having realised she'd moved, she was lying beneath him. A fire lit beneath her skin.

A DRIZZLE of summer rains preceded the twilight, turning the barren fields beyond Qulha Palace to mounds of mud and canals of slurry. Himation slung over her head against the weather, Medea slunk across the desolate landscape, though she need not have concealed herself, she supposed. She was far enough out from the palace no sentries upon the wall would have seen her in daylight, much less now, with a deepening gloom stretching across lavender skies.

No, and Father did not set any watchmen over this land. Why would he? For he had already, enslaved to his will, the perfect guardian for his precious Fleece. Atop a distant hill, a bent and gnarled oak rose, a solitary beacon to the foolish and the greedy. And to Medea, who dared fancy herself neither of those things, though she made for the hilltop, nonetheless.

The Fleece hung within those branches, glinting in the last light of the sun, taunting any foolish enough to brave the hill and climb to the prize.

The tree's bark was a mottled grey-green that reminded her of gangrenous flesh too diseased for even the best of chirurgeons to have saved. Its boughs twisted like a crone's lumpy arms, its branches like a thousand broken fingers. The oak's leafless upper branches might have reached almost ten times her height, and indeed, the husk of it cast frightful shadows, even in daylight. Now, at dusk, those shadows stretched as if reaching for her, yawning and grasping to snare her soul.

But it was not the tree itself that kindled the horror simmering in Medea's breast.

It was what she knew lurked within the hollow shell of its trunk, no doubt already watching her ascend the hill, eyes hidden within that rotten cavity. It was this guardian that had her reaching into the satchel at her side to grab a handful of powder that, she prayed to Hekate, would work as she imagined. She could not well get the creature to drink the Honey of Morpheus, so she'd concentrated and desiccated a batch, turning it into a loose dust. The Sands of Morpheus, she had read some works name it, and, in theory, if she had made no error in its creation, it ought to induce enduring dreams even in a drakon.

If her heart now threatened to climb out of her mouth and run screaming back toward the palace all on its own, well, that was because it knew the price of failure. Had she made the least mistake in her alchemy, the drakon would soon sink its venomous fangs into her flesh.

As she drew closer, Medea hefted the powder up before her face, careful to keep her palm bent away. Inhaling the stuff would prove ... an embarrassing way to get herself killed.

Then she crested the hill. She felt the drakon's presence, looming and ancient, spawned, no doubt, within the lightless bowels of Gaia. Or perhaps somewhere beyond this fragile world entirely. The musk of it saturated the air, even before she heard the slithering of coils over coils.

Already, it was too late to run, even had her legs not turned to water beneath her. Even were her knees not trembling with atavistic dread of the thing shifting within the hollow. Flickers of luminosity flared in those depths.

She had to keep her hand up. She had to remain steady.

It could have lunged already, but it was playing with her. Maybe it scented her fear and savoured the aroma like a well-aged wine.

She dared another step.

The snakelike drakon peeked its head forth. The shadows still concealed the better part of its head and made it hard to be certain of its colour or aspect. She had the sense of something as sickly green as the trunk, as though the drakon had infected the oak with its essence, made it an extension of its putrid form.

The tension in her broke like a cord pulled too taut. Whether it was too early or not, she could not stop herself. She opened her palm and blew, spraying the Sands of Morpheus into the hollow.

A forked tongue flicked out, reflexively tasting the air. The next instant, those glowing eyes disappeared back into the shadows within the tree hole.

Was it asleep? Did it toy with her still?

No answer seemed forthcoming, and yet Medea found herself powerless to move. She needed to climb the tree, grab the Fleece, and run like Tartarus itself was opening behind her. And yet her sandals seemed rooted to the muddy hillside. Rain continued to fall in sporadic drops, the only sound she could hear over her frantic breathing.

She needed to go now.

Now, Medea, she told herself. *Go, now.*

Such fear could have suffocated her.

Move!

With a gasp, she lurched forwards, grabbed the lowest branch. Every instant she felt certain the drakon would lunge. She could almost feel its fangs sinking into her abdomen. Instinct demanded she drop the branch and curl herself into the smallest target possible.

Hades, she was going to piss herself.

She tried to pull herself up onto the branch but had not the strength.

Damn it, damn it, damn it all.

She kicked off her sandal, and caught her foot upon the trunk. The drakon was going to bite off her leg now. Pushing off it, she had enough leverage to climb.

Keep moving, Medea.

She did. She kept climbing, branch to branch, until she could reach out and grasp the Fleece. It was cool, as if the summer's heat had never touched it, and slickened by the rain.

She yanked. The damn thing remained stubbornly tangled about the branch. "Hekate, help me now," she mumbled, though she'd no idea if the goddess could hear or would do aught if she did realise Medea's need. Another tug. The branch groaned and bent, creaking.

"Oh, Gaia's rocky arse." She'd wake the drakon like this.

But what choice had she? Climb back down without the object of her quest and let all this be for naught?

Another heave. The Fleece tore free. Next Medea knew, she was flailing, pitching backwards, the sudden removal of opposing force costing her balance. With a shriek, she toppled from the tree. A lower branch smacked her between the shoulder blades. A hit like getting kicked by a horse. It blasted the breath from her lungs, and she fell again.

She landed hard upon the hill and rolled, slipping and wheeling in the mud. The Fleece wrapt itself about her arms. She could not draw breath to even scream at her maddened tumble. Blow after unseen blow pounded her until, at last, she crashed down at the base of the hill, coming to rest in a knee-high pool of mud.

Muck rushed up her nose and she thrashed—the terror of drowning proved nigh as profound as the dread one feels of drakons —wriggled loose from the Fleece and managed to push up on one arm. Mud squelched beneath her fingers and the ground gave way, but still she got her head far enough above water to choke and sputter and, at last, catch a breath.

Too exhausted, pained, and still too shaken even to weep, Medea dragged herself from the mudhole and collapsed upon a mound beside it. She could not sob at the ordeal, but she could moan.

And that she did.

❦

MUD HAD CAKED Medea's peplos as she made her way down to the Phasis River where the Argo awaited. From what she could see of her dark locks, her tumble in the field had all but dyed them a filthy daub colour. She imagined she looked like aught save the elegant princess Jason had promised to carry away hence and make his queen.

And yet, she had the Golden Fleece draped over her arm, and for that alone, she had to hold her head just a bit higher. That alone deserved a smidge of pride. She had done what even her mighty father thought impossible: she had overcome the drakon, climbed its tree, and stolen the prize out from under his nose.

Night had fallen, and Thoth's gleam was high in the sky, reflecting off the dark waters of the Axeinos Sea. This was it. She was really about to flee her home, to leave beyond all she had ever known.

On the riverbank, the Argonauts were prepping small boats,

preparing to row back to their ship, moored out in the deeper waters at the river's centre. The men shoved one of the lesser vessels off the sands even as she approached, none glancing back at her.

It took an effort of will, despite her love—despite that she had already gone well past the point in which she might turn back—to call out. Sometimes, the first step is the hardest. But sometimes, that final, irrevocable move into the unknown proved the weightiest of all. "Jason," she managed, her voice trembling with more than mere exhaustion.

A young man spun to face her then, not Jason nor any of the men he'd brought into Qulha Palace. He stalked closer to her, hand upon the pommel of his sword in threat, though he eased off it as he caught better sight of Medea.

"Theseus?" someone asked. "Who is that?"

"Must be the princess Jason spoke of," this Theseus said. He reached a hand toward her, seemingly untroubled by her sodden, dishevelled appearance. "Come, I'll take you to him."

Medea did not know this young man. But nor could she afford to mistrust one of Jason's people now. So, she took his hand, and he helped her into the rowboat. A moment later, other men shoved it into the river with a splash that sent droplets of water spraying over her. Medea winced. She'd never been on a boat before, and the rocking, as the men set to the oars, left her unsteady and nigh certain any moment the whole vessel would topple over sideways.

But the boat made its slow, steady progress out to the Argo. Once alongside the larger ship, the boat was drawn up with ropes, and someone took her hand, helping her aboard.

"Aunt Medea," the man said, gripping her elbow.

A reflexive sigh of relief escaped her on recognising Phrontis, the sight of any familiar face enough to unwind at least one of the knots inside her chest.

Medea allowed herself but a moment before looking around for her beloved. "Jason?"

Phrontis pointed to where the Argonauts' leader stood on a higher deck, beside the helmsman, preparing to make way. Jason must have noticed their attention, for he spied her, raced to the ladder from the upper deck, and scurried down to meet her.

His gaze at once alighted upon the Fleece, and he eased it away from her. "You have it!"

"Yes, I ..."

Jason hefted the mud-strewn fabric for all the crew to see, or perhaps just to glory in his prize himself. "It's mine. Ahh."

"Yes, I brought it," Medea said. "Now we must flee, first, and escape my father before ..."

A murmur ran through the crew, and heads turned toward the riverbank, where a string of lights sprung up. Like a flaming serpent, they slithered down toward the shore, announcing the arrival of soldier after soldier, all come to bring her back so that her father could avenge his wounded pride upon her flesh. Those lights would converge upon the Kolchian ships moored nigh to the city, and some would speed to the sea, bringing word to the fleet of her crime.

Medea found herself struck speechless.

Jason handed her off to Phrontis without another word to her. "Make way! Make way and get us onto the open sea!"

Phrontis guided her down into the hold as the Argonauts rushed about the ship. Many sat at oars, preparing to send the vessel speeding toward the Axeinos whilst others grabbed great shields to ward the side of the ship. She saw men preparing javelins and bows, and the thought struck her, with an abrupt coldness, that Kolchians would die over this. The Argonauts would kill men loyal to her family in order to escape with their stolen prize and their stolen princess.

And their deaths would fall, in part, at her feet.

Settled before a porthole, she watched. For it was far too late to consider such things now.

THROUGH ALL THAT remained of the night, her father's fleet pursued the Argo. Medea watched through the tiny portal available to her, catching sporadic glimpses of Kolchian biremes closing the distance.

Her stomach heaved with the surging waves—the sea proved worse even than the river—and more than once, it tried to empty itself despite her having eaten not a bite since the day before.

When morn came, over Phrontis's objections, she made her way on deck and up to where Jason still stood beside his helmsman. Her beloved held the Fleece close by, beneath a cloak, casting the occasional glance about as if he feared his own crew might try to sneak up and take it from him. Did they have something to fear from the other Argonauts? Had she unwittingly wandered into a moil of conflicting egos no longer united by common purpose?

"Medea," he called when he spied her. In his voice all her doubts were erased. If he saw her, if he knew her and held her close, she need fear neither her father nor the Argonauts. In the recesses of her mind, she knew, of course, that such thoughts were born from the love she had mistakenly woven about her own heart. But the knowledge of the truth blessedly did not ruin the comfort Jason's presence provided.

She came to him and took his hand, and together they walked to the gunwale, where she could see the Kolchian fleet converging upon them. On the lead ship, she spied Absyrtus, his silhouette stern and damning. Her father must have sent her brother to bring Medea back for punishment. The king might not risk his own safety against these warriors and demigods, but he would not spare any of his own men, nor even his son, should they fail to retrieve her. Because of Medea, the Kolchians were left with very few choices, all of them bad ones.

"You have sworn not to disgrace or forsake me," she whispered to Jason and wondered if he had ever said those words, exactly. Oh, he had promised to make her a queen. Their bodies had promised more, still, and sealed that promise forever.

Jason raised a hand to draw the attention of those closest to the two of them. "It is because of the princess we escape with our prize, and thus I have sworn an oath to take her into my house as my wife. And you, Argonauts, must protect her too, for without her our quest might well have ended in failure!"

No one disputed him, but then, no one said much of aught. They watched Jason, and more, they looked to *her*, with their stern eyes concealing unknowable thoughts. Of the faces she saw, each looked grim now. They knew a bitter battle would ensue because of her. Worse even than if they had come as thieves in the night and stolen the Fleece. Maybe—she imagined they told themselves—King Aeëtes would have forgiven such an affront. Maybe he'd have let them sail away, unmolested, had they not corrupted and stolen his daughter.

Medea looked again to her brother, and from the way he stared hard in her direction, she could not help but imagine he saw her, too. His fleet was like a flock of birds, swarming, flanking out around the Argo. They would cut them off and either force them to make land at some island or perhaps even attempt to ram them, though even Medea knew battles at sea proved uncertain enough no one relished such encounters. That was a sure way to wind up feeding the sirens.

The thought chilled her and had her shivering, despite the morning sun.

But her brother did not chance such a thing. Rather, his ships outmanoeuvred the Argo, forcing her to thread the narrow straits betwixt the tiny islands northwest of Kolchis. When his flagship moored alongside the largest of these isles, he made it plain enough he intended to parley with the Elládosi.

Medea listened as the Argonauts argued amongst themselves about whether to talk first, before turning to violence to escape these circumstances. But Absyrtus had many more ships and many times their number in men, and caution won out even over this crew of demigods and champions.

Jason took ashore some of his finest warriors, including the brothers Telamon and Peleus she had seen in Kolchis and others. Kastor and Pollux she heard named, and an older man named Autolykus, who Phrontis assured her was well known for his craftiness. Be that as it may, it much distressed Medea to be left behind while Jason went to meet her brother. But her beloved dismissed any notion that she could accompany him.

"Your presence would only further inflame raw nerves," he said.

And maybe there was truth in that. Though, too, she heard the whispered mockeries among the crew, about what fool would send a woman to a negotiation. Medea held high her head and pretended not to hear their scorn.

So, in the company of her nephews, and under the watchful eye of Theseus who assured her she'd be safe, Medea waited. She paced the deck until she was certain she'd wear treads into the planks. She wrung her hands over the gunwale and stared at the shore where tents had been pitched and men decided between peace or war.

Using buckets of seawater and rough combs, she sought to scrape the mud from her dark locks and scrub the worst of it from her dress. Had she another garment with her, she'd have changed. But she had brought naught save the Fleece. And trying to cleanse herself as strange men watched only increased the self-conscious waves that crashed over her again and again.

She wanted to scream for the sheer, unbearable impotence of her situation.

Then, at length, the Argonauts returned. Jason looked not to her —nor even to his crew—but first to the locker where he'd stowed the Fleece. Only after inspecting his prize did he make his way to the gunwale and lean heavily upon it. He did not speak.

Telamon filled the silence. "Prince Absyrtus says we can leave these waters. They'll even let us keep the Fleece."

"They value their lives," a man said. Iolaus she thought someone had called him, earlier.

"No doubt," agreed Telamon. "And hers." He pointed to Medea. "The prince will leave us be if we surrender his sister, to be turned over to her father."

Medea felt the blood drain from her face. For a moment, she was not even certain she remained standing. She felt her mouth flapping, but words were as far beyond her as they were beyond those of a fish protesting at being hauled from the sea.

And Jason still had not looked at her. Had not met her gaze. Her beloved could never countenance such a bargain. Surely, even to save the lives of his men, he would not break his oath to her. Surely ... He ...

But she must act, before doubt and the harshness of reality could sway him. She grabbed his elbow and drew him away from the others.

"Jason." When he did not look to her face, she tightened her grip on him. "Jason, what do you intend for me? Surely not to revoke the promise you gave me! Has your prize made you forget all you swore when in need of my help?" His eyes fixed upon hers, and she could almost swear she saw qualms rising within those sky-blue depths. "*Jason*. Please, beloved. Was I a fool to pin my honour upon yours? I left my family for you. My *country*! I betrayed all I knew and left behind all I loved because I loved you *more*. I ... I gave you my body, my maidenhead ... my ..." Her honour.

Her fragile, crumbling heart.

Still, he refused to make an answer and she could have screamed.

Her voice was rising into a shriek, and no doubt those closest, Telamon included, heard her. But she could not still the growing agony inside her. How dare Jason even contemplate abandoning her after all she had done for him? "It is because of me you ever escaped Kolchis! If I am returned to my father, do you think he will show me mercy? Show me love? I have wrought an unforgivable stain upon his honour! Have you the least idea what noble families do to girls who marry without their consent, should they get their hands upon them? We are prizes to be sold to the highest bidders, and if we give ourselves away, we are thus treated as thieves!"

Aeëtes would make an example of his wayward daughter, such that no girl in the whole of a generation would dare so much as think of going against her father's wishes. That Jason could abandon her such, it had never crossed Medea's mind. The utter profoundness of such a betrayal left her hoping Poseidon would open a hole in the sea and devour her and the Argo itself with some monster.

"You know I am blessed with secret knowledge of the hidden worlds, Jason. Treachery now must be met later with the wrath of vengeful spirits." An idle threat, but she'd have thrown aught within reach at him to sway him now. His face darkened, but in fear or anger at her threats, she didn't know. "Just let me speak to my brother," she interjected before he could say something either of them might regret. "Let me appeal to his brotherly affections for me." If Absyrtus had any. He revelled in his authority over his sisters and would no doubt have eagerly fulfilled Father's vengeance upon her.

But maybe ... maybe ...

"Convince him, then, Medea," Jason said. He moved, and she thought, for a moment, he meant to embrace her. Instead, he stalked past her and once more peeked inside his locker, checking to make certain his Fleece remained where he'd left it.

HER BROTHER, despite her misgivings, received her within his tent. He sat at a low table, taking his repast on fish and nuts. Absyrtus offered Medea not so much as a sip of his wine or a bite from his table.

It was well, though. She wasn't certain she could have kept any of it down.

The churning of her gut had little to do with the sea, now. Not anymore.

"You cannot really believe Father would allow you to go," he said around a mouthful of almonds. "Do you know, he swore that were you not returned to his lands for punishment, he'd have the heads of every sailor on these ships." Absyrtus snorted, still crunching, though whether his amusement came from Father's cruelty or the idea Medea might escape, she did not know. "Yeah." He threw back a swig of wine from his goblet. "That put some iron into the backs of the rowers, I tell you true. As if you'd ever had a chance to escape."

"I am your sister, Absyrtus."

Another snort answered her. "Seems you forgot that last night, didn't you?"

"I forgot naught, Brother. I ... the sons of Phrixus tricked me into meeting with the strangers." The lie came easy enough. "These Argonauts seized me as but one more prize and carried me off."

A shadow of doubt crept over Absyrtus's face. "Huh." His gaze darted back to his goblet and he sighed to see it empty. With an affected huff, he crawled from the table to an amphora and began filling his glass. "Well, if that's so, I pity you. Of course, there'd be no salvaging your virtue or returning to court, but if you can convince Father of it, well, maybe he'd let you live in secluded exile ..." He threw back another long swig. "Who knows, maybe he'd even find an aristos desperate enough to accept damaged goods."

Medea wrapt her hand around the hilt of the knife she'd concealed within the folds of her filthy peplos. He'd sneered to see her wearing such a thing but otherwise had paid so little attention. It was beyond the scope of his world to imagine he might have something to fear from a woman.

Don't think. Don't delay. He's no brother to you, he made that plain with his words.

As he swallowed yet another draught, Medea lunged. The point of her knife bit through his jugular. A cataract of wine spilt from his lips, mingling with the sudden fountain blossoming from his neck. Crimson upon crimson.

She collapsed back onto her arse, not even pulling the knife out.

Absyrtus, too, pitched over. Clumsy fingers brushed over the wound in his neck, but he could not scream. Could only flop about like a dying fish.

And then lay still.

They'd find him soon. They'd find him, and they'd have to return him to Aeëtes. The death of the prince would outweigh even the concerns of his daughter's betrayal.

This she told herself as she walked from the tent, head held high, wondering how long it would be before one of the Kolchians went to check upon their prince. Before that happened, she needed to be back aboard the Argo. They would shelter her now, culpable as they were in the murder of the prince of Kolchis.

They would shelter her, and they would fly hence, forever fearing the wrath of Aeëtes.

PART II

Out of a Primordial Abyss came Nyx, the dark night that held the World in its timeless embrace until, at break of day, Ouranos emerged, a shining sun to conclude the Time of Nyx. Broken, Mother Night fled to the fringes, daring to show but a hint of her former glory, peeking forth only whilst the sun slumbered.

— Polyhymnia, Analects of the Muses

11

PANDORA

726 Bronze Age

Upon one of the verdant hills beyond the sea rose the mighty stonework of Qulha Palace, towering above the town. Whilst climbing the winding path toward the barbican, hoping to make it before the sun finished setting, Pandora spied a pair of women wandering the hillside. Tall grasses tugged at their dresses as they drifted amid a field of irises. While one had dark hair, making her origin harder to determine, Pandora would have recognised the fiery locks of the other most anywhere.

Trudging up the hillside, breathless despite the stamina the Phoenix bestowed, Pandora realised that, though she had travelled across the sea to find her daughter, a part of her still had not expected to look upon her. A thousand mental rehearsals of this conversation could not have prepared her for how to handle it once it resolved into the pellucid clarity of the present.

But neither had she ventured so far to give up. Pandora would never give up, least of all on her family.

"Pyrrha," she said.

Her daughter spun, eyes widening upon her mother. Bedraggled and weary, having come direct from the riverbank where she'd taken a boat from the Argo—the others planned to wait for full dark and sneak in like the thieves they were—Pandora must have presented a pathetic sight.

"Pandora ..."

None of it mattered. Not the mountains of recriminations her daughter had for her, not the unparalleled horror of the future Pyrrha would unleash. How could aught measure up to the relief of seeing her daughter and the boundless capacity for a parent to look beyond the gravest faults and see naught but an infant's hand reaching out for their own?

And she was rushing forwards, throwing her arms around Pyrrha, holding her tight, though her daughter but stiffened within her embrace. Finally, Pandora pulled back, looking deep into Pyrrha's eyes. That her daughter—for whom this meeting must have come much farther apart than even it had for Pandora—still would not acknowledge their bond ... it was a hammer blow upon her heart, the impact so jarring it took her a moment to find words.

"There are so many things I have to tell you," she managed.

Pyrrha, though, merely nodded, her eyes still overflowing with recrimination.

PYRRHA GUIDED Pandora through the grandeur of Qulha Palace. Reaching it had meant navigating a mazelike cave city of clustering homes lit by flickering torchlight. But the palace rested atop the cliff, claiming a commanding view of the hills and the Phasis River. Upon the threshold, Pandora had studied the horizon to seek out the Argo, but Phrontis had known where to moor to keep the ship out of sight.

Her parting with those men had been tinged with sorrow and bitterness. What Herakles had done at Ilium had served as a sanguine reminder of the nature of these warriors. They took what they wanted and killed those in their way, then expected the World to laud them for their violent pursuits. For Theseus alone Pandora had offered a clasped arm of farewell. But even he, she feared, would one day accomplish his dream of becoming so like his idol. No man could live a life of violence and remain unchanged by it, she thought.

Nor could Pandora herself. The Phoenix gave her power, and she had *used* it.

The palace was a wonder of marble and gold-plated reliefs and crackling braziers. It fair dripped with Titan wealth and ostentation. A giant golden disc of the sun bedecked one wall, announcing Aeëtes's descent from Helios. Elsewhere, frescoes depicted further the glory of the Heliad genos. In the courtyard, grand fountains burbled, with statues of bronze bulls rimming the walkway.

At last, they came to a private chamber Pandora assumed to belong to Pyrrha. Her daughter seated herself upon a divan and called for servants who brought welcome bowls of wine. Pandora settled on the floor before the couch, accepting the wine with a nod for the servant. After she'd downed a few sips to calm her raging nerves, the servants offered her a bowl of bean soup. Its warmth seeped into her fingers, its aroma welcome after so long at sea. This, she drank as well.

Pyrrha touched neither wine nor food, only stared at her with her father's unreadable gaze, though she had Pandora's eyes. And yet, while Prometheus oft inspected Pandora thus, in his eyes there was mystery and compassion and hints of sadness deep as the ocean. In Pyrrha's eyes, behind the golden mask, there lay a seething moil. Pandora could not judge her daughter's thoughts, but neither did Pyrrha quite manage to mask the sum of her pain, clenching her jaw, creasing her brow.

The soup gave Pandora the excuse to steady herself, to grasp at words that kept slipping from her tongue. Pyrrha shifted, her mouth opening as though she might speak, then snapping shut again once more, as stripped of the ability to ford the torrent between them as Pandora herself.

How did one bring up such a perverse twist in Ananke? How was she to relate to one she loved best in the World the abject horror which lay ahead?

History is merciless.

Leaving the empty soup aside, Pandora took up the wine bowl once more, daring to hope the answers must somehow lie within the glint of firelight upon the draught's ruby surface. Maybe there was no tactful means to broach something so obscene. Maybe, to give voice to ideas of damnation was already to breach all pretences of pleasantry and trod into lands where words could not comfort.

"The path you're on ends in darkness," she said, unable to bring herself to look up from the wine.

"What?" Pyrrha's voice sounded raw, forcing Pandora to lift her head to meet the woman's gaze.

"You will ..." Speaking such things was like carving out her own heart and casting it into the brazier. "If you continue down the sorcerous road, you will become a *curse* upon the lips of Man. A blight, an incarnation of death itself, hated. And feared, Pyrrha."

"My *name* is Hekate, Pandora."

"I am your mother!" Pandora half set, half dropped her wine bowl and shoved it aside, glaring at her daughter, demanding with her gaze the woman acknowledge their relationship.

"And yet I am by far your elder." The calm behind Hekate's words stung more than any shouted rebuke. Hers was not a seething anger but a frozen one, cold as the future from which Pandora had escaped. Her scars had sealed over with ice, and Pandora would never thaw through such a mass to dress the wounds beneath.

Sighing, she let her face fall into her hands. Damn the Moirai for the convoluted maze they had woven of Pandora's destiny. Damn them all for the price their Tapestry inflicted upon her and her family. Damn herself for not finding a means to cut through this trap.

History is merciless.

Much though she wanted to give in to the wracking lachrymosity that wrapt its fingers around her heart, her tears would have only stung Hekate all the more. Talk failed, and yet, it was all she had, so she forced herself to meet her daughter's gaze once more. "Somewhere in the dark of all this, I have to believe I could find the words to reach you, to bridge the gap and save you from the end I've beheld."

Hekate's eyes widened a hair. "To thwart the weavings of the Fates without unmaking ourselves and all we hold dear."

She knew. She *knew*! She had seen the Tapestry, had felt its choking threads tightening around her throat, denying her choices. The thought her daughter could, in fact, at last apprehend the depth of Pandora's travails, it offered such unexpected hope, she felt tears trying to well once more. The relief and fear of knowing her child could look upon her and see her.

Rising from the divan, Hekate drifted to her hearth and slid something out from behind it. "You fear I will damn myself with the Art, only because you have not seen enough of the Ontos to realise what lurks just beyond your perception."

Pandora crawled across the floor to look upon a leather-bound book Hekate now spread open before her. Her daughter turned page after page, giving Pandora bare glimpses of strange sigils and diagrams, of foreign letters. Amid the text were scrawled occasional illustrations, depictions of faces lurking in shadows, the sight of which had scorpions skittering along Pandora's flesh.

Her daughter paused on one page, and Pandora leaned forwards, trying to gauge what was so important in this passage. The flowing script seemed to squirm before her eyes, alien, beyond any ability to parse. Pandora was about to tell Hekate she could not read the language when she noticed the illumination in the margins. No, not just the margins but rather a sketch that flowed among the text itself, intimated as much by the positioning of the words and by empty spaces as by any explicit rendition.

There were ... hints that something vast beyond imagining squirmed down from the sky, tendrils grasping at the World and all upon it. Despite all the innominate horror Pandora had beheld in Tartarus, despite the forsaken, frozen Earth she had seen in the future, in this hint of a sketch, she saw perhaps the most obscene sight imaginable.

That sudden clenching of her heart stole her breath even as her fingers rose to her mouth. Now, a tear did tumble down her cheek. To speak of the abomination before her seemed a violation of some tacit agreement handed down since the dawn of Man. And yet, here was her daughter, so clearly desperate for the chance to share this with her. To make Pandora understand her, even as Pandora strove for the same from Hekate. "Is that ... a demon?" she managed, voice a whisper. "Or is this supposed to be an Elder God?"

A shudder wracked her daughter. "I am no longer certain ... there is a difference."

Revulsion rose in Pandora, strong enough to smother the crushing weight of her panic. She seized the cover and slammed the profane tome shut. The very feel of this thing disquieted, as though the cover seethed with profane, tormented life. What was this book? What madness did her child seek from it? "Turn from this, Hekate! This thing, wherever you got it, it reeks of the darkness! It is like the horror told of in tales of the Nyxlands."

Hekate glared at her and snatched away the book as though it were one of her children. "I have been to the Nyxlands. There is a dark city there, a ruin built upon yet older ruins. They—those inhab-itants—understood more of the World than those of our Era. I think they realised something, tried to harness it, perhaps. And I think they *failed*."

Oh, Gaia. Another iteration of the Earth, a fallen civilisation. Pandora knew of what Hekate spoke. "Vulgeth ..."

"What?"

"A ruin upon ruin." Pandora tapped a finger upon her lip. "The answers ...?"

Her daughter scoffed. "You cannot think to go there. Despite whatever power you wield as Nike, you are woefully unprepared for the Dark."

"I have to, Hekate. Kronos told me this all began in Vulgeth, and if there is *any* chance at escaping from beneath the heel of Ananke, it must lie within the origin of these circles of madness."

Wrath, or something akin to it, flashed over Hekate's visage. A fury Pandora could not understand. "I found the Box there!" her daughter blurted. "I found it buried amid millennia of rubble!"

"What?" The Box? Hekate knew of the Box? But if the Box was in there, it must mean Pandora would lose it there, in the very past she sought after. How could she risk venturing to a time and place where history already demanded she fail?

History is merciless.

"Where did the Box come from?" Hekate demanded.

So Hekate knew of the Box but did not realise her own father had made it. Of course, Prometheus had done so based upon his seeing it when Pandora had brought it from the future. The Box was predicated upon itself, though Prometheus had also asked if it was based upon the Time Chamber of Vulgeth. Through one of these chambers, Kronos had fled to the future. No matter the risk, she had to *try*. She had to have the answers if she was to save her family or the future.

But telling Hekate that Prometheus had made this, had started this—at least in a sense—would only have pained the woman and driven her apart from the one parent she still connected with. All she could do was shake her head; pretend she didn't have the answer.

From the growing ire limning Hekate's face, her daughter was not fooled for a moment. "Get out," the woman snapped. "There is naught for you here in Kolchis."

And all Pandora could do was flee.

SHE TRAVELLED NORTH, skirting the shores of the Axeinos Sea, her lone footprints cutting a long trail through black sand beaches. Each sunset, flames would limn the lapping waters before winking out, leaving behind an inky curtain to remind her of the emptiness around her. These were wild lands where Man rarely trod, flanked by a wall of aspens. The forest provided forage and game, but always, Pandora returned to the sound of the sea, keeping her course true.

Sometimes she wondered what had become of her companions among the Argonauts. But they had their aims, and she had hers.

Despite the loneliness, maybe she was better off facing the travails ahead alone.

Always, she pushed further, deeper into the unknown lands, deeper into the weavings of Ananke. For there was no turning back.

There had never been *any* turning back.

AS ANOTHER DAY SLOWLY DIED, a smear of clouds obscuring the sunset, thunder rumbled in the distance. Pandora had just set to heading in toward the forest, seeking shelter, when she realised it was not actual thunder but the pounding of hoofbeats that set even the land to trembling. A curtain of dust billowed on the horizon moments before horses surged onto the black beach, not in any sort of formation but rather as a whooping horde.

Most of their riders guided the animals with their legs, hands occupied with drawn bows. Pandora backed up against a tree, hand going to her kopis behind her waist. Though she didn't expect she could hold off more than two score warriors, neither would they seize her without losses.

Burn, the Phoenix implored inside her breast.

The riders soon banked, spotting her. Without any obvious command, the flow of horses split like a river breaking around rocks, doubling back to encircle her. As the riders drew nigh, Pandora started. They were women. All of them were women. Some had painted faces, some tattoos. Fur cloaks had disguised their features from afar, and these women wore leather trousers and woollen tunics, but there was not a man among them.

Amazons ... The Amazons of Themiskyra.

Releasing the kopis, Pandora slowly raised her hands, showing them empty. "I am female," she said in Phrygian, the closest language she could think of.

One of the riders skirted forwards, face twisted in something between sneer and snicker. "Which is why arrows do not yet sprout from you like hedgehog quills." The woman had hair as raven dark as

Pandora's own, woven into several braids, held back by a gilded tiara. Gold embroidery trimmed the fringes of her woollen shirt, indicating a woman of wealth and prestige. Their leader, perhaps their queen.

"I seek after the Muses College in Themiskyra." It would serve as a starting point for her trek into the Nyxlands and, with even a dollop of luck, perhaps give her a better chance of pinpointing the ruins of Vulgeth.

Though many bows remained pointed in her direction, she noted that most of the Amazons eased off their draws.

"Are you a scholar, then?" The sneer had not quite left the lead woman's face.

Once, maybe, but then, Pandora had an excellent memory and could quote many of Urania's Analects by heart. "'Supposing, then, that you had spent your entire life trapped within such a cave, witness only to shadows cast by those passing between you and the light. How could you not mistake these shadows for the substance of reality?'"

Now, at last, the distrust that had creased the woman's face fell away like a discarded shawl, replaced by an openness that *almost* qualified as a smile. "You know the works of Urania. That alone proves you have a mind of your own. Elládosi?"

"Phoenikian," Pandora answered, "though I lived long in Elládos. I am ... Nike."

A murmur rumbled through the women now, and their leader's burgeoning warmth melted in an instant. She did not know the word they mouthed again and again, though she guessed it must be their equivalent of *Titan*. "An ally of Zeus."

"No longer." And never by choice. "Circumstance forced me down paths I misliked. Now I make my own way."

Still, a shadow had settled over the woman. "I am Queen Hippolyta, blessed by Themis herself. And you, Nike, can only be judged by the Great Lady. You will come with us to the polis, and you will speak before her. She alone shall decide your fate."

As if anyone, Man or Titan, could decide the whims of Ananke.

But Pandora bowed in acquiescence. There was no turning back.

12

ARTEMIS

726 Bronze Age

Maybe Artemis ought to have fled Oeneus's palace once she'd spoken to Queen Althaea. Yet, she could not leave without seeing the results of the queen's kindled wrath against her son. What aspersions would she cast his way to shatter his celebration? What pains would they share in pale shadow of the pain Artemis felt at Orion's loss?

Thus, trembling with both her weakness and anticipation, Artemis lurked in the hall where the feasters gathered. Long tables laden with fruits and nuts and meat—*boar* meat, an unspoken pretence of having come from the object of the hunt—ran the length of the hall. Already, would-be heroes gathered, snatching up the rich fare King Oeneus offered. Red wine flowed in troughs, poured by servants from amphorae almost as tall as the women who bore them.

In an alcove, she leant against the wall, a statue of some great champion of Men seeming to peer over her shoulder. Woozy and feeling the incessant slap of tendrils of the God's power at the edges of her soul, she watched.

This altercation she must see.

It did not happen as she had imagined. No spewed words of vitriol, nor hurled goblets of wine. No accusations resounding through the hall, spoiling the mood. Queen Althaea stepped up behind her son and placed a hand upon his shoulder.

Artemis struggled to send Pneuma into Perspicacity to catch whatever whispered recriminations the queen would have offered. Drained as she was, she found her control of her Pneumatikoi flimsy. There was so little Pneuma left for her to spare. In shattering the staff, she had allowed her own vitality to be siphoned away, and it would take long days and rest and meditation beneath Thoth's glow to replenish her energies.

But Althaea did not speak. Rather, with a snarl, she drove a glowing brand she had claimed from the hearth directly into her son's eye. Meleager collapsed onto the table, his inchoate shriek of agony cut off as his brain was skewered. His hair burst into flame. Even from across the room, Artemis saw the sickening charring of the flesh around the eye socket.

Screaming madness enveloped the hall. Arms wrapt the queen and dragged her from the prince's corpse. She did not fight her husband's men. Rather, an inarticulate wail erupted from her, as if the screams of the damned poured from the very bowels of Tartarus to swirl about the chamber and offer forewarning of the horrors that awaited all gathered here.

King Oeneus flung himself over the body of his son, his words of anguish—if he managed any—lost in the chorus of shouts and fear enveloping the feast.

And all Artemis could do was stand, paralysed and befuddled at how far things had gone. For it had taken but a single, swift turn for anger to spark into uncontrollable violence. And once unleashed, that violence took on a life of its own. Men hurled themselves at one another, wrestling upon the floor, smashing amphorae, hurling plates. Bones snapped. Skulls were cracked upon the benches. Blades were drawn by revellers with manic, wild looks in their eyes.

Rivers of spilt wine streamed along the floor, far more than every last amphora in the room ought to have held. The current fed into itself, forming a circular channel that flowed over her sandals. The wine—Bacchic wine, the scent made plain its nature—became a moat enclosing the guests within.

Trembles shot through her limbs at the thought of the precious, life-giving draught that stood so close within reach. Then she was upon her knees, heedless of the wine staining her tunic. With cupped hands she raised it to her lips. Heady warmth teased her tongue and trickled down her throat, an almost orgasmic relief surging down into her core. Sip after sip. Here lay the answer to her enervation.

Here, her salvation.

"The queen claimed an *Olympian* herself revealed her son's crimes to her," Atalanta accused. Artemis's adopted daughter cornered her in the courtyard, cutting off her progress back to Dionysus. Her God called to her, and she must return to him. Oh, how she ached for the touch of his glory. She needed it, upon her flesh. Upon her *soul*. Artemis fair chittered with anticipation of taking the God inside herself and letting him fill her with his unrivalled power.

The Bacchic wine had tinted the World rosy. Tittering, she reached unsteady fingers to stroke her daughter's cheek. A voice inside her core told her Dionysus wished for Atalanta to join his Maenads, as well. The God would soothe away the coarseness of life and leave behind a soul polished and gleaming, free of mortal woes.

"You betrayed Meleager!" Atalanta spat.

Dimly, in the back of her mind, Artemis wondered that she could be accused of betraying a man whom she had not met. One who, in supposed valour, had in fact slain her own lover. Artemis might have killed him for this but had contented herself with ruining his revels by tearing away the curtain of anonymity behind which he had hidden his crimes from his own mother.

Help her see Truth.

The command rose up from her soul, undeniable in its urgency. Yes, she must help her daughter, for such was her duty as a mother. The benighted eyes of all the World must be opened to the glory of God. Only Dionysus's caresses could assuage Atalanta's burdens. His penetrations would leave the girl so full she would have no room left inside herself to harbour the least dolours.

Atalanta's eyes widened, her face stricken as though she had seen something inside Artemis that troubled her beyond words. And indeed, God was beyond words. Beyond all description. His glory must have shone from her silver eyes. But Atalanta did not understand that, though it was right to approach God with fear and reverence, his glory was not a source of apprehension.

"You are drunk," Atalanta accused.

Oh, she *did* understand. Artemis found a wonderfully wide smile creeping upon her. She cast about the courtyard, drawn to the scent of Bacchic wine now flowing from the central fountain. "In wine flows the Truth, my child."

It was strange to hear God's voice spill from her lips. Strange, but not unwelcome, for how could God's presence ever be unwelcome?

Atalanta backed away. Children so oft fled from what was best for them, dreading the momentary discomforts and failing to see the greater rewards that would lie beyond such transitory hardships. "I'll help you," she said in sweet promise to her precious child. "It will feel so much better soon."

Fear won the battle waged within the girl, and she broke into a run, fleeing from God's embrace. But the Bacchic wine had restored —nay, enriched—Artemis's Pneuma, and it flooded into Alacrity and Potency off its own accord. A rush of wind, and she'd crossed the courtyard and seized up Atalanta, hefting her over her head.

"Mother!" the girl squealed.

"Shh, darling," Artemis assured her. She carried her daughter to the fountain, twisted her around, and shoved her face into the burbling flow of God's bounty. Atalanta's hands caught on the fountain's marble lip. She tried to resist. Tried to push her head out of his cleansing bath. That was of no matter, though. Artemis would not allow her beloved child to suffer or deny herself salvation.

She was saving the girl, so said the voice in Artemis's soul as Atalanta thrashed. Her resistance flagged, her struggles waning as the crimson redemption flowed into her.

Artemis gave her daughter the most precious gift a parent could offer: the gift of belief. Such presents must always be bestowed lest children risk learning *wrong*.

Why, then, was there still a dark corner of Artemis's own soul that wept at her actions? Why could she not still that lingering whisper of doubt?

But she would burn out even this shadow of disbelief, within herself and within Atalanta. Only then might they have peace. For she knew another truth within her soul: God abhorred a faltering heart.

As death's fingers brushed across Atalanta, Artemis jerked her daughter up into the air. With a single squeeze on the girl's abdomen, she pushed the wine from her lungs. "Thus, do I anoint you into God's grace."

Eyes wild with rapture, Atalanta looked to her. And she smiled.

13

ATHENE

716 Bronze Age

*A*thene could not stand the thought of calling in on Kirke's father in Helion once more, so she'd returned by way of Phoenikia, resting Nephos in Byblos. Later, she'd taken hospitality from Laomedon, the prideful king of Ilium. Much though she misliked the man, he offered her reception she could not spurn. Last, out of Ilium, Nephos had borne her back to the slopes of Olympus.

Looking upon these slopes, after seven centuries away, Athene was not certain she could have explained her feelings to anyone who had asked. Her palms had grown clammy with anticipation, the beat of her pulse erratic. That breathless feeling was more than the thin, chill air.

Time had cast its shadows over her memories of this place, darkening the grandeur that had once seemed fitting. But home, even one rejected, held an undeniable *weight*. Though she'd tried to smooth it away, this place had left its impression upon her, and seeing it now left an ache within her chest.

She could not stop herself from trailing fingers along the marble facades of the temples bedecking the peak. Every flute in the columns, every caryatid watching her with marble eyes, tried to whisper to her this was where she belonged. Athene had been first cast from here, then rejected it in her heart. She *must* reject the place, for there was a rot here, lurking beneath the very stones. To rule here, above Man, induced cosmic narcism and an inevitable apathy for the plight of those seen as beneath Olympian cares.

All this she knew.

And still, *still* home beckoned. Still, there was the temptation to slip back into the comfort of familiar patterns, even knowing they must poison her once more.

With a shudder, Athene forced herself to focus only on making her way toward her father's palace on the summit, aptly named the Throne of Zeus.

Slaves and Titans alike watched her. Most probably did not realise Zeus had sent for her. Mayhap they thought she violated her banishment and stood there aghast at her temerity, fearing her father's wrath. Or perhaps they secretly craved his displays of fury, hiding that perverse thrill so many took in seeing another brought low.

Some of the temples had fallen into disrepair. Demeter's once grand pavilion had its gable defaced. Whilst no one had torn down the structure itself, it was overgrown with brown creepers that somehow survived the chill air. Hephaistos's temple, though not defaced, fared little better. Looking at it now, Athene pursed her mouth. His unspeakable crime against her had sent her down a path of bloody vengeance she had struggled for so long to dig herself out of. That he should die for his crime was justice. But her retribution upon his entire genos had been vanity, cruel and petty. For that, she would ever think of his line with shame.

She had ruined so many lives, not least that of his daughter. Mother had been right, of course. Athene had pleaded with her to revoke the curse upon Medusa. On realising the horrific injustice of punishing the child for the crimes of the father, she had gone to

Hekate and beseeched that Medusa should be released. But such a curse could not be broken, and Athene had been powerless to go to her. Mother had claimed Medusa's unending torment would serve as Athene's true lesson. Thus, even when ages of that torment had driven Medusa to utter insanity, Athene could not reach the woman or offer succour. And then Mother was gone without a trace. After that, the only respite Athene could offer to Medusa was death. In the throes of her agony, Medusa had even struggled against that, too. There were no easy answers.

She forced herself to stare up at the worn facade of Hephaistos's temple. She could do so now, without pain. After hundreds and hundreds of years, the hate had burnt out of her.

With a steadying breath, Athene moved on. She, too, had lost her status in the Olympian Order, and yet someone had maintained *her* temple. Its columns sparkled, immaculately clean. She could even see the flames of lit braziers within, glinting off the polished marble floors. Had Father ordered it upheld all these years? Or had he demanded someone restore it after deciding to revoke her exile?

It didn't matter. She told herself she had not come here to live in palaces or reclaim a place she no longer wanted. This, she told herself.

But then, home had its weight.

"I COULD SCARCELY BELIEVE it when that platinum-haired ox turd announced your pardon," Hera stated the moment Athene stepped through the enormous archway into the Throne of Zeus. Her sneering voice echoed through the vestibule, seeming to bombard Athene from all sides. The woman emerged from an interior archway, folded her arms over her chest, and stared hard at Athene. About her heels, a peacock milled, strutting with its tail unfurled.

Perhaps Hera thought the bird a reflection of her grandeur, but Athene could not help but imagine it a mockery. Her stepmother was a puffed-up prancing twit, thinking herself a queen, yet, in the end, no more master here than the bird.

"My father sent for me, so I have come." Once, she'd have fled from Hera. She had hidden from that lacerating gaze, always so keen to flense away at Athene's confidence and see her reminded she was but a bastard child.

Strange, now, how standing here with so little pride remaining, she did not feel the need to cling to the pieces of it as tightly as she had done when haughtiness had fair burst from her. The self-important guarded their image as jealously as any miser watched his every drachma.

Was that Hera's problem? Or did this woman insist on showing everyone she was queen because she clung to the last vestiges of her pride?

Hera huffed. She unfolded her arms, though, as if somewhat taken aback that Athene had not winced and retreated at her barb nor risen to meet it with anger. She was not used to anyone simply ignoring the knives of her wit. "Of course you did. His loyal pet. Eager to replace your mother as his top bitch, perhaps?"

The queen's voice carried, and yet no slaves or courtiers crowded the vestibule watching this confrontation. Perhaps they all knew well enough to stay clear when Hera's temper flared. Perhaps Athene, too, should have bowed and made her withdrawal to await Father's summons. He would know she was here and would send for her when it suited him.

Maybe she should have run now as she so oft had from such vitriol. When a viper hissed, the wise did not try to engage it in conversation.

Athene spared a glance at the peacock. "Your birds are as beautiful as ever."

"Of course they are." Her stepmother, it seemed, hardly knew what to do with a compliment. Her wary response bespoke one looking for the hidden thorn behind a gift. Or a punchline soon to follow.

"It must take great skill to see them thrive on this mountaintop."

Those Tethid eyes narrowed. It seemed almost to offend her, that she could not find the insult buried within Athene's compliments. "You think you know something of birds?"

Athene nodded. "My grandfather had a penchant for the raising of them. He imparted a few titbits, here and there, in the days when we travelled together." An understatement. Athene could probably name every species of bird native to Elládos, Phlegra, or even Kemet. Grandfather had refused to speak of Athene's grandmother, save in his elusive comments. But through those rare, wistful remarks, she thought perhaps his love of birds had come from knowing *she* loved them.

Hera frowned, obviously uncertain what to say to that. Prometheus had, in the years since the Gigantomachy, managed to avoid drawing Olympus's eye to himself. Though he still paid others to tend the Aviary on Ogygia, so far as Athene knew, he spent most of his time still wandering far and wide. She doubted anyone alive had seen so much of Gaia as he had. By making certain he stayed away from Elládos, he managed to keep from drawing Zeus's ire once more.

But no one would forget what Father had once done to him. The peace between them since the Gigantomachy was a tenuous one at best.

Athene had learnt so very much from Prometheus. So many lessons she could not quite put into words. He was, perhaps, the wisest, most haunted man she had ever encountered. Grandfather so oft approached every problem at oblique angles, that, on those occasions when he spoke plainly, his words would burst through one's defences like the sharpest of spears. His insights could pierce the strongest of armour, oft because one did not see the blows coming.

"Why do you hate me?" That startling directness, when used sparingly, had served Athene on some occasions, as well. "What did I ever do to you, Stepmother, that there has never been peace between us?"

Blanching, Hera swallowed. "I ..." The queen took to pacing about the vestibule, the slap of her sandals the only sound. Aristoi did not speak to one another thus. On Olympus, one hid poisoned daggers beneath silken threads. And Hera sputtered as though Athene had stripped naked before her. "Y-you ..." After a moment she spun upon Athene. "You were *born*."

Athene could have rolled her eyes at that. She could have sneered at the absurdity of holding one to account for matters far beyond their control, merely because of their proximity. Instead, she forced herself to nod in sympathy. "Surely the culpability for that lies with my father." She could well understand that, in Hera's eyes, Athene represented a perpetual reminder of Zeus's infidelity.

Then, of course, so would Hermes, Zeus's bastard by Maia. And Hermes was an Olympian who still lived on this mountain with Hera. Discounting him, Father had innumerable other bastards, too. Not least Herakles. There was Minos, too, and Pollux, and many others over the ages. Maybe Hera held venom enough within her breast to poison the lot of them.

"It lies with both of your blighted, detestable parents, you bitch."

Athene shuddered at the wrath in Hera. Because she had seen it in *herself*. For years, she had simmered in such similar smouldering fury, always ready to burst forth upon any convenient target.

But Hera could not take out her anger upon Zeus. Men called him Almighty, and whilst that might have been a stretch, no living Man or Titan could challenge his power. Athene's father held more Pneuma than anyone she'd ever heard of, and that was not accounting for the unassailable might of his lightning. Nor could Hera bruise his ego with her barbs. Her father, she knew, could not perceive veiled insults, because he could not imagine anyone seeing fault in himself.

She knew who her father was. This, she always told herself.

"I was a princess of Thebes," Hera said. Her voice, though a whisper, still echoed through the empty vestibule. "I was a ..."

Burgeoning sympathy had Athene striding closer. Almost close enough to reach out and touch her stepmother, though she knew Hera would have slapped away her hand rather than accepted the comfort she intended. "You regret marrying him, king though he is."

"Regret?" The sound that spilt from her lips was something

between a sob and a chortle. "Naïve bitch." She shook her head as though Athene were once more a toddler, too stupid to understand the simplest of lessons. "Regret implies *choice*." Hera closed the remainder of the distance between them now. "Do you think a man such as he takes it well when a woman refuses his marriage proposal? Rack your brains, child, difficult though it may prove for you to rely upon those rather than your brawn." Her smile was cruel. And trembling. "How would such a man ensure a woman could no longer deny him? What method do you imagine he'd employ to both, in his mind, punish an 'insolent bitch,' his exact words I shan't ever forget, and to force her mother's hand? Hmm? Can you think of some condition a princess might be left in which would ensure even a queen married her off in a hurry to the one who'd done it?"

Despite herself, despite her intent to bridge the gulf between them, Athene balked. She fell back. Hera was lying. She *had* to be lying.

Except, Athene knew better.

She knew she wasn't.

The queen nodded, that malicious smile still cracking. "Oh, you do see it." She swallowed. "That I gave him your brother Ares. Gave him Hebe ... it was never enough for him. He shamed my marriage bed before it was ever a marriage bed. He has defiled it, time and again, since the day I first laid eyes upon him." She was shrieking now, no longer caring in the least if the whole of the palace heard her. "He fucks every last cunt from here to Lydia, and Men *praise* him for his rapes! They laud him for his lusts and think him a paragon of manhood for such. They call him their glorious god! And despite it all, still I remain faithful. But that's not enough. No, I must tolerate the products of his betrayals walking beneath the same roof I am forced to live under.

"So, Stepdaughter, you dare ask why I hate you?"

Athene trembled in place, unable to even speak before Hera's explosive tirade.

"I do not hate you. I hate you no more than I would shit stained upon the wall. My loathing ... that I reserve for the one who insists on *flinging his godsdamned faeces around like a baboon!*" Hera was panting.

But it was Athene who could not catch her breath. Not even when the queen stormed from the vestibule.

IT WAS through Athene's half-brother Ares that Zeus summoned her. Once, Hermes had served as messenger for their father, flitting to and fro like a pigeon. Now, though, Athene passed Hermes in the halls and he stood idle, muttering under his breath, and sparing her only the barest of glares.

Ares grabbed his own stones in mockery of their brother.

"Is that necessary?" Athene asked, though she knew no fraternal loyalty existed between any of Zeus's offspring. Father had oft pitted them against one another in competition for his affections. It had stifled any chance at sisterhood that had ever existed between Athene and Hebe, and she had to assume the same was true between Ares and Hermes.

Her brother snickered. "Always best to remind the winged little shit where real power lies in the family." He flashed her a wild-eyed grin. "It's in my cock."

Because Athene had needed her brother to clear that up for her.

She sighed. The relations betwixt them were all but hopeless, she feared. The Olympians were, all of them, drunk on Ambrosia and power. It was not enough to rule the Elládosi world beneath their oppressive heels. Too, they must forever bicker with one another in these petty games.

So why, then, did it mean so damn much to her, the hope to see pride in Father's eyes when he looked upon her?

Athene's encounter with Hera had left her shaken, and she had not the strength even to chide Ares. Especially not as she knew, all too well, her sadistic brother feasted off agony and anguish as though they were the finest of delicacies spread before him.

Ares led her to the tunnels beneath the Throne of Zeus and

paused before an orichalcum-banded door. Once, so, so many years back, after Father had bound Prometheus, Mother had brought Athene here, to the Seeing Pools. Or rather the Oracle Mirrors, Mother had told her, saying that Kronos had crafted them from quicksilver by means unknown and lost to time.

Back then, Mother had warned that her father held an obsession with the Mirrors. Hekate had told Athene that Zeus hunted for something, hidden with the past or future. Something that haunted him.

Pausing before the door, Ares rapped his knuckles once, with affected drama. A moment later, Zeus opened the door and glared at his son with narrowed eyes.

"I brought—" Ares began.

"Get in here," Zeus commanded Athene, snatching her elbow and yanking her through the doorway. As Athene glanced back, Zeus was looking to Ares, who lingered upon the threshold. "And you, do not tarry in these halls. Be gone until I send for you."

Her brother, the self-styled God of War, stiffened at the coarse dismissal. He stood, mouth half agape, struggling for some retort. His mind never had been the swiftest of rivers, Athene knew. Ares earned Father's favour, when he managed it at all, through his epic propensity for violence, prowess in battle, and unfathomable sadism.

Their father slammed the door in his face. Then the king looked to Athene.

"Speak of the gossamer threads of Ananke, Daughter." Though the chamber was cool, a sheen of sweat dribbled down her father's brow and ran off into his beard. "Long have I sought for answers in the darkness. And you ... you must have them." Zeus mopped his face with the back of his wrist. "You are like her, your mother. You *see*."

Athene frowned at his words. Obsession could well turn to madness, she knew, but she could not believe such would happen to her father. Not to him. Whatever his faults, he ruled the World. He was a bastion of eternal strength, mighty upon his throne. Surely, if he had lost himself, the other Olympians would have noticed.

If they were not so caught up with their own petty pursuits and selfish fancies.

No, no, she would *not* entertain such thoughts, for the path they led down was too terrible to countenance. Instead, she turned her attention to the chamber. She'd been in here once only, so long ago. It was more cavern than Man-made place, though carved archways framed the numerous quicksilver Mirrors inset into the walls. Each glistened like a vertical pane of standing liquid, an almost frozen waterfall beckoning her with secrets just behind their veil.

Slowly, Athene paced the cavern, glancing at the Mirrors but careful not to gaze too deeply into them. She was not certain losing herself in pursuit of such things would prove wise. She had gone down that route, once, using Kirke's Nectar, and it nigh destroyed her. "I cannot help but note that a ... distance ... has grown up between you and your sons sometime during my centuries away."

"Bah! One of those simpering little bitches will betray me, one day. He'll think, in witless self-delusion, he can strike down the rightful King of the World. A fucking patricide! I've but to find the face of the traitor, and I'll have his limbs strewn from here to Argos. I swear upon Styx I'll let Poseidon feast upon his stones!" Athene had no idea whether the mer-Olympian did such things, but she quite hoped not. "What contemptible son would ever dare raise his hand to his own father?" Her father's eyes crackled with sparks, the sharp tang of his power saturating the still air within the cavern.

Athene might have pointed out that Zeus had, in fact, struck down his father. Were she to say such a thing, he would no doubt brush over it as being entirely unlike in nature, or otherwise irrelevant. Maybe it was. If Ares—she found his rebellion easier to credit than Hermes's—were to strike against his father, it would be for his own vanity. Father had always said he had overthrown Kronos to spare the world his tyranny. He had explained, time and again, that the Ouranid League had pressed its heel upon the throats of all on Gaia.

"I will have the traitor's identity," her father said, striding closer to her. His meaty hand fell heavy on her shoulder, and he guided her toward a Mirror with a roughness born of his obsession. "You already possess the Sight, and thus you are primed to derive even more within these mercurial pools. Tell me, Daughter. Give me the name of the one who will betray me."

A chill shot up her spine. Had not he spoken very similar words to her grandfather, seven centuries prior, before imprisoning Prometheus in Tartarus?

I have no names for you this day, King.

"Only," her father said as though struck by an afterthought, "have a care with the Mirrors." He tightened his grip upon her shoulder. "Do you know, I've reason to believe it was peering into these depths that first drove my father to his madness? His writings, such as he left, speak of obsessive fears of his own death, beheld beneath a Mirror's damning surface." Her father snickered and shook his head. "Those of weak minds risk fracturing themselves when faced with unpalatable truths. Fortunately, my own mind is forged of adamant, as well everyone knows. I alone have the will to thwart prophecy and prevent my ending." With his free hand, he pointed to the Seeing Pool. "You need but find me a name, and I shall deal with the traitor."

He allowed her to shrug free of his grasp, and Athene moved to the Mirror, bracing herself on either side. The stone was cool and smooth beneath her palms. A tether to the now ... even as the shifting liquid of the Mirror reached up to wrap its tendrils around her mind.

THE BLOOM OF PEONIES, unfolding in bursts of pink and pools of brilliant white. A spring breeze, sweeping down from the mountains, cool without being cold in the evening. This hillside she knew too well; had once thought it home.

Blighted now.

Stained with blood of purest innocence.

The house was an empty husk. There was a sense, as she lingered upon the threshold, of hope dying a slow, painful death.

No, no, no. Not there, where she'd been forced to dig tiny bones from the ashes of the hearth. Not there.

But she stepped through the doorway and collapsed in a heap against the wall. Fatigue and despair. Heedless of the grime—dust and soot caked the whole place now—she settled to watch another day dwindle. An intimation arose, of gnawing dread that oft seemed to claw its way out of the twilight, as if sorrow born from the rifts the setting sun tore open in the sky.

Loneliness.

A wonder what she was doing.

Tears blurred her vision. She could not endure this. It had gone on and on, and her fragile hope ... What if it had been birthed in her own disquiet mind all along?

Then a shadow fell over her, obscuring the moonlight spilling in from the doorway.

She looked up. And he was there.

He had come, as though he too had escaped the rifts of dusk. Or been reborn from the blooms of spring flowers.

THE URGENCY OF HER VISION, distorted though it was, shot through Athene like a blow. It sent her tumbling backwards, flailing. She collapsed onto her back, smacking her head upon the cold stone floor of the cavern. The impact sent motes of light skittering across her eyes even before the pain of it registered.

Athene groaned.

Her father bent over her prone form, his dangling beard obscuring her view of his face. Could he not have caught her, standing so close behind her? "The *name*. Give to me the name of the one who shatters all filial bonds, that this can be ended. Which of my recreant sons would dare to strive against Almighty Zeus? The ranks of Olympus must be thinned one last time, my daughter. Give me ... the name."

Wincing, Athene probed at the back of her skull. Her fingers did not come away coated in ichor, which, she supposed, was a good sign. "I saw naught concerning any betrayal." Unless one counted Kirke's betrayal of Athene, in brewing the Nectar. She rolled over onto her side. On hands and knees, she took a steadying moment to gather her senses. "I saw only something from, I think, my own future." A hope to find her son, at last, whatever might have befallen him. Her beloved son.

Who was also Zeus's son.

A sudden, sick fear twisted her guts into knots. Was there even the remotest of possibilities that Herakles could be the one to strike down her father? Such kinslaying seemed unthinkable, but she could not quite suppress that awful churning in her now. "How do you know it's an Olympian?" She almost dared not voice the question.

Zeus snorted. "Am I surrounded by imbeciles?" He threw up his hands and began pacing around the chamber, leaving Athene to regain her feet on her own. "Only an Olympian, steeped in the power of Ambrosia, would have the meagrest of chances of standing against me." He paused, then whirled on her. "And only if he had the element of surprise. Which I shan't give either of those curs. No ... No, my eyes see all. I will know their treachery even before they dare to act. Still ..." More pacing, and now he wrung his hands. "Could the culprit have conscripted allies toward his treason? Hmm. I can trust no one, Athene. No one save yourself." He pointed at her. "The one advantage to your gender—you've not the stones for politics. And bless you for it."

Athene willed her face to impassiveness. Though her father had oft reinforced his lessons—that she was no equal to a male Titan—such offhanded remarks remained slaps in the face. Striven though she had, she had failed to ever impress him with her prowess or intellect. He had called her here, not because he missed her or regretted her banishment. Not because he valued her wisdom. But because he needed the Sight she had inherited from her mother.

Zeus would never trust Hestia; not after what he'd done to her former teacher, Prometheus. He'd called Athene back from banishment for her Sight. Which meant Apollon, as the only other true Oracle amongst the Olympians, had either failed to give him the answers he sought, or Father's confidence in the Heliad had waned.

Maybe, one day, she could learn which of her brothers would betray Father, and maybe *that*, at least, would win his respect. Maybe.

It would not be Herakles. No, she would not indulge such fears. Her son had not the means, motive, or intent to assault an Olympian, much less to kill Zeus himself. Surely even her father must suspect Ares most of all. The God of War ... yes, he could have attempted a coup. She would not put it past him. But Athene would not condemn him until she knew for certain.

"I need time," she said, proud of how she kept her voice even despite the insults her father had just hurled at her. At all womankind. "Between now and then, in the spring, I've somewhere I must be."

A growl rumbled from her father's chest. His fingers curled like claws.

"You cannot compel the Sight," she warned.

His face darkened further still. Perhaps he took it as a personal affront that aught upon Gaia, even a gift of the Moirai, was not his to command.

Athene risked his ire, but she would not miss the chance to find Herakles. "If I am to aid you, Father, I must be free to come and go as I will."

"Why?"

"Because the mind needs succour. It cannot bear the strain of peering into the future, time and again, without reprieve. The senses must be soothed with the sights and sounds and smells of the present, or prescience risks becoming stifled. It pulls back into recursive patterns until an Oracle beholds only madness." She ought to know. Drunk upon Kirke's Nectar and desperate for an edge in her obsessive vengeance against Hephaistos's genos, she had nigh broken her own consciousness. Had a falling out with Kirke not cut her off from the drug, she might have been reduced to a simpering shell of her former self, unable to distinguish present from the future. "I will walk the face of Gaia, Father, and on each return, I shall look once more until we have the answer you seek."

Her father's dislike of her conditions was writ plain upon his face. But he did not argue. Just stormed from the chamber and left her to breathe a weary sigh.

14

THESEUS

726 Bronze Age

"You murdered your own brother," Theseus accused Medea.

Despite her red-rimmed eyes and bedraggled appearance, the gaze she cast him was so baleful Theseus fell back a step. Could the witch work her Art upon him with a mere look? Could she, with a spiteful thought, lay a curse upon him and all his endeavours?

Before Medea responded or Theseus could decide what to do, Jason shoved him. "I slew Absyrtus with my own blade." The Iolkan prince bore the Golden Fleece draped around his shoulders like a glittering cloak. Or a funereal shroud.

That Aeëtes's armies had failed to catch the ship thus far did not reassure Theseus overmuch. They had stolen the sorcerer-king's great treasure, run off with his daughter, and slain his son. Theseus did not think Aeëtes, vain as only a Titan king could be, was like to let such affronts pass.

"I saved us," Medea protested. Her golden irises, hallmarks of her Heliad lineage, seemed to flash with her fury. Even now, stricken as she was with grief and—unless he missed his guess—no little terror, she wore an unearthly beauty about her in much the way Jason wore that damn Fleece.

Pirithous had drawn nigh when Jason accosted Theseus. With a raised hand, Theseus forestalled his friend. The last thing any of them needed now was to break into strife amongst themselves.

Still, Theseus misliked all that had unfolded in Kolchis. This was not the glorious quest he had sworn to bind himself to. Treachery and potions and kinslaying ... None of it fit with what he'd sought on this ship. He could see why Nike had parted with them the moment they reached Kolchis. He was beginning to wish he'd stayed by her side instead of chasing glory.

He stalked away from Jason and his witch bride, Pirithous at his heels, making their way to the forecastle where Herakles stood in grim counsel with Telamon. From the look upon the demigods' faces, neither of them much approved of bringing Medea or what she had done either.

"Jason has agreed to take us home by way of Themiskyra," Herakles said when Theseus drew up beside him. But Theseus noted the grim glance Herakles cast back at their leader.

"Amazons will not let us moor in their lands," Telamon objected. "I know you cannot back down from the task Eurystheus set for you my friend, but if the Argo draws too close to shore, we'll have a hail of arrows raining on us. Such things make for ill weather and sour mornings."

Herakles sighed and scrubbed a mighty hand over his beard. "Tiresias told me you, Theseus, must accompany me ashore for this labour to succeed."

Stealing a girdle from an Amazon queen ... Theseus had to admit to a certain titillation about such an endeavour. Men oft told tales of the land where women ruled themselves. They spoke of it in fear and condemnation, yes, for such women perverted the natural order of the World. But still, what Man did not dream of seducing a wild

Amazon, of taming her and making her a proper wife? Such things he had heard, even before joining the Argo. No few among the crew would have leapt at the chance, however dangerous, to see the fabled polis.

"Is it true what they say?" Pirithous asked with an idiot grin. "Is it true they abduct men to give them offspring and then do away with them once they've taken their seed?"

Theseus raised a brow. "Are you hoping to become such a victim?"

"I heard they go about their city unescorted," Telamon said. "Can you believe that? Women, even noblewomen strolling the streets *alone*."

Pirithous snickered. "I heard it they go both unescorted and un*clad*."

Herakles rolled his eyes. "I rather doubt it."

So did Theseus, though he loved a salacious story as much as anyone else. "If the seer claims I ought to go ashore by your side, then I will do so. I'd not abandon you if there is any way in which I can aid you." Not least because Theseus had begun to think Herakles a friend, but moreover, because it would mean joining his own name to the legendary demigod's. How better to enhance his legend and thus his reputation when he should return to Athenai than to be associated with one of Herakles's labours? Something less sour than what had unfolded in Kolchis.

Even now, when men spoke of the slaying of the hydra, Herakles's nephew Iolaus warranted mention. It earned the man renown and wine aplenty, both during the Kalydonian hunt and in the days whilst the Argonauts had awaited the completion of their ship.

"How long until we can draw nigh enough to those shores to take a small boat?" Theseus asked.

"I don't ..." Herakles began, then lulled about, as though in the midst of some dream. With languid steps he wandered to the gunwale, peering beyond the ship's wake and out, toward small rocky islands rising some distance off the shore.

Even as Theseus watched, the ship slowed and began to bank toward those islands. "What ...?"

Telamon too pressed against the gunwale, swaying, his heavy-lidded eyes fixed upon something on those rocks. And Pirithous as well.

Then Theseus heard it.

A song, lilting across the waves as if ephemeral enough to dance upon the surface of water and flick droplets about in its passing. The aria swept over him, like a balm upon his soul, soothing all the anxieties that had so long wracked him. What matter, in the end, who his father had been? Why should Theseus so strain himself to carve a legend for himself? Why not, instead, drink in the simple pleasures of life?

Upon those rocks lounged three women, sunlight glistening off the water that dripped from their naked flesh. The haunting, alluring song came from them. They reclined in perfect repose, one straining a pearl-coloured comb through the golden hair of another, whilst the third waved her fingers as though slowly stirring the waters of the sea. As though massaging away all the pain that had ever creased Theseus's brow.

Across the shrinking expanse of water separating them, somehow her fingers traced his temples, the lines of his neck, and his collarbone, sending tingles rippling along his whole body. Never, in all his life, had he beheld such perfection as the song that now wrapt around his soul.

What matter, came the passing thought as the ship drew ever more nigh to those rocks, if it seemed the women might have had flapping gills hidden beneath their sodden tresses? Why should it trouble him that hints of aquamarine scales broke from the surface of their perfect legs?

It was no matter, for they offered all he could ever want from life. Theseus had a foot up on the gunwale, dimly aware others too made to leap the side. He must be the first to reach these women, he realised. No other could be allowed to trammel his joys.

Another melody cut through their song, discordant at first. The intrusive lyre song drowned out the women's wondrous, enchanting calls, and Theseus spun, hand upon his sword to strike down whoever had such temerity.

There Orpheus stood upon the deck, strumming his accursed instrument. His pellucid voice rose high and ringing, joining his music in perfect accompaniment. Theseus's palm slipped from the hilt of his xiphos and, for the life of him, he could not explain the wrath that had gripped him an instant prior. He stumbled, took a knee, and looked up at Orpheus.

It felt as though a wine-haze dripped from his senses. An abrupt sobering that disoriented for the sudden loss of pleasure. When he looked back, he realised the Argo was about to crash into the rocks.

Only, no, the oarsmen banked once more. On the port side, several oars slapped the rocks, snapping in twain, but the Argo eased away from the women who, no longer languid, had risen to glare at him and the others with wrathful, nictitating eyes. One woman hissed, baring sharklike teeth as the Argo passed.

Sirens.

Theseus swallowed. The Deep Ones had nigh shattered the entire hull, and he could only imagine everyone onboard would have found themselves drawn into the murky waters of the Axeinos.

Only now, when he looked back, did he realise Medea stood behind Orpheus. Had the witch called upon the bard to free them from the siren's song? From the look upon her face, ashen and yet still smug, Theseus imagined she had.

She had saved the whole of the ship, then.

And still, Theseus could not bring himself to trust one such as her. He could not help but think that, sooner or later, great evil would come from Medea's presence among them.

BENEATH THE COVER OF DARKNESS, Thoth's glory obscured by drifting clouds, Herakles rowed their small boat ashore. In the stern, Theseus sat with his forearms resting upon his knees, watching the hulking demigod. The man threaded the waters with ease, not the least straining himself at the oars, and even the slap of wood on water was so soft no lookout could have caught it over the sound of the waves.

Theseus wanted to ask if Herakles had a plan for this endeavour, but something about the grim set of the other man's face forced him to silence. On occasion, Theseus might have sworn Herakles's gaze settled upon something else in the boat, something past Theseus, impossible though that seemed. Whatever it was, it creased his face in consternation. What dark musings so haunted the hero? He supposed he would not ever know the real depths of his friend's pains.

At last, as rain began to drizzle around them and Theseus pulled his himation over his head, Herakles drew the boat close enough to shore the hull scraped sand. Without a word, the demigod rose, hopped into the shallows, and moved to grab the prow. Once Theseus too had leapt into the cool waters of the Axeinos, Herakles heaved, yanking the vessel all the way up onto the beach.

Theseus rubbed his arms, though the real chill came from his now sodden khiton. "How shall we go about this?"

Herakles grunted, his grim gaze now settling upon Theseus with such weight Theseus might have almost thought the demigod blamed him for something. But he could not, for the life of him, imagine how any part of this labour was his fault. "According to Tiresias ..." Herakles sighed and shook his head.

Theseus quirked a smile. "In tales, I had always thought famed Tiresias a man, but I could have sworn that—"

"He's man so long as he so wills it," Herakles cut in. "And possessed of a tongue sharp enough to cleave flesh from bone if you cross him."

Theseus raised a brow. Herakles spoke as though from painful experience.

The demigod pressed on, letting the matter lie. "According to the blind seer, the Amazonian queen will be hunting in the woods at dawn. Alone. If she comes across you, she might take a fancy to your handsome face." The way he spat the words only reaffirmed that Herakles somehow held it all against him.

"Me?"

"Lay with her, and whilst she is distracted, I'll sneak over and claim the girdle."

Theseus felt heat rising in his cheeks. Was this some bizarre teasing spawned by Pirithous's words about Amazonian customs? Did the others watch in secret, waiting to see Theseus make a fool of himself? Surely, Tiresias would not have uttered such instructions. "You jest with me."

Herakles folded his arms over his chest, his dour expression making plain he found none of this the least bit amusing. In fact, Theseus did not recall ever hearing the demigod jest. "Perhaps you do not realise it, boy." Boy? "But the gods blessed you with princely looks and bearing. One day, perhaps, battles will scar and scour the handsomeness from your countenance, but for the present, it runs to your advantage."

A memory flashed, a moment in Pirithous's arms, his voice a husky whisper. *Your body seems chiselled by Olympian sculptors ...*

Theseus shook that away. He could not deny a certain rush of anticipation at the thought of lying with an Amazon, much less an Amazonian queen.

"Go and wash yourself in the stream," Herakles ordered. "We've been too long at sea."

❧

LIKE IN A DREAM, Theseus fulfilled the role Tiresias had laid out before him. He washed himself in a stream that fed the great river upon which Themiskyra sat. He swam in the waters, scarce aware of what he did.

But if the seer had foretold it, if Ananke decreed such a thing, would it still prove as sweet? Did either he or this Hippolyta actually choose the other if they served but to fulfil a prophecy?

Worse still, he had come here only because of that prophecy. Which meant, at least for him, his volition never entered into account. On the other hand, the sense of blood rushing to his nethers reminded Theseus he wouldn't pass this chance for half the gold in Atlantis. His whole body seemed atingle with the thrill. And the wonder if lying with a woman would prove even sweeter than his few times with Pirithous.

When he rose, water streaming down his chest and legs, feet still in the shallows, the woman was there, fierce eyed and clad in a loose tunic suited for hunting, her hair tied back. In one hand she bore a bow, a spear in the other, and beyond her, a large horse neighed in apparent irritation at the interruption. Dangling from the horse's bridle was a patchwork of leather napkins sewn together.

The Amazon followed his gaze and broke into a disconcerting grin. "Scalps of men I have slain," she answered the unspoken question. "More than any of my sisters."

Dozens of them, in fact.

Only now did his gaze at last catch the glint of a gold-plated girdle cinching tight her khiton. "Is there a reason your scalp aught not join my collection?"

Even now, even with her spear pointing at his breastbone and the heavy look of murder in her eyes, he could not shake the sense of having fallen into some fanciful dream. His words spilt from his lips as though called from the depths of his hypnagogic trance. "I am a single man, alone, and surely no threat."

"Who are you?" the Amazon asked. She made no effort to disguise her appraisal of his naked body, and Theseus had to suppress the urge to hunch up and cover himself. Never had a woman seen him thus, much less looked upon him so brazenly.

"I ... um ..." His body betrayed him, his manhood stiffening at her regard without his least intention. And still, the sense that all of this flowed around him, as though he were caught up in puppet strings, his words and deeds pulled upon by the unseen hands of the Moirai. "I am Theseus, son of King Aegeus of Athenai, come wandering to these lands in search of adventure."

"And how old are you, oh Prince of Athenai?"

"Seventeen ..." Even as the words slipped from his mouth, he wondered if he ought to have lied to make himself seem older.

The Amazon snorted lightly under her breath, her mouth quirking in a hint of a smile. "So young, and I can well see which adventure you seek." With a jerk of her spear, she motioned him free of the river. Theseus bent to snatch up his khiton, but her spear barred the way. "I know what you want, and I'm of a mood for a diversion. So, you may count yourself doubly fortunate you can keep your head and see what you've been missing."

"D-diversion? Wait, what do mean, what I've been missing? What makes you think I ... that I never ..."

A raised brow answered him. "We do not live as you live, Prince Theseus. In *your* world, a woman learns her desires are shameful and that so-called modesty ought to curb her animal instincts, though a man is entitled, even encouraged, to give in to his. Here, in this land, we lie with whomever we feel inclined to do so, when it suits us, and no time other." She motioned with the spear again, and Theseus realised she intended him to lie on his back on the beach.

He did so, scarce able to breathe for the anticipation. "You never told me your name."

She shrugged, tossing aside the bow, then began to unbuckle the girdle. "What care you for that? Take what's offered and then flee these lands before I decide to execute a trespasser." Still holding his gaze, she rammed the spear into the sand and left it quivering there as she unfastened and tossed aside her girdle.

For an instant, his gaze lingered upon the belt, which glinted like a brand in the harsh light of the rising sun. When she yanked her khiton up over her head, he found his attention drawn elsewhere.

THE LAST VESTIGES of dawn's flames still streaked the sky as Theseus hurried back for the rowboat. The woman, the Amazonian queen Hippolyta he had to assume, had ordered him gone mere moments after she was finished with him. And though she had lingered in quiet repose—part of him had longed to idle beside her and lose himself in meaningless talk—he could scarce afford to be there when she bestirred herself. When she went to dress and found her golden belt missing, she would be after him, and Theseus hoped to be well away from Themiskyran lands before that happened.

As he scrambled for the seashore, he found his thoughts roiling. The casual way in which she spoke of having executed men left him somewhat shaken, especially now that he found himself no longer thickheaded with the rush of lust that had taken him. Hippolyta, so far as he could tell, would slay any man she came upon, unless he took her fancy.

Perhaps she later slew some of those as well. Even if they did *not* steal from her. A nervous chortle broke from his chest then. He could not shake the sense of utter disbelief at what had just happened.

He found Herakles waiting for him in the boat, fingers wrapt around that belt like he thought to squeeze the life from a snake caught in his grip. Such deceit seemed to sit ill with the demigod.

For Theseus's part, though, he found it all a rush. Lying with Hippolyta had offered a euphoric pleasure only heightened by the fear of the crime unfolding around him. The thrill of it left him shuddering, almost ready to burst into bouts of raucous laughter he suspected would have earned him no little ire from Herakles.

But Theseus could not shake away the sheer joy of his adventures. This feeling lending heat and lightness to his chest that he knew he would now live for.

15

HEKATE

1587 Silver Age

Minos, the bastard son of Zeus and Europa, was set to wed Pasiphaë. Though Hekate could not well blame Minos for his father's crimes against Pandora's adoptive mother, the mere sight of his visage served as a bitter reminder of Hekate's culpability in that assault. She had very much considered refusing to attend the wedding, however much Zeus might have taken umbrage at her absence.

It was Keuthos—now in possession of the corpse of a nineteen-year-old boy slain in a pointless scuffle over a girl who had probably forgotten him in a fortnight—who had convinced her. "You do not want the King of Olympus's attention upon you ..."

No, that was the honest truth. Hekate had not decided what, if aught, she would do about Zeus. Having learnt he had seduced—or coerced—his own daughter had only further deepened her mislike of the imperious bastard. But she had created in him something powerful almost beyond measure, and, should she decide to dethrone him, it was best she do so with him having never imagined a chance of her disloyalty. A direct challenge would never do, no.

Besides, these past eleven years, she had been forced to direct a great deal of her attention to ensuring Hades could not come looking for his vengeance against her for freeing Keuthos.

So, she sailed to Helion, let herself be known in the vile celebration, and did her best to avoid contact with the newlywed couple. Thus did Athene find her and offer her the reprieve of a walk on the wide balcony rimming the upper floor of Helios's megaron. After idle chatter and pleasantries, Hekate leant against the balustrade, peering into the depths of the sea far below. She had wrought for herself a great many enemies to attend to, though some, like Zeus, did not even seem to realise themselves her foes.

And both of her daughters had crafted rather messy plights for themselves, too. Athene had poisoned herself with Kirke's damn Nectar and, worse, blamed her sister for her hungers and withdrawals. "You still crave it," she said, not looking at Athene.

Hekate sighed, wondering, as she so oft did, had she made a mistake in ever aiding Zeus. But then, had she not, she never would have had Athene, either. Her children were the one good thing to come of her life.

"What?" Athene demanded. "Her actions jeopardised Pandion's authority by damaging relations with Mnemosynia."

"Or perhaps you judge too harshly. Both you and your sister." When Athene made no answer, Hekate pushed on. "You must find it easier to blame Kirke for your perennial need for what she provided, as if she forced it upon you, as if you yourself are not culpable for your choices. But in the shadowed recesses of your soul, you already know that, Daughter, and thus you languish under your guilt as much as your loathing for your sister." Still, silence answered her. "Absolve yourself, and her along with you. The self-deception of boundless strength, that need to project an amaranthine facade—it ruins us, abrades our hearts one poisonous deceit at a time."

Athene scoffed, a petulant brat despite her long life. In that moment, Hekate desperately missed her own father. Would she have turned to him now? Sought his advice in the handling of a fractious child? As if he had done so very well on that account ...

Either way, she could not forgive what Zeus had done to him, either.

"Is that the sum of your wisdom, Mother? Forgiveness? Shall I offer it to Hephaistos as well?"

Hekate cast Athene a solemn look. She knew well enough forgiveness did not lie in either of their natures. Still, Athene might have been better off if she *could* have let the past remain dead and buried.

Athene threw up her hands. "I can't. I won't."

Still, at Hekate's prompting, Athene had sought out Kirke, leaving Hekate alone with her thoughts.

SOMETIME LATER, Athene returned, whilst Hekate remained leaning upon the balustrade, lost in the dark maze of her thoughts. In Mu, some few witches were known to tattoo their flesh with sigils, which, if prepared properly, could fortify Pneuma. More importantly, these techniques could be used to ward oneself against potential threats from the Realms beyond. Such tactics might serve to shield her from Hades and his inevitable striving for vengeance against her. Still, always she came back to the question: how was she to help Persephone?

As a shade, had Persephone the strength, perhaps she could possess a corpse in similar vein to how Keuthos had done. But every time she and her Hyperborean friend had discussed it, they had come to an impasse. For neither believed Persephone had the will necessary. A spirit required energy, Pneuma or souls; revenants—and wraiths holding corpses like Keuthos—must feast upon one or the other. She was not certain she could envisage Persephone living thus in the Mortal Realm. That the woman must have done something akin to it in order to persist in the Underworld, she preferred not to dwell on.

More concerning still, she doubted she could slip inside Hades's fortress in Kek unnoticed. It mattered little if they could find a way to aid Persephone if they could not enact her escape in the first place.

Her daughter leant her back upon the balustrade, forcing Hekate to meet her gaze. "I've thought of a fitting fate for Medusa, assuming your Art can handle warping of the flesh."

Two years back, when Hekate had returned to Athenai and met with her daughter, upon the edge of the rocky acropolis, Athene had haltingly asked after Persephone, as if afraid to give voice to such fragile hopes. Back then, Hekate had advised Athene to abandon her revenge against Hephaistos, or at least against the other Kreiads. Steadfast, Athene took no heed, and had insisted on crushing the one who had violated her by first destroying his child.

Hekate felt her mouth twitch in frustration. None of this would assuage the pain Athene felt, and one day it might deepen the ache within. The compounding of bitter deeds must invariably weigh upon the soul. Pursuit of the Art had flensed away too much of Hekate's humanity for her to feel the depths of guilt another person might have. Athene, though, she would have to reckon with all she did.

Still ... still, as her mother, Hekate too seethed at what had been done to Athene and would not deny her daughter vengeance when she came asking for it.

"Curses can achieve such things, but not with ease, and the cost will be high, for the both of us, Daughter." She hesitated. "Perhaps it is better to slay her and spare us all."

Athene glowered. "I will take from her that which she values above all else: her precious, vaunted beauty and the pride she derives from it. I will make her a monster. Whatever the price, I'll pay."

"Only those who do not fathom real cost can claim they would pay any price." Hekate swallowed. Athene had not the least idea the prices Hekate had paid for the Art over the years. Most of all, the price Aeshma would yet extract from her when death at last wrapt its icy fingers around her throat. "I will do as you wish. I even know a wretched hold to which we can send her to pass the ages. But Athene ... this is the sole time I will use the Art thus for your retribution."

Her answer was a grim upturn of Athene's mouth. So be it. "Get me some of her hair."

ABOVE THE NETWORK of caves worming through the mountain that formed the better part of Kolchis rose the fortified hill of Qulha Palace. Outside the city, Hekate had learnt, Kirke now dwelt in a small estate purchased by her half-brother Aeëtes. No doubt Hekate's daughter found refuge here, beyond the Thalassa world, hiding from Olympian eyes whilst still tinkering with her Nectar brews.

It was this that prompted Hekate's perilous crossing of the Axeinos Sea to far Kolchis. The truth was, Kirke had long since surpassed her in alchemy, and for the curse Athene had chosen for Medusa, a transformative brew would work better than a traditional curse. With the strands of hair Athene had procured, Hekate could bind the workings, but it was Kirke's Nectar that would effect the physical changes in the Nymph.

"A petty waste of your time ..." Keuthos commented, skulking by her side as they trekked over the hills toward Aeëtes's estate.

"Helping my daughter is never a waste of time."

"This ... shall not avail her ..."

Hekate grimaced. Even the wraith, a being consumed by loathing of all things living and dead, could see Athene's plan offered risk without potential gain. "I have learnt many lessons from my father, old friend. The greatest, perhaps, was that some things a person must discover for themselves. The hard-won truths linger longest."

So she told him. But still, she had warned her daughter, even knowing Athene would not take heed.

Kirke received them with warmth and smiles, effusive as ever in her greetings and inquiries about the goings-on in Elládos. Despite the hospitality—she plied them with sweet breads and wines, with olives and figs—Hekate's daughter cast a wary eye upon Keuthos more than once and no doubt took note that he failed to sample any of the delicacies she brought before him. Even in her cups, Kirke had an astuteness that brought a faint smile of pride to Hekate's face. Whatever her suspicions, Kirke asked no questions about Hekate's companion.

"I need you to make a potion for me," Hekate said as they later sat beneath the waxing moon, savouring the crisp night air. Keuthos had retired to leave her alone with her daughter, though Hekate suspected he hunted the city for a soul to devour. It was, after all, the only way he could sustain his mortal form.

"Yeah, sure. Kirke make this, Kirke make that ... Kirke stop making so many tonics. I hear it a lot."

"This one is for your sister."

"Because she definitely needs to imbibe a bit more. I mean, you could just piss in an amphora, sprinkle some saffron in, and call it a potion. Athene would down it and ask for seconds, bet you Zeus's stones, she would."

"Kirke," Hekate said, treading the line betwixt sternness and imploring her daughter to give aid. "I need to make a potion that will transform one of Athene's enemies into a snake."

Kirke whimpered and let her face slump into her palms but dared to peek at Hekate through her splaying fingers. "Mmm. Why don't we just make a love potion for her? Or a lust potion, even? Surely a good romp would offer more satisfaction than this absurdity. It's damn hard to predict an exact effect like that. I mean, yeah, sure, I could mix snake blood into the brew and *mayhap* it would work."

"Not just a snake, Kirke. I want you to make a monster. Something vile beyond words, that will leave all who look upon her aghast."

"Mother ..."

Hekate looked away from Kirke, staring at Thoth's face, high above. "Do you think I have no inkling of what you do here, Daughter? I know what you strive for, if not why. Consider this a test of your ability to craft whatever monsters you hope to give rise to here. Through my sorcery, I can enhance the efficacy of your brew."

The quiet answered her, and Hekate knew Kirke was mulling over the possibilities. To accomplish her profane aim here in Kolchis, the chance to test her draughts, particularly with summoned spirits guiding the process, might prove invaluable.

At last, Kirke blew out a long breath. "Yeah. I'll do it. I always do these things, huh?"

⁂

SITTING in Athene's personal chambers in her palace in Athenai, Hekate handed her daughter a ceramic phial. Athene turned it over in her hand, examining it as if the bottle itself might reveal some clue as to its contents.

"Should you cast this upon Medusa, the curse will take effect."

A dark smile tugged at Athene's lips. "I'll do so the next moment in which I find her alone." This had so consumed her she could see naught else. Would this represent the culmination of her vengeance? Would effecting the curse free her from the spite that choked her? Hekate doubted it.

"I have dreamt somewhat of days ahead, Daughter. There will come a day when you shall beg me to undo this wretched deed, and I will remind you of this moment, when I tell you that such lies beyond my power."

But Athene, of course, waved it away, her mind no doubt abuzz envisioning the horror she would wreak upon the Kreiad genos.

⁂

IN HER DREAM, Hekate walked alongside Athene as she stalked Medusa through the moon-silvered streets of Byblos. In the way of dreams, Hekate did not know what had brought Medusa so very nigh to the desolate remains of the Lodge of Whispers, but she passed along the fringe of the necropolis. Phantasmagoric images of Hekate's erstwhile companions in the Circle of Goetic Mysteries flitted into view beyond the thornlike gates. The ephemeral aspects of sorcerers she had long ago betrayed watched and judged her.

They were the sisters, Deino and Oizys and Pephedro, marked by the spiralling tattoos upon their cheeks. Medusa and Athene did not see them watching, but the apparitions glared at Hekate with judgment for all she had done to them and her many crimes in the ages since her theft of the Sefer Raziel. Behind the haze of their empty eye sockets, she saw their malice. Their desire to drink in Hekate's suffering. So eagerly did they await the fulfilment of her damnation.

When a silken-clad figure emerged from a doorway, his figure silhouetted by the flickering light of an oil lamp in the room beyond, Medusa's purpose here became clear. The flame-haired daughter of Hephaistos sashayed toward her tryst, and blatant anticipation of the encounter stiffened the man's posture.

Artemis herself had taught Athene the arts of stealth, and neither Medusa nor her lover took note of her. At least not until Athene stepped forwards, hurling the phial from the shadows such that it shattered against Medusa's back.

Medusa hissed in annoyance and spun to search for who had accosted her. A bare, trembling moment, her gaze met Athene's own. Before Medusa's paramour could spot her, Athene stepped back into the shadows.

The next instant, Medusa convulsed, dropped to the ground, and sputtered. Her hissing took on another, far more bestial note as she writhed. Her legs kicked in wild thrashing, soon stuck to one another as though bound together.

Scales wormed their way out of flesh, slicing skin in the process. Ten thousand tiny rivulets of blood oozed from Medusa's lower half, a weeping crimson cascade. Before Hekate's horrified eyes, the woman's hair fused, becoming a wriggling, hissing nest of spitting serpents.

When at last the afflicted Nymph looked up, meeting the gaze of her agog lover, he too convulsed. His flesh seized up in a rictus of agony. His skin took on a glistening sheen in the moonlight. It calcified, becoming marble.

Hekate slapped a hand over her own mouth, unbelieving what she had just seen.

Before she even had time to consider how her curse had

produced so wretched a side effect, Medusa shrieked, the sound ringing with unending agonies. Her pain went beyond the physical torment, mingling with laments over what had become of her once vaunted beauty and perfect life.

Hekate imagined she felt it as Medusa's mind snapped in twain. For sanity could not remain in the face of such a vile metamorphosis.

Medusa's dire cries drew more men into the streets. As each looked upon the monster Athene had created, they too shared the first man's fate. One by one, statues sprang up along the streets of Byblos, a dozen men destroyed forever.

And in the dawning revulsion that began to spread over her daughter's face, Hekate saw that, *at last*, Athene now knew the price of her vengeance.

IN TRUTH, Hekate could not say for certain whether her dream had already transpired or represented something soon to come to pass. In either event, she had rushed to barter passage to Byblos for herself and Keuthos. They had been on Phoeba and sailing to Phoenikia would take time. Nyx alone knew how much chaos Medusa would wreak in her rampage along the way.

Hekate had—before ever cursing Medusa as Athene begged— considered imprisoning the monster in Sarpedon. But she had not expected Athene to act so soon, nor Medusa herself to have left Lydia. Slunk into the ship's hold, crouched amid carefully tethered crates that still shifted with every lurch of the trireme, she sat with Keuthos.

He kept his hood up, even here, in the dark, rendering himself almost invisible to passersby, should there have been any.

"Why should I take this risk ...?" he demanded.

Hekate reached over to grasp his hand. It was chill as the grave, and beneath her thumb, she could feel a patch that had taken on a flaky, necrotic texture. Even consuming souls, the wraith could not hold this stolen corpse together forever. "I don't think it much of a risk. You are not a Man to be affected by her gaze."

"You do not know that ..."

"Fine. At worst, it destroys this decaying husk you now inhabit and I bribe a gravedigger for a new vessel."

"Being discorporated ... weakens ..."

"Keuthos." She squeezed tighter. Others might have demurred to touch the corpse, but Hekate knew well the soul within, and they had been through so much together. "You alone have the power to subdue her so we can transport her to Sarpedon. Once within the Circle's refuge, I can bind her there to harm no one else. If we do not, Medusa will ravage Phoenikia and anywhere else she roams. She is utterly consumed with rage, driven to madness and the need to avenge herself against all life."

"Empathy ...? You seek empathy ... Such was excised from me the moment a Titan heel crushed my throat ... Let damnation spread ..."

Hekate shuddered. She could not stand to let go of her fallen friend, but times came when his malice seeped from him in waves that churned her gut, and she would imagine—for a moment—he might be better off if claimed by oblivion. No. Such vile thoughts would not poison her mind. She only tightened her grip upon his hand. "Help me contain Medusa. Or I will do so myself, and you risk losing your companion."

When he leant forwards, a cruel light glinted in his eyes, so sharp it could slice. He gripped the back of her head, pulling her close enough the putrid reek of his rotting insides choked her. "You would have my aid ... Then I name a price ..."

Cold spite lurked behind those words. And yet, she needed him. "Name it."

"When you bind Medusa ... within the Circle's bastion ... you will also ward it against entry ... by *any* Titan ..." She opened her mouth to ask why, but Keuthos pressed on before she could. "You wanted your daughter ... to learn a lesson ... Let her learn it *well* ..."

Because once her spell was done, Athene could never change her mind. She could not enter the bastion to put Medusa out of her misery nor ask Artemis or even Hekate herself to do so either. Keuthos would see Athene's guilt, when at last it arose, dragged out over the course of impotent years in which she would find no one with the strength to overcome Medusa. And the cursed Nymph herself? Her isolation would deepen her madness until she drowned in an eternal sea of self-loathing. Derangement would turn her monstrous in more than body. Already, her victims were manifold, but this ...

Hekate breathed out a heavy sigh. If she demurred, Keuthos, turned bitter himself by centuries of torment as a wraith, would surely refuse to aid her. Hekate might well get herself killed—and her soul sent screaming down to Aeshma—if she tried to overcome the monster she had created by herself. Besides, she owed Keuthos far more than she owed to Medusa, a woman she did not even know.

She knew well enough what her answer must be.

16

KIRKE

701 Bronze Age

*W*hat had she done? This question paraded through Kirke's mind, again and again, in endless permutations. Wandering out of the woods had brought her to Knosós, and she had hidden on its periphery. Had watched as her past self made her pained way back to the city, intent to soak in the palace baths.

It was all real, and she had—overcome by wrath, as so oft happened with her—become the architect of her own exile. Yeah, Pasiphaë had betrayed her, but Kirke had betrayed her sister, as well. Worse still, the implication had settled into her soul that such had been inevitable. Kirke had experienced the interference with her sorcery back then, and Pasiphaë had birthed the Minotaur. Was this the weave of the Fates?

What had she done?

Filthy and broken, she'd sat on the edge of the wood, cradling the Box in her lap like a fragile infant whilst casting furtive glances at it and imagining it a viper, coiled and poised to strike. Mother must have *known* what it did. Had she failed to inform Kirke for fear Kirke would try to use this thing on purpose? Yeah, Kirke would have done it, too. Would have seen a means of escaping her exile, maybe of stopping the rise of the Olympians from ever happening.

Now, though, having borne witness to the trap that was the Box, all she wanted was to get home. Even Aiaíā didn't seem too dire compared to the merciless currents of history she found herself mired in.

What had she done?

When the sun had risen high, she hefted the thing in front of her eyes, peering at it. A little Box that had unmade her World, revealing a more inescapable prison than even her island. Or could she yet use this as Mother seemed to intend, to escape the grasp of the Moirai and change Fate?

No, she needed to get home. She would tell Mother what little she had learnt of this thing, hand it over, and be well rid of it. The Box had wrought enough chaos in Kirke's life already.

So, if she reversed the means of opening the top, perhaps she could return whence she came.

Of course, Kirke could not say with absolute certainty what she had done, as she hadn't planned to need to recreate those steps. Her best guess ...

The top cracked open and another vertiginous wave enveloped Kirke, light bending backwards.

❧

"What have I done?" Ino moaned, shaking her head while sitting on the straw-laden floor of the chamber the merchant had given them. "My children ... What if I cannot ever see them again?"

Kirke rocked the infant in her arms. "There is a child who needs you now. A nephew whose life is like to prove as difficult as those who have fled. And, yeah, I know it's hard, but you're the only one who can save him." Kirke handed Dionysus to Ino, who took the babe with more tenderness than she'd expected, as though the child might replace the two she'd lost. "Can you take him somewhere beyond the reach of the Olympians?"

Ino held silent before at last nodding. "My sister Autonoë, her husband holds some lands in far Nysa, in Kumari Kandam. I could ... They would not come for us there. No one would come so far."

Kirke nodded. It would be far enough, that seemed certain. "Swear to raise him as your own. Swear to see him safe."

"I swear."

Bilious and disoriented, Kirke found herself slumped against the wall of an alley. The stench of humanity assaulted her, mingling with the reek of brine from a not distant sea.

"Ugh. Always pleasant," she mumbled, rising. And this was *not* Aiaíā.

The sun had grown brighter even than what she'd seen outside Knosós, late in the afternoon she thought. So ... she was in a different city, covered in grime from the forest, and had not a thing on her save her clothes and this damn Box.

"Gotta love a challenge," she said and stepped out into the bustling street. Down the road, she could make out a congested harbour thick with biremes and triremes, as well as at least one Neshian bagala. Was this Phoenikia? Indeed, she followed the breezeway in the other direction until it rose up into an arching bridge crossing over to a fortified island. This was Tyros, the etiolated city-state in southern Phoenikia. Though, at the moment, given the bustle of the harbour, she had to imagine it closer to its zenith than its decline.

Had the Box brought her yet *further* back in time?

Right. Unless she missed her guess, she had found herself several centuries in the past, in a foreign city, without a single drachma on her person. Because her day had been going so well before that, and the Fates would never kick a woman when she was down. Maybe

Kirke ought to find another alley, pop the Box once more, and try for home again.

Except, twice she'd used it and twice she'd wound up worse off than before. Mayhap the Moirai could guess where next she'd find herself, but Kirke had no idea. Rather, the best she could do now was call upon the king—whoever that was at the moment—and try to learn about her situation. And to do that, she needed attire fit for a court.

It did not take long to find a tailor, as it turned out, and her stature and golden eyes must have announced her as a Titan, for the man dropped into an obsequious bow the moment she ducked into his shop. Ducked, because the roof was a hair too low for her to stand up in, with the man himself sitting upon a wide shelf, a dozen fabrics spread out before him. Kirke scooted up beside him.

She tried on her best possible smile, which she figured was pretty good, and folded her hands in her lap, tucking the Box in the folds of her khiton before it drew too much attention. "This seems a lovely shop, you know, and I'm in need of a new outfit and, hmm, a nice satchel if you do that, though if not, it's all right, I'm sure I could find one in the market."

"You mean for Agenor's symposium, mistress."

She cleared her throat. "Yeah, that. But, you know, I've had a spell of unfortunate luck of late and don't happen to have so many drachmae on my person. By which I mean actually no drachmae, on account of said misfortunes, which you would not believe if I told you, so I'll spare you the telling and disbelief and just say you ought to offer me your wares on credit."

"Of course, mistress," the tailor said, sweeping another bow.

Huh. Well, that worked out better than she had expected. Titan blood got you rather a lot of hospitality most places, but she hadn't realised she could convince the poor shopkeeper to garb her without coin. Or perhaps the man thought refusing might cost him more than the price of some fabric and a bit of labour. Either way, Kirke resolved to see him paid if ever it lay within her power.

While the tailor took her measurements, Kirke turned his

words over in her mind. King Agenor had lived, unless she misremembered, in the final decades of the Silver Age, some seven hundred years back. There was some fame to him, though Kirke found it hard to remember what. Perhaps fatigue and hunger jumbled her mind, or perhaps the strain of her sojourn had addled her memory.

By the time the tailor, Ithobaal, had finished her fitting, the sun had already begun to dip and the eve drew nigh. The man stepped outside to give her the privacy to change, and when he returned, he offered her a satchel.

"I'll see the king hears of your generosity," Kirke said. Any mortal king would have to welcome a Titan, even a Nymph like her, into his home and give weight to her words. Kirke did not much like using her heritage to lord over Men, but circumstances left her few options.

"Ba'al bless you, mistress," the tailor answered. Kirke supposed, at this point, she'd take the help of any god inclined to offer it.

Dropping the Box inside the satchel, she made her way over the causeway and onto the island. Agenor's palace lay upon the Hill of Epaphus. It was a vibrant hall into which a multitude of guests now flowed. Those who took a long enough look at her to recognise her as a Titan gave her a wide berth, allowing her easy access.

Whilst she needed to present herself to the king, Kirke hadn't eaten in days now and so made her way into the great hall, where tables lay laden with flamed baked cod and so many sweat breads her mouth watered from the smell of them. Grabbing a bronze plate, she filled it with a slab of fish and as much bread as it could hold.

"Pandora, get back here!" a woman called.

The name sent a shudder through Kirke, and she spun, half expecting to see the woman Prometheus had once brought to Ogygia, the very image of Nike. She had been in her dream, too, hadn't she?

Instead, she saw a girl, perhaps five years old, squealing and giggling as she wended around the legs of grown men, sweet roll in each hand. A Phoenikian woman chased after her, while another looked on and laughed.

Pandora ... a child?

"She's here, Europa," the other woman called when the girl raced behind her, still giggling.

Europa?

Oh, by Hyperion's fiery cock. Agenor was famed as the father of *Europa*, whom Zeus abducted as his pallake. This woman chasing after the young Pandora was Princess Europa. Was that Pandora's past, too? Kirke had judged her one of Nike's bastards and misliked her on sight, but if she had been here, suffered through this …

Despite her empty belly, Kirke set the plate of food down and wandered from the hall, stumbling into another woman, who caught her by her arms.

"You wonder if the unravelling threads of time shall reveal truth or madness," the woman said, and Kirke looked up into the aureate eyes of another Heliad.

"Pandora?"

She was here, grown, and fiercer now, the look of grim determination clear upon her visage.

Involuntarily, Kirke glanced back toward the hall, where Europa chased young Pandora.

"Because it seems too much to grasp," Pandora said.

Kirke found herself unable to swallow. "Y-you …"

She had seen this moment.

Pandora took her by the arm and guided her out into the courtyard, pausing beneath the shade of a cedar. Fortunate, as Kirke found herself needing to lean upon the tree for support.

"Until now, I've not seen you at a loss for words," Pandora said.

Against the tree, clutching it with one hand, Kirke at last managed to still the World that seemed so intent to shift beneath her feet. "You speak as though you know me."

"I have and I will." Hints of quelled emotions warred across her face for a bare instant. Her eyes widened at something she had seen behind Kirke, but when she looked, she saw naught save the crowded party. Pandora looked back to her. "The child was me, as I know you've surmised. I—" Pandora fell silent once more, looking beyond Kirke to two well-dressed Phoenikian men approaching.

Kirke thought she might have known them but could not recall for certain. This time had been so long ago ...

The mortals both dropped to a knee, one after another.

"Goddesses," one of them said, voice thick with awe. "We did not know you were among us."

And what to say to that? "Are not all welcome at this symposium?" Kirke asked. These were the princes here, weren't they?

"Of course they are, my lady," the same one said.

The other was staring hard at Pandora, in rapture or terror or both.

"Hello, Kadmus," Pandora said, and Kirke thought some pain lurked beneath the surface.

"My lady," he answered, jerking his head down in forced obsequiousness.

Pandora grabbed Kirke's arm and pulled her away from the men with such haste Kirke would have almost thought her afraid of them. Oh. Because she had known them as a child and now ... now ...

"He referred to you as a goddess, too," Kirke said. Certainly, the woman had a Heliad aspect to her, though not quite so tall as a Titan and lacking the Pneumatikoi of even a Nymph, so far as Kirke knew.

And she had travelled through time, just like Kirke. It seemed the only possibility to explain her presence now.

Pandora grimaced, glancing about the courtyard before answering. "The Tapestry's weaves are complex, sometimes gossamer threads we do not always see."

"Yeah, kind of like that answer." But another thought welled up. "This is it, isn't it? This is the moment when Zeus will come for Europa. And ... and you'll be swept up in the chaos?"

"It is." The words seemed to rip Pandora apart and Kirke wondered that the shreds of her did not blow away in the wind.

"Can we stop it?" Her question tumbled forth, though, in truth, she had no idea if she even ought to try. What might unfold if they succeeded in unravelling a pivotal event in history, more than seven hundred years in the past?

A melee of thoughts passed over Pandora's face in the space of a heartbeat. The woman blinked at tears welling in her eyes, and Kirke found herself overcome by the sudden urge to wrap her arms around her, to comfort her, though she had once disdained Pandora. "History must unfold as it always has, or all that has gone would collapse in on itself, Kirke. Some things ..." A choking sob swallowed her words. "Some things we think unbearable must be borne, regardless."

And even Kirke felt apt to burst.

17

PANDORA

726 Bronze Age

*I*t was a day's ride to Themiskyra, though the Amazons offered Pandora no horse and forced her to trot alongside them at a pace that would once, before the Phoenix, have left her gasping for breath. Even now, sweat streamed down her back and plastered her hair to her neck. But they came at last to the light defensive walls that framed the polis. At regular intervals, stone watchtowers broke those walls, and atop each, archers watched their approach. The city lay off from the sea, reachable by a river that fed into the Axeinos. The forest ran up, almost to the wall's edge on the side opposite the river. The route Hippolyta led them along, however, brought them instead to a wide grassland and up to a gate set within that wall.

Those gates were thrown wide at the queen's approach, and Pandora was led within a modest city that seemed constructed with one eye ever upon defence. The streets were laid out in funnels that would force invaders to pass through chokepoints into which archers on rooftops could rain death. Wooden bridges spanned the spaces between the outer wall and these roofs, creating a maze the defenders could navigate above the heads of their foes. Even some of the civic buildings further in had crenelations behind which archers could mount further defence of the agora.

Without pausing, Hippolyta led Pandora beyond that agora. Rather than upon an acropolis as one might see in Elládos, the palace they approached lay in a valley, nestled alongside a lake shaded by pines and birches. As they descended the slope, the songs of larks filled the air, muffling any sounds of Man. Here was a peace Pandora could well understand. A place she could have long lingered, had time and Fate permitted such diversions.

The palace itself was framed by long, two-tiered arcades broken by regular arches. From the upper balcony, a Titan woman watched their approach. Ebony-haired, with skin the deep colour of eastern peoples, the woman peered at Pandora with an intense gaze.

As Hippolyta guided Pandora through an atrium and on into a courtyard spotted with aspens, the Titan on the balcony vanished. She emerged from an archway, gliding across the distance between them with effortless grace.

Even the queen of the Amazons bowed to the Titan.

"Thank you, Hippolyta," Themis said. "You may leave us." Perhaps the queen would have offered some introduction, but instead she accepted the Titan's words without question. She and her warriors disappeared out the way they had come.

After they had left, Themis meandered around the courtyard, fingers brushing against the trunks of trees. Should Pandora break the silence? Uncertain where to begin, she watched the Titan.

The choice was taken from her when Themis spoke first, turning to appraise her. "Do you prefer Nike or Pandora?"

A surge of panic jittered up Pandora's spine, pinched her chest, and stole her breath. How could this woman know such a thing? Of course, she had long been the Oracle at Delphi, but Artemis had driven her from that home during the Titanomachy before Nike had come to Delphi and helped her and Apollon slay Python. Yet Themis seemed to know the depths of her, leaving her naked and trembling in the morning breeze.

"The others know me as Nike."

"Hmm." Themis nodded. "I would be lying if I claimed to have seen the whole of your road, Nike. But the pieces I have seen are enough to rattle even one as ancient as myself. These winding paths upon which you venture are shaded by eaves filled with nesting vipers, and you, I think, never know when venom will dribble down to scorch your flesh." The Oracle paused. "Or is it not so much the striking serpent you fear ... as the one devouring its own tail?"

Pandora rubbed at the ache in her chest. Though she willed the pain away, it refused her. No amount of mental demanding nor flooded Pneuma allowed her to soothe these attacks of nerves. Themis's words came perilously close to the sensation of helpless wandering amid unseen dangers that had so long plagued Pandora. "How do you know so much?" Her words seemed more wheezed than spoken, and she doubted Themis could have missed it.

"You already know most of the answer to that. Besides my visions, in truth, I've had some dealings with your daughter, though not in long ages now. Once, I considered your lover a dear friend, though I've rarely seen him since I left Delphi. In ages gone ... it was he who brought me from Dangun." Some place so far off Pandora had never even heard it named?

What mattered more, rather, was that Themis knew both Pyrrha and Prometheus. Her revelation that she realised who Pandora was meant she knew more than she ought to, yet Pandora still doubted even this Oracle understood the full scope of Pandora's plight. Themis played at being so forthcoming, but Pandora could not help but detect a ruse. Give away what is known and thus lull the other person into assuming one knows everything. Thence would come mistakes, Pandora speaking too freely, and Themis's knowledge would compound.

"You have some training as a warrior, yet barely more than a foundation, I think."

The Phoenix inside her—wriggling and burning at even that

minor slight—gave her power, but Themis was correct: Pandora got by more through sheer depth of Pneuma and force of will than martial abilities. "I trained with Artemis, once."

"Oh, she too has ventured here, many times over the years. She trained Hippolyta, some decades back, and others who watched them."

"Decades?" Hippolyta must be older than she appeared.

"She's a demigod," Themis confirmed. The Titan woman quirked a smile. "Train with the Amazons, Nike. Let them make you stronger even than you are now."

The knot in her chest began to uncoil at the kind offer. "Why? Why help me at all?"

The Oracle's gaze darted around the courtyard before returning to settle, heavy, upon Pandora. "Because those whom you strive against are my foes, as well. Perhaps the foes of all who walk upon Gaia."

Understanding shot through her like a thunderbolt. "You are part of Kronos's Gnostic Cabal."

"Kronos is gone." Indeed, he ventured into the future and was beheaded for his troubles, not that Pandora could explain any of that to Themis. "So many of us are gone. The chains that bind Man to Fate remain. If you are the hope we seek, if you are the one who might break those chains, I would see you armed with every advantage I might ever bestow."

Pandora had no idea if she could be that person, determined though she was to try. After all she had witnessed, all the ages she had seen, history seemed immutable. But she had sworn to bring the light of hope first to her loved ones, and now, having seen the shape of the future, to all Man. The Deluge would destroy this world, giving way to Era after Era, before finally resulting in Hekate's misty, poisonous future. Unless Pandora could heal the vicious wounds of time.

"I welcome your insight and training," she said.

For all knowledge could become her weapon, and she would seek it wherever it lay.

FOR TWO SEASONS, Pandora resided in Themiskyra. In the mornings she would expand her knowledge at the Muses College, where she met her idols, Urania, Kleio, and all the others. They were daughters of Mnemosyne, come here, to a place beyond the Thalassa and the Axeinos, where women reigned over their own futures.

In Themiskyra, one saw men on occasion, though only those kept for menial tasks or as breeding stock by Amazons who sought daughters of their own. The women here had taken the patriarchal affronts of Elládos and other lands and responded in kind, keeping males in servitude, locked away and powerless. Those men she saw kept their eyes downcast, and many bore scars of the lash, a reminder not to step out of line.

Here, she saw women from across the breadth of Gaia living together as sisters—or sometimes as lovers, Pandora noted. Skin tones ranged from fair Hyperboreans, to the ruddy complexions of Thalassa dwellers, to black Inumidians, or brown easterners like Themis. All were welcome, save males.

Pandora could not deny a certain peace, but still, she wondered if the inversion of oppression in Themiskyra would not sow all the same woes suffered in her own homeland.

In the afternoons, she would train with Amazon warriors, learning the arts of bow and spear. The women expected her to be able to ride and shoot with accuracy, even at speed. To fight from horseback or chariot. To stand shoulder to shoulder with other women in a hedge of spears, or to hurl javelins in a rain upon their targets.

Hippolyta, perhaps due to her demigod nature, could almost match Pandora in physical strength and, due to her superior skill, oft sent Pandora sprawling onto the sand of their training circles. The wrestling moves she taught seemed similar in nature to the handful of pankration manoeuvres Artemis had shown her, yet the Amazons went deeper, drilling over and over until Pandora's muscles remembered the motions even in her sleep.

After her first month, Hippolyta's belly began to show. The queen said naught of any liaison, but her sparring with Pandora ended, and she was replaced by her warriors, or sometimes by Themis herself, who proved an even greater challenge, even if she had not quite the sheer physical might of Hippolyta or Pandora.

Pandora attended to every lecture, read every papyrus scroll, soaked up every beating, and cleared every obstacle. There was no challenge she refused to attempt, and, on failing once, no obstacle she would not push herself until she could overcome it. By deliberately avoiding the use of Pneuma to strengthen her body, she found she could hone her muscles naturally. Pneumatikoi like Potency, she had come to realise, did not simply add to her physical strength, they multiplied it.

Small wonder Kala was so much stronger than her. But Pandora was growing stronger. With each passing season, she grew fiercer.

Most times, the women trained here wearing naught save a loin cloth, if that. It was how Pandora had heard men practiced in gymnasiums in other poleis, and here, inside the College walls, males were never permitted.

Drenched in sweat, despite the winter afternoon having threatened snow for hours, and panting with exhaustion but refusing to call upon Pneumatikoi, Pandora faced off against Themis once again. She escaped one hold and then the next, before Themis caught her wrists, twisted around, and hurled Pandora over her shoulder and into the Earth with dazing force.

As her senses returned, someone cleared her throat, and Pandora looked up to see the golden eyes and auburn hair of Kirke, of all people, staring down at her.

"I would speak with you ... Grandmother."

Still prone and panting, Pandora's eyes widened. Had she heard that correctly?

When Pandora had washed and dressed, she walked with Kirke, along the colonnades outside the College. In the interim, snow had begun falling, coating the whole of the polis in a dusting of fresh powder. The other woman seemed to know her way about well and pointed out a low building. Kirke hopped up, caught an eave, and pulled herself onto the roof. After Pandora followed, the Nymph jumped across a narrow alley to reach the overhang of an entablature.

Though no one seemed to have noticed, still Pandora found herself casting wary glances about before making the leap herself. How much would the Muses appreciate her stalking amid the College roof, she wondered? The entablature formed a narrow perimeter that Kirke followed until she reached a spot where she could climb the sloping roof to a flat shelf at the peak.

Once perched atop this, Kirke offered Pandora a hand. While Pandora had little need of aid to scale the roof, she accepted the gesture and the warmth it represented. That Kirke knew who she was —who they were to each other—meant the burden of concealing the truth from her was lifted, and that alone offered a profound relief that soothed her nerves and left her almost giddy.

Pandora settled, suppressing a faint chill as the snow soaked through her khiton and she felt the cold stone beneath. The Phoenix burning in her breast meant the cold would pose little threat, but it reminded her of the frozen wasteland Gaia would one day become. The future Hekate, Kirke's own mother, would create.

"I used to come up here with Kalypso and watch the stars," Kirke said, her words sluggish, lacking their usual effusiveness. The drawn, languid voice, the stooping posture: something had wracked the woman, left her despondent, faltering. Desperate enough to come to Pandora for something. For answers? For aid?

Kirke shuddered, looking not to Pandora, but out over the city. "I'm afraid to ask how much you already know."

"I know you are Hekate's daughter by Helios. I know you are my granddaughter."

Flakes of snow cast motes of white amid Kirke's fiery hair. In her, Pandora could see writ plain the lineage of Prometheus. But Kirke's eyes—those golden irises—those were Pandora's eyes. And Hekate's.

"Yeah, I think we established that." Kirke opened her satchel and withdrew the Box, holding it up before Pandora's face.

Pandora sucked in a ragged breath. Again? First she'd seen Hekate with it, and now Kirke? The nested weaves of the Tapestry seemed almost too convoluted to parse. She caught herself tapping a finger against her lip, then peered over the Box to Kirke. "You too?" It seemed all she could manage in such a heavy moment.

Kirke snorted. "Sums it up, I guess." A single, abortive sob wracked Kirke. "I can't ... I can't ... do *this*. How the fuck did we get here?"

History is merciless.

Like Hekate, Kirke was thousands of years older than Pandora. But still, still she was her grandchild. Pandora laid a hand upon the woman's shoulder. Squeezed, in whatever shallow comforts she could offer. "We've always been here."

Kirke scrubbed at her eyes and sniffled. "What does that even mean?"

"These tangled paths of past and future are predicated upon themselves. They created us, created everything we've ever loved. It's why we cannot simply cut through the threads, no matter how they wear at us, how raw they scrape our flesh as they slide by."

Her granddaughter huffed. "Yeah, Ananke cannot be denied, right? So, we just line up for the whipping, wipe off the blood, and wait for our turn to come round again."

"There's still hope."

"Oh, yeah?"

Pandora forced a smile. "Always."

"Psh. I wanted to *hate* you. First, I thought maybe you were Nike's bastard child. Then, I realised you must be Nike, and I couldn't fathom what Prometheus was doing with you. But I kept thinking, you made Father surrender to that despot. You and Artemis, you built this wretched future." Pain cracked her voice. "And here I go, betraying my own friends to uphold the same appalling timeline you crafted."

"I didn't craft it. I cannot escape it."

"Yeah, well, I have to blame someone, don't I? Blaming myself appeals about as much as swimming in a latrine, which I try to avoid."

"You should," Pandora agreed.

Kirke scooped a handful of snow and let it dribble down between her fingers. "I, uh ... I never *fit*, you know? Sometimes I talk too much, without hardly knowing what I'm saying, or what I'm supposed to say, so I just ramble." The woman had begun tracing intricate patterns in the snow where it settled on the roof between them. "Yeah. Like, other people have this sense of people, where they can catch all the whispers that are supposed to lurk between words, and I feel like I need these things shouted at me. Only, if you shout at me it feels like stones hurled against my skin. But all this I time, I just thought, sure, I'm lonely because Mother barely acknowledged me for, maybe, the first five decades of my life. In the throes of melancholy, my heart blamed her, too. And now ... now, come to find out, even if I didn't *cause* that, I had a hand in some of the worst things she's ever done."

So far as Pandora could tell, Kirke did not so much need her to speak as simply listen. While she had lost track of her exact age, she couldn't be more than thirty, and here she was meant to assume the mantle of grandmother to a four-thousand-year-old immortal. Her granddaughter flailed in the dark, in search of aught she could cling to, and all Pandora could do—maybe all she needed was to be there. So, she clasped the woman's hand, stilling the nervous twitch of her sketching in the snow.

Kirke sighed. "Our family is wrapt up in this tangled weave, I think. Blame. Right? We want someone to blame, but how can anyone be held culpable for events without beginning or end?"

"Time is an ouroboros." Even Prometheus, for all he knew and failed to share, followed the paths he had always walked, his own actions compelled by a future beyond his control.

Kirke chortled and shivered. "Urania said, uh ..." Sniffling muffled her words. "She said in this lecture that well-being is a product of well-living. Our happiness predicated upon our goodness. I wanted to save Mankind, to save Nymphs, to save *women* from the fuck-awful rule of self-righteous men. I thought that was good, but I don't think I've ever been happy. Now, I think I might even be close to my own time, but if I go back to my island and they realise I ever left, I'm dead."

While Pandora had read Urania's dialogues on ethics and could agree with Kirke's interpretation of them, she had no idea what the woman was on about now. "What do you mean?"

"Yeah." Her chuckle almost masked the sob beneath it. "Father exiled me to Aiaíā for brewing the Nectar. Among ... other things. And Zeus, he knows. I mean, I don't know how he found out, but he knows about it. So, if I defy my imprisonment, one of them would take it amiss. It means, if I wind up back even a year or two after I left, they'll know I was gone. I guess I could hide in the past, but isn't that kind of like denying myself a future? And if I live long enough to reach the point of my own exile, then what, hop back again?"

Pandora blew out a long, slow breath. She had been studying the Box for all this time. With each use, with each permutation, she closed in upon a clearer understanding of its intricacies. With every passing year of her meandering jaunt through time, her picture of its workings deepened. "I believe the Box has a kind of memory to it. If we can trace your steps we can find the moment you left, and with luck, send you back within a few days of then."

Kirke's golden eyes widened. "You understand its workings."

"I'm starting to. Together, we can find a way to get you back to Aiaíā. If that's what you truly desire for yourself ... Granddaughter." The word tasted more than passing odd upon her tongue. She felt herself not old enough for her own child to be grown. And yet she had a grown grandchild.

Kirke squirmed, though Pandora did not release her hand. In the other woman, for the first time, Pandora could see bits of herself beyond Heliad eyes. That same furiously spinning mind. The jitters that accompanied it. The desperate need to fix everything and the helplessness that chased that need. If she had lived Kirke's life, would she have made any different choices? Probably not.

Her granddaughter sighed, clapping her free hand over Pandora's, squeezing as though afraid she might tumble from the roof if she let go. "I can't do this anymore. Even now, I'm afraid to tell you all the things I've seen and done for fear of rupturing our family line. I cannot know which of those events have already unfolded for you, and which are still to come. If I … If I were to ask, even …"

"We can solve the Box together," Pandora assured her.

And with the insight of another who had used the device, Pandora felt certain it was the truth. That this would open new possibilities for the both of them. Another chance for a better throw of the dice.

For hope.

INTERLUDE: PROMETHEUS

Gloaming Era, Dark Age

*L*ong years had passed since Amirani had last set eyes upon the Gnostic Cabal's strange device. The orrery was set into a pool that descended deeper than Amirani could guess. A narrow walkway surrounded the circular chamber, with the device itself set upon a platform, at the heart of which stood a raised astrolabe. A wonder of interlocking gears and mechanisms connected everything, including catwalks that linked the outer ring to the inner circle. From the look of them, the catwalks could rotate, much like the arms of the orrery.

Within the astrolabe lay a multitude of adjustable gears that seemed to control the orrery. Even if this chamber were naught but an astrological study, it would have proved a marvel of engineering unlike aught the world had seen. Truly, Vorsanos and the Gnostic Cabal had outdone themselves, and Amirani could scarce imagine how they had built such a thing.

He knelt beside the astrolabe, running his fingertips over the gears while mentally tracing the interlockings of so many components.

A Time Chamber, Vorsanos called this place. They had built identical devices within each of the ruins of the four cities of Dark Faerie, claiming the chambers need work in unison to allow passage through time. Veles claimed to have even tested it.

That they had built it upon Falias and the other ruins of Dark Faerie spoke volumes in Amirani's mind. Those four cities—the greatest, most terrible civilisation in history—had tapped vile powers from the Otherworld. From here in dark Falias to the soaring city of Murias, they had constructed devices to bridge worlds, and he had to imagine the Time Chambers drew upon such boundless fonts of energy. Which was, of course, utter madness, as Vorsanos and the others knew better than most.

The fallen Watcher's visions of the future, perceived in the Oracle Mirrors, had driven him into paroxysms of desperation. Oh, Amirani knew all too well the damning force of prescience, but he liked to imagine he weathered those as best as might be managed. That, if his mind sometimes frayed upon the edges, still the centre held. The fragile Gnostic Cabal ...

As if summoned, Veles burst into the Time Chamber. "You gave the uriași the Flame of Agni."

Amirani rose, taking in his old friend. The fallen Watcher had an unnerving glint to his eyes. The look of one shaken by having seen too much. The look of one *broken* by it.

"What, exactly, did you see in your sojourns through time, my friend?"

Veles waved his hands in the air as he strode toward Amirani. "This city is under siege! You have started a war and we shall all burn in the chaos!"

Either Veles had not heard his question or had no intention of answering it. And, though it clenched Amirani's gut and scoured his soul, he suspected he knew why. If the future he beheld in prescient visions existed, and prescience accounted for itself, why then would the future not *also* account even for time travel? If this device could change aught—which seemed doubtful—Amirani suspected it would not do so with any ease. Mostlike, the timeline already accounted for its existence, and always had.

The Gnostic Cabal had built these Time Chambers at great cost and risk, all in their determination to break the Wheel of Fate. And Veles had, unless Amirani missed his guess, learnt Fate was forged of adamant. He might sooner have pushed aside mountains than altered the flow of history.

"The siege was inevitable," Amirani said. Everything was inevitable, for history would not be denied. History was merciless, binding all of them—him most of all—in chains most were fortunate enough not to perceive. "And Men already suffered under the horrors Erlik unleashed into this world."

"He paid for those mistakes!"

Amirani nodded. "The whole world has paid for them."

Veles turned about as if seeking some unseen enemy in the shadows. "Someone has come through time. Maybe he works for *them*. He hunts me now, wherever I flee."

Yes, and Amirani had seen hints of growing paranoia in the Gnostic Cabal. A fear that some other force moved through time, or at least moved *with time*, countering them. Amirani had not been able to ascertain if such fears were founded. If Veles knew who—*what*—Amirani himself had sworn to, they would certainly not be having this conversation.

But there could be others, still.

Maybe others were inevitable. Maybe, the moment time travel existed everything changed. Back and forward ripples, like a stone cast into an otherwise still pond. Wasn't that how prescience had seemed to work? There were times his visions not only accounted for themselves, but in which they became predicated upon themselves.

So how could other factions *not* arise, trying to control the flow of history?

Veles seized him, the derangement behind his eyes now laid plain. "There was a woman pursuing me, and a man, too. Clad in aureate plate, as if from another Era. She is relentless and yet walks unseen."

For a moment, Amirani looked deep into the desperate, faltering gaze of his erstwhile brother. One of so many who had stood by while Aditi died. Who had condemned Amirani for daring to doubt their blessed Truth.

With sudden violence, he shoved him away, sending Veles sprawling down onto the catwalk with a clatter.

"Do not mistake me for one of you, Narada." Amirani glared down at him. "You did not listen to my warnings when I offered them, and it is far too late now." Oh, it was always too late, as Veles was no doubt beginning to understand. Time *existed*.

History was merciless.

"You cannot change aught," Amirani said, staring grim faced at Veles or Narada or whatever name the Watcher preferred. "Only the Destroyer might do so."

"It is him, isn't it? The one after me?"

Yes, and it had occurred to Amirani such might unfold in the very moment he had first seen these Time Chambers. The Destroyer was part of the cycle of history that the Gnostic Cabal had hoped to oppose. They might have—or someday would—set themselves in opposition to his drive. And now, thanks to these Time Chambers, conceptions of causality had become far more labyrinthine than they once seemed. Veles and the others might have to pay *now* for sins they would commit in the future.

"Once more," Amirani said, "as ever, you have delved into things you do not understand. Do you seek my pity? My help? I have little of the former and even less of the latter to offer you. You will reap what you have sown, Veles."

And once more, the World would die. Oh, they would all suffer for their sins.

Amirani most of all.

PART III

Certainly Titans—with their Pneuma enhanced by Ambrosia—have the greatest potential Pneuma-related feats commonly called Pneumatikoi. I would argue, however, that mortal Men, especially those of Titan descent like the aristoi, can still achieve similar manifestation with proper training of the body and, crucially, the mind.

— Second Chronicle of the Circle of Goetic Mysteries

18

PANDORA

726 Bronze Age

Though Pandora and Kirke spent days mulling over the Box, examining every possible permutation of its workings, and tracing Kirke's own roaming through time, in the end, Kirke would have to take a chance. This they both knew, and thus, in the quiet of Pandora's chambers in the Muses College, casting a last, desperate look at Pandora, Kirke activated the Box and vanished into streams of time once more.

Pandora's ears popped as the bubble collapsed, leaving her chamber emptier than it had ever seemed before. The silence slithered up the walls until it had become a looming presence, blanketing her in its oppressive shadow. For a moment, she'd had an ally in her ceaseless quest. She'd had, perhaps, a friend and, at the least, kindred who could understand the burdens she bore.

Kirke was a bundle of nerves and eccentricities pulled so taut she seemed primed to snap at any moment. Yet the woman had endured millennia of hardship and despair. The weight of ages had bent her, leaving so many cracks beneath the surface. It had not, however, broken Kirke; a reality that left Pandora sanguine that she, too, could endure whatever tribulations the Moirai laid before her.

She would find her answers, she would save herself, Kirke, Prometheus, Pyrrha, all of them. All the World.

When spring came, she would go. She would go and face whatever peril lay within the Nyxlands.

PERHAPS, given her deepening understanding of the Box and its wonders, she might have used it to move not through time but space, to bring herself closer to the Nyxlands and the ruins of Vulgeth. Yet she had no means of setting the Box for a place or time she had never witnessed. Any attempt to do so risked her hurling herself wildly off course.

"Follow the river north," Themis said, standing beside Pandora beyond the polis. She had packed as many supplies as she could carry into her satchels and informed the Titan of her plan. As if she had known already the time had arrived with the first azalea blooms —and perhaps the Oracle did know—Themis had nodded and bid her await the next dawn for leaving. "It will lead you through the steppelands." They clad her in Amazonian wools and trousers, thus any riders she met would take her for accepted by one of their clans. "Beyond there lies the Hylean Forest, and the river traces its periphery. You can hunt and forage there, but do not venture deeper than you must. Kimmeria remains wilder than Elládos. Centaurs and chimeras lurk in the woodlands, and who knows what else."

Centaurs, according to the Muses, were a breed of half-horse, half-Man creatures that had sprung up at the end of the Silver Age and since become a plague across the lands for their savagery. And chimeras were monstrosities she would have considered flights of fancy not so many years back. Pandora nodded grimly, having little desire to encounter such beings.

"Beyond the Hylean Forest, you venture past all lands of Man.

The Gryphonpeaks frame the wilderness of Arimaspia, where the last of the Cyclopes seemed to have retreated after the Gigantomachy. I can offer you no assurances there. Sorcerers sometimes venture to the Nyxlands, making profane pilgrimages in the hopes of augmenting their dark knowledge with forgotten and forbidden lore. Most never return."

"Hekate returned." And so would Pandora.

"The Nyxlands lie further north still, past Arimaspia, and to the west. I cannot guess what you will find there. Just remember how we trained you. Keep your wits, Nike. The future of Man may well depend upon you."

"You could always come with me."

"We both know that were I to leave this polis, an unending cavalcade of warlords would flock here, so eager to bring to heel the women brazen enough to defy their world order." And yet, she could see the temptation war over Themis's face. There was truth to her fears—once word spread she had left Themiskyra, Titans and Men would strive to come here, eager to claim treasures and slaves.

In quiet conversations, whispered before her hearth fire, Themis had told Pandora bits and pieces of her time with the Gnostic Cabal. Kronos had, along with others, founded the Cabal in a prior Era. A time that, unless Pandora missed her guess, corresponded to Vulgeth, the ruined heart of the Nyxlands. "He recruited us," Themis had said of Kronos, "in the years following the dispersal of Nyx and the establishment of the Titan order. Several of us, meeting always in secret. Always searching for a way to break the hold of Ananke upon all our lives. But we never found such a path, and the Cabal is broken. If any of the others yet live, I do not know what became of them."

Pandora had, at last, revealed to Themis Kronos's ultimate fate. She thought the Titan woman deserved to know that the man she'd so admired would not return.

Now, the thought of venturing across the unknown wilds alone appealed very little. But neither could Pandora be responsible for endangering this place by drawing Themis away from her polis. Oh, Pandora scorned their use of male slaves and wondered what it said of Man, that, wherever she went, *someone* always knelt in the dirt. In every society she found, some insisted upon elevating themselves whilst pushing others down. People would latch onto the pettiest of distinctions between themselves as an excuse for oppression.

Even Urania had admitted the hypocrisy of Themiskyran society, while making plain the Muses would not and could not change that society.

"I go alone," Pandora said. "I hope I see you again."

"As do I, Nike. And you are not alone. You carry the hopes of many."

As Themis instructed, Pandora had followed the river upstream through the steppes. Once, riders had stopped her but, on seeing her Amazonian garb, released her with well-wishes. Days stretched on, and she took to singing to herself to pass the drawn-out hours. In times long gone, she had once sung so many old ballads for the pleasure of her clients, or for her own amusement in the empty chambers of her house. Now, she sang only to hold the quiet at bay.

Sometimes, she wondered what had become of that home on Atlantis, that place that had, back then, meant all the World to her. It had represented a slice of the city that was hers, and hers alone, where her solitude had become a shield against the buffeting gales of her life. Now, now she would have given away her last drachmae for someone to talk to, to share her burdens.

But so few could understand the weight that pressed upon her. Most people, blessedly, remained oblivious to Fate's threads playing them like puppets.

Spring had summoned riots of colour and fragrance along the steppes. Fields of daisies and carnations offered her moments of awe to break up the press of isolation. She passed through the woodlands, keeping to the edges for fear of the creatures Themis had spoken of. Pandora sought no conflict with monsters and doubted centaurs would offer the sort of company she would have relished.

Sooner or later, she would have to head west, and thus, when she came to a shallow in the river, she forded the waters. Despite spring's warming sun, the shock of ice ripped through her legs as water lapped over them. Once on the other side, she used the Phoenix's spark to light a small fire, wrapping her arms around her knees and willing heat to seep back into her extremities.

Days became fortnights, trekking through the foothills nestled around the Gryphonpeaks. The snows now graced only the distant summits, with verdant grasses sprouting along the slopes and gullies, and fields of azaleas carpeted the hillsides in pink.

Each morn, dawn would break over the mountains, a searing fire shooting through the sky, wakening the Phoenix inside her. But in the wild, there was little for it to unleash its tumultuous emotions upon, no enemies to burn. So, rather, it smouldered within her breast, engendering a pervasive disquiet.

She could not shake the sense that Gaia went on and on, that she might walk for years without reaching the Earth's edge.

At night, despite the day's fatigue, she would lie awake for hours, her mind whirring with a moil of apprehensions and half-formed conversations with all those she had left behind. She would try to explain herself and her intentions to beloved Prometheus, only to sputter and sigh, for he would have always understood without need for elucidation. Or she would seek after some justification, some turn of phrase that might reconcile her with Pyrrha. Oh, how many times she replayed that last, bitter encounter in her mind. How many variations of the conversation, in which she would manage to say something else, to prevent the schism that had torn them apart.

There is naught for you here in Kolchis.

Words became vicious barbs worming beneath her skin, burrowing into her heart, defying any attempt to extract them. Now and again, Pandora mused, one suffered wounds that time failed to heal. Injuries inflicted by those who mattered most that, rather than mend, festered with the passing of days and months.

Isolation gave one too much time to ruminate, stewing in the miasma of all the might-have-beens.

On such a night, tapping a restless thumb against her thigh, deep grumbles came to her, carried on the night breeze. Only when the discordant sounds struck her did she realise the nightingale songs had vanished, and she could not say how long back.

Pandora kindled fires only to cook, dousing those as soon as she might to avoid drawing attention. Now, jolting upright and blinking in the moonlight, she desperately wished she had a blaze going. Turning her hand into a torch would illumine her immediate surroundings but destroy her night vision and thus ruin her chance of spotting whatever had made the throaty sound.

More growls came to her, closer now.

Pandora's hands closed around the haft of a spear Hippolyta had given her. They had provided a leather cuirass, too, but trying to don it now might leave her compromised if whatever stalked her closed mid-process.

Instead, she rose, slow as she could, hefting the spearpoint.

A chorus of bellows greeted her, echoing off two different hilltops.

Dark shapes rose, silhouetted in moonlight, forms Man-like and yet stretching ten, twelve feet tall. The Arimaspians of which Themis had warned—the Cyclopes. Some bore clubs, broken branches making plain the weapons had once been small trees, while others held naught in their grasping, massive fingers. More than a dozen of the creatures had risen, forming a half ring around her.

Cyclopes were Gigantes. Man-eaters.

Another bellow, and whatever had held them in place snapped, the giants surging toward her like rocks in an avalanche, whooping and slavering, swinging those massive clubs in wild arcs.

Grasping her spear in both hands, Pandora swivelled, keeping each of the giants in view as they descended upon her. But they were too many. Whatever training she had received in Themiskyra did *not* include facing a small army of Cyclopes by herself.

Familiar pain twinged in her heart. Not again! She thought she was done with such torments brought on by the churning of her own soul.

A deep breath.

If she could not fight, that left only fleeing, though neither could she escape the long-legged predators in a race. Knowing it madness but seeing no other way, Pandora broke into a dash toward the closest group, shrieking.

Perhaps it was her imagination, yet she smirked when the lead Cyclops seemed to falter at her brazen response.

The wrath that simmered within her, the fear, the hope, the desperate *need*. All of it she poured into in the Phoenix and she leapt. Flames spurted from her legs, propelling her skyward, even as fiery wings erupted from her back, offering greater altitude.

She wished she could have seen the looks upon the Cyclopes' misshapen visages as she soared over their heads, blazing like a meteor. She wished even more that the ambush had not forced her to abandon most of her supplies.

The flaming wings immolated her woollen tunic, ashes of which tumbled off her even as she landed in a crouch, past the hill over which her foes had come. Immediately, she broke into a run and leapt again, her wings once more hurling her up into the air, flying beneath the stars.

A piercing shriek cut through the night, covering even the irate bellows of the Cyclopes as they turned to trace her path.

In midair, as she began to plummet once more, Pandora twisted to see the source of such a cry.

A dark form surged down toward her from above, an eagle with a thirty-foot wingspan, diving for her. More of the birds cast black shadows before the moon, before banking.

Panic shot through Pandora. Her wings sputtered out, sending her flailing, pitching back toward Gaia.

Her wild motion saved her, the bird screeching by within a foot of her as she fell.

And it wasn't a bird, for though it had eagle wings, head, and foretalons, its back half was that of a lion, probably almost ten feet long.

Gryphons!

Shock raced through her, at least for the brief instant before the earth lurched up to slam into her with more force than any giant's blow. Pandora smacked upon the mountainside, the impact blasting thought and wind from her.

NEXT SHE REALISED, she lay in the dark. A hundred burning agonies crawled over her, each breath revealing a fresh pain, a new injury. She was slick and wet and cold. Bolts of lightning shot up her left arm. With every attempt to move, red explosions formed before her eyes, despite the blackness that had swallowed her.

Ragged, choking breaths scoured her throat like so much sand. A convulsion had her retching up some sticky warmth.

Pandora groaned, mired in too much misery to even think of moving again.

She had broken herself.

THE SUN'S harsh light punctured the darkness, a beam of radiance falling upon her face and illumining her prison. Above her rose jagged walls of rock on either side, the space between not more than a dozen feet across. She lay upon a stone shelf at the bottom of a crevasse. Her tumble into the mountain must have sent her pitching down into this void.

She tried to sit, and another bolt of lightning coursed up her left arm. Needles jabbed into her neck as she tried to turn her head. With teeth gritted against the pain, she managed to look. Her arm lay wedged beneath her, twisted around the wrong way, and almost certainly fractured.

"Fuck ..." It seemed about the only thing to say in such circumstances.

The sad irony was, falling into the ravine may have saved her from the gryphons and Cyclopes. It had also damn nigh killed her, broken her body, and left her trapped beneath the mountain.

Prometheus had told her once that the Phoenix held so much

Pneuma, it could restore her body from most any wound in which she had not lost a limb. She had seen Kala save Mundilfari from fatal internal injuries. Assuming she had not destroyed her entire arm, it ought to heal.

The thought alleviated some of the growing tightness in her chest, letting her catch a breath that had begun to get away from her.

Perhaps it was but fancy, yet she imagined she could *feel* the bone trying to knit back together beneath her flesh. Trying and failing, for it remained out of place. Pain yanked a moan out of her as she forced herself to turn over. Even when she managed to roll onto her side, off her arm, it refused to obey her commands.

Searing swells of hot agony.

Her body betraying her.

"Help," she whimpered, the sound as hollow as the empty ravine. There was no one to hear her. No other person around for miles upon miles. She squashed a burgeoning fantasy of Prometheus showing up to save her once more, as he had done so many times before. But she could ill afford such fancies now.

Pandora would live or die by her hand alone.

Again, her breath sought to run from her, escaping in ragged pants, dimming her vision in a haze of black spots. What had she done in coming here alone? Why had she thought she could do this?

Now she had no choice. Live or die.

Live or die.

Flooding Pneuma into Potency, she pushed herself up on her right arm, hissing against the surges of pain every motion sent thrumming through her. Sitting allowed her a look at her arm, the joint hyperextended in the wrong direction, the bone of her forearm protruding, oozing crimson wetness.

Gaia, she wanted to retch.

She could heal from aught. Prometheus had told her that. She could heal, but in this case, she might have to help the process along.

A fresh whimper sputtered from her as she prodded at the bone where it jutted from her flesh.

Only her arm was broken. Not her soul.

Her shriek—as she jammed the bone back into place—ripped through the crevasse, bouncing off narrow walls, until it filled her head, the only sound she could perceive. On and on, a slowly dying wail.

Maybe she fainted, for she was lying on her right side, next she knew. Slowly, she rose, realised she still lay in the damned gorge, and groaned. Morning light still spilled down from above, so she had not lost too much time.

By Nyx's unholy arsehole, Pandora did not want to have to set the joint. She would have paid most any price to turn from the pain she would have to inflict upon herself. To surrender.

Except, she never would.

She knew that now. Somewhere, through all of time's wracking cruelty, through the abuses visited upon her flesh, through the debasement of her heart, she had seen something. She had seen herself.

She would set her arm, she would climb from this cage with one hand if needs be, and she would venture on, into the forbidden wastes of the Nyxlands. She would find her answers amid the ruins of Vulgeth. And she would strive against the Moirai, time and again, until even Fate must crumble before the relentless onslaught of her determination.

Pandora would never, ever surrender.

She wrapt her hand around her elbow.

19

ARTEMIS

726 Bronze Age

A trail of torches slithered through the darkness, worming their way up mountain paths, toward the fig groves scattered upon the plateaus. Into this train, Artemis and Atalanta flowed. Like all the others, they had cast aside their clothes and donned wooden masks set with curling antlers. The pounding beat of mighty drums gave pace to their climbing, broken by sporadic exultations of the faithful. Briomos, "the Roaring," they named God, for deep and feral was his voice.

Deep as though it rose up from the very bowels of Gaia. From beyond.

One by one, the followers of the God reached the glade and staked their torches into the dirt. No one instructed any of them as to the geometric pattern which was to be traced by the burning of so many lights. No one needed to. All touched by Dionysus knew his will and were overjoyed to bend to it. Torchlight filled the glade, dancing in time with the music.

A hundred bodies writhed and bucked and leapt, all naked save for those wooden masks. Even the trees themselves swayed in acknowledgment of the puissance that saturated the air this night. For something sacred now awakened into the World, and they were, each of them, divinely blessed to bear witness to its nascency.

The wood convulsed with birth pangs. Each beat of the drum had become a labour pain. A corridor of fig trees opened into the deeper wood, trunks forming arcs and boughs entangled to roof the tunnel. Streams of wine, glistening and nigh black in torchlight, dribbled from splits in the trunks like so much sap. The wine pooled around the roots before flowing over in fountains and running in canals between the torch designs.

From this corridor strode the God himself, seven feet tall, naked save for his own mask, this one of bone and antler. The whorls painted upon his skin shifted now, joining in the convulsions of the World. In his hand he bore a staff, not unlike the one he'd once given to Artemis but wrapt with strands of spiralling ivy. Wherever the butt of the staff struck, springs of burbling wine rose from the ground.

Dionysus came to them then, pace as erratic and wild as the gyrations of his faithful. When he stood in their midst, he raised high his ivy staff. At once, half his followers dropped to their hands and knees and began to buck and bleat like goats. Some mounted others, rutting in time with the drums.

Upon his knees, another male plodded over to Dionysus. The man wore a bull mask, shaking his head and snorting like the beast his mask implied. The God lowered his staff until the cusp of it rested upon the bull-man's neck. "Behold the glory of the God of Life and Death." A shudder ripped through the creature bowed beneath his staff. Flesh rippled like turbulent water.

Dionysus shoved his staff downward, piercing the bull-man's too-pliant neck.

Even over the beating drums and creaking wood and the moans of the faithful, Artemis heard the rupture of bone within the man's flesh. His head thrashed too far to one side then the other, each twist echoing with crunching vertebrae. All at once, he fell still, a lifeless heap of shattered bones, limbs askew at unnatural angles.

The drums ceased. The lurid convulsions of the wood and her denizens paused. All heads swivelled to gaze upon the sacred, macabre wreckage of Man-flesh upon the forest floor.

"I am the Voice of the Wood." And, indeed, his voice came not from the towering form in the glade's heart but from somewhere deeper still. It emanated from every tree, root, and creeping vine. It ran *beyond* the scope of Gaia, rumbling up, spewed from eldritch sources old before the dawn of time. That voice reverberated within Artemis's soul. "I am the living and the dying, the beginning and end of all that burgeons upon the Earth."

And Dionysus once more struck his staff upon the ruined corpse before him.

In answer, the broken bull-man's back ruptured. With a sick tearing, flesh separated from bone. Sinews stretched and snapped. From the husk of empty skin, a living, skinless bull burst. The creature bucked and leapt, thrashing about the glade. Its glistening horns caught a woman kneeling too nigh, and the air filled with the reek of offal as its horns ripped through her belly and tossed her aside in glorious offering to God.

A pounding of that staff, and the drums resumed. The faithful seized one another, no longer confined to paltry limitations of societal mores or conceptions of gender, no longer bound to the limits of the mortal. For within the grove of Dionysus seeped divinity.

A riot of flesh erupted, more hands upon Artemis than she could have counted, had she the least care for such things. A pile of bodies, grasping, clawing, thrusting. Biting. Gnawing away pale weakness. The dead would serve as sacrifice to the grandeur of God.

"Althaea!" Dionysus's command ripped through the orgy, and the queen's form, sticky with fluids, was thrust above the mound of moaning bodies. Dimly, Artemis knew it as God seized his chosen vessel and plunged himself within the queen. Aching jealousy bloomed within Artemis's desperate soul, and she saw it reflected in the eyes of every person within that rutting pile, woman or man. All longed for the consuming love of Dionysus.

Briomos, the crowd cried. His answering roar of climax split the night sky. It cleft the heavens, leaving an iridescent streak across the firmament. Within the rift, inchoate tendrils lashed at the stars, as though they might feast upon those pinpricks of light. The forest spasmed.

Hints of a memory crept up on Artemis.

In the wide Phrygian plains, grasses turned umber by autumn's first crisp winds, Artemis exulted in the rivers. Her ebony hair streamed behind her as she swam after Aura. The Heliad Nymph had joined Artemis as an apprentice some years before, and she had trained her in woodcraft and the hunt. But Artemis's fondest memories were of times such as these, languid days stretched for all they were worth, their laughter ringing beneath clear skies. They would joke of the pomposity of Apollon, or the fool styles of the courts that would forever wax and wane like the face of Thoth. Or they would sit beneath the moon and watch its glinting upon the countless placid lakes of the Arad Mountains.

Aura was the daughter of Eos and thus a cousin to Artemis on her father's side. Long years had the Nymph wilted upon Aiaíā. Until, at last, unable to stand it a moment longer, Aura had set out on her own. A chance encounter with Artemis in Phoeba had led to a fast friendship.

This wasn't right.

Artemis had last had Orion as an apprentice. Centuries after Aura's death.

The ugly head of her grief wriggled its way up from the mound of prurience in which she writhed. She managed a single, bitter, free breath before the writhing orgy drew her down once more.

*W*ITH A SWEEP OF HER ARM, *Aura sent a wave splashing over Artemis. Not having expected it, Artemis sputtered, sucking down half the river in the process. "I'm going to string you up by the ankles from a tree," Artemis shouted after the Nymph. "I'll leave you there to freeze your tits off all night, I swear it!"*

Aura only giggled and dove beneath the river, daring Artemis to catch her.

Ah, but Artemis was a full Titan, and her Pneumatikoi made her a faster swimmer as well as enhanced her senses, so she could find the hiding Nymph. She followed Aura underwater, caught the girl around the waist, and dragged her ashore.

"No, no, no," Aura blurted as Artemis heaved her onto the sand. She made a worthy—if futile—attempt to escape using a pankration throw Artemis easily reversed. One more twist, and she had Aura pinned and yelping. Though even her cries of discomfort did not quite put a stop to her mischievous snickers.

"I swear to Thoth," Artemis panted. "I'll never quite know what to do with you."

A*URA WAS GONE.*

One day, Artemis had woken had and found herself alone.

T*WO YEARS LATER*, Artemis had found her, in the woods just outside Thebes. She'd hung herself. But so much chaos had unfolded in Thebes in those days.

She had heard then the tales of Dionysus. How he'd swept through half Elládos with his frenzied Maenads. They'd come to Thebes and rent limb from limb King Pentheus, grandson of

Kadmus. They'd spread madness ... until it had broken like a cresting wave.

And no one had known where Dionysus had gone.

﹩

A Tethid girl—just shy of twenty if Artemis had to guess—danced within a windowless hall. Torchlight flickered from sconces set into columns rimming this subterranean chamber. But it was to the floor Artemis's gaze drifted. For it was carved into lurid geometric patterns, like a map of a madman's mind.

The girl smiled, sea-blue eyes glinting. Impossible though it seemed, Artemis almost fancied the girl could see her. Here was a woman enraptured by the sheer joy of her solitary dance. She moved for no one save herself, and in that choice came freedom.

Beneath the maze-carved floor, a bellow sounded, echoing up through the whole chamber.

The Nymph dropped to her knees and placed her palms upon the carving, her smile replaced by a look of grief. "Ease, Brother. It is not yet time." The words were a whisper, drawn from the girl in pained wheezes. "Not yet."

﹩

Orgasmic release crashed through Artemis, stealing thought and time. Eternity wailed in vain protest, its veneer cast aside by powers that ran deeper than mere conceptions of days or hours.

This was a different hilltop. Where was she? Still, it was night, still the torches. Some of the Maenads were the same. Some had discarded—or lost—their masks, revealing faces contorted in the throes of ecstatic pleasures beyond naming. Bacchic wine flowed in rubescent cataracts across the landscape.

This was a different night ...?

Atalanta's belly was heavy with child, beside her, even as her daughter's hips bucked beneath the ministrations of some woman's probing tongue. Someone was sucking upon one of Artemis's breasts. A creature, somewhere between man and goat, she realised, and wondered if the thought ought to have alarmed her. Should not there have been horror to be touched thus?

The trees awakened, mucous eyes creaking open, filmy slits all peering at the God in their midst.

And God ... The World around Dionysus had deepened, as if his form was an impression pushed into the sand. As if the sum of him were too vast to be contained within so shallow a vessel as the Earth. Gaia yawned to receive him. One hand yet bore that ivy-twined staff, the butt of it driven into the ground as if it was a sapling.

Althaea shrieked, now in the centre of the circle, on hands and knees between God's straddling legs. Her own abdomen had grown many times the size of Atalanta's. Birth pangs spasmed through the kneeling queen.

The Maenads danced a wild circle around their God, and Artemis was swept into their wake, though she had no memory of standing. Back and forth, hair flung wild in time with her swirling motions. The dance consumed her.

She saw it as Dionysus reached down a vine-like hand, arm bending the wrong way. His grasp stretched up inside Althaea, clasping onto the infant within her womb. With a squelching plop, he yanked free a mewling babe, and Althaea collapsed into an unmoving heap.

Dionysus hefted the babe by her back, holding her up in a single massive hand. Her flailing limbs glistened with afterbirth, the uncut placenta still dangling from her abdomen. "Behold my child." His words boomed through the forest as if all of the wild spoke to her with a singular voice. There were male and female eidolons—dryads —within the trunks of the trees, singing the praises of God. Artemis did not know what they said, though she recognised the discordant, mind-rending intonations of Supernal. "Behold the blight upon the accursed bloodline of Zeus."

It was too soon for Althaea to have borne his child. The thought sat heavy in her mind, a splinter she could not dislodge.

"She must be made ready to embrace Ananke," Dionysus said. He yanked free his staff from the dirt and raised it toward Thoth's face.

No, not Thoth. For there was something of an Elder God in Dionysus, of that, Artemis was now certain. The God of the Wood. Pan was rising in Dionysus, lurching itself closer and closer to the Mortal Realm with each Bacchic frenzy Dionysus induced. The essence of it ran deeper than the scope of the World. Its fearful eyes settled upon her, peering into the depths of her insignificant soul.

That thought, too, ought to have invoked terror. Yet all she could summon was a sense of revelation. The joy of knowing she was privy to secret knowledge denied the rest of Mankind. The feeling of being sanctified by divine insight.

She was blessed to witness the imminent collapse of the facade of civilisation.

Dionysus rammed his staff into Althaea's skull, splattering it. Her corpse quivered. Slurping tendrils of wet, grasping flesh burst from splitting seams along her back. All at once, that corpse liquified. It flowed about the staff like a spring. It flowed *up* the staff, a stream of squelching semisolid goo, drawn forth from the mother of God's child. Like a delta, the stream split into so many branches, flowing over Dionysus's bare arm and chest, only to join along his opposite bicep. Wet smacking sounds followed, the goo that had been the queen latching onto the placenta before flowing through it into the child.

The infant fell from God's hand and landed with a thwack upon the hilltop. Artemis's breath caught, but Dionysus seemed unconcerned with the fate of his offspring. Those snapping, squelching tendrils of flesh wrapt about the girlchild, forming a shell around her. No, not a shell, but a cocoon.

Time slipped from Artemis.

"Ariadne," another girl called. The other was a Tethid too, so alike in aspect as to make plain she must be the younger sister of this Ariadne. This dancer

in the darkness. "His hunger quickens," the younger girl said. In her arms she bore a heavy bucket, glistening with hunks of raw meat Artemis could not identify. "Asterion will not content himself with feasting once in nine years for much longer. This prison cannot hold him forever."

The dancer drifted through the torchlit hall with preternatural grace and wrapt an arm around her sister's shoulders.

A grumble shook the stones beneath their feet. They clutched each other tighter.

"Ariadne …" the younger girl said again.

"I know it all, Phaidra. I know it … I …" Ariadne drew the younger girl off the carved floor and into the shadowed peristyle beyond. "Daedalus told me it can be ended."

Phaidra screwed up her face in the sort of mocking sneer only a teenager can manage. "That man is crazier than a goat who's eaten a whole damn poppy plant."

Ariadne frowned but did not deny her sister's claims. She took the bucket from the girl and paced down a hall until she came to a tiny windowless room. A cell? It stank of rot and refuse, sensations Artemis was shocked to feel within the vision.

A grate in the floor opened into utter darkness below, the openings just wide enough one could have gotten an ankle trapped in there. When Ariadne upended the bucket, the mess of meat slopped down with wet plops, tumbled through the grate, and fell into the blackness.

"Sate yourself for now, Brother," Ariadne said.

"Zeus's arse," Phaidra swore, having refused to enter that putrid cell.

20

THESEUS

726 Bronze Age

The Argo sailed from Themiskyra in Kimmeria, and Jason had hoped to skirt the Phlegran coast and return to Iolkos. But on the very day in which Jason's home polis ought to have come into sight, a wild storm arose. For the better part of a day, the Argo was tossed and thrashed, hurled one way and the next, until not a man among them could have said where the wind and currents had borne them.

Theseus fought with the oars once more until blood ran from the bursting blisters upon his palms and stained the cypress wood umber. Time and again, Jason called upon them to remain steady. But, in the spaces between exhausted pants and heaving struggles with the oars, he heard the whispers run amok among the crew. They said that Medea had damned them all with the murder of her brother.

Whether her sorcerer father had laid a hex upon the Argo or whether the gods themselves now turned their ire at ill-done deeds upon the crew, they thought themselves cursed never to return home. And when it was revealed that the winds had hurled them beyond the Axeinos Strait and out beyond even Lydia, those whispers turned to cries of outrage.

For how could a ship pass so many miles in a day? Something foul had wrapt its loathsome claws about all of their fates, and the crew looked to Jason for answers. In assuming the mantle of leadership, he had taken responsibility for all that befell the Argonauts. To Theseus's eyes, watching the Iolkian prince squirm upon the deck in hushed consultation with the sorceress of Kolchis, Jason seemed not a leader but a frightened man out of his depth, only a few years older than Theseus himself.

"We ought to throw her overboard," Euphemos stated. Theseus had heard the others voice such thoughts before, but Poseidon's son was the first to speak so openly. "Give her to my father and perhaps he will see whatever curse lies upon us broken."

Jason whirled upon their helmsman. "Or maybe that was your intent in taking us so far off course? Are we not now in the waters claimed by Poseidon?" The Iolkian strode toward Euphemos, gesticulating in time with his surging temper. "Are we meant to believe you, the supposed finest helmsman in the Thalassa, managed to navigate the Axeinos Strait and get us to far Lydia *by accident*?"

"You question my skills now, boy prince?" Euphemos puffed out his chest. "Think you could do better for yourself?"

Jason shoved the demigod, who stumbled back, crashed into the gunwale, and steadied himself lest he pitch over the side of the ship. "You think I'd sacrifice the woman I am sworn to marry?" Jason bellowed.

"She's just a fucking woman," Euphemos shot back. "There's more of them around, I swear."

Autolykus pointed an accusing finger at Poseidon's son. "Euphemos, you pig's runny arsehole—"

Euphemos sneered at the thief. "Someone shut the old thief up. The real men are talking now."

"Enough!" All heads swivelled to see Medea, fuming, golden eyes flashing and hair glistening in the afternoon sun. "Enough bickering. If we are nigh to Lydia, then we are not so far from the island of Aiaíā, where dwells my aunt, a sorceress who might break any curse upon us. Make for the island, and we can be purified before we come to any further travails."

"Aunt?" Autolykus demanded, now looking to her with a discerning glint in his eyes. "As in sister to your mother—or your father?"

"My father's older sister," Medea admitted.

"King Aeëtes's own sister!" Laertes blurted. "Why in Zeus's name would she aid us when we betrayed her brother and murdered her nephew?"

Beside him, Autolykus nodded grimly. "Unless she doesn't know."

"We don't know what she knows," Jason argued. "We have no reason to believe word would have reached so far from Kolchis as yet. So, we don't tell her what we've done, only that a curse carried us so far awry. Yes?" He looked to Medea.

"She knows me well and would not turn me aside." To Theseus's ears, the girl seemed to be trying to reassure herself as much as the rest of them. Even filled with doubts and as bedraggled as the rest of them, Medea had a haunting beauty. Was that why Jason listened to her over the advice of his own men?

He would not bow when Talaus bid him moor at Phoeba and beg purification from the priests of Artemis at the temple there. Nor would he cave when Peleus and Telamon tried to convince him to return to Elládos, or even Atlantis, rather than sail far afield of their homes in pursuit of this wild aim. But Jason looked to Medea as though lost in the glitter of her aureate irises.

Such were his misgivings that he could not quite ignore it when, on the evening watch with him, Kastor wondered aloud whether Medea had ensorcelled their leader. To this, Theseus had no answer, and he could not say when next the Argo would find home in Elládos.

But in the middle of the night, he heard Medea whispering

prayers to Hekate and had to wonder whether the Goddess of Witch-craft would deign to aid them.

THEY MADE SAIL FOR AIAÍĀ, as Medea had chosen, and the crew kept the grumbles to a minimum. Perhaps the sudden rise of another storm made such arguments moot. For surely they could not have crossed the Thalassa now. Elládos might as well have lain at the far side of Gaia for all their chance of reaching home whilst such weather persisted.

At last, the rocky shore of Aiaíā rose on the horizon before them, and when the ship had weighed anchor, Jason proclaimed that he and Medea alone would go ashore to find the sorceress Kirke and beg her aid.

So, Theseus sat on the deck with Pirithous, refusing to answer his friend's questions about his encounter with Hippolyta. Instinct demanded he brag of lying with her, but something else stilled his tongue, and he refused to confirm or deny aught that had happened that morn.

A pensive restlessness had settled upon the now-idle crew, and Theseus suspected that, if Jason did not return with good news, he would find himself no longer captain of the Argo.

He took to pacing the ship, but he found little solace amid any of the others. Rowing through a storm or intent upon a destination, the Argo felt spacious enough. But at anchor and yet forbidden to go ashore, the ship now seemed cramped. When he wearied of Pirit-hous's tales of centaurs and the wild lands held by the Lapiths, Theseus found himself drawn to the bow. There, perched precari-ously against the curling prow, Orpheus plucked at his lyre without seeming aware of any song.

"You saved us from the sirens," Theseus said. "I didn't have much chance to thank you before."

The bard quirked a sad smile. When he met Theseus's gaze,

Theseus saw something haunted in his eyes. The look of a man who had seen things others could not fathom.

"Did you find what you sought in Kolchis?" Theseus asked.

Orpheus blew out a long, strained breath. "I may have. Medea herself has proved some aid, but I will not know for certain until ... Ah, well, once we've returned to Phlegra, I've another journey to make."

"Where are you going?" Theseus ought not much to have cared, but even the strange bard's conversation provided reprieve from wondering what went on upon the island. He had little trust for Medea and even less for her sorceress aunt.

Orpheus hopped off the prow and set down his lyre. "What if you could look again upon the face of one lost to you? What would you risk for such a chance?"

"Lost?" Theseus took an involuntary step backwards. "You speak of ... seeing ghosts?"

Orpheus snorted, perhaps at Theseus's discomfiture. "Given the chance, I'd do more. I would venture to Hades's very gates to reclaim what Fate has stolen from me."

A hollow had opened in Theseus's gut. A chill, despite the summer heat. "You are mad ... There is but one road to Hades, and no one returns from it."

"Someone once did return, though Hades took it amiss and has since taken on a new guard dog." Orpheus chuckled. "As for madness? Well, perhaps I am. Pray, then, you never suffer such madness. For in its grip, a man would chance any peril to body or soul."

No, no. Theseus did not think so.

And he wanted off this ship more than ever.

WHEN JASON and Medea at last returned from calling upon Kirke, both seemed pale and somewhat shaken. At first, taking this as an ill sign, the crew bristled, and Theseus would have sworn mutiny brewed.

With their leader away, Theseus had asked Herakles—the one man among them who might sway the crew to one side or the other —whether he would speak for or against Jason. "The murder of Absyrtus was ill done," Herakles had said. "And I too must return to Mykenai." The big demigod had not, however, made plain if he would support any move against Jason.

Saying naught, Jason made for the bridge. Medea, however, paused at the ladder. "We are purified," she announced. And though the Argonauts breathed a collective sigh of relief, Theseus could have sworn something haunted Medea's golden eyes.

THE SHIP MOORED AT ATHENAI, and like a breaking tide, the Argonauts flowed from her, all too eager to be free of the wooden hold and of one another. Try as he might, Jason convinced but a few to sail back to Iolkos with him, and only those with business still in Phlegra. Few others bothered bidding him farewell, and, despite the purification she had received, Theseus noted several baleful glances cast at Medea. Nor could Theseus deny his own disappointment with this whole endeavour.

Oh, indeed, they had cleared the way for crossing the Axeinos Sea. They had trod in the fabled lands of sorcerers and Amazons. They had faced dangers of sea and sky. Why, then, did the Argonauts leave here feeling stained?

Pirithous was one of those few who sailed on with Jason, and Theseus would miss his friend. But the time had come when he must climb the steps to Athenai's acropolis, greet his father, and claim his birthright.

Alone, heart aflutter with nerves, he made that climb up the mountain, passing aristoi who cast disdainful glances at his haggard appearance. Their stares had him suddenly self-conscious. Not all the bloodstains had washed from his khiton, and the stitches where he had repaired the garment now seemed all too apparent. Besides, he no doubt stank of brine, sweat, and too long without a bath. Halfway to the top, Theseus paused upon the stairs and considered turning back, using his few drachmae to find a bathhouse, and returning the next morn.

But he came here bearing the sword and sandals that Aegeus had left for him, the sign of his heritage. He was of the blood of Pandion, the blood of Athene herself. He came here now, to at last fulfil his destiny, and after such a long road, the idea of delaying even a moment more tasted bitter upon his tongue. Let the courtiers cast their scorn his way, then. Let them sneer and whisper as they passed. Soon enough, they would know him for their prince.

Thus, head held high—even if he could not quite still the trembling in his chest—he strode into the palace as though he belonged there. For he did. This was his home now, and he had every right to walk these halls, proud.

He made it all of three steps inside the vestibule before one of Aegeus's guards, a brawny man with a missing ear, moved to bar his way. "State your business here."

Theseus allowed himself a bare hint of a smile. What would the man say, should he proclaim himself the son of Aegeus? He had heard the man's wife had died childless, so the guard would no doubt name him a liar, or at best assume him a bastard clamouring for scraps. "You have heard of the voyage of the Argo," Theseus said instead. "I am come from that ship, with news for the king."

That managed to shake the haughtiness from the guard. Theseus could almost see him pondering whether a man might lie about such a thing. Apparently the guard decided no one would, for he ordered Theseus to follow. He led him to the very heart of the sprawling palace—and Theseus struggled not to gape at the vast marmoreal halls and the fine painted frescoes—past the central courtyard and into another anteroom. Beyond this, massive double doors stood ajar, granting a view of the megaron proper.

From within, voices rose in barely civilised argument. The guard growled at the disturbance, but it did not stop him from escorting

Theseus into the throne room. Within, upon a fine-wrought wooden chair, an ageing man sat, his eyes creased by lines of worry. His hands griped the armrests like he clutched them for fear of what he might do if he released his hold.

Before him, three young men stood, one in front of the others. It was these men who badgered the king, the foremost of them demanding Aegeus name his heir at the coming festival in honour of Athene.

So, then. These must be some of the sons of Pallas. Well, they would find themselves in for a rather stiff disappointment, and all too soon.

"King Aegeus has an heir already!" Theseus boomed.

A thick silence settled upon the megaron; every eye turned toward him. He felt the rising heat in his chest, threatening to flush his face, but he ploughed on, for Ananke had surely woven this course for him.

The guard at his side had stiffened at his interruption and already looked to Aegeus for permission to have Theseus escorted out and, mostlike, thrashed for his impudence. But the king raised an indulgent finger to forestall the man, and Theseus jumped at the implied invitation. After unstrapping the xiphos he'd claimed from beneath the rock, he hefted it high, so the light spilling in from high windows could glint off the gilded hilt. "I am Theseus, son of Princess Aethra of Troezen. I have come here after many travails. I have cleansed the roads of beasts and bandits. I hunted the great boar of Kalydon. I sailed with the Argonauts across the Axeinos Sea to far Kolchis. And at last, I return to you the gilded sword you once buried. For I am also the son of my mother's secret husband, King Aegeus of Athenai. And I come bearing the token of my birthright."

Theseus's father rose from his throne now, mouth agape, lip trembling as though he could not believe such a change in fortune possible.

"Secret marriage?" The one Theseus took for the eldest son of Pallas scoffed in his direction. "At best, this boy is a bastard, and even of that I have my doubts. Rather, I name him a fraud come to steal what is mine by all rights."

"No." Aegeus did not shout, yet his voice filled up the vast space of the megaron, soaring into the vaulted ceiling. "It is true I wed the Princess Aethra when my now late wife could not conceive an heir. With her father's blessing, our union was kept secret. And only her son could know of this, much less come here, bearing my own sword."

The elder Pallantide looked to his brothers for support, but their faces were stricken with the same shock that had settled upon all the guards and courtiers gathered in the megaron. In the wings, Theseus heard slaves and servants whispering and guessed news would fly from here like a stone from a sling. Before Hyperion dipped beneath the horizon, every tongue in Athenai would know the name Theseus.

"This is not to be borne," Pallas's son blurted.

But no one was still listening to his bluster. As the Pallantides fled the throne room in failure, Aegeus strode forwards. If his aged bones ached, he showed no sign of it. And when he embraced Theseus, his arms were still strong.

A deep, shuddering sigh was torn from Theseus then. For the first time in his life, he had a father.

21

HEKATE

43 Bronze Age

The setting sun glinted off the canals of Babilim, almost blinding. Beneath the shade of the cultivated Hanging Gardens, Hekate watched the day slip past, awaiting the rise of night. Night had always been her time. The king of Babilim welcomed a visiting Titan, granting her freedom to roam their arboreal wonder. Tiered gardens created a scalable verdant mountain beside the castle-ziggurat of Etemenaki, where both king and his supposed sky gods dwelt. A cascade of small waterfalls poured down from one tier of the garden to the next in pleasant burbles.

Not long after the last glint of the sunlight winked out, a faint padding over leaves announced Keuthos's arrival. The wraith-revenant wore the body she'd found him long back. Oh, the first one, the teenage boy, that one he'd lost during the chaos of the Gigantomachy, but it had taken little effort to find a corpse in decent condition following *that* insane battle.

Sometimes, Hekate wondered if she had done right, telling Demeter that Persephone had died and could never return to the world of the living. Sometimes, she wondered if the Inumidian Titan might have chosen another path, might not have launched her ill-fated war, had she not known such painful truths.

Keuthos crouched beside her, the Phoenikian perfume he wore masking the faint scent of decay that might otherwise emanate from even a well-preserved corpse. His vessel had, after all, once taken a spear through the throat, forcing Keuthos to always keep a cloak wrapt around his neck concealing the wound. The ghost misliked the daylight and most oft wiled away the hours until nightfall hidden in crypts or abandoned tenements. In the dark, as with her, he was free.

The lesser arcana of Tongues meant Hekate could freely travel and speak with any she met, but Keuthos had worked harder to learn to speak so many differing languages, some of which had changed in the years since his death.

"I found an old friend of yours," Keuthos said. Riding this husk, his voice still rasped, but it had lost that nerve-shredding ephemeral quality of other wraiths.

In the back of her mind, Mormo cackled. *One day ... he shall feast upon your soul ...*

No, Hekate did not think so. From their first days together, she knew, Keuthos had loved her. Despite all that had befallen him, despite his sorceries damning his soul and transforming him into a creature of utter hatred and self-loathing, some part of him loved her *still*. Thus, he had not left her side in the century since she had freed him from Hades's grasp. When the Gigantomachy had heightened Zeus's paranoia and led to him insisting his remaining Olympians dwell beneath his gaze in their palaces, it was Keuthos who suggested they travel to far Mu.

There, Hekate had consulted the Seven Queens. She had studied the magical dances and sacred songs, had smoked herbs in the Dreaming Desert, and walked in a space that, according to the spectres of her dream, had existed before the coming of Man. Ever she sought answers, ever she dug deeper. There had to be some means of escaping the damnation of her soul and the fate Aeshma held over her head like a quivering sword, ready to plunge.

"What old friend?" she asked, turning to Keuthos.

"He claims, the same one who saved you from Hypnos not so far from here, ages back."

The words took a moment to fix in her mind, to form into something beyond the haze of shock. This man claimed to be Mithra? She had not seen the stranger—who had himself claimed to know Enodia—in thousands of years. Not that she had seen much of her former mentor in centuries, either.

And here Hekate was, back in Kumari Kandam, seeking the deepest of knowledges, and once more he appeared. She and Keuthos had spent more than five decades on Mu. They had scoured the depths beneath Mugedang in hunt of the ruins of Murias, and Hekate had scribed all she learnt in her grimoire. She'd spent years more in the isles of Nusantara, before at last passing through Yueshang and on to this continent. Had Mithra lingered in the vast Kandamian wilds for so very long?

"I will meet him," she said.

Keuthos stood without further prompting. He did not beckon her to follow. Disregarding sporadic conversations that sometimes stretched until just before dawn, Keuthos oft spoke very little. Nor need he say much, after their years together, for her to apprehend his intentions. The revenant guided her out of the gardens, and beyond the royal sanctum, into the city proper.

The River Ufratu bifurcated Babilim, creating two districts joined by numerous bridges. Keeping to the shadows, no doubt more by instinct than intent, Keuthos led the way into the western district. Within this one lay the Sanctum of Belus, a place she had gone to study all the priests' lore on the Otherworld and demons, paltry and error ridden as those teachings had proved.

It was not to the sanctum Keuthos headed, though, but rather along the whitewashed colonnades toward one of numerous opulent palaces. No guards watched the gate to the walled yard, and Keuthos pushed it open without knocking. The revenant stalked up to the alabaster building but paused beneath the eaves, tinged with hesitation she could not understand.

Waiting for her to make the move? Hekate strode forwards and rapped upon the door.

A heartbeat later, a steward ushered them inside a hallway lit by twin rows of braziers. As ever, Keuthos recoiled from fire, keeping as far from either side as the narrow corridor permitted. Since she could do little to comfort the revenant, Hekate kept her eyes locked ahead.

The steward guided them to a central courtyard. From here, they could see the almost-full moon amid a field of stars, though the peaks of ziggurats obscured her view of some constellations. Once, she and Keuthos had debated just what the stars represented, or if they were even real. While she had posited a possibility that they were punctures to some Otherworldly source of light, even she had no way to know for certain.

She felt Keuthos swivel, though she heard naught, and followed the revenant's gaze to where a man emerged from a doorway, his form silhouetted by the light within. Once he strode out enough the moon's silver glint highlighted him, she could see he was indeed the one who had saved her long back, in the Empty Desert. Black haired, with a beard as trim now as it had been millennia ago. Only his clothes seemed changed, for he dressed now in the fashion of Babilimian aristoi.

"Hekate," Mithra said. He walked not to her but past her, circling as if carried upon a dilatory breeze. As if they had chanced to pass in the street after but hours rather than ages. "Welcome to my abode." The man—Titan, obviously by his longevity, even if his height was not as great as that of most Titans—offered her a wry grin as he drifted around her once more, forcing her to turn to keep him in view. His accent seemed a perfect mirror of local nobility, more than a bit changed, she suspected, from their last meeting, though her memories had somewhat blurred with time.

"I must admit, I was taken aback when Keuthos told me you were here."

"Why?" the strange Titan asked.

"Because I do not oft see people disappear for thousands of years at a time."

"And you think, because I did not deign to become involved in the great wars for Elládos, I must have disappeared? You cannot imagine a person having other concerns than wars waged on the far side of the ocean? Hmm. Perhaps I met a woman, made a life. Perhaps I raised a family. Perhaps I may yet do so."

A point, she supposed. Naught compelled every Titan of power to involve themselves in politics. Naught, save the ever-present need for Ambrosia. One way or another, Mithra had maintained his immortality, and that meant he'd received shipments from Atlantis. Still, prying would little avail her.

"Do you know why I showed myself to your companion now?" Mithra asked.

"No." Though she'd intended to ask.

The Kandamian, if such he was, at last paused in his aimless wanderings about his courtyard. "I know you have a keen interest in the Elder Gods, those great powers at the fringes of the World, far beyond our faltering Realm. I know you lust for the secrets they hold, the wisdom locked away from the prying eyes of Man."

"Enodia." The sorceress must have told him of her encounter as a young woman and the impression it had left upon her.

Mithra inclined his head in agreement. "Indeed."

Hekate folded her arms over her chest. "I seek all knowledge. All the secret lore, the buried truths. I will understand not just *this* world, but the World as a whole." And in that knowledge, perhaps she might find meaning for horrors she'd be forced to inflict upon her mother, for the suffering she'd caused so many others. Perhaps, most of all, escape from her own fate. There had to be a way out, a way to slip the noose Ananke had placed round her neck.

With thumb and forefinger, Mithra stroked his beard. "Well, knowledge may sometimes come at a cost higher than you think.

Still, rumour claims a man down in Nysa was touched by the hand of an Elder God."

"Which?" Hekate asked, taking an involuntary step toward him. "What man?"

"Which Elder God? As I said, it's just a rumour, and you'd have to investigate that yourself. As for the man, he's gathered quite a cult around him, so he ought to prove easy enough to find. Name's Dionysus, and last I heard, he lurked in the deep jungles west of the Sumeru Mountains."

"Why help us?" Keuthos rasped. "Twice now."

"Why not? Enodia will appreciate it."

Though Hekate considered mentioning she'd not seen her mentor in years, she saw little advantage in pointing that out. "Thank you."

THE INTRICATE SUN temples of Nysa never failed to evoke hints of a time lost to the mists of history. In her wanderings through the cities here before, Hekate had mused that, were she to sleep within those vaunted walls, if she might have dreamt herself back to the days even of Dark Faerie. North of here, within the Empty Desert, lay the etiolated remains of once-mighty Gorias, the jewel of Kumari Kandam.

What remained of Murias she had seen beneath the city of Mugedang. Falias lay somewhere within the Nyxlands, a place even sorcerers spoke of with dread. Findias, she knew, had lain upon Hy-Brasil, lost perhaps in the Rainwoods, though she'd failed to ever lay eyes upon it.

But to dream of the sun temples here were but idle musings; the pandits would never consent to her dwelling within their sacred spaces, least of all if they perceived the taint of sorcery upon her soul.

When the sun had risen, Keuthos had disappeared off into the nearby jungle, no doubt hiding from the burning light beneath the dense canopy. As the day dragged on, she found herself counting the hours until dusk, when she could confer with him once more. Oh, the locals had heard indeed of this god-touched one, Dionysus, and rumours of his wanderings had spread throughout Nysa.

They said where he went, drunkenness and debauchery followed like a spreading plague. Some claimed his eyes were black as the bosom of Nyx. Others claimed him a prophet of the Elder Gods, a messiah come to set right a World askew. "Witness the ever-increasing chaos," a pandit had told her with an expansive wave of his hand. "The Wheel of History turns toward corruption and immorality, toward war and perfidy even amid kin. Only when it reaches its darkest point, when Man stands upon the precipice of annihilation can we pass through the crucible and reach a new Golden Age."

What would he have said, Hekate had wondered, if she had told him she had witnessed the whole of both the Golden and the Silver Ages? There had been war then, too, and betrayals aplenty, most all amid kin. Was the Golden Age, in fact, better than this time, which the Muses named the Bronze Age? Perhaps, but not by so much as this priest seemed to think.

Finding no answers at the temple, she had walked the town further, soaking up gossip as if such petty pursuits suited her. A madness, some termed the Cult of Dionysus that had arisen in the south, down in Barbarikon. Washerwomen claimed painted hordes had thronged the streets, dancing naked beneath the moon and howling like wolves. "Not just that," another insisted. "There were orgies on half the rooftops in the city. I heard it from my son's master's wife, and she never lies, you know."

As if any of these people had ever seen Barbarikon in their lives.

One claim, though, persisted. Stories that the jungles had become more haunted than usual. From time immemorial, Nysians had known not to venture into the sylvan expanse at night when spirits of the wood and rivers stirred and ghosts prowled. Now, though, some claimed to have heard chanting and moaning, sounds carried all the way across the fields and into town.

So, crouched in the shade of a peepal tree, Hekate watched the fading light limn the elaborate facade of the sun temple. As soon as

Keuthos returned, they would make for that jungle themselves. If this Dionysus had answers, had truths about the World, about Fate, about any of it, Hekate would have those answers from him. She must.

"There is something ... of the Otherworld here ..." Keuthos said as Hekate ducked beneath a branch that swept so low it nigh brushed the protruding roots of another tree. "It saturates the air ... it seeps into the Ether ..."

Hekate turned to look at him, the light from her oil lamp barely enough to hint at his cloaked features. "That's why we are here."

"You may find ... more ... than you expect ..."

But then, she wanted *everything*. Embracing the Sight, she peered into the deepening shadows of the Penumbra. Indeed, as Keuthos had observed, a tension thrummed through the Spectral air. A welling, not of psychic echoes of the past so much as psychic reverberations of the now. Pulses so deep they seemed to ripple out from some unseen drum.

"Follow the current," she instructed.

Using the Sight to peer into the Penumbra whilst navigating such a dense jungle would have proved like to send her sprawling on her face, so she blinked it away, trusting the revenant to guide them toward the source of the emanations. After perhaps a quarter hour, she caught wind of faint drumbeats in actuality.

"You hear that?"

"For some time now ... It is louder ... in the Echo."

Which removed any doubt that they had found the source of the psychic disturbance.

Once they had navigated a maze of roots and a tangle of vines, they came to a glade encircling a lake. The space sat within a depression; the lake fed by burbling streams carrying runoff down to the water. Upon the shoreline, a dozen naked men and women danced, several thumping rhythms out on handheld drums. Amid them, a woman straddled a man, grinding her hips in time with the beats while flinging her head round in wild gyrations.

A whole cellar's worth of discarded amphorae were scattered about the glade, making plain these people had imbibed enough wine to sate a small village.

When she and Keuthos drew closer, she realised many of the participants had painted their skin in white streaks. Their faces, especially, bore an abundance of red and white colouring, like eerie masks.

All of this seemed familiar, in a way she could not quite place ...

Had she dreamt this before? She didn't recall.

From the wood strode another figure, taller than a Man, pushing seven feet. The whole of his nude body bore blue paint, twisting into strange, somehow erotic, spirals. The Titan—she assumed he must be—also wore an antlered mask of bones. In each hand he carried a new amphora.

With one amphora the Titan beckoned, and Hekate found herself plodding toward him, legs jumbled, chest quivering in wanton anticipation of something ... glorious.

"Hekate ..." Keuthos's voice came to her on a distant wind, too far away to distract from what lay so close ahead.

"Dionysus," she purred. The Titan cupped her chin, then began to dribble honey-sweet wine from the amphora into her mouth. A warm rush surged through her, pooling first in her gut then her nethers.

Dimly, she realised only two drummers still beat their instruments, while the remaining cultists had joined the copulating couple in a writhing mass of flesh.

"Hekate ..." The chill, dead hand upon her shoulder jolted her from her daze. Hekate gagged on wine, suddenly aware she had reached inside her khiton to touch herself. More irritated than embarrassed, she jerked her hand free of her clothes and cast a glower at the Titan who had somehow mesmerised her.

Dionysus turned his gaze upon Keuthos. An instant later, the revenant fell back several steps, leaving Hekate to wonder what silent contest of wills had taken place.

"I came to you for answers."

"All Truth lies within the best vintages." Dionysus's voice was deep as the jungle itself, throbbing through the land and back into Hekate. It might, had she allowed it, have unmade her then and there, and even so, her body responded in a spontaneous orgasm that had her stumbling in place.

Next she knew, that wine was wetting her lips once more.

"Leave this ..." Keuthos implored, voice a somnambulant intruder into the sea of passion that had engulfed Hekate.

The land itself bucked, arcing in throbbing need. A presence pushed into her, not just into her flesh, for so many had penetrated her already, Dionysus included, but into her soul. A mammoth will, eldritch and consuming, glorious and terrible. It swallowed her whole, bored through the tiniest fractures in her psyche, and, with each groaning, grinding movement, lurched a little closer to her Realm.

Or perhaps the line between Realms was never so distinct as Men wished to believe.

Her mind, her soul, it flitted about, dancing round the souls of the others, spiritwalkers all. Mediums trained by Dionysus to reach further and further.

Maenads, he called them.

"Return to yourself ..." Keuthos implored.

That behemoth intellect brushing over her turned its regard—some fracture of it—onto the revenant, decaying abomination that it was. The walking corpse fled then, vanishing into the jungle upon recognising its impotence against the enormity of what unfolded. This marvellous manifestation of nature in its purest form.

Oh, *yes*, Hekate knew this, for it had tried to induct her into the great mysteries even in her youth before fatuous Artemis severed the connection. She might have had all the answers back then but had lost the chance and could no longer understand why. Only, she knew with a certainty, she would not turn from it again. Through the revelation of all, she would grow so far beyond herself none would ever know her.

Yes, Hekate knew this Elder God, from way back, and had at last come home to the embrace of Pan.

22

ATHENE

724 Bronze Age

$\mathcal{E}$ach spring, she would tread the road from Olympus to Thebes. Father had granted her Nephos to keep, but Athene cherished the walk itself. She would linger upon the snow-capped peaks in her descent, and revel as she spied the first anemone blooms upon the lowlands. She would pause in villages and drink beer with the townsfolk. Sometimes, she would help with the planting, though not so long as to be late in arriving at Herakles's abandoned home outside Thebes.

Whilst daylight lasted, she would aid Theban farmers with their tasks. Sometimes she would disguise herself as a huntress and bring wild game to their tables. Once, she fixed a broken plough, and many times tended to the animals. Another time, she brought herbs to treat a sick little girl. When that failed, she had given the family drachmae and sent them to meet Asklepoius, son of Apollon and master chirur-geon, in Phlegra. She had been the one to introduce Asklepoius to the wise centaur Kheiron who had taught him much, and Apollon's son would favour her for it.

When dusk drew nigh and Nyx began to spread her dark wings, Athene would return to the gloom of Herakles's house. And she would sit. And wait. And imagine that, at last, *this* would be the night her son returned.

It never was.

And the years rolled by.

He had not returned.

Each time she came to Olympus, her father pleaded and bribed and raged at her, driven by wild swings of mood and fervent desperation. He needed her to find the answer to his demise within the Mirrors, but she could not do it. She saw glimpses of her own future, yes, but not his.

So many visions raced past her in fevered blurs, and so oft, she misliked what she saw.

❧

Bright blood and golden ichor were splattered so thick upon Ares's panoply Athene could scarce make out the bronze of it. His crimson cloak billowed behind him. Here stood one well aware of the striking figure he cast amid the carnage of a field strewn with uncounted dead and dying. But carnage was Ares's great love in life. No pleasure of the flesh or mind could compare, for Athene's brother, with his exultation at violence.

Perhaps that was how they had come to this.

Her brother traced lazy circles in the air with his burnished spear, scattering blood drops from the tip of it. He beckoned, taunted. He dared her to face him. Even with her fierce ally, Ares thought her but a stumbling block in his path. One he, clearly, delighted at the thought of removing.

Athene approached, cautious, her shield up, her xiphos at the ready.

❧

*H*AND TO HER MOUTH, *Athene choked upon sobs she could not stifle. Already, the pyre had become an inferno, a blazing beacon against the black curtain of night. Smoke billowed up from it to vanish against the darkness. She could not make out the body beyond the flames. She couldn't see him.*

Somehow, impossibly, she still expected him to stir. To leap from the pyre and deny even this could be the end of one so great.

She knew Hyllus needed her. He needed her to be strong to keep himself from collapsing in the crushing press on unfathomable grief. She knew it, but she had no strength left in her.

*T*HOSE TOWERING *walls were so thick, so high, perhaps the Elládosi would never have breached them. No ladder could stretch so tall as to reach the top. The warriors could have landed blow after blow upon the gates without the doors cracking.*

Hence the gift. A horse, the royal symbol of Ilium, standing nigh thirty feet high, wrought of wood salvaged from broken ships. And upon great wheels, they rolled it through gates thrown wide. Pride was ever the most human of failings.

*W*ITH DAWN'S *first flame upon the sky, the silhouettes of triremes appeared on the horizon. Raven dark, a murder of crows clogging the Strait and closing in upon the last tiny island that stood between death and Elládos.*

More and more ships joined that fleet, leaving Athene's heart clenched in her chest. Cold sweat beaded upon the back of her neck and dribbled between her shoulder blades, leaving her armour clammy.

If they failed here, her homeland would burn. Even as, across the Strait, Athenai still smouldered. The people of her city—of her own namesake— they had needed her, and she had failed them. Athene clutched the pommel of her sword, drawing a pale comfort from its solidity. This day, she would give not another foot of ground.

This day, the seas would run red with Babilimian blood before she let more of Elládos burn.

⸎

Aᴛᴴᴇᴧᴇ *sᴛᴀᴿᴇᴰ defiance at the self-proclaimed king of the world. "My father will not ransom me."*

Now, Mithra leaned forwards, offering her a hint of his features, from his trim black beard to his intense eyes. "But it is not your father I am interested in, Goddess." With ponderous import, the man rose, giving the sensation of a river changing its course. "No, I had you brought here for something far more momentous than Zeus's petty struggles. I have summoned you forth from the farthest reaches of this world in order to bestow upon you a gift. The greatest of all gifts, in fact, Athene. I am going to give to you ... Truth."

She wanted to laugh in his face. She wanted to dismiss his pompous claim for the self-serving arrogance of all Men who claimed divine insight as justification for following the courses that suited them. It was the great deception of the powerful, convincing those they trampled that a deity willed it thus. For the love of a god, for the fragile hope of pleasing someone that might have their interests at heart, Men would welcome the heel upon their throats of those who so plainly did not.

Such things flitted through her mind. Yet she could not deny a tremble that shot through her at the utter certainty with which he spoke. Fanatics oft blinded themselves most of all, she knew. And yet ... "What Truth?" she could not stop herself from ask.

Mithra paced over until he stood before her. With a finger beneath her chin, he lifted her gaze to meet his own. "That our lives exist not in insolation but as cogs within a mechanism that ensures the continuation of the cosmos. That we are, all of us, a part of the ever-turning Wheels."

⸎

Aᴧᴏᴛᴴᴇᴿ sᴘᴿᴛᴧᴳ cᴿᴀᴡᴸᴇᴰ oᴧ. Once the summer solstice arrived, another year would have died, and still Herakles had not returned.

Hers had been such a vain hope, Athene knew. Whatever she had beheld in the Oracle Mirrors, years back, could well have been the vague musings of her own desperate mind.

And since, she had seen such frightful visions. She remembered Babilim from long back. And seeing it again, the vision deepened and unchanged, it sat heavy upon her shoulders. All this time, all she had been through, and still she saw herself brought in orichalcum fetters before the Babilimian king.

But such musings were distant worries compared to the drowning sorrows of the now.

Sat against the hearth, knees on her chest, she let the tears come. They came every spring. Not on the first night, and not every night, but sometimes the swell of memories grew so momentous it burst forth from the dam of her. A thousand half-formed recollections would dance in front of her. A childish voice, calling "Mama, Mama, Mama." Laughter, in halls now thick with pregnant silence.

Such was the peril of memory. Beautiful and terrible and each one worth more than all the drachmae hoarded in every vault in Elládos.

When there were no more tears, she folded her arms over her knees and let her weary head rest upon them. Some nights, when she had wept herself to emptiness, a hollow ache would rise inside her head, as if to protest the void her tears had left behind. It would throb and throb, and she'd sit without moving for hours and clutch onto the pain as if it were a piece of her son.

A sandal creaked upon stone, and Athene looked up. He stood there, in the doorway, silhouetted. Looking at her. He stepped inside, tentative, as frightened as she was.

Hope warred with terror. For how could he be but an apparition after so long? But this was the moment she had seen. And she would not allow this to be some dream, no matter how pleasant.

"You're back. I ... knew you'd come back one day."

"Mama?" Her son shook with the anxieties that wracked him. He slipped down before her and allowed himself to reach for her. But he dropped his hand before they connected, sat, and shifted backwards. "Why are you here?"

This was real. It had to be real, for she could not bear to have it snatched from her.

"I saw, in the waters, that you'd return one spring night. So ..." Athene swallowed, almost ready to break into tears once more. "Each year, when the first blooms would waken, I travelled back here. Every night I wait and hope that ..." Now she crawled toward him, but Herakles pulled back. His rejection was a lash upon her face. What could ever sting worse for a mother than for a child to forbid her to comfort him?

"How long was I gone?"

He needed her to be strong, it seemed. He needed her, not to hold him but to anchor him. That he could ask such a question implied a whirlwind of possibilities, but one rose to the forefront, no matter how incomprehensible it remained. She had seen him, centuries before his birth, when he saved her during the Gigantomachy. She could not say how or why, but if he had vanished for so long and did not know it, had not even changed ... Had he somehow reached that ancient war and now returned?

She rose, forcing herself to calm. She would be his anchor to the world. She would be aught he ever needed her to be, this she swore. "It's been nine years, Herakles." She offered him a hand. "Son ..."

Now he accepted her grip and pulled himself to his feet. "I have to tend to something. I'll return." With that, he stepped outside.

Guilt stooped his shoulders. He didn't realise that all that had happened was something *done* to him by Kirke's poisons. It was something inflicted upon him, mostlike through no fault of his own.

"The madness was not your fault!" she shouted after him. "It was a curse which befell you, Herakles."

But he only winced, refusing to turn to meet her gaze. To him, she knew, it mattered naught that a drug had induced the madness by which he'd slain his boys. No details of his affliction would assuage his guilt. This she knew without doubt. Even as she knew that, had something happened to him through her—be it her fault or otherwise—she could not have forgiven herself. No parent ever could.

"Whatever drew that savagery from me," he said, staring out into the night, "came from some dark, broken place within the depths of my soul. That brutality, that unforgivable rancour needed but a nudge to rise once more to the surface. I have *always* been a murderer, Mama, as well you know. These hands ..." Herakles choked, looking at his hands. "These hands are only good for carnage."

Those words cut like knives. Herakles vanished into the darkness before she could find a fair response for him.

ATHENE'S SON returned not long before dawn, worn and weary. She had kindled a fire outside the house for him, thinking perhaps he would sit beside her and confirm where he'd been these nine years. Instead, he bent to snatch a brand from the blaze.

"This can never be a home again. A place stained by such crimes remains forever tainted."

And what was she to say to that? She had longed and feared to return to her home on Olympus. Even now, she felt the pull of her father's desperation, calling her back. She had sworn to save him. Oh, Athene knew well enough who and what her father was. She knew what kind of man he was.

She knew, too, he was her *father*. She could not abandon him to the merciless hand of Fate that had already so crushed her family within its grip.

Herakles, perhaps, took her silence for approval and hurled the flaming brand onto the rooftop of his former home. By her side, he watched the house burn.

When all was ash and Hyperion had begun to creep over the eastern horizon, Herakles had pleaded with her to turn to hydromancy. Such pangs strained his voice when he spoke of redemption.

So fragile, so close to breaking. He needed her, he said, to find him some means to appease the souls of his murdered boys.

He did not want her to tell him it wasn't his fault, much as she wished to do so. He wanted her to give him some means to *fix* the horror. Or perhaps what he really sought was the means to forgive himself. Therein, she had learnt over the passing of an age, lay the only redemption available in life. It had taken Athene centuries to manage that feat. She'd been forced to let go, not only of her anger but also her guilt over what it had brought out of her.

So, she had stared and stared into the waters, suddenly wishing for the Seeing Pools beneath Olympus. Dangerous though they were, they served as stronger catalysts for the Sight than any other medium she had ever looked into. Mayhap they could have given her better answers. When next she returned, she dared hope they would.

Because what she saw herself telling her son, it did not well please her. Oh, the peril and suffering would serve as a crucible through which he could reforge himself, she had no doubt. If he survived such harrowing tasks as lay before him, perhaps they would give him the chance to work through the war raging inside his breast.

Perhaps, but she was far from certain of it.

She found him wandering a dew-moistened field that had once been part of his farmland and now lay fallow and overgrown with waist-high weeds. "Herakles," she called. If his road to acceptance—to returning to life—lay through the extraordinary suffering and shame and struggle she had seen, she would give that to him. She would hand him such burdens and hope that, through them, he might ease the greater weights already borne by his soul. "I looked into the future."

Her son swallowed, pensive, as well he should be. He did not understand what he'd asked of her. She did not want to make him understand. Oh, Gaia. All she wanted was to throw her arms around him, shelter him. Whisper to him that he must forgive himself now. Say it, over and over, until he let go the anguish. Which, of course, he could not do. "Tell me."

"You were cursed, Herakles." If only he would listen. If only he would accept it. But she already knew he would not. He did not want to hear about Nectar. He did not want to know it was not his fault. His self-loathing was the only pillar upon which he had left to lean, and without it, he might collapse into utter despondency.

He needed someone to blame.

"Whether someone ..." he began. "Even if another, in malice, brought the madness out of me, still my children's shades haunt me, Mama. I know they are there. I *see* them each time I close my eyes."

Athene could have died from the pain in his words. "I cannot see ghosts to make an answer for you." Not the way Mother had been able to. She could not say, with utter certainty, that his children did *not* haunt him. Such things could happen, she had heard. The dead sometimes lingered, restless and resentful of the lives stolen from them.

"How might I cleanse myself?" He was already falling apart.

If she told him, it might aid him. Or it might break what little remained of the man he'd become.

"Mama ... I will *lose* myself if I cannot find a way. No man can endure such guilt."

With a trembling sigh, Athene looked about. How she did not want to utter these words. "Submit yourself to the will of your greatest enemy."

"The Minyans of Orchomenus?"

She sighed. Oh, if only. "No, Son. Your foe is closer, one of your kin. Your uncle, Sthenelos, ruled Mykenai after his brother Elektryon's death. Perseus had chosen Elektryon as his heir." Because she had told him to do so, because her visions revealed that was how the future ought to play out. But *ought* implied the Moirai's weavings were beneficent. And Athene simply did not know anymore. If Father was right, they seemed inclined to destroy her family. Perhaps her father was ... not a good king. Shit, he was not even a good man. But she would not let him fall. Nor was she still certain she had done right by Perseus's kin, though she had tried. And here Herakles was, Perseus's great-grandson. She *had* to do right by him. She had to.

"Sthenelos too died in your absence and left the city to your cousin, Eurystheus, who rules there now."

Herakles rubbed his palm over his eyes. "Why should my cousin be my enemy? Should he not welcome me if I called upon him?"

She almost laughed. Families were more complex than her son seemed to realise. "The last surviving legitimate child of Elektryon, Alkmena holds claim to the throne of Mykenai. As a woman, she cannot inherit, but you, her son, could do so. You are a threat to his rule, Herakles."

"I care naught for thrones. I seek only penance for my crimes."

Be that as it may, she doubted others would feel the same. "As your kin, outwardly, Eurystheus will no doubt welcome you, as you say. But if you ask him this, ask he task you labours to purify yourself, he will throw before you such impossible feats as to ensure your death."

"So, I must make for Mykenai."

"Herakles ..." Athene grabbed his hand and squeezed. There had to be a better way to assuage his guilt. "I never got the chance to thank you for what you did on Olympus. I was waiting ..."

He sputtered, at a loss for words and clearly unable to speak of it, so she pulled him to her and held him close.

GLAMOURED *to look like an old woman, her face concealed beneath a threadbare himation, Athene stood beside the bank of a river, staring at it as if at a serpent. Its current was swift, breaking upon the few bits of rock that rose above the surface level. There would be more rocks below, and slippery ones.*

From behind, the expected young man approached. She turned to look at him, a Kroniad, though his hair was more a sandy blond than the platinum of earlier generations. Last she'd seen him, he'd been but a babe she'd given to Kheiron to raise into a hero rather than let his uncle murder the child.

Now, she had begun to question the visions she beheld. She saw herself shaping and aiding and mentoring heroes. But did she truly help them, or Mankind, or was she but some pawn of Ananke? Still, she was not ready to turn her back upon the future. What if Man needed these heroes? What if the future could be so much worse without them? Had she not followed her vision, the babe would never have grown into this man at all.

"Do you need help?" the man asked.

Athene nodded. "The rains came heavy this spring, and the waters rose. There was a bridge, but it washed away in a flood." She pointed to where the remaining foundation was still stuck in the ground on the far side. On the close bank, the surging waters had swept away any sign of the bridge.

"This is the fastest road to Iolkos," the young man said, folding his arms in what might have been a pout.

"Yes," Athene agreed. "The next crossing is miles upstream, and I've business in Iolkos this day." Because, of course, she had seen this, too.

The man huffed. "Well. I suppose I'll carry you then."

Athene nodded and allowed him to heft her into his arms, dropping her own arm around his shoulders. The young man was strong enough, though he wheezed as he stood. The glamour disguised Athene's impressive height and build, but it did not change her weight, and the man clearly had not expected an old woman to present such a burden. Stepping into the swift river, he staggered. Chill waters splashed up against him, some rising high enough to dampen her peplos and spray over her heels.

Halfway across, the man jerked to a stop, gasped, and teetered. Athene tightened her grip around his shoulders before he pitched her into the river. "Ahh," he growled, tugging upon one leg that seemed stuck in the mess of wet rocks beneath the surface.

With a heave, his foot came free, and he resumed their passage over the river. When he set her down, she saw he had lost one of his sandals. The young man looked back at the river, glowering, and clearly debating whether or not swimming under the water would offer him much chance of reclaiming his footwear.

In the end, he huffed and shook his head. "I suppose that's that, then." He cleared his throat. "I can see you on your way to Iolkos, my lady, if it pleases you."

"It would indeed," she agreed, careful to maintain a slight affected limp as they plodded along the road.

A few days back, glamoured as an Oracle, she had warned King Pelias of Iolkos that his death would be heralded by the arrival of a man with but one shoe. The king had chuckled at the absurd prophecy, and Athene might almost have pitied him, had she not known him for a vile creature who had tried to murder a babe. She did not, in fact, know how the king would die, but she knew the man she brought here would have a hand in it.

For the throne was his by right.

The young man announced himself to King Pelias, naming himself Jason, son of Aeson, the king's brother. And Pelias was no longer smiling. At least, not until he goaded Jason into promising him a grand undertaking to prove himself worthy of the throne. For this task, Pelias demanded the Golden Fleece of King Aeëtes of Kolchis ...

Athene found Jason, afterward, mulling over his challenge into a bowl of cheap wine. It had to be cheap, for that was the only sort served in the kind of tavern she found him in. No stools or benches, just a crimson-stained stone bar against which the patrons could lean.

Jason looked up at her approach. "Old woman?"

"I heard the task Pelias set before you."

"An impossible one," he said with a sniff. From the slur of his voice, it was not his first bowl of wine this night.

Athene leant against the counter beside him. "Not with the right allies, it isn't. There are those with the strength to aid you, if you can find them. The Olympians enjoy their dalliances with mortal women, and Elládos has no few demigods." Sometimes her brethren seduced their women. Oft, they did not bother with that, a thought that had Athene brittle with hints of that old rage. "You've heard, perhaps, of Herakles? The son of Zeus who slew the Nemean Lion and the hydra of Lerna?"

Perhaps it was the wine, for Jason looked at her as though the sun itself poured from her mouth. "It is a grand idea."

For him, she imagined so. For Herakles, she dared to hope that in helping another achieve his ends, Herakles might too ease his own conscience. Because Athene had to do something for her son. She had to try.

ATHENE SHOOK herself from the Mirror, pressed her palms to her aching temples, and blinked. It took a moment to reorient herself within the cavern. This Jason ... she had seen him in times past, too, and he was one of many mortals she knew she was meant to help achieve their grand quests. Mentoring these heroes gave her purpose and gave them hope, though she found herself, at the moment, always dwelling upon the pain Herakles felt.

She knew about the lion, though not about this hydra. Apparently he would succeed in slaying even so fell a creature. She supposed that meant she ought not worry over it. A feat easier said than done for any mother. Either way, if aiding Jason meant giving Herakles purpose as well, she needed to make for Iolkos.

She had to help her son however she might. She had to pull him through his guilt and grief. Because otherwise ... she had seen it in his eyes. She had beheld the longing for his own death there. That, she could not abide. No parent could see their children surrender thus.

"Well?" her father demanded behind her.

Athene turned, still woozy. For a moment, she had forgotten he was even there. "I saw naught of your future, Father. I'm sorry ..."

"Why?" His roar was a sudden eruption that shook the cavern. Ribbons of lightning coruscated along his arm for an instant. The air convulsed with his rage. "How many years am I to endure these failures, Daughter?" Like a storm cloud, he drifted toward her, looming and furious. "Or perhaps you too are in league with whichever of your brothers schemes against me?"

"Never," she said, and meant it. Whatever his faults, Athene would not betray her own family. That, she could not do. "My loyalty is absolute."

A puff of air blew out of her father, and he sagged, seized by a sudden dolour every bit as powerful as his momentary anger had been. "There is an answer, in these lustrous pools. And if you cannot find it, Daughter, what then? Will you allow one of your brothers to claim my throne, not through will but sheer neglect?"

Athene sighed and leant back against the wall. She was so tired. Her head ached and she needed to make for Iolkos to ensure her vision played out. She could not afford to miss any thread that might aid Herakles. But what if Father was right? What if Ares did plot against him? She could not name him without proof. She had seen herself prepared to come to blows with her brother. But still, that did not guarantee he had betrayed their father. Rather, it meant one day his violence would put them at odds, and that hardly came as a surprise.

She rubbed at her temples, though it did little to abate the pain. "Most Oracles have limits. It's different for all of us, but many see few visions not of their own futures."

Zeus threw up his hands. "Well, I need to know *my* future! And how to avoid it."

"My Sight doesn't work that way ..." But her Sight had been largely rarefied by Nectar. Kirke had given her that. Maybe she could give it to Zeus now. Athene had always kept Kirke's secret, even now, years after what the woman's poisons had done to Herakles. Why was she protecting her? She was no longer a sister to Athene; she had severed those bonds herself with her lies and awful results of her actions.

But if Athene handed Kirke over to Zeus, he might kill her for violating his laws. So far as she knew, Olympus had given over any active attempt to stamp out Nectar propagation centuries back. But the substance remained illegal. Few knew the secret recipe for the creation of Ambrosia. During the Silver Age, the Pleiades had guarded the secret. Either Father knew it too or had discovered it before he acted against Atlas's daughters. He'd passed the secret on to Athene's half-sister Hebe.

With Nectar, Kirke had come dangerously close to replicating true Ambrosia. Father might well execute its creator for the years of inconvenience she had posed.

If she handed Kirke over, was she doing it to punish her because of Herakles?

Athene weighed that. She could not live with herself later, not if she cast a woman into danger for such petty reasons as vengeance. Was that it? She did not think so. The truth was, she just wanted her father safe. She needed him to know that, if no other Olympian, he could count on her. And he certainly would not kill Kirke if she gave him what he wanted. He was not one to throw away someone who might prove useful.

"Father ..." Athene swallowed. "My Sight may not be able to ever find the answer you seek." She raised a hand to forestall his rising ire. "But I might know a way *you* can gain the Sight to seek out your own future."

23

PANDORA

727 Bronze Age

Through lonely days and lonelier nights, Pandora walked. Across the hill lands, amid meadows and valleys, and through trackless sylvan expanses. Her arm healed to full strength in just over a day, making plain Prometheus had not exaggerated about the healing effects of so much Pneuma. The Phoenix gave her strength and stamina, the ability to push on for more hours than others could have dreamt.

Sometimes, she hunted game. The Amazons had instructed her well in woodcraft, and in these lands where Man dared not walk, wildlife abounded. She slew deer or rabbits, sometimes fowl, and on one occasion, a bison left behind by its herd.

In time, the lush greenery of hill lands gave way to pale, withering grasses and the desiccated husks of trees that had endured long beyond the time they ought to have turned to dust. The bent trunks stood like faded grave markers, memorialising those whose names were long forgotten by the World.

She must have drawn toward Vulgeth, for a chill wind seemed to blow from the northwest, bearing upon it the reek of decay. The sepulchral stench evoked the winding catacombs beneath Delphi, where the Old One, Python, had laired. Not a memory Pandora had sought to relive.

The days grew shorter, the nights darker. Game vanished, replaced by scattered predators that watched her with abhorrent intellect glinting behind onyx eyes. One night, as she pushed on—unwilling to make such fleeting progress as the limited daylight permitted—a pack of wolves gathered on a hillock, watching her progress through the valley below, still as marble sculptures in a garden. A dozen or more of the animals locked their shining black gazes upon her, and Pandora could not gauge whether they thought her prey or mere curiosity.

In rapid succession, they lifted their heads toward the crescent moon overhead, howling in a chorus that lifted the hair upon her arms and neck.

Nerves jolted through her, threatening to steal her breath. She would not give in to this. She snapped her fingers, the spark igniting a torch upon her hand. Unless starving, she could not imagine animals closing with one bearing an open flame. And indeed, she passed by the pack unmolested, but ever with the feel of their eyes upon her.

ANOTHER FORTNIGHT of travel and she came, at long last, to the decrepit ruin of once majestic Vulgeth. For surely, the crumbling wonder spreading out before her must have been a grand city. Its great spires had collapsed into towering heaps of rubble. Its cobbled streets were clogged with debris from a thousand broken structures.

Standing upon the threshold of the fallen city, Pandora blew out a long, slow breath. Once, this place must have gleamed with the light of gaslamps like those in Kronos's vault. Once, she imagined, intricate stonework upon soaring buildings had created a maze of grandeur, shadowing streets, and striking awe into all who beheld the wonder of Vulgeth.

Even now, looking upon its corpse, still the city struck her almost breathless. Rather than head towards the city's heart, Pandora skirted the periphery. Where she could catch glimpses beyond the mounds of broken stone, she realised the streets pitched inward, as if the polis had collapsed upon itself, imploding into a rent at its very heart.

The thought chilled her, had her looking over her shoulder, as if she might turn back. Naught forced her to tread into this defiled, accursed place. Naught save herself. She could, even now, use the Box and flee from here.

Tempting though that sounded, instead, she pressed onward, threading around debris, and into the husk of Vulgeth. The reek of a tomb washed over her, growing stronger the further she pressed in toward the heart of this place.

If there were answers here, she would find them. Whatever had befallen this place, she would uncover it, and through it, find the way forwards. Always forwards.

There had to be a solution. There had to.

Kronos had claimed all of this had begun in the city of Vulgeth. Yet sifting through the rubble, walking the dilapidated streets, Pandora could not shake the creeping sense that something vile had seeped into the very stones of this place. Once, she might have assumed the sensation a product of her own nerves, but she could hardly dismiss the existence of the Otherworldly, given all she had seen.

Some catastrophe had destroyed Vulgeth, that much was plain. But was the unshakeable sense of the land being poisoned a result of the cataclysm or something deeper? A rot that lurked at the very heart of this fallen city?

At the heart of the ruin lay a vast pit, as if some monstrous hand had reached up from beneath the Earth to yank Vulgeth down into the depths. The destruction had ripped the walls off buildings, torn at foundations, and sent Gaia-alone-knew how much broken stone spilling into the black abyss.

Nearby, a shattered wall revealed the interior of a structure, in the cellar of which lay the remnants of a library.

"That's something," she mumbled, scrambling over to the ruined side. She wended her careful way amid the debris. Most of the tomes lay in heaps where they had tumbled from the shelves, though some few others sat splayed on the ground as if, even in the city's final moments, someone had paused to read. A blanket of dust covered everything, so thick she imagined none had walked here in centuries.

Kneeling beside one of the opened tomes, Pandora blew the dust off, then wiped what remained away with her palm, careful of pages turned brittle with age. The script below had faded, nor did it seem to be written in any of the numerous languages she knew. Maybe a slight resemblance to Phlegran, but far from enough for her to translate without more time and study. Besides, with the amount of damage done here, and the ravages of time, she doubted she'd find aught resembling complete records.

And still, still she could not help herself from combing through tome after tome, seeking any clue that might aid her. A single grain of Truth that might offer her a chance of crossing the chasm of Fate that lay before her.

PANDORA SPENT hours in the library, enough time to deduce the meaning of a few words, to guess at others. After all that time, sat amid piles of books, cross-referencing one to the next, she had little else to show for it save an aching neck and fatigued eyes. Following a long stretch, she rose.

Maybe she could find more information elsewhere in the city. If not, she could always return here and start again. Her growling stomach reminded her of her hunger, so she took to gnawing on the last of her smoked rabbit meat. It was cold and chewy, far from something one might describe as palatable, but it would mute the burbling in her empty belly, at least for a while.

Twilight had settled upon the city, so she would probably need to find a place to shelter soon, little though she felt like sleeping in this blighted corpse of a city. She made her way down darkened alleys, seeking any structure that looked sound enough to use as a base.

On rounding a corner, she abruptly drew up short, sucking in a muffled breath at the sight before her.

Monstrous roots had ripped through the cobbles, splintered buildings, and created an impassable barrier along the street. Dirt and rocks clung to frayed bits of fibre, as if this plant had erupted from the ground rather than grown out over the course of ages. As her gaze roamed over the maze of roots, she hissed a second surprise. Corpses lay entwined by the root tendrils, some crushed to pulp, others impaled. Still more seemed swept up as if by a storm, held frozen by bands of wood, some thick around as a Gígas's chest.

Why hadn't the passing of ages turned these bodies to dust? She drew closer, examining the macabre spectacle from multiple angles. She hadn't seen any other bodies in the city. Did the roots themselves prevent decay? But then, some of the corpses did show signs of rot, foetid stenches wafting off them now she was close enough to catch the reek over the general putrescence that saturated the ruined city.

Maybe this plant had—

One of the corpses' eyes popped open, empty sockets glinting with an Otherworldly red gleam. It bared fangs at her, hissing, even as it reached for her with clawed fingers.

With a yelp, Pandora toppled over backwards, landed on her arse, then scooted away without the least concern for dignity.

The creature remained held fast within the root cage, straining toward her, yet making no progress in its attempts to escape. Panting —and fighting those first twinges of pain in her chest—Pandora scanned the rest of the plant. Some few of the other corpses had also turned to leer at her with rubescent gazes, mouths agape in hunger for her flesh.

Pandora scooted even farther away before rising to her feet. What in Nyx's bosom?

24

———

KIRKE

1550 Silver Age

"*I*f we cannot risk changing the past for fear of rippling repercussions," Kirke said, "then my presence here serves no purpose."

"To say that, if Fate cannot be changed, we have no purpose in it, seems an oversimplification," Pandora replied, pacing alongside Kirke in the shadows of the courtyard, well away from Agenor's guests. "We cannot change what will happen—perhaps not even if we tried—but that does not mean we cannot affect it. Or be affected by it."

Indeed, because this night had already flensed Kirke down to the pith, and Zeus had not yet showed up. He would, though, any moment, with Mother alongside him. He would come for Europa and, as Pandora had confirmed, for Pandora's young self. The woman admitted she had been taken and sold as a slave on Atlantis and had thus come to meet Prometheus. More than that, Pandora refused to explain, whether out of pain or further concern for the timeline, Kirke did not know.

Either way, her impotence here made witnessing this seem like crawling through a briar patch, each passing moment a new laceration upon her soul.

A commotion rose up in the grand hall, and Pandora strode for it, perhaps unable to help herself from watching the horror of her own childhood. Trauma drew the eye, even when one might not wish to see.

Yeah, but Kirke did not belong here. With every gaze drawn toward the growing tumult, she withdrew the Box and once more began twisting panels. Maybe, if she got just the right combination, maybe she could find her way back to her own time.

A pleasant self-delusion.

"Kirke?" Mother asked, ushering her inside and embracing her. "I thought you'd gone to see your sister in Kronion." A tremor, almost suppressed, ran through Mother, noticeable only because of their contact. A reminder that Persephone had been a close friend to Mother, even as Io was to Kirke.

And still Gaia refused to swallow Kirke. If she took her own life, if she cast herself into the sea, could she abrogate this duty?

Her voice refused to work, but when Mother's gaze drifted down to the phial, Kirke pressed it into her hand.

"What's this?"

"Yeah, um. It's a lust potion."

When next Kirke awakened, she found herself beneath the cliffs of Thebes, lying like a drunk in the harbour. This led her, of course, to stop by a wine vendor who proved all too happy to offer a Titan lady a bowl of his local vintage.

Fortified with the pleasant warmth—though it served to remind of her empty belly—she'd asked who ruled here.

"Old Kadmus yet rules, for more than fifty years now. People claim he's got the blood of gods to have lived this long already." That, or perhaps his wife, the Nymph Harmonia, had shared a drop or two of her Ambrosia with her beloved husband. Her father Zeus would have had her head if he learnt of it, but still, Kirke could almost see it happening. People did mad things for love.

So, then. Demeter had granted Thebes to Kadmus not long after Zeus had taken Europa, Kadmus's sister, which meant Kirke had wound up some fifty years after she'd left Tyros. Bringing her closer to her own time, true, though still several centuries off.

Would Kadmus recognise Kirke now, after so much time? Would he help her? To survive, she needed drachmae to survive long enough to figure this Box out, and circumstances had prevented her from asking Kadmus's father Agenor for much of aught. Strange, though, to think that, for her, she had seen Kadmus a couple of hours back, and for him decades had passed.

More than a bit maudlin, Kirke climbed the cliffside steps up to Thebes proper, then made her way to the palace of Kadmus, which, unlike those of his Titan predecessors, lay below the acropolis. Whether Kadmus chose to live among his people or Demeter had forbidden a mortal to live on the divine space, she didn't know. Huh, actually, if fifty years had passed, Demeter might well be dead now, slain in the Gigantomachy. Had that happened yet?

Yeah, Kirke should have had more than one bowl of wine. Her mind spun in vain attempts to reconcile the moil her life had become.

The steward announced her with all pomposity of a peacock, such that Kirke had to wonder whether his pride in his own position outstripped his belief in the lie of Titan divinity. Either way, Kirke found herself escorted into a lounge where Harmonia, rather than Kadmus, waited for her. She'd met the Nymph a handful of times over the ages, never with more than a few words for her. Though Harmonia bore no blame for her parentage, as Zeus's bastard child, she remained a hair closer to that lineage than Kirke preferred to cross. In truth, she avoided the whole of the Kroniad genos when she could. Athene had been the exception to that ...

"A woman whose works destroyed the life of my son has no right to name me sister."

Some words carved themselves into one's heart, wounds that never ceased to weep.

Queen Harmonia rose from her divan and threw a perfunctory embrace around Kirke, patting her back. "Welcome to Thebes, daughter of Helios. Your coming is fortuitous indeed."

"Yeah, I mean, I try for that. You know, spreading fortune everywhere I walk. It kind of bubbles out of my sandals. Just *poof*, here's some ... good luck. Um, what do you mean, actually?"

Harmonia snorted with the daintiness of an amused bunny. "We'll speak of such things later, I'm sure. You seem to have come a long way and must be hungry."

"Yeah, feels like it took me years to get here." And she still hadn't had aught to eat, so ... "Feels like I could down a bite or two. Maybe a couple of pigs. Or whales, or something."

With a too-knowing smile, Harmonia laid a hand upon Kirke's back and guided her to another divan, then summoned servants who carried out platters of dates and figs, followed by cabbage and then roast pork.

"We're out of whale," Harmonia said.

No, but they'd had pig already on the fire it seemed. Had Oracular insight told Harmonia she would need it? If so, if her gifts were strong enough, could she learn the truth about Kirke's presence here? Had she figured it out *already*? Or was the idea of someone bouncing around through history too absurd for Harmonia to grasp onto, no matter what her visions unfurled before her?

Either way, with a relish she'd not found in years, Kirke tore into the pork, giving little care for the hot juices dribbling down her chin. Prim and proper eating manners didn't apply to the famished, or they shouldn't, anyway. "You wanted something from me," Kirke said around a mouthful of meat.

Another servant waddled in, her arms laden with a heavy

amphora from which she filled bowls of wine to wash down the food, one for each of the Nymphs. Kirke took both, one in each hand, flashing a wicked grin at Harmonia, though the other woman smiled with indulgence and motioned for her servant to bring another.

Once Kirke had thrown back both bowls of wine—and covered her mouth to hide a small belch—Harmonia reclined on the divan beside her. "You're an oneiromancer like your mother."

"Ha, not even close to her mastery." Despite the light buzz, Kirke found herself craving another bowl. Should she grab the amphora and pour one more? "Yeah, I have some talent, I suppose."

Harmonia laid a hand upon Kirke's knee, a bit too familiar. "Though an Oracle, my gifts remain limited. I cannot uncover the answer to a question that troubles me. Even our adviser Tiresias fails to find the truth, though foreboding almost crushes him."

Oh. On the other hand, maybe Kirke was a bit *too* buzzed for this conversation. Though glimpses of the future seeped into her dreams, she couldn't control it and most oft could not say whether what she beheld was even truth or metaphor. Or nightmare. And since she'd started using the damn Box, they were only getting worse. "I can't just pull answers to specific questions out of my dreams. I mean, you have to go to Delphi for prophecies."

"I'm not looking for answers about the future," Harmonia said. "My youngest, Semele, is with child, soon to give birth. She says a man came to her in the night, over her balcony, though I cannot see how, and she does not know him."

Right, and Thebes couldn't well have her princess whelping a bastard child with no idea who the father was. Harmonia must think only a Titan or a demigod could have reached the girl, and losing her 'virtue' to such as them was less shameful than to a Man. "And you think, if I got into her dreams, I could uncover his identity."

"Tiresias foresaw your coming and believes it presages something. My family has …" Her grip tightened upon Kirke's knee. "We've faced more than our share of misfortune, Kirke, and it has worn upon my husband, left him stretched thin almost to breaking. I need to offer him some answer so that he …"

The battle the Nymph fought to steady her voice had Kirke wondering if she, rather than Kadmus, had not become the brittle one. "I can try," Kirke said, clutching the other Nymph's hand. "I can try." She cleared her throat. "Yeah, though I could use a few things from you. Some drachmae, first and foremost. I find myself far from home and somewhat on the wrong side of fortune. Too, a place to stay and a change of clothes would not prove amiss."

"All you need will be yours, Kirke," Harmonia said. "Help my family."

Funny, Kirke had wanted to help Kadmus's family back when Zeus took his sister. Wanted to and realised history would not permit her kindness.

THE PRINCESS SEMELE WAS YOUNG, not more than seventeen Kirke would have guessed, and possessed of a grace that had permeated her chambers, even with the girl but lying abed, hand upon her bulging abdomen. A fortnight, at most a month, and the child would enter this world, born a bastard like Kirke herself. Unlike Kirke, however, unless a Titan father claimed the child, it would find itself hard-pressed in life.

Almost as hard-pressed as Semele would, bereft of her so-called virtue.

The girl's bed divan did not allow room for the both of them, so Kirke had told servants to lay mats alongside it and now settled down beside Semele.

"You're going to sleep with me?" the princess asked.

"Yeah." Wait, that didn't sound right. "I mean, no! Er, sleep with you ... in the room, we'll both be sleeping. Like asleep together. In the same dream." Because that sounded so much better. "Just try to rest and relax. I'm going to try to slip inside you and it won't hurt if you ..." Oh, damn. That really did not sound the way she meant it. Damn words. Kirke hated trying to make words fit together out loud. "Ahem.

Princess Semele, I'm going to try to share your dreams and direct them."

So Kirke could watch Semele getting seduced and bedded. Because that sounded much better.

In truth, it proved somewhat difficult to sleep beside the princess, knowing what she intended. Whilst Mother had trained her mind to master oneiromancy, Kirke's own came to her more or less of its own accord. Still, she focused her mind, running a mantra through her head to build a connection with Semele, until at last, she found herself not watching the princess but rather having become her.

Dressed in a simple shift despite the impending winter, she stood upon the balcony, wind ruffling the garment against her legs and prickling her flesh. There was a luxurious sensuality in the chill, a promise of life, leaving her senses tingled with anticipation.

In front of the moon soared an eagle. Or no, not an eagle, but a pegasus, Kirke realised, banking and turning, until it flew some distance above the balcony. A shadow dropped down, down from above, plunging onto the landing outside the room and landing in a crouch. It rose, a hooded figure, and Kirke felt herself swallow a yelp.

The figure rose, ice-blue eyes shining within the canopy of shadows framing his face.

No.

"You are a goddess," the figure cooed.

No!

Yet Kirke felt herself flush and titter, giving in to banal flattery that ought not to have swayed a simpleton. Zeus's rough fingers stroked her cheek before grasping her chin. His grip tightened, his other hand going to her shift. A single yank ripped it away, and Kirke was shoved up against the wall.

No! Fucking no, this was his own granddaughter, Nyx damn him!

She felt it as the King of Olympus slipped inside her, and though her body thrilled, Kirke fought it down, gagging within, screaming against the bounds of her mind for escape. The connection refused to break, however. Panic surged as her soul lurched in silent shrieks despite the moans of her body, despite her hands grasping in salacious desire.

Not this, not *him*! She had to focus, had to pull herself out of—

§

HER OWN RETCHING hurtled her awake as wine and half-digested pork spilt over Kirke's shift. With a violent groan she rolled over to the side, ready to heave up what remained in her stomach, though naught more billowed forth. Then a gasping breath and a mangled sob.

"What!" Semele asked. "What?"

Oh, Nyx's fathomless darkness. Oh, Hyperion's blistering arse.

Wiping her mouth with the back of her hand, Kirke slumped down and looked at Semele, heart torn apart by pity. Maybe she ought not to even tell her. Maybe no one ought to know they had been made a party to such violations of nature.

But Harmonia had needed to know, and did she not owe Semele the truth? The poor woman—demigod, Kirke supposed—had no idea what had been done to her. The child had thrilled at her midnight liaison, giving in to pleasures of the flesh without the least idea who had so violated her. Though the king had known, Kirke had no doubt.

"It was ... Zeus who lay with you."

Disbelief in her eyes lost out to a spreading radiance, a curling up of her lips. "My child will be a son of the King of the Gods." Her chittering giggle slashed through Kirke's nerves like a sword, and she fled in horror, wondering just how long it would take Semele to remember Zeus was her grandfather. That he had raped her grandmother Elektra.

His lusts never ended, did they?

§

Rumour buzzed through Thebes with the speed of the zephyr, and it seemed all the polis knew Zeus had spawned another demigod. The girl herself continued to brag of it, though her mother had warned her against drawing attention, for Hera did not take well to such offences. The queen could not vent her grievances upon her husband, but they had all heard of her vengeances against Zeus's mortal lovers and demigod offspring.

Women torn apart, limbs cast into the sea, children fed to sharks or offered up to Pontus in sacrifice.

And Semele boasted.

It was not Hera who came to Thebes, however, but Zeus himself, his pegasus descending upon the palace unannounced save for the rumbling thunderclouds that preceded him. His arrival sent the servants scrambling to accommodate him, even as Kirke clung to a column and hid from his gaze. The king burst through the doors to the palace and Kirke trailed behind, apprehension for Semele over-ruling her desire to be as far from Zeus as possible.

She came round to Semele's room and found the doors shut, the king already within.

"I don't need this now!" his roar came, bellowing from within Semele's chambers. "You were meant to open your legs, not your fucking mouth, you bitch!"

As she approached the doors, Kirke's hair stood on end, the air crackling with unspent energy an instant before the blast ripped through the chamber, its roar deafening.

Her heart and mind refused to parse what had happened. For a long time—or it felt long, at least—she remained mired in place, staring at the door. When she noticed the screaming within, she could not say how long it had gone on for.

The doors were flung wide, drawing her from her stupor, and Kirke beheld Semele's maid, ashen faced and trembling. She raced into the room, knowing what she'd find but unable to stop herself. Semele lay hurled against the wall, charred flesh smouldering, blood oozing from a thousand rents in skin and muscle turned to ash. Her eyes had melted, and her hair had sizzled away into dust. Though it defied reason—and mercy—the girl rasped a pained, wheezing breath.

"Get the midwife," Kirke managed, hoping the maid would listen. Despairing, she dropped beside the princess.

SEMELE DID NOT LIVE LONG ENOUGH for the midwife to arrive, and perhaps that was a blessing, for her existence must have become utter torment. Still, the midwife cut the babe from her and found it drew a wailing breath. A demigod son of the King of Olympus, pulled from the ruination he had made of the princess.

Looking at the child, Harmonia fell to her knees, weeping. The Nymph beat impotent fists against the floor, and Kirke had to wonder if the Oracle had known something like this must unfold. Naught Kirke had done had made aught any better here.

She could think of naught to do save join Harmonia in her tears. Maybe despair was all that had ever lain before her.

Such was her lot. Such was the lot of all Nymphs.

25

THESEUS

726 Bronze Age

Though he had loved the thrill of adventure, Theseus too found the comforts of palace life much to his liking. He slept upon a padded divan, draped in the smoothest blanket he had ever laid hands upon. His new room was painted with a vibrant fresco depicting the coronation of King Pandion I, the son of the Olympian Athene. His floors were laid with plush carpets woven in what the servants told him was the latest Phoenikian style. He supped on pheasant and fish and succulent dates and drank the finest of wines. He bathed in heated pools in echoing marmoreal halls. Servant girls massaged his muscles with scented oils and no few of them came eagerly to his bed.

One, a girl his own age by the name of Sofia, hailed from Phlegra, and wrapt in naught save a blanket, she lingered in his chambers one languid afternoon. Earlier, during one of those oil massages, they'd spoken of her homeland and his journey there. Afterward, he'd asked if she wished to join him in his chambers.

"I would not be permitted to refuse," she had said with what he took for feigned demureness.

Her words had punched through his gut like the thrust of a blade, leaving him breathless. Had any of the others he had invited felt they had no choice save to accept his invitations? Did they believe, as slaves or servants in the palace, the prince had claim to their very bodies? Whilst that was no doubt the law, it left a queasiness in his stomach which he found he could not still.

Theseus had left her, apologising for the encounter, and telling her she would never be under any such obligation to him. But Sofia had later come to him herself, and though a certain pensiveness had gripped her, she assured him it was not from any lack of desire to lie with him. When she'd begun to disrobe, well, Theseus had not been enough of a fool to pass his chance.

Now, though, something creased her features, and she sat there, staring not at Theseus but at the unlit hearth, as if something lay within its quiescent embers.

Did she regret coming here? Hades's Underworld, Theseus had thought he'd made clear he had not meant to compel this of her. "Are you cold? I can kindle the fire if you wish." It was a banal and useless thing to ask, but he could think of naught better.

The girl looked to him now, clenched her eyes shut a moment, and shuddered.

Still naked himself, Theseus scrambled from the divan to her side and gripped her shoulder. "What happened? Was this not what you wanted? Was it not ... pleasurable?"

Her eyes, when they met his gaze, didn't even seem to register that. Sofia swallowed. "You know Damastes?" Her voice trembled, thick with unspoken fears.

Theseus released her and nodded slowly. "My cousin, yes. The elder son of Pallas, who sought to be my father's heir."

"He is not content to surrender that birthright."

Theseus caught himself glowering and, rather than risk frightening Sofia, forced his face to placidity. "It was never his in the first place."

"It would be if you were dead." Unbidden, the glower returned, and Sofia flinched but pressed on. "My brother works as a herald for them. He told me the brothers, the whole of the Pallantides, plan to ambush you the night before the festival. They will slay you in secret and leave King Aegeus with no other heir save Damastes." Sofia swallowed down a choking sob. "My brother told me Damastes has the cruellest of predilections. Men who vex him, he has them brought to his home and bids them spend the night. If they are short, he takes them to a large divan, and claiming it not the right size, stretches them upon a rack to fit. If a tall man comes, Damastes takes him to a child-sized divan, and when the man's feet overhang it, he lops them off. H-he ..." Tears dribbled down her cheek now.

Not every bandit preyed upon the roads, it would seem. Some dressed in fine khitons and soft sandals, bedecked themselves in gold ornaments, and hid behind a civilised veneer.

"The festival is two days from now," Theseus said.

Sofia nodded.

Theseus cupped her cheek and she clutched his hand. "You may have saved my life. Go and tell your brother not to return to his employer. Here." Theseus rose, fetched a bag of drachmae from his trunk, and handed it to her. "Find somewhere to stay until such things are resolved, one way or the other. If you see me on the festival, if I yet live, you'll know it's safe, and I will ask my father for your freedom." He could have seen her freed now, but it might give away too much to Damastes and his brothers. The Pallantides must think their plan unrevealed, or they would adjust and he'd lose this advantage.

PALLAS HAD fifteen sons from three different women. All grown men and all warriors. Theseus might have liked well enough his odds against Damastes alone, or perhaps against him and a few of his brothers. But against fifteen men, even with the element of surprise, he misliked his chances. No one, maybe not even Herakles himself, could win against such foul odds.

Fortunate, then, that some few of the Argonauts had lingered in Athenai these past many days. The Argosians, awaiting the arrival of their own ship to carry the princes home, had taken hospitality from Aegeus and decided to stay and enjoy the festival. Thus, Theseus came to them in their chambers and found not only Kastor and Pollux but Amphiaraos and Talaus as well. From the looks the four of them cast his way, all had expected him, and Theseus was not certain whether he ought to praise or curse the seer for that.

Arms folded over his chest and back leaning against the wall beside the window, Pollux smirked with his usual arrogance. "Come to us for aid on a matter?"

Theseus glanced behind himself to make certain no servants lingered in the halls that might overhear. Thanks to Sofia, he had information from inside Pallas's household. He could not assume the Pallantides would not have spies of their own in the royal palace. "The sons of Pallas scheme to murder me. Did any of them intend to challenge me with honour, I'd have gladly faced them. But this—they plan an ambush, with fifteen of them against me alone."

Talaus chuckled, fingers tracing the wrap along his sword's grip. "So, you thought, perhaps, it would be best to even the odds, yes? Five on fifteen does make for a *somewhat* fair fight."

"Sure," Pollux said. "You each take one man, and I'll manage the other eleven."

Was he really a son of Zeus, like Herakles or Perseus? Or was his bravado mere affectation or arrogance?

"You'll come with me then?" Theseus asked.

It was Kastor who answered. "We fought the boar together, yes? Sailed the forbidding waters of the Axeinos and braved all the vileness that unfolded in and after Kolchis. However it all turned out, I doubt any of us would turn our backs upon any other now."

Theseus nodded, the knot in his chest loosening. "Thank you, friends."

NIGHT FELL, and with sunset came an incessant drizzle that proved enough to drive indoors all but those most desperate for a drink. Rain slickened the cobbles and had the gutters running with filth, but Theseus supposed it would help with the stench in the long run. Either way, he had not quite accustomed himself to living in such a large polis, and he found clusters of buildings rose like unfamiliar boulders on a mountain path. How easy to get lost, wandering this reeking maze. Though he was grateful the citizenry was not about this night—the warm light of oil lamps glowed in many windows, rooms within bursting with chatter and camaraderie he would have preferred to take part in—the emptiness in the roads lent Athenai an eerie atmosphere that had him casting furtive glances about himself.

Praise Zeus that the Argosian princes and their followers had chosen to join him, at least. Young Amphiaraos led the way and seemed, despite hailing from Argos, to know these streets better than Theseus himself. Was that Oracular insight or the mere fact he had more experience with cities in general?

A hand fell on his shoulder and squeezed, and Theseus looked back to see Kastor offering a reassuring nod. Perhaps the prince mistook Theseus's apprehensions for nerves about the coming battle. A surge of pride had him wanting to protest, to claim it was the strange maze, not the conflict that unnerved him. Theseus misliked feeling lost, that was for certain. But any objection he offered would have made him look more foolish, so he simply returned the nod and pressed on.

When they came at last to the Pallantide estate west of the Colonnades, all four of his companions gathered up and looked to his face. Awaiting his orders, or just making certain he wanted to follow through? It was not murder when these men intended to waylay and kill him. A thought Theseus had run through his mind, over and over, all the way here. They were the ones planning murder.

This was not murder.

"Amphiaraos and Talaus, go around the back. Drive them toward me," he said, "but try to ensure they cannot approach more than one or two at a time." And what would the populace say of this night? That the prince had broken into their house and slaughtered them in the night. "Let none of the Pallantides escape to speak of this."

The rush of adrenaline muddled thoughts, even as it sharpened instinct. Pollux kicked in the estate door with such force the hinges ripped clean from the stonework. A shout went up among the household, cries of alarm. Servants ran amok in their frenzy to escape. The Pallantides dashed one way or the next, each striving for knives or clubs or, in a few cases, actual xiphe. By unspoken accord, Theseus and the Gemini twins allowed them to arm themselves. He had not come here for coldblooded murder but to thwart an attempt at such a crime.

The first of the sons of Pallas came at him, fast, though his slight wobble meant drink must have dulled his reflexes. The man hurled an amphora at Theseus's head. Theseus ducked under the projectile and it shattered on the wall above the doorframe. His attacker tried to tackle him, but Theseus braced himself, caught him in a pankration hold, and drove his blade between the man's ribs. His attacker's eyes widened in disbelieving horror as his blood burst over Theseus and drenched his khiton. The inexplicable urge to apologise rose in Theseus, mad though he knew it was.

He jerked his blade free as more of the brothers rushed him. The Gemini had fanned out, doing as he asked and slowing the sons of Pallas such that no more than a handful could close in on Theseus where he fought in the heart of the vestibule. Another man swung a club, and Theseus danced from it, then twisted out of the way of a knife thrust from a different brother. His backswing ripped through the knifeman's cheekbone, and the poor brute fell, shrieking and clutching his ruined face.

The club wielder swung again, and Theseus was not fast enough. The weapon clipped his left arm, sending bolts of lightning shooting up it, leaving it dangling in agony. The man moved in to smash his skull and Theseus rammed his xiphos up into his foe's throat. A geyser of blood erupted over Theseus. It stung his eyes and filled his mouth with the taste of copper.

Half-blind, he yanked free his sword and spun as another knifeman swiped at him. Theseus jumped back but earned himself a gash along his chest in the process. With a bellow, Pollux crashed into the man, and both the demigod and the Pallantide tumbled into a heap. Given Pollux's strength, Theseus doubted the prince would need help. Indeed, already, he heard the sound of crunching bone.

Then Damastes himself was on him, face slick with blood that did not look to be his own. The eldest Pallantide held a xiphos, a crimson droplet pooling at its tip. As he moved, the drop fell and splashed upon the mosaic floor. Then he lunged, making a vicious swipe for Theseus's neck.

Theseus parried and fell back. If he could have used his left arm, he'd have scrubbed away the blood stinging his eyes. It was hard to counter Damastes like this, and the Pallantide kept him on the defensive. Iron rang as their swords clashed again and again. Damastes pressed his advantage, faced limned with what seemed an almost lascivious excitement at the thought of Theseus's death. With something between snarl and cackle, he thrust, intent to skewer Theseus.

But Theseus rolled to one side and swiped with his own xiphos. The blade bit into Damastes's shin, sheared through the bone, and lopped his leg clean off. The twisted bastard pitched over sideways, shrieking, and fell into a bloody heap.

Still prone, Theseus hurled himself atop Damastes and rammed his xiphos into the man's ribs again and again. A third time, even.

Until his breath was spent and his adrenaline ran out and he was left to collapse upon his arse, panting. He looked upon the chaos he had wrought here. Fifteen men lay dead or dying, their bodies horribly broken. Bones were snapped and limbs hacked off. Servants and slaves were huddled in the corners, weeping, and screaming, and trying to shrink into inoffensive little balls in the hopes the marauders would spare them. Blood and viscera lay strewn across the mosaic floor, imbruing the tiles crimson. The whole vestibule stank of shit and terror and perhaps an undercurrent of vomit.

Theseus, too, found himself suddenly inclined to retch. Bile scorched his throat at the sight of what he'd participated in. Amphiaraos came staggering over, hand pressed against a severe gouge upon his cheek. A hair to one side and he'd have lost an eye. Theseus took stock of his comrades, saw they all lived, and tried to unclench the fist wrapt around his heart.

Talaus moved to check on his future son-in-law, though Amphiaraos waved him away. The Argosian looked back at Theseus. "No witnesses, yes?"

A half dozen servants were backed into the far corners, all stricken with absolute horror at what had befallen their masters. Maybe, like Sofia's brother, they had overheard the Pallantides's plans. Maybe, if a case came before the courts, they would back Theseus's claim that he had acted in self-defence. Or maybe they would speak about how he and his Argonaut allies had burst in here in the night and murdered fifteen brothers.

Expedience demanded he order them slain as well. Should anyone save the Argonauts walk from this place, it could turn ill for him later, he knew. To say naught of straining relations with Argos if anyone realised the Argosian princes had aided in such a slaughter.

Theseus opened his mouth to order their deaths, much though he hated himself for it. The words caught on his tongue and refused to pass his lips. They needed to die, though innocent of any crime. But if he let them live ... "We ..."

Before he could give the command, Pollux grabbed one of the servants and smashed him against the wall, splattering it with brains and blood.

Theseus's heart caught in his throat.

More screams and chaos and blood, though it was over faster this time.

And Theseus watched, paralysed, afraid he would never know for certain if he could have uttered such an order himself. Afraid he would never know what choice he might have made.

INTERLUDE: MEDEA

731 Bronze Age

along the Strait of Korinth, on the outskirts of Troezen, Medea and Jason had raised their estate. Though the glorified farmhouse paled in comparison to the Qulha Palace of her youth, at least here Medea remained the absolute mistress of her domain. With little Tisander clutched to her breast, Medea sat upon the stones of the boundary wall, watching the path for Jason's return. He'd been gone overlong, she thought, having headed to Korinth with a pair of their labourers several days back, intent to trade the best of the harvest at market.

Their lands, though modest in her estimation, still allowed them to raise several groves of olive trees. The oil their workers produced kept her larder and wine cellar both well stocked year-round, and the olives themselves had come out particularly succulent this season.

The babe stirred himself and Medea gave him her breast, still watching, as if she could bring Jason plodding back by force of will. Behind the wall, she could hear the twins cavorting. By the sounds of it, they once more were Argonauts, reliving their father's so-called adventures. Jason had named Thessalus for Theseus, and his 'uncle' remained ever the boy's favourite, even if Medea had never shaken the sense that Theseus harboured a secret disdain for her and perhaps even for Jason. Her son bemoaned that Theseus had vanished from his throne some time back, though the boy had not even known the prince of Athenai. Rather, Thessalus's young mind had snatched upon Jason's tales of the warrior and woven them into illusions of remembrance.

It was true that Theseus had seen to it his grandfather granted Jason this Troezen estate, after they'd been driven from Iolkos. But Theseus had looked at Medea askance, as if Jason had not asked—pleaded upon bent knee, even—that she help him revenge himself upon King Pelias. The crusty old wretch had, on believing Jason dead in Kolchis, forced Jason's father Aeson to suicide. Jason's mother, Polymede, too had taken her own life out of grief.

Polymede had been Autolykus's daughter, and the famed thief, upon learning of her fate, would have joined Jason had he stormed Pelias's hall in Iolkos. Maybe many of the Argonauts would have come. Or maybe not. So many had thought Medea vile, she knew, for what she'd done to her brother, no matter that Aunt Kirke had purified them for the crime. They wanted as little as possible to do with either her or, because of her, Jason himself. She felt their stares, their harsh judgments raking over her skin, though she held herself like stone, impervious to such abrasions.

Jason would not settle for killing Pelias. He rightly blamed the king for the deaths of his parents, and for sending him to Kolchis in the first place. He blamed him for all the woes of his life, and he begged Medea to make the man suffer. Who was she to deny the earnest pleas of her grief-stricken husband? *How* was she to deny him, when her very life in this strange land hung so precariously upon his favour?

So, she had done it. She had convinced the ageing king's insipid daughters she could restore their father's youth. That she, using her Art, could galvanise his flesh and give him the vitality of a Titan. The credulous pair bought the lie, even going so far to do her bidding as to dismember vile Pelias, that she might boil his limbs in a cauldron before "re-assembling" them.

Pelias's son, Akastos, on learning the truth, had turned ashen and driven her and Jason from Iolkos, denying Jason his claim to the throne.

Medea's husband had blamed her, when so many turned against him for the horror of the crime, forgetting he had *demanded* horror, and she had but delivered it. And by then, she was carrying the twins. Medea had never shaken the sense, had she not been heavy with Jason's sons, Theseus might have refused to shelter her, self-righteous little shit that he was.

Tisander grew fussy once more and Medea rocked him. When he still wouldn't settle, she huffed, rose, and began to pace along the top of the wall.

Well, nigh five years had passed, Theseus was probably feeding the worms on some foreign shore, and Medea remained.

She was no queen. Jason's promise of her future had been as hollow as so many of his boasts. Still, she could not remain cross with him for long. Besides, they had the farm and wealth enough. And thanks to Kirke, Father had never found them with his Art. Medea supposed she ought to feel grateful the Moirai had allotted her at least that much.

From the shouts, Thessalus and Alkimenes's games had grown heated and Medea considered checking in on the boys, though Jason encouraged their roughness and competition. But now, at last, she saw her husband's approach, plodding down the dirt path from Korinth. His labourers led the empty cart some distance behind, which meant he must have sold every amphora of olive oil.

The trip had gone well.

Medea ran her tongue over her teeth, quirking a smile. After several days away, and a successful run to the market, Jason would no doubt find himself amorous tonight. He'd not seen the new khiton she'd bought herself from that trader yesterday. Perhaps, after supper, she could surprise him and let things run their course. A pleasant warmth rose in her cheeks. Yes, she could scarcely wait for evening and the intimacy it promised.

WITH THE TWINS ASLEEP—FINALLY—AND Tisander snoring in his cradle, Medea had lounged upon her divan, watching Jason meander about their private room. He was not a man to delay over-long in seeking out his pleasures, and thus his occupation with whatever troubled his mind might not have been feigned. Perhaps events in Korinth had not gone as smoothly as she had first thought. Though she longed to ask, Medea forced herself to silence, waiting. Watching. Her husband would broach the topic when it suited him.

Without taking her gaze off Jason, Medea stroked Tisander's cheek inside the cradle. His rhythmic breathing always brought such a comfort.

Jason paced about, undressing. He bothered to hang his belt in its reserved spot, though most oft she was the one to pick it up from the floor and put it away. He set his rings upon the table beside his divan with reserved deliberateness, before sitting and tucking his sandals in their proper place beneath his bed. One more thing he was wont, on most nights, to leave for her to tend to.

Barefoot, he then plodded over to the amphora upon their low table and poured them both a cup of Korinthian red. Medea found herself now apt to burst with questions—and nascent concern, for when did he ever before act thus? —but she accepted the goblet he offered without comment.

Finally, with a great huff, he collapsed upon his couch and threw back his wine in a single gulp before letting his goblet clatter upon the table. The noise drew a wince from Medea, though Tisander gave no sign of stirring. Still, if Jason woke the babe, she'd have some choice words for him.

Looking at her now, Jason mopped his lips with the back of his hand.

The silence had grown unbearable. Her resolve to let him speak first melted like clarified butter in a cauldron. "What happened?"

Jason cleared his throat. "I had an audience with King Kreon." After a momentary pause, he added, "of Korinth." In case he thought her fool enough to assume he meant the recently re-instated ruler of Thebes. "He consented to a most profitable proposal of mine."

Medea leant forwards, leaving her own half-drained goblet on the table, her smile returning. If Jason had secured a contract with the king of Korinth, they'd be needing to harvest more olives than their fields had ever produced. It would mean hiring new labourers, maybe even trying to purchase a grove or two from the neighbouring farms. The logistics of such an undertaking would certainly keep the both of them busy enough in the coming months, preparing for the next planting season. But already, she could see the streams of drachmae rolling in, pouring over the hills, and filling their estate. One day, maybe she would even once more find the luxuries of her youth available to her.

The aristoi of Korinth would come calling to see her grand estate, and Medea might once more enjoy the society of high ladies. Oh, before that, she'd need new tapestries for the hall. Those worn, faded decorations Jason had bought her from that overcharging Theban merchant would never do now. Not if she was expecting the wives of the great men of Korinth to sit and admire her home.

"Korinth has suffered a steady decline in the centuries since the death of Hephaistos, you know. The whole Kreiad genos has begun to falter, some claim. Kreon fair jumped at the chance to unite his bloodline with the line of the kings of Phlegra, you see."

A chill she could not quite explain ran up her spine. This was not about trade deals. And, she decided abruptly, she was going to need to finish that cup of wine. "He wants to marry his daughter off to one of the boys," she said after taking a long swig of the red.

Jason scoffed as though she were a fool. "You'd have one of our sons marry a woman *older* than himself? Even were Kreon keen to wait years for Thessalus or Alkimenes to come of age, they would be mocked the whole of their lives for marrying Glauke. Men would say a woman ruled them." Another snicker. "They'd claim the wife kept her husband's stones in her jewellery box."

His condescending tone left her with that queasy feeling one got from eating porridge that had just started to spoil. Besides, Glauke could not have passed more than sixteen or seventeen years. If she waited for the twins to be eighteen, yes, she'd be older than was customary for a bride, but not beyond childbearing years. "What are you saying, Jason?"

He grunted. Rose. Poured himself another goblet. "It's simple enough, I think." Another drink. "Even if you refuse to see it."

"To see what?" she demanded, now climbing to her feet as well.

Jason sighed. "Oh, must I spell it out for you, Medea? I've come for your consent to dissolve our marriage. Through the princess Glauke, I have a chance to reclaim somewhat of the birthright I lost when you used your Art upon Pelias. It's hardly fitting for you to make a fuss over it."

Medea felt the heat in her cheeks. She knew her mouth hung open, but still, she could not quite form words. Not yet. She took a stumbling step backwards, bumped into her divan, and collapsed back onto her arse. "What about our love?" she said, the words so insipid even in her own mind she might have laughed, was her heart not now cracking like a shattered amphora. She felt those spiderwebbing fractures spreading throughout her core, certain that any moment now her insides must begin to spill out upon the floor.

No one could hold herself together with such destruction run through her.

Jason heaved an affected sigh and slumped down upon his own couch once more. "Well, of course I'll always be fond of you, Medea, but when Ananke offers up such a chance, I can hardly spit in the face of the Moirai. And one cannot expect the princess Glauke to accept me keeping a pallake, at least not in the early years until she'd offered up an heir or two."

"You have heirs ..." Her sons' faces danced in her mind, already fading from the fair future destiny had dangled before them all their lives. To inherit a thriving estate, marry well, to live in relative comfort ...

"What, to a farm? Medea, do try to be reasonable and approach this issue with some logic."

This was some nightmare. It had to be. His cruel indifference could not exist within the waking world. Deep in the hidden depths of her soul, she could still feel the knot she'd woven between them. The way she'd doomed herself to pine for his love. "I gave up everything I ever had for you. I betrayed my father, Jason. I killed my own brother!"

Jason folded his arms over his chest. "You did that for yourself, because you sought to escape your father's punishment." He paused, his affected sympathy so insincere a child could have seen past it. "You think it easy on me, saying these things? But surely you've seen the looks of mistrust these long years. Men do not trust a witch, Medea, and I can hardly find fair weather in these lands as long as I attach myself to a woman who crafts potions and brews poisons rather than bakes sweet breads."

He could not say such things to her. Medea was a princess of Kolchis. Heat rose in her. It burnt behind her eyes, and she knew her Heliad blood would have them flashing with hints of lambency. Indeed, Jason recoiled, perhaps suddenly aware he spoke thus to a Nymph. "If you so fear my Art"—her voice had dropped low and feral —"perhaps you ought not make mockery of it."

Taken aback, Jason pushed away from the table, glanced about the room as if seeking support from the shadowed corners, and then looked back to her. With uncertain steps, and never taking his eyes from hers, Jason backed to the doorway. "You would threaten your own husband with vile crafts?"

Medea sputtered, a sudden exhalation caught between tears and mocking laughter at the rank absurdity of Jason's indignation. And still, that knot of love refused to untangle. Still, her treacherous heart urged her to cast herself at his knees and beg him not to leave her. Only her last vestiges of pride kept her rooted to her divan, clutching its sides for support.

"Get out," she managed, at last.

&

THE INTRUSIVE FINGERS of the waking world tugged at Medea's senses, clawing her back to reality no matter how she sought to hide her face beneath the blanket. Her eyes stung, parched like deserts from sobbing herself to sleep. Her head throbbed with the cruel, empty aching that followed such lachrymal bouts. And still, still she found herself grasping at some desperate hope all this had been some nightmare born of soured wine. That she would sit and see Jason sprawled across his own divan like some beached whale, one arm dangling in the air, his snores a gentle thrum through their chamber.

But, though the blackness engulfing the room told her Hyperion had not yet summoned dawn's gleam, a perverse silence now choked her bedchamber. Reflexively, she reached over to Tisander's cradle to place a hand upon the babe's chest. A subtle reassurance to herself as much as her son, and one she must have repeated a dozen times a night.

Jason was not here, and that meant it had all been real. Their argument, his ... complete betrayal of her. Of all she had ...

Tisander was so cold. The thought cut through the weave of her anxieties like the sharpest of knives. It carved away all other concerns, and Medea was standing at once. That little chest did not rise and fall. She stumbled over. Her bare feet squelched in some thick dampness that coated the carpet.

What in Nyx?

She couldn't see! She couldn't see her baby!

Frantic, Medea swept Tisander up in her arms. Cold wetness caked his frigid skin.

Medea screamed. She wailed, stumbling, the whole world heaving from side to side like a storm-tossed ship.

This wasn't happening!

Little Tisander against her breast, she half ran, half fell from her bedroom into the balcony that rimmed the house's upper floor. The embers of the hearth glinted like the eyes of Erinyes, mocking her suffering. In their red-tinged light, she beheld the still form of her child. A hole in his throat. A hole ... as from a blade. Run through with precision enough the babe had not been able to cry out in its agony.

Medea's shriek was not a human sound. It was primal, a world riven in twain and collapsing in on itself. A death knell for the whole of the cosmos, consumed in the bitterest of icy flames. On and on she howled until all breath had fled.

And no one came. She crashed through the door into the twins' bedroom. Their widow was open, and now the first rays of Hyperion's golden light spilt over their empty beds. Thessalus and Alkimenes lay not in them but sprawled upon the floor in pools of their blood, their hands clutched around wounds in their necks, identical to the one on Tisander.

Still holding her babe, Medea collapsed into the blood of her other sons and knew not what she did. She knew she shouted their names, having found breath she thought was gone from her. She knew she shook them, begged them not to cross the Styx and leave her behind. She must have shouted a thousand imploring calls to uncaring gods. She did not think any answered her.

The impossibility of this morn told her she must be trapped in the nightmare. Such things could not transpire in life. Such cruelties were beyond enduring. No one withstood having her beating heart ripped from her chest and stabbed before her eyes. How then was she to endure such happening over and over, suffering her own destruction with each passing moment? Every breath in which she yet existed mocked her.

Not even the Moirai could have imagined such patent depravity as had befallen her. Even Fate must have limits to its tortures.

"What have you done, Medea?" a voice asked from behind. From far, far away, outside the broken world in which she now dwelt.

Dimly, she felt herself look. Saw the shadow of Jason—it wore his face, but it was not him—and behind him their labourers, all gathered and gaping at the massacre of three children. They looked at her, condemnation in their eyes, as if they thought it even possible a mother might slaughter her own young. As if she might cut out pieces of herself, her flesh, her very *soul*, and cast them aside.

Her tongue was too heavy to even form words of objection at the absurdity of their silent accusations. All she could manage was to raise her blood-soaked empty fingers and reveal she held no knife. To beg, with her imploring gaze, that they ought to ask themselves what mother could have done this.

Some distant part of herself realised it when Jason had the labourers seize her arms. When they dragged her from her house and cast her into the field, to blink beneath the dawn's searing brightness. Soaked in the life of her own flesh and blood, she knelt in the mud, staring dumb at her husband and the gathering throng of onlookers.

"Burn her," someone said. "Burn the witch!" A chorus quickly stifled by her husband's raised hand. He would speak for her. Whatever their differences, he would know all this stood beyond the realm of possibility for her.

"What foulness have you wrought?" Jason demanded. What? He too thought she could have ... "I ought to have realised a woman who could steal from her father and knife her own brother in the throat capable of the unspeakable. But your own *children*, Medea? No mother, not one with even a drop of maternal instinct, could have committed such obscenity."

"Burn her!" One of the labourers shouted once more.

Medea tried to object. Tried to make her mouth work, to protest her innocence. All she managed was a moan of indignation. How could he think this of her? How could he imagine, even for an instant, she was the murderer here?

"Burn her!"

"No!" Jason shouted. "No, I'll not taint myself, as she has done, by the killing of my own family. No." He shook his head, face grim, eyes dark. "No, this woman is to be exiled from these lands, banished from Troezen and Korinth." Each word struck her like a blow. He believed this of her. "For her crimes, I *renounce* Medea as my wife. Escort her to the road and see she follows it far from here. If she dares set foot in the domains of King Kreon once more, she must be whipped."

The same knife that had struck down her children felt lodged in her gut. He couldn't do this. He couldn't do it ...

But already, one of the labourers—she didn't know his name, but she'd brought him wine a time or three, and spoken to him of his own children, had laughed with him—he had a whip in hand. Harsh leather bands coiled around his knuckles. His visage turned cruel, as though the once kind man relished the thought of inflicting such pain upon her.

"She must be punished," someone said.

"The Erinyes punish kinslaying," Jason stated, his voice calm. Almost ... as if he'd known he would spout such a claim.

Barefoot and clad in naught save her sheer nightgown, Medea found herself hauled to her feet and herded toward the road like some criminal. The labourer snapped the whip between his hands by pulling it taut, the sudden crack enough to make her jump.

JASON HAD ORDERED his men to whip Medea *if* she returned to his lands. Later, bleeding and alone by the side of the road, she wondered if he'd known they would do it regardless. The sudden, unexpected crack of the leather had ripped through her nightgown and torn a bloody gouge into her arse. It had sent liquid fire racing over her body.

Her screams and pain and shame had only served to entice her attackers, who *laughed*. They chortled at her suffering.

"Run, witch, run!"

And she had. She'd run over the beaten dirt path, blood trailing down her leg, tears in her eyes, heart pounding for fear. A thousand horrible things they might do to her flashed in her mind, but the men did not chase her beyond the road. And still, she'd run, wearing raw her feet until they too bled. Until, at last, exhausted and drained from the seeping away of her adrenaline, Medea had collapsed amid the rocks and juniper shrubs. She had pulled herself through the dust, heedless of any further filth, and lay against a boulder.

Though her breath calmed, her reeling mind refused to do so. Someone had murdered her children. As Jason had said, they had been slain in the exact method she had used upon Absyrtus, details she had shared only with her husband. Was it possible some spirit of vengeance had, despite Kirke's purification of her, avenged her brother upon her children? Would the Erinyes do such?

She could not utterly discount such a possibility.

But there seemed another, more plausible if equally unthinkable, explanation. Her husband had wanted her cast aside, and she had refused him. Threatened him, even, with her Art. He alone knew how she'd slain Absyrtus. He could have killed Tisander and Thessalus and Alkimenes in mirror of her own crime. That is, if he could have brought himself to murder his own offspring.

Princess Glauke would not have wanted him coming to the palace with existing heirs who might serve to challenge any son she bore him. The more Medea considered it, the more the hateful possibility clarified into a damning certainty. King Kreon would have demanded Jason set aside Medea and send away her children by him. Send them away ... at best. Maybe the king would have supported Jason in his unthinkable act. Maybe he had even demanded it.

A blade had slid into her babies' throats.

Medea rubbed her neck, feeling it cut through her flesh as well. It cut through her very life. It cut through the knot of love she'd mistakenly woven for Jason within her breast. The truth of vile, unimaginable betrayal sliced through the bonds between them, and she felt them snap with almost physical recoil within her chest. It left her gasping, flailing about, limp fingers digging rivets in the hard dirt.

Trembles shot through her, left her a quivering wreck beside the road. Her husband had not only murdered her children, but he'd also seen to it the world blamed her for the deed. How badly she had misjudged his character, in those days back in her father's palace. How sorely she had wronged Kolchis, wronged *herself* when she, by her Art, bound herself to the wretched Iolkan.

Jason and his Argonauts had come as thieves in the night, and Medea had failed to see that was *exactly* what they were. These men thought they could take aught they desired, have any*one* they lusted after. And why not? Their very gods walked the earth and seized women for their pleasures whenever the mood struck, then cast them aside as new pursuits drew their eyes. How could she expect better of men who *worshipped* such knavish bores? How could it surprise that the very sons of the loathsome, unprincipled Olympians would walk the tracks left by their fathers?

Medea choked upon a wretched sob. She could not go back to Kolchis, now. There was no forgiveness for what she had done when the Argo had sailed to her homeland.

No forgiveness.

But vengeance. That, perhaps, she could arrange.

IT TOOK TIME. Almost a year, in fact.

Of course it did. She'd come to the villages south of Korinth with naught save a tattered nightgown. Medea could not even count how many men had sought to take advantage of her. Some saw a woman alone and thought, if no man was there to claim her, surely her body was his right. Others at least tried to trade for her flesh, offering food or lodging or clothing.

Medea had, in turns, fled and hid and lied, and once, in desperation, caved a man's head in with a rock and left his body in a ditch. Only after the rush of fear had faded had she thought to climb down there and take his drachmae.

So, it took time and degradation and pain and hunger, through the months before she came to Athenai, and longer still before she'd gathered the money she needed to purchase the ingredients she could not harvest herself in the wild. Metics—female metics at least —could find but one occupation in the poleis of Elládos, she learnt.

It affronted her dignity to take custom as hetaira. The unwanted penetration was like another knife, once more defiling her flesh. She asked herself, over and over, why she had refused to whore herself in the villages, only to come to the city and sell her body thus. In those dark times, she pictured the still forms of her children, crying out for justice.

She had prayed for Erinyes to visit the very justice upon Jason that he had threatened her with. If those creatures of vengeance existed, they did not seem to hear her invocations.

So, she did what she had to until she had the means to brew once more the Honey of Morpheus. The distance between them would make finding Jason harder, she had known. Still, she sat in her tiny, rented apartment in the slums, surrounded by the handful of candles she'd managed to afford. The room stank of urine as though some wild little boy had pissed the walls not long before she'd claimed it. She thought it best not to even question the nature of the stains in the corners. She pretended she did not see the roaches scampering into the dark when she lit the candles.

Poppy was harder to find here. It had cost more drachmae than she'd wished to part with. Enough she'd be forgoing supper—for more than one night, perhaps—in exchange for smoking the brew. But the Honey of Morpheus had cost her more, far more, and she would not see it go to waste. All that remained to her now was to punish Jason and his Argonauts for the ruination they had made of her life.

So, she drank the draught and she smoked the poppies. And she breathed deep, in search of the dreams of a perfidious husband.

It outraged all conceptions of rightness in the World that Jason's dreams should see him happy, living in a palace. Awaiting the arrival of a new heir, his accursed wife already showing. As if a man might so easily replace the sweat and pain and living soul a woman must pour into birthing. Medea had carved pieces of herself out to breathe life into each of her precious sons. And Jason had cast them aside like rotten driftwood.

Thus, she stalked his dream, an unseen spectre skulking the shadows between the columns of his palatial home. She mocked and chided and engendered a disquiet in his soul that he might feel some fraction of the ravaged ruin he had made of hers. She drove him, with whispers of times past, to lose himself in memories of deeds done aboard the Argo.

His supposed heroism, in sailing to foreign lands and stealing from foreign kings, had availed him naught in the end. He had never sat upon the throne of Iolkos. It had earned him only Medea's eternal scorn. It had earned him *wrath*.

So, she plucked at the strands of his mind.

And when it wasn't enough, she came again the next night. And again, though her Honey and poppy stocks dwindled. For her nights had no reprieve from grief and rage, and so his would offer no reprieve from the madness she kindled in him.

There could be no peace for one such as him.

Unwittingly, the Argonauts had declared a private war upon the princess of Kolchis. And if she could not overcome them with swords, there were other ways.

There were times when strength of arm offered no benefit. Thus, in the fields of the mind, Medea would face her foes and repay the affronts they had committed against her. Thus, in the depths of their own souls, would they face her vengeance.

IN THE DAYS THAT FOLLOWED, word came to Athenai of the ignominious end of Jason of Iolkos, newly named Prince of Korinth. Men said, in a fit of melancholy-induced drunkenness, he had come once more to look upon the rotten hull of the Argo. He sought, so stories claimed, to relive his days of glory whilst drowning his sorrows at the crimes the witch Medea had committed against him. But deep in his cups, he had fallen and drowned not sorrow but himself in a tidal pool that had seeped into the wreckage.

Perhaps that was the truth of it, but Medea preferred to think it otherwise. She told herself, with goblet raised in silent salute to her efforts, that though the Erinyes themselves had not come upon Jason, she had *created* them for him. Drunk though he may have been, she rather thought he had chosen to let himself be swallowed by the rising tide in the Argo's hull.

Men mourned the death of one of the great heroes of the so-called Bronze Age. Bards sang his praises for sailing the black waters of the Axeinos, overcoming the strange, vile dark lands of Kolchis, and winning back great prizes for the Thalassa world. Stories, too, told of how Jason, with his princely charms, had won the heart of treacherous Medea for a time. How she had, in the end, true to her faithless nature and not knowing the proper place of a woman, betrayed her husband.

And when she could endure the sting of such barbs no longer, Medea wove armour from her wounded pride. She held her head high, exulting in the truth, and telling herself her love for Jason had never been more than a fouled working of the Art. Stately aristos ladies would hold Medea up before their daughters as a spectre, a warning to girls who refused to play the role laid out before them. How Medea longed to slap those self-righteous women, more even than the men, so culpable they were in the perpetuation of their own enslavement. How she longed to stand before those young girls and say to them, *it was not I who was in the wrong.*

But such were useless thoughts. No one would hear her side.

Once, on first coming to Athenai, before turning the Art against Jason, she'd thought to call upon those vaunted Athenian courts, so famed for their justice. She'd gone to inquire, only to find she could not even speak in the court. She must return with a male relative to plead her case, the officials had told her, their mocking disdain writ plain upon their faces. She ought not even be out, wandering the city unaccompanied, they had warned her. Her father or brother could bring a case against her husband, but no *woman* could speak for herself. "These are not the barbarous lands of the Amazons," the official had chided.

Medea was damned to forever remain the cautionary tale against women who dared rise above their stations. Men feared—and rightly so—the Art and misliked that a woman could wield power they could not understand nor ward against with brawn and bluster. Turning to the arcane to wriggle free of subservience was, in the eyes of the masses, Medea's greatest crime.

With a grim and determined smile, did she resolve that it should be through the Art she would continue her vengeance. Jason was dead, but those Elládosi men who'd sailed with him, thievery and murder in their hearts, had suffered far too little for their black deeds and blacker intentions.

Theseus had vanished, and so she could not strike at him directly. Perhaps he had died, even. Either way, she could not forget the disdain with which he'd looked upon her all these years.

Thus, he had offered a fair target to vent her wrath. Earning a chance to visit the royal palace of Athenai had proved, in truth, more difficult than actually lacing her love potion in King Aegeus's wine. Under the name Eriopis, a rising hetaira, Medea earned her invite to come and recite poetry and entertain the guests of the king, who sought distraction from his grief over his missing son.

Men stared at her golden Heliad eyes, and she knew they imagined taking her to their beds. For such a trait meant she was of the aristocratic genē, a descendant of the Titans, and yet, as hetaira, they could claim her flesh without need for weddings and formal alliances with other aristoi. Even Aegeus proved not immune to her charms, in his desperate loneliness.

Almost, she might have pitied the king, were he not Theseus's father. Had he, too, not betrayed his wife in days gone, when she had not given him the heir he'd hoped for? And men called him valiant and wise for taking another woman in secret, leaving her alone to raise a son in shame. No, any real pity Medea had for Theseus's bloodline would have gone to his mother.

So, Medea had dosed Aegeus with her love potion and gotten the old man to wed her over the objections of his counsellors and courtiers, naming the hetaira Eriopis the new queen of Athenai.

Without a drop of blood spilt, she had stolen Theseus's throne out from under him. Part of her hoped he was dead, and she could live here and have peace. Part of her thought perhaps now she might bury those last traces of Princess Medea and become Queen Eriopis in truth.

But in the grim, bitter depths of her soul, she hoped Theseus returned. She wanted to see his face when he realised that the girl they had brought from Kolchis, the one whose home they had come to with ill intent, had taken back from him the destiny once stolen from her.

❦

IN THE SPRING following Medea's wedding to Aegeus, Theseus returned. Though she had not spoken of it to Aegeus, had told no one, Medea suspected she already carried the king's child. Not so long ago, she had imagined Theseus's return with grim satisfaction, thinking of the suffering he would find on seeing his father besotted with Medea. Now, on hearing of his approach, Medea's gut churned, hollow and bitter.

His coming heralded a disruption in the life she had once more begun to build for herself, as if Ananke scorned any idea that she might ever live in peace. Not for this one, the Moirai must have said, are the idylls of marriage and the passing of carefree days. Though no Oracle, she felt a dread premonition when sitting beside Aegeus on her throne. Whilst she would not show for months still, she realised she had laid one hand upon her belly as if she might shelter this one. As if she might keep this child safe, even after having failed the others.

The draught she'd given Aegeus would blind him, even to his own son. Using her husband thus sat ill in her breast. Not so long ago, Medea had sworn to bring suffering to the Argonauts by the means available to her. She could not fight men and demigods with blades, but through Art and intellect, she could have her vengeance, even if she must take it in part upon their loved ones. Vengeance seemed so plain, such a pure-burning flame whilst consumed in her own torments. But a moment of reprieve from anguish cooled even the brightest of blazes. Try as she might, she could not quite summon the fierceness of her anger that would let her assure herself she remained in the right here.

Neither, though, did Fate leave her many choices. Even if she need not to have acted as she had for her own sake, she would not risk losing her babe. Not another child. Never that.

The slap of Theseus's sandals upon the marble floor announced his coming with more force than the cries of any booming herald. Each echoing tread was a gong in Medea's skull, a tremor in her chest. The warrior was older than when last she'd seen him, worn by the years and by cares she could not guess at. His face, first filled with joy at looking upon his father, darkened as his gaze swept over Medea.

"Who are you, warrior?" Aegeus demanded.

Whispers sounded from those few courtiers present, though Medea had striven to ensure most of those who might recognise Theseus be elsewhere for this meeting. Still, she could not well empty the whole megaron, and some here knew their prince. What they thought of Aegeus denying his heir, she did not know.

To his credit, Theseus did not balk, though his look grew even grimmer as he stared at Medea without answering.

"You are bold, boy, to stare at a king's wife thus," Aegeus rumbled.

Theseus looked back to his father. "Forgive me, my king. I mean no disrespect. I am Theseus, recently come here through ... some hardships."

Aegeus, perhaps mollified, settled back on his throne. "What hardships are those?"

"Ah." Theseus shook his head. "Those would be rather long in the telling, my king."

It was her chance. She had no choice but to do away with Theseus. None, if she was to protect herself and her unborn child. Besides, this man had sailed with Jason. Together they had plotted against her and against Kolchis, and then, for years, Theseus had scorned Medea using the very Art the Argonauts had begged her to use for them. They were, all of them, wretched hypocrites deserving of their fates.

"Then you must join us for a meal and regale us with your adventures."

Now. It had to be now. "Despina," Medea called. "Bring the wine for our guest."

Despina, a serving maid, had been desperate to conceive with her husband, and Medea had given her the needful brew. For that, the girl had sworn eternal favour to Medea. She had clearly misliked it when Medea had told her to ensure their coming guest, and he alone, received wine from a specific amphora. No fool, Despina would have known Medea had tainted the brew. When Theseus took ill and fell to the fevers, maybe Despina would know that Medea had poisoned that batch. But that was a problem for another time. First, Medea had to survive the day. Then she could bribe or, if that failed, threaten the maid.

The servant brought wine first for Theseus, and then for Aegeus and Medea, and the three of them retired to a table that was soon laden with fish and fresh breads. Aegeus remained ever eager to show off his hospitality and would not turn away Theseus, though he did not know him. As Medea suspected, the king even offered their guest a room for the night. She sipped at her wine, watching Theseus, who had not yet touched his, so intent was his gaze upon his father's eyes.

"Have we met before?" Aegeus asked after draining his own cup. Medea's new husband was not shy with the wine, she had noted.

With a sigh, Theseus looked to his goblet, then to Medea. "Memory is a strange, slippery eel. We think it lurks well contained within known hollows, only to find it has freed itself through unseen passages." Medea caught herself leaning forwards as he raised his wine. Her hands trembled, so she set them in her lap beneath the table. "Sometimes," Theseus said, "we recognise the eel only when it has crept around to bite us upon the arse." The prince downed his poisoned cup in one long swig before letting the goblet clatter upon the table. "Such is the peril of memory."

Aegeus cleared his throat and rubbed a hand against his chest.

"Ah. Well. I'm not sure I follow that." The king coughed and waved to Despina to refill his goblet. "In any event, I believe I was promised a tale."

Theseus nodded, watching the maid as she refilled the king's goblet. Filled it from an amphora painted to depict Bellerophon's slaying of the great chimera outside Phoeba.

No.

What in Tartarus? Why was she serving the king from *that* one? That one was for Theseus alone. Aegeus already raised it to his lips. Theseus must have seen the horror writ upon Medea's face, for he lunged at his father and smacked the goblet away. Wine sloshed over the king, staining his robes and the table.

Medea slapped a hand to her mouth to stifle a gasp. Not like this.

"What the—" Aegeus blurted. He rose, swayed unsteadily, then collapsed forwards upon, catching himself with both hands on the tabletop.

No. Not *him*. Medea shut her eyes and allowed the despair to wash over her. A moment of pure denial—as if she could spite Fate. Maybe she'd been wrong. Maybe Kirke had failed to ever purify her for the murder of Absyrtus. Maybe the Erinyes *had* targeted her, squeezing slow, damning ruin from her life.

Gasping, the king pitched over, his noisy crash jolting Medea from her forced repose. The hall broke into a bustle, servants running for their lord. Someone screamed for the priestess of Hera to come and bless the king. Others wept for fear.

Medea rose and edged her way from the table, toward the shadowed recesses of the megaron. Aegeus had not the youth or health of Theseus. The dose she had prepared to poison a man in his prime had stricken the old king much more quickly. Too quickly, and whatever Theseus had seen upon her face—

A strong hand seized her by the back of her neck and shoved her against a column. Next she knew, Theseus stood before her, sword pointed at her breast. "Even along the lonely road I walked to reach Athenai, tale reached me of what you did to Jason and his children. Give me one reason not to run you through here and now, *witch*."

She might have pleaded her innocence for the murder of her children. Might have said that, after all she had sacrificed for him, Jason had abandoned her. Might have tried to convince Theseus that Jason, not she, had done the unthinkably foul deed. She might have tried any number of tacks, but he would not have believed her. Like the courts in his city, he saw a woman, her words amounting to less than dust before those of a man. Besides, in Theseus's eyes, her witchery blighted her. It was a stain upon her very soul.

How dare a woman use her mind to brew potions and poisons that made her a match for a man?

"I carry your father's heir in my womb," she said instead. "Your brother"—though she supposed it could have been a sister—"would die too should you make good on that threat."

Theseus's sword trembled in his hand. She could see in his eyes he plainly considered running her through anyway. His haunted gaze darted to where his father convulsed upon the floor, dying. At last, he lowered the blade, unwilling to strike down a child of his father's line. "Pray to whatever dark gods you worship that, once you have birthed the child and can no longer use it as a hoplon to hide behind, I do not again lay eyes upon you."

She fled.

What else was there for her to do?

RUMOURS OFT PROVE IMMORTAL THINGS, impossible to quash and godlike in the speed with which they soar across the world. Thus, even in the far reaches of Kissatu, word came to Medea. Medos, her son, heard it from silk traders in the covered bazaars, who had it from fishmongers in the harbour, who themselves claimed it the talk of sailors out of Phoenikia. The great sorcerer-king Aeëtes, son of Helios himself, had repented of his anger.

Tales said that he sought across the world, sending messengers far and wide, hoping for reconciliation with his lost daughter, the princess Medea. Such tales she found hard to credit, much though she wanted to believe they held truth behind them.

Sitting in the parlour of her small Neshian abode, Medea chose not to look up at her ten-year-old son, though she knew he shifted impatiently from foot to foot. Instead, she kept her gaze upon her worktable, where she carefully adjusted her alembic to distil the allwing root extract. It was a painstaking process, one that required attention over the matter of a fortnight to prepare even a small decoction. But once readied, the allwing had uses in a variety of tonics, aiding in the healing of various kinds of indigestion and bowel irregularities, as well as helping balance the humours.

Such drugs, though less lucrative than the poisons for which she was sometimes hired, drew less attention and thus constituted the bulk of their income here in Kissatu. Building her reputation here, across the Thalassa and away from everything she had known for the second time in her life, had not come easy. Her name was known among the great families now, though, and they came to her with their ills. When a matron's eyesight failed, it was for Medea she sent to anoint her eyes and restore her vision. When chest pains troubled men who ought to drink less and eat better, they came calling upon her at home. And yes, sometimes, when one family troubled another beyond endurance, they sent someone in the dead of night, come seeking a permanent remedy for such grievances as well.

"Mother." Medos's voice carried that unique self-important gravitas only children could muster. "This is our moment. Right now, we've a chance to reclaim our birthright. We are of the royal blood of Kolchis, and we sit here in this"—he gestured to the profound lack of ostentation in their mudbrick house—"hovel."

Medos was, thankfully, too young to recall what living in a real hovel had been like, when she had first reached Kumari Kandam, heavy with child and all too light on silver. Those first few years, his life had been filled with tribulations he would never know. Medea clucked her tongue and looked to her son now. Maybe she ought never have told him the truth of his origins. Since his earliest days she'd suckled him on tales of the grandeur of her homeland. To reminisce upon all she'd lost had been more balm to her soul than aught for his benefit, and it had sparked in him a yearning for palaces and dangers and hidden secrets. Time and again he implored her to teach him what she knew of the Art, and each time, Medea promised him to teach him the secrets of alchemy when he was old enough.

For now, it was letters and mathematics and astronomy, and all the myriad disciplines that would separate a learned youth from his peers. He watched her, sometimes, at work with her decanters and phials and alembics, and maybe he understood more than he ought to have.

With a sigh, she shook her head. "Rumours have lives of their own, Medos. My connections with my kin in Kolchis I severed myself, at the end of a knife." A haunting face. A brother betrayed, his unquiet shade forever seeking ingress into her dreams. "Whatever the truth, I cannot believe my father would forget, nor would he forgive all I've done."

"You let fear control you! You won't even take the chance to claim what's yours."

Medea felt her temper rising. What was *his*, he meant. She snapped her jaw shut before she could form a retort. No doubt Medos thought that, with his uncle dead and Medea's nephews fled to Elládos all those years back, Aeëtes might name him heir to the throne. As if her father did not plan to imbibe enough Ambrosia to rule until the end of time. For her part, she'd not tasted the brew since leaving Kolchis, and time had begun to wear upon her at last. Hints of crow's feet, unknown to most Nymphs, had begun to carve their way upon her once immortal visage.

Medos spoke like he had the least idea what it cost *her* to stay away. Her Titan blood would give her a longer life than a mortal, but not forever. Age would have its due, sooner or later. "It's a foolish risk." It was the only thing she trusted herself enough to say at the moment.

The boy stomped his foot. "Your craven heart keeps us crawling in the dirt!"

"Enough!" Medea rose, staring down at the boy. She had to clench her fist to keep from slapping the insolence off his face. "I will not tempt your grandfather's wrath by setting foot within his domain."

"Then I'll go myself!"

The patent absurdity of his claim first had her wanting to laugh. But he was in earnest, that was plain by the set of his jaw. A fevered, panicked vision arose in her mind. A thousand, thousand deaths for the boy on attempting such a voyage. For he had within him the stubbornness to run from his home here, flee in the night, and barter passage on some northbound ship in a fool voyage to Kêr-Ys. He could be lost at sea. Even more probable, men might take him aboard, then sell him as a slave in some foreign port. But even supposing he made it to Kolchis, what welcome could Medea's son expect from her betrayed father? Perhaps he was right, and Aeëtes would embrace him, name him heir, and give him a lofty throne.

But Medea could not say that for certain, and she would never allow her child to gamble his life thus.

She envisioned chaining him to the hearth at night. All the manifold actions she might take to keep him from making good on his illconceived threat. But she could not watch his every breath. No one can stop another person from pursuing a course upon which they have truly bent their wills.

Except by pre-empting that course.

"I will go," she said. The words felt ripped from her. "I will go, and if we are welcome there, I will send for you, my son."

"We ought to sail together—"

"Push me no further, Medos." Broken though she felt, she managed to lace her tone with such quiet iron he snapped his mouth shut.

HOPE WARRED with rising panic as Medea walked the halls of her former home. More than fifteen years had passed since last she'd come here, and at once it seemed both smaller and more towering. The shadows had deepened, thick with perils she had not before feared. The eyes of every soldier and courtier in Qulha Palace traced her progress along her father's throne room.

And the great and powerful Aeëtes, he sat upon his throne, face impassive, limned with neither wrath nor quite welcome, though a keenness lurked within the depths of his lambent eyes. They flashed with such certainty Medea dared imagine perhaps he truly had sent word that she was to be forgiven.

Her father leant forwards upon his throne, hands clasping the armrests as she drew nigh. Did he still himself from rushing forwards to embrace her? Could she really, truly come home again, after so much time?

Despite her fears, her heart leapt into her throat. Home. Forgiveness for the awful mistake she'd made so many years ago, betrayed by her own heart and thus driven to betray her family.

"Father," she said, bowing low. The word almost choked her, so much did she desperately need it to convey. All the churning emotions of her tortured soul, come back at long last to where it belonged. Medos had been right in the end. Her future had always lain along her kin.

"You received word of my offer of leniency," her father said, pushing off his throne and stalking closer. Close enough she could have sworn she could feel the heat of his eyes.

"I scarce dared to believe it," she admitted.

Aeëtes nodded solemnly, then looked her up and down. "It is not the first time your desires overwhelmed your judgment, Daughter."

"Father?" But she knew, already. His gaze eviscerated all her protests, leaving only the certain knowledge of the torment to come. She might have told him of his grandson, but then, perhaps he would have sneered. Perhaps he'd even have sent men to punish Medos, too, no matter how far from Kolchis her boy dwelt.

"Did you, possessed by your desires to believe redemption possible, delude yourself into thinking I could ever forget the *shame* you brought upon my name?" Aeëtes seized her chin, his grip so tight she could not have spoken, even had she words left. "Did you think you could forever escape the righteous judgment of an immortal king?

You want forgiveness, Daughter? You shall have it. When the flames have cleansed the impure flesh from your bones, then shall I show your ashes leniency and hold you absolved of your betrayal."

With a single shove, he sent her sprawling upon her arse. She sat stunned and yet not shocked. For a part of her had known it must end thus. She ought never have left. She certainly ought not to have returned.

Medea did not weep as the king's men seized her limbs and dragged her outside, onto the cliff above the caves of Kolchis. She cursed herself for a fool for daring hope, but she did not weep. No tears spilt from her eyes as she was stripped naked in front of the populace. No sobs or cries for mercy when they bound her, alive, to a pyre.

Do not come here, Medos. If I have taught you aught in your life, let it be some measure of caution.

She would neither weep nor beg.

But when the flames licked at her flesh, still, she could not stop the screams.

PART IV

There is a known truth of which Titans have long feared to speak, whether out of fear of censure or, rather, the tendency toward wilful ignorance of that which proves inconvenient. Nevertheless, I must name it. Consumption of large quantities of Ambrosia certainly enhances Pneuma and thus power, yes, but it also degrades compassion and drives one toward a precipice of madness. Are we to pretend it coincidence that the most powerful Titans in the world suffer from a total lack of empathy and, often, outright megalomania?

— Thalia, Dialogues of the Muses

26

PANDORA

727 Bronze Age

She wandered far, retracing her steps back toward the library. By the time she returned, the sun had winked out and an oppressive darkness had settled upon Vulgeth. Still, she dared not rest anywhere nigh to where she'd seen those ... creatures.

Thalia's *Compendium of Gaia* had referenced a Kandamian superstition about ghosts in the desert, possessing their own dead bodies and craving the flesh of Man. Ghuls, the Muse's writings called them, but not even Thalia seemed to take such wild stories seriously. Then again, Thalia had never seen the horrors of Tartarus, either.

Past the library in the other direction, Pandora found a house that seemed stable enough. The wooden door barely stood any longer, so weathered by rot, but the foundations remained free of severe cracks. When she kicked the door, it burst inward, breaking into splinters.

Waving away the dust that stirred up, she ignited a torch on her hand and ducked inside. A maze of cobwebs clogged the fringes, obscuring much of the room. From what she could make out, a table and chairs looked no sturdier than the door had proved. Stone stairs wrapt around behind a hearth. Little wood remained within, so Pandora snapped the legs off a chair and shoved them into the fire pit, then sparked a blaze with her burning hand.

The crackling fire didn't offer so much warmth—the wood was too old—but its flicker managed to grant a reprieve from the darkness that had begun to choke her. When she sat before the hearth, the needle of despair she'd tried to ignore until now wormed its way through her heart. She had come so far, certain she'd find the answers she sought in Vulgeth.

But what she found, instead, was the leavings of an apocalypse, and all myriad questions echoing through empty halls. The voices of those who had lived here wanted their stories, their lives to be known, she had to believe they did. But the darkness of the Time of Nyx had swallowed all they had ever been or dreamt of, and they could no longer tell Pandora aught.

What terrible insight had come upon Kronos here that he and his brethren had founded the Gnostic Cabal in defiance of Fate?

Warming her hands against the fire was more symbolic than necessary, given the Phoenix within and that the summer night was not so cold, yet holding them against the blaze offered a comfort she could not pass up. Caught in the whirlwind of momentous events, one realised how crucial were the simple pleasures. Moments of peace, stolen from Ananke, and so oft undervalued until they had flitted through one's fingers like vapours.

She sighed.

It was doubtful she would find any divan fit to sleep on upstairs but checking never hurt. After pushing herself up from the hearth, she drew a handful of fire back into her palm and made her way up the stairs. Dust caked these as well, her Amazonian boots leaving impressions in the centuries-old coating of grime.

As she ascended, a noxious odour seeped into the air, like a whiff of a bog. The reek grew denser atop the stairs, which let out onto an open sleeping chamber. Rather than a divan, the room featured a large flat bed, its head and foot framed by intricately carved woodwork. Posts rose taller even than she was, cut into delicate spirals, and joined by beams at the top.

Her gaze rose, taking in tattered remnants of cloth that must have once draped over the bed in a canopy. The fabric tangled with a mess of spiderwebs that ran up to the ceiling. Her breath caught. The webs netted together into a meshy lump dangling overhead. Numerous dark, chitinous appendages of some sort protruded from the mass, segmented joints folded, talons boring into the ceiling. Beneath the webs, some sort of fleshy object expanded and contracted, like a languid heart beating every so oft. It was from this obscene mass the putrid stench emanated.

Her free hand went to her mouth, even as she backed away toward the stairs. Dread crept in around her, bid her flee and pretend she had never looked upon whatever Tartarus-spawned foulness dwelt within these walls. Her pulse pounded in her temples as she stumbled, bumping into the wall.

Then came a tearing sound, like snapping mucus, as the cocoon ruptured, the foul odour growing so dense Pandora might have retched had horror not frozen her in place. A form pitched out of the husk, spilling not to the ground but dangling in midair, suspended by those purplish appendages. The figure was all the more abhorrent, for, despite the alien extremities jutting from its back and shoulders, it bore the face and aspect of a Man. Its flesh was sunken and distended, taut against protruding bones, its colour somewhere between mauve and ashen. She could see its spine through its shrivelled abdomen.

Its eyes opened, the fell incarnadine glint behind them reminiscent of the ghuls bound in roots, and yet, somehow infinitely deeper, as though she peered into a darkness beyond the stars.

With a muffled gasp, Pandora flooded Pneuma to Alacrity and Potency, leapt the banister, and landed on the stairs. Even as she jumped again, launching herself for the spear she'd left by the hearth, she heard the chittering shriek behind her. The clatter of too many plated appendages striking stone resounded as the creature must have flowed over the space between them.

Pandora flew, landed in a roll, and came up bearing the spear an instant before the abomination streaked through the air at her as though hurled from a sling. Her spearpoint punched through desiccated flesh and scraped against ribs yet did naught to abate the creature's momentum. Its weight slammed into her like a hammer blow, hurling her against the back wall.

A rain of those chitinous limbs darted into her spear, pierced the wood, and tore it to kindling. Even as Pandora pulled herself from her daze, another of those appendages bored through her shoulder, pinioning her to the wall. A scream burst from her, then died as a Man-like hand shot out, squeezing her throat, cutting off all air. The creature opened its mouth, baring overlong fangs, even as it yanked her head to the side. Those teeth pierced her neck, and a sudden coldness suffused her limbs, draining them of struggle. She felt it as her lifeblood seeped from her, drawn into the creature, carrying more and more of her Pneuma.

There was a soothing peace in welcoming the encroaching blackness.

Deep within her chest, the Phoenix smouldered. A burst of heat erupted through her veins, filling her, invigorating her with surging, burning Pneuma.

The creature feeding upon her blood staggered away, its spidery leg ripping from her shoulder as it stumbled, hands to its mouth. Blood oozed between fingers that almost seemed suddenly less gaunt. The horror toppled to its knees, wailing. Incandescent flames roared inside its maw, liquifying its insides.

Gasping, struggling through each breath that passed her bruised throat, Pandora too stumbled. It seemed the monster did not like the taste of Phoenix, else she would be dead now. Though dizzy and with blurred vision, Pandora snatched up the broken blade of her spear, then lunged forwards. What Pneuma remained to her she poured into thrusting blow after blow, punching the spear into chest and throat and glinting ruby eyes. Wheezing, she bore the creature down backwards and ground the spear inside its skull until, at last, its convulsions stilled.

Then, woozy, she pitched over sideways. Her sight had narrowed to a pinprick, even that fading in and out. With what little strength she had left, she dragged herself across the floor, close to the hearth.

Just a little rest. Just a little.

❧

WHEN NEXT CONSCIOUSNESS intruded upon her, Pandora sucked in a deep breath that only stung her throat rather than scoured. The wound in her shoulder had sealed, at least partially, now only weeping a trickle of blood when she moved. Bizarrely, the hearth had gone out, though not all the wood was consumed.

Had she drawn the flame inside herself without realising it?

Profound weakness had wrapt its fingers around her limbs. The creature had drained so much of her Pneuma, not even the Phoenix had managed to heal her injuries all the way. How had it ... The creature!

Pandora looked to where it had lain. Now, only mounds of dust lay there, gristle and broken chitin poking out from beneath the collapsed husk of the monster.

If that was another type of ghul, Pandora truly hoped never to witness any others. Were these the creatures that had destroyed Vulgeth? Was that thing the source of the vileness that seeped into the whole of this place?

She tried to sit, but her strength gave out, and she managed only to roll over and groan. It had taken too much from her. She needed time and rest to renew her Pneuma. Most of all, she needed food, and she would not find aught to eat in this ruin.

What then? Were all her efforts in vain? Must she leave? She could use the Box to return to Elládos and seek shelter with any friendly aristoi. She could do all that. If she was willing to admit defeat, to give over the hope her answers lay in Vulgeth.

But then, what she sought had never lain in *this* shell of Vulgeth.

If she wanted to find the Ontos, if she wanted the chance to overcome Ananke, she had to go back to the real beginning of this mad spiral. If the ouroboros had been birthed in the Vulgeth of the past, it was there, in the Time of Nyx, she must go. No matter the cost, no matter the dread implication of Pyrrha's warnings.

There was always only forwards.

WHEN SHE HAD RECOVERED what strength she might by a few hours' rest, Pandora rose, took up the Box, and began the careful process of trying to send herself backwards in time. She could not know just how far back she needed to go. Thousands of years, certainly, but she also needed to maintain her rough location in space. Working with Kirke had further refined her conceptions of how to use the Box, but she wasn't sure she'd ever be able to achieve complete precision.

Regardless, she saw no real choice in the matter. If she was to unravel the threads of Fate, she needed to understand what had begun in Vulgeth, all those ages ago. Time Chambers, the Gnostic Cabal, all the intricate weave of history seemed to converge upon this blighted place.

Circles upon circles.

Time is an ouroboros.

More than once, the trembles in her fingers made fine manipulation of the Box's intricate gears so difficult she had to set it aside and concentrate only on breathing. In the end, life reduced down to breath, each one worth savouring.

Then, at last, the moment came. She had tuned the device as precisely as she was able, given she had no knowledge of an exact time period to shoot for. She supposed, with a bit of luck, she might use whatever she learnt from one jaunt through time to prepare another. But such musings only served to delay the path she knew she must now take.

So, she activated the Box.

27

ATHENE

728 Bronze Age

*I*n the days of the Titanomachy, Hestia had been an apprentice to Prometheus. With Athene's grandfather so oft absent from Elládos and thus beyond her reach, Athene had somehow developed a rapport with his erstwhile student. Most times, Hestia remained in the palace situated just beyond her temple. She cared little for court politics and thus did not oft deign to visit the Throne of Zeus.

Her home, like her temple, remained shadowed, lit only by the flicker of her hearth fires. As a pyromancer, she saw something in those flames, Athene had no doubt. But Hestia had established no name for herself as an Oracle, and thus Zeus had long ago given over any attempt to glean useful information from the woman. After what he'd done to her mentor, he no doubt mistrusted Hestia, though she had given him no reason to oust her from the Olympians as yet.

On her return from Iolkos, Athene had stabled Nephos. Now, she plodded through the open archway of Hestia's home. The Olympian welcomed women from across the peak, slave and free alike. They brought her food and wine and companionship, and sometimes helped her tend her palace. She did not keep slaves herself, though, so it was no unusual to find Hestia busying herself with chores. She would cook and clean and do whatever else seemed needful to her. Athene was probably one of the few other Olympians who understood, or who even knew how to do such things for herself.

This day, she found Hestia alone, stirring a burbling soup cauldron over a fire. Not once did the woman's gaze drift to her work, though. It remained locked upon the tiny flames beneath her pot. What secrets did the flames speak of to her?

Having no desire to disturb an Oracle in her trance, Athene walked silently to sit beside Hestia. Their friendship over these past few years had been far from a natural one. When Athene had first walked through those doors ... Well, Hestia was Kreios's daughter. Which was to say, Pallas had been her uncle and Hephaistos her cousin. She had been there, in the wake of the Gigantomachy, when they found Athene kneeling beside the body of Hephaistos, wondering at the brutal murder she had just committed.

Athene had come here to beg for forgiveness she'd well known Hestia would never offer. It had taken an almost unbearable toll upon her, striding through that door and looking the woman in her crimson-striated eyes. Hestia had watched her, no sign of emotion upon her face. She had waited patiently whilst Athene had, voice shaking, made her feeble, useless apologies.

Then she had laid a shockingly warm hand upon Athene's cheek. "They brought me a Delphic vintage this morn," she'd said. "Drink with me."

Athene could hardly refuse.

"Of my cousin," Hestia had said, voice thick with three cups of wine, "I will speak only once. I know what he did to you. The law would have given you little justice, we both know. And what you did to him, I count as his due." The words hung between them, her implication clear. If Hephaistos had deserved his fate, so many of the other male Titans must deserve the same. But too, Athene had carried her wrath far beyond its source, spewing venom upon all with the least passing connection with Hephaistos.

To Athene's shock, though, Hestia had sent for her again after that day. She had called her once more into her private sanctum, and they spoke again of the past and pain, though this time of Persephone and Demeter and the many people they had lost in their long lives.

Athene wished, uselessly, that Demeter had never risen against her father. She had liked the other Titan, but she could never have let her bring down Zeus. Hestia, it seemed, had warned Demeter against such a course, but wracked by her own fury, Demeter had gone down the same path as Athene. And lost.

"You return," Hestia said, her gaze torn from the flame with startling abruptness. "How went your attempt to aid the Iolkan prince?"

"I don't know," Athene admitted. She'd not had the time to gauge Jason's character well. No, but if she had to guess, the man had more of the arrogance of Bellerophon than the self-effacing humour or quiet valour of Perseus. Even now, some eighty years since his death, her mistakes with Bellerophon still haunted her. "My visions tell me I'm meant to help all these demigods and heroes. Through them, I strive to aid the whole of Mankind. But my heart ... it wants only to watch over my son and shield him from all his woes."

She might have said, too, she began to fear whether the visions in fact aided anyone save the Moirai and their schemes. But to give voice to such doubts was to make them too real. It would mean surrendering the foundation upon which she'd based her life, these past centuries since leaving Olympus.

Hestia nodded, then peered inside the cauldron she was still stirring. "It would rather defeat the purpose of setting him labours through which to battle his grief if you then resolve his challenges for him."

"So, you understand a mother's plight."

Hestia chuckled. "In theory, I suppose. I've not had the pleasure."

"Why did you never marry?" Long back, before Athene's exile, she'd heard the rumour that both Apollon and Poseidon had asked for her hand, and Hestia had refused to countenance either offer.

The pyromancer sucked air between her teeth. "I could never tolerate being beneath a man's ... authority." The way she cast a hooded glance Athene's way, Athene thought she might have said more.

And Athene nodded, for she thought she understood well enough. Fortunate Hestia was, like Artemis or Athene herself, that as an Olympian no one could compel her to marriage.

"You will continue to aid these mortal heroes, Athene," Hestia said with the air of a pyromantic foretelling.

She nodded. "They need me."

"As does your family?"

Athene blew out a frustrated breath. She still could not say whether she wrought weal or woe in betraying Kirke to Zeus. Certainly, she'd owed the woman no further loyalty, not after what she'd done. But ... but ... "He's my father." That meant something, no matter his faults. She had to believe that. "I will not turn my back upon him, either."

She told herself she cared naught for Kirke after all the woman had done. The words rang hollow.

With an iron poker, Hestia churned the hearth. "No. I don't suppose you will." A pause, and those rubescent eyes turned toward her, glinting in the firelight. "I saw something that haunts me now, Athene. Something I cannot shake from my mind. It lingers waking or sleeping. And so I look, again and again, dreading what I must see and compelled to witness it nonetheless."

Though she knew she ought to ask, Athene found it hard to speak. Hard to even move beneath the weight of the other woman's dread.

"Great wars ended the Golden Age and the Silver Age alike." Hestia did not seem inclined to await Athene's questions. Did not seem able to spare her this foretelling. "And now, I think, this one too draws ever closer to its terminus."

"What ...?"

"I saw ..." Hestia clutched her hand, so tight Athene reflexively flooded Pneuma into Steadfastness to ward her bones against crunching. "I saw the land stained red with the blood of your heroes. I witnessed the fall of the last of these demigods in whom you place your faith and your hopes for Man." Hestia leant in so close her breath ruffled Athene's hair. "I ... foresee no blissful endings to these threads. They are all, finally, cut, their frayed ends drenched crimson. And with them, we too, shall come undone."

Much though Athene pried, Hestia offered up no further answers about her dire prophecy. And Athene still had mortal heroes she needed to watch over.

ATHENAI WAS THICK WITH CROWDS, come to hear the hateful words of Minos's herald. Most of the public remained outside Aegeus's palace —though that too bristled with irate aristoi. The common folk, though, they pushed the fringes, waiting to see who would be chosen this time for profane sacrifices.

Athene ought to have put a stop to this long back. Ought to have, but found her hands fettered by circumstances. Athene had resolved to let the poleis of Elládos govern themselves. She would not be a Titan who swooped in and issued dictates or killed those who opposed her. Besides which, her father would not have taken kindly to her inference with the cruel games of his son Minos.

Everyone knew the tragic tale of Minos's birth, much as Athene had always preferred not to dwell on it. Zeus had kidnapped the Phoenikian princess Europa from Tyros. By him, Europa had borne a son, Minos, Athene's half-brother. Long had the demigod ruled Knosós. Much longer than any demigod ought to have lived, such that Athene had to assume Zeus favoured his son with sporadic draughts of Ambrosia. It was a violation of Olympian law, but then, who was there to call Zeus out on such a breach?

What common people did not realise, what not even Athene had known until speaking of such events with Prometheus during their wanderings, was that Zeus had returned to Europa some years later. Had taken her again, and she had borne him another bastard son,

Rhadamanthus. The boy had lived long enough to wed and sire heirs of his own, before a spat with Minos had led to his death.

Minos, in a show of guilt but what, in fact, probably resulted from him having no children of his own at that time, had taken Rhadamanthus's line as his heirs. Twenty-seven years back, one of Rhadamanthus's descendants, Androgeos, had been slain in Athenai. Some said the young man had been murdered in cold blood. Others claimed he died attempting to wrestle a bull, perhaps in some drunken challenge.

Athene had her suspicions that Minos, upon the birth of the monstrous Minotaur, had sent his heir to Athenai as more of a deliberate, if unwitting sacrifice. It had offered him the excuse he needed to sail against Athenai and plunder the city in revenge. And when the fires had burnt low, Minos had promised to leave the citizens in peace. They could live if they would agree to his conditions of tribute. But Minos wanted not only an annual donation of silver and goods. Once every nine years he demanded that the Athenians should offer up seven boys and seven girls in sacrifice to his son, the Minotaur.

To avoid the wholesale slaughter of Athenai, Aegeus had consented to let the parents of Athenai die withering deaths, slowly consumed by dread their child would be next.

Glamoured to look like any other aristocratic mortal, Athene sat in the assembly, watching as the young prince Theseus, seated beside King Aegeus, took in the assembly in his father's court. This man, the descendant of Pandion, had his ancestor's bearing, if not quite his aspect. The way he surveyed the gathered aristoi—and that pompous emissary of Minos—it reminded her of a leopard. He was more than his father had ever been, and Athene couldn't help but quirk a smile at that.

Ah, but then, she had seen this moment, hadn't she?

"The nine years have passed," the emissary intoned with the air of a speech he had given before. "And upon this, the twenty-seventh anniversary of your crimes"—he stretched the last word with such arrogance Athene rolled her eyes— "the time has come to once again send your seven boys and seven girls to sate the beast."

Theseus rose, his chair scraping noisily along the stone floor. "No."

"No?" the emissary asked as if the very word tasted alien to him and his tongue could not quite wrap itself around the sound of it.

"No," Theseus repeated. "No more sacrifices. I will walk the Labyrinth. Find this Minotaur. I kill it, our debt is paid. I fail, your king has claimed the son of his rival. Fair recompense for the loss of his own heir. Either way, Athenai owes no more sacrifices after this."

The men and women gathered in Aegeus's throne room gaped at the young man, as if unable to imagine their prince would put forth such an idea. Indeed, Aegeus, too, paled. Perhaps, had he suspected Theseus of such a play, he would not have invited his newly found son to this assembly.

No, but Athene had known it would come to this, long ago, and it was as it should be.

Whatever resulted in the Labyrinth beneath Knosós, Theseus had saved his polis. This was the true heir of Pandion. Athene's heir.

Some twenty generations removed, yes. But there was pride in looking upon this young man, and Athene found it hard to tear her gaze from him, wondering what he might accomplish in Knosós.

So she rose, offered her blessings and fair wishes to the young man, and watched him go to ready himself for the voyage. Maybe she ought to have descended into the Labyrinth herself, even if it would have enraged Minos and thus vexed their common father.

But Athene had to trust Theseus could accomplish this. If he did, he would unite Athenai behind himself. He would be a hero to Man.

She had to trust him.

ATHENE RETURNED to Olympus only to see her father, upon the steps leading to his palace, hurling insults at her brother Ares. Far as she was, the swirling winds of the perennial storm above the mountain swallowed her father's bitter words, whatever they may have been. Of a sudden, Zeus shoved Ares with such force Athene's brother hurtled through the air, flying dozens of feet before crashing back-first upon the marble steps in front of her.

For a single heartbeat Athene gaped in a stupor at the violence of it, unable to believe Father had done this to his own son. Ares groaned. Had he been a Man, the impact would have shattered his spine. His pain drew Athene from her own shock, and she dropped down beside him to inspect her brother.

As soon as his eyes opened, he waved her away, shame clearly outweighing whatever pain his Pneumatikoi failed to suppress. "Get the fuck off me," he grumbled through gritted teeth and rolled onto his side before pushing himself up. As he managed his feet—and clearly saw no use for her aid or concern—Athene left him be. She watched as he limped away from the Thrones of Zeus and off toward his own palace lower down the mountainside.

She had seen herself squaring off against Ares, prepared to engage him in a battle that could easily go either way.

When she looked back, her father had already disappeared within his expansive manse. Overhead, lightning crackled. Islands of Skystone drifted amid the thunderclouds, their shadows rolling over the acropolis as if in momentous omen of darkness soon to come.

She could not quite suppress the sense of apprehension that had settled upon her. Of course, she still feared for Theseus and whatever he must face within the Labyrinth. But more, a foreboding crept over her. What did Father turning upon his own son portend?

In the grips of heavy melancholy, she climbed the steps and made her way within the Throne of Zeus. Perhaps she ought to have instead left this mountain. Much though she still, despite it all, could not shake the need for Father's approving nod, the disquiet upon her soul almost choked her. Too, came the temptation to instead head to Hestia's manse and sit in the play of shadows and light cast by her fires. In that hall, she could whisper her misgivings to a woman who would understand without need for explanation. Or maybe it was Hestia's prophecy that had first kindled these fears in Athene's breast, fears that now burst into open blazes of doubt.

She found her father not upon his throne or in the great hall but once more within the cavern of the Oracle Mirrors, pacing and muttering and casting aspersions upon the shadows.

Kirke had given him Nectar. Athene did not know what effect it had produced, nor how oft he imbibed the dangerous draughts. But it *had* seemed to offer him visions of one sort or another, for he spent the better part of his time here, staring into the quicksilver pools set into the walls. He no longer hounded Athene for answers about the future.

Now, he delved deeper and deeper himself, so deep she feared he might drown in quicksilver waters.

"Ares could have died from such an impact," Athene said, keeping to the chamber's periphery. Interrupting her father's pacing might well provoke his ire. Like an incensed bull, he misliked anyone ever standing in his path. "Was it not, perhaps, harsh treatment for your own son?"

Unless Father's visions had at last revealed the answer he'd sought and confirmed Athene's suspicions that Ares would be the one to strike him down. But then, would he not have ended the self-styled God of War that very moment? Would not he have called the lightning and left his son a smouldering ruin, allowing his ashes to swirl upon the eternal winds of Olympus?

"One of them will murder me!" he bellowed, voice booming through the cavern. "One of them will *try* to catch me unawares and usurp my birthright to the World's throne! Oh, no, but they shan't succeed. I will smite the traitor before he has any such chance." Zeus shook his head, his ice-blue eyes wild when he looked to her. "I need but be certain of his identity." He resumed his pacing, though only for a moment, before spinning upon her once again. "Unless the best step lies in destroying them both before either can advance their plot ... They would not expect that. They would if they had half my intellect, but I am surrounded ever by my lessers. Fools, the both of them!"

Athene found herself at a loss for words. Her heart was hammering. Her face hot even as a chill ran down her spine at his words. That he would even consider murdering both his sons on the theory that it would guarantee he'd finish off the one who might have betrayed him —such a thought left her feeling as if the mountain had begun to cave in around her. It ought not to have surprised her. Cleft from sentiment or empathy, it made a cruel sort of sense, she supposed. But the idea he could cast aside her brothers thus ...

"Are they not your heirs?"

"Bah! What need has an immortal for heirs? My reign shall endure until the end of time."

Athene shut her eyes a bare moment to steady herself. She would have defended her father from either of her brothers, should they have moved upon him. He was her father. Indeed, such a case might have finally earned her his genuine respect. Father had always favoured her, in his way, but he saw females as of such limited use, that a measure of disdain always tempered his affections.

So, yes, should Ares come here with arms drawn and bloodlust in his heart, she would strike him down to save her father. Maybe that was what would lead to her baring her blade against her brother, although the battlefield she'd seen was not on Olympus.

Yes, she would fight him if she had to. But the idea of her brothers dying—of them *both* dying—for something that one of them might do ... This she could not abide. "If you kill the two of them," she warned, "you will lose both a foe and a loyal supporter of your eternal reign." Would such an argument sway him? "That's to say naught of how it will look to the mortals, to see the Olympian Order further sundered in open war. They must see us as a united front." Even if naught could have been further from the truth.

Part of her even imagined that, could Man have won such a battle, they would have been better off to throw down the Olympian Pantheon and rule themselves. Man worshipped gods because it seemed, within the framework of their lives, better than accepting the truth they had only themselves and one another on which to rely against an apathetic and oft cruel World. The self-delusions of faith in deities, though perhaps comforting, availed them little in the long run. They enslaved themselves to petty gods and convinced themselves Olympians answered prayers, despite evidence to the contrary.

But at the moment, Athene needed to keep her family from tearing itself apart. Much though she wanted to see Mankind's lot improved, she was not willing to watch her own kin die for such a cause. It was one step too far. One sacrifice she could never make.

And her argument appealed to Zeus's pride, for Father cared ever so much that the masses thought him an omnipotent ruler. Strife within his house would show a weakness, and that he could not abide.

Her father growled and grumbled and paced back toward one of the Mirrors. "Then still I must search until I find the traitor among us. When I do, that worm shall envy even Prometheus his Fate."

Athene shuddered as Zeus gripped the Mirror's edge and peered within once more. Maybe thus came the awful sense of foreboding that had seized her. For no matter what track she took, she could see no way to help Man, her father, and her brothers all at the same time. No matter how things played out, some would suffer and die.

She could not save them all.

28

THESEUS

728 Bronze Age

With black sails unfurled, the Athenian ship made for Knosós, threading the waves in a journey Theseus found at once took too long and was yet over too quickly. Before he'd had time to order his thoughts, before he'd had the chance to make peace with this madness. Aggrieved to learn the plight of his countrymen—how were they to bear having their young fed to a creature such as this Minotaur?—Theseus had hurled himself forwards with brazen folly, insisting he would take their places.

Clad in his burnished panoply and bearing his father's sword at his side, he had tried to remain at the ship's bow, proud and tall. He had an image to uphold of the noble prince, venturing into darkness and peril on behalf of his people. If they saw him tremble now, if they realised his courage could falter, they might force him to turn back, refuse to send him to his doom. He must seem confident, or else he condemned children to their deaths in his place.

Theseus had fought bandits and monsters, had sailed with the

Argonauts. He had battled alongside Herakles himself. In a moment of weakness, he found himself desperately wishing the demigod were here. Much though he longed to seal his name into the epics alongside Herakles's, part of him would rather if Herakles had slain the Minotaur as one of his labours and obviated any need for Theseus to descend into this Labyrinth.

For two years he had stood beside his father, prince of Athenai. Now he must earn the title anew.

Knosós lay along the north shore of Atlantis, and, despite his apprehensions, there was a thrill at laying eyes upon the famed island. Were circumstances other than this, Theseus would have sought to visit the legendary polis itself, to gaze up at the towering statue of Atlas, to marvel at the orichalcum walls in what bards named the greatest city in the world. But such pursuits must wait for another voyage, assuming he lived through his appointment in Knosós.

Theseus remembered his mother telling him, once, that Knosós was so old it dated from the Time of Nyx and none could say who had built it first. For centuries, Zeus's bastard son Minos had ruled here. Minos was the son of Europa, a mortal, and was thus a demigod who ought not to have lived a fraction so long as he had managed. Perhaps Zeus had favoured his get with some blessing to allow him to endure so very long. Or perhaps Minos had received long life after marrying the Nymph Pasiphaë, daughter of the Titan Helios. In truth, Theseus had no idea how these sorts of things worked.

He had been told that Minos dwelt within the Palace of Elektra, upon the acropolis that dominated Knosós. The Athenians were met by Minos's grim-faced warriors, all of which carried spears and shields. Small wonder that Minos, having no doubt received word from the herald of Theseus's intent to slay his monster, had misliked such a response.

The terror beneath Knosós must have proved equal parts shame and pride to the king here. For who would not fear the monster that stalked the dark and feasted upon the flesh of Man?

It was his son, tales said.

Theseus pushed the thought away. What matter whence came a beast that ate *children*? It was an abomination, and he would do well to ram his sword through its black heart.

One of the Knosians stepped forwards, glaring at Theseus like it was his own offspring Theseus had come to slay. The man's arrogant sneer made Theseus's palms itch with the need to grip the hilt of his xiphos. How could a man provoke such violence with but a look?

"The prisoner must surrender his arms and armour," the Knosian said, managing to speak at once both to Theseus and past him, as if in address to his Athenian escort.

Theseus frowned. He cracked his neck from one side to the other. Were he to order it, his men would fight for him, he had no doubt. Of course, doing so would start a war, and he could not say whether Athenai could win such a conflict. Even if they did, more mothers would grieve sons than had wept for those sacrificed to the Minotaur these past decades.

Malice glinted in the Knosian's eyes, as if he wanted Theseus to refuse his terms. These men were experienced warriors, Theseus could tell from the way they held their spears. Experienced, yet their leader seemed more thug than soldier.

If Theseus gave over his sword, how was he to battle the monster? Without his panoply, the creature might well gore him in the dark halls of the Labyrinth. Almost, he would have refused. Almost, he would have spit upon the ruffian's sandals, drawn his blade, and ordered his men to follow him into battle, rather than facing his prey alone and, apparently, unarmed.

Almost. But that would open yet another road to war. He must show Athenai and Knosós alike that the son of King Aegeus was more than a match for the monstrous get of King Minos. So he unclasped the buckle of his belt, loosed the scabbard of his xiphos, and handed it over to his belligerent captor.

Theseus's own men helped him unstrap the panoply, which too was claimed by Minos's men.

"Should we attend?" his man Hypatious asked.

But Theseus raised a hand to warn off the Athenians. They would linger in the harbour until they could be certain, one way or another, whether it was Theseus or the Minotaur who lay stricken in the darkness.

The Knosians clapt Theseus in bronze fetters and paraded him through the agora on their way up to the Palace of Elektra. Rather than meet the gazes of the many who stared at him, tracking his progression, he mused on the changing of ages. During the Silver Age, Knosós, so tale claimed, was ruled by the Pleiad Elektra, once among the greatest of her sisters. But she was taken by Zeus, by force, and later executed for treason against Olympus, and Zeus's bastard son by Europa now ruled this place unchallenged ... Was that why Minos had been granted seeming immortality? That Zeus wanted his offspring controlling this ancient polis?

He was led through the smoke-choked halls of Minos's megaron. It was perhaps coincidence the king favoured crimson paint upon the walls and columns. Surely it was not a deliberate attempt to evoke thoughts of the bloody spectacle that unfolded beneath their feet every nine years?

The king sat upon a slightly raised dais, his face given an unearthly gleam by the light of twin braziers just below the steps. His beard was stark white, and lines creased his face. Age had touched yet not ravaged this demigod who, if Theseus had the right of it, had to be pushing eight hundred years of life. Indeed, there was an almost fearful vitality behind Minos's icy blue eyes.

"You think to challenge the monster of the depths, do you, boy?" Minos asked. His voice was too deep for a Man, sounding more like Theseus imagined a bear would if it spoke. Perhaps it was even a trick of the firelight, but he fancied he saw in that mouth hints of ... fangs.

"Do you doubt the might of that monster?" Theseus challenged. In such situations, even feigned bravado seemed preferable to revealing his honest terror. What *was* King Minos to have lived so long? Had Theseus seen what he'd thought he'd seen, or did his fears transform the man before him into a monster himself?

"Hardly," Minos grumbled, then looked to his guards. "Have him taken down to the Mistress of the Labyrinth." His words, spoken with dark relish, held the finality of an executioner's falling axe.

THE MEN who ushered him down stair after stair, into the bowels of Minos's palace, did so none too gently, as if in coming here and declaring his challenge to the monster, he affronted their pride, as well. And why not? They sought for Men to cower at the mere whisper of the Minotaur's name. The bathed in the revulsion and horror the sick legend of its birth had engendered.

Some bards claimed Pasiphaë had slept with a bull that the god Poseidon had sent rising up from the depths of the sea. Lurid tales spoke of her donning a cow-apparatus to get the creature to mount her and sate her blasphemous desires. Theseus was not certain he put much stock in such tales. At least, he hoped them vulgar inventions of men eager to earn a few drinks for their efforts.

The steps grew narrow, twisting their winding ways into musty depths, the small breadth of the stairs forcing his guards to walk behind him rather than flank him. They bore no lamps and, with each bend around the central pillar, the darkness grew every more consuming. A wild thought arose: what if there was no monster? What if Minos's men simply sent their prisoners stumbling down darkened stairs until they broke their necks?

But such was a fanciful musing, and Theseus did not think he would avoid facing the creature with such ease. Just when the gloom had deepened beyond the point he could make out his own sandals upon the stairs, hints of flickering light crept round the next bend. The illumination, however paltry, was a balm for his soul, and Theseus found his pace quickening without need for his guards to push him forwards.

Theseus misliked being blind almost as much as he hated feeling lost. It was, he supposed, a poor choice to volunteer to fight a monster in the pitch black of the Labyrinth.

The stairs emptied onto a landing. Beyond a peristyle of columns, each bearing a sconce with a flickering torch, a wide-open floor lay, forming the heart of the chamber. The floor bore a mosaic of a geometric pattern. His guards made no move to pursue him past the staircase, so Theseus wandered into the ring of a torch's light to examine part of the design. It was a perfect square sliced up into the branching pathways of a multicursal maze of impossible complexity. Dare they display a map of the very Labyrinth itself in taunt of the victims? For no man could memorise such a pattern in order to find his way to the centre, much less back out.

Silken fabric whispered over the tiles, and Theseus turned to see a woman gliding from the shadows. She did not so much walk across the floor as dance to unheard music, a floating spectre claiming this sepulchral hollow as her domain. Tall enough to perhaps be a Nymph, she had eyes the colour of a stormy sea, and her raven-dark hair billowed about her, unbound. The fabric she wore might have been a peplos, but she'd more tossed it around herself than clad herself, leaving her left leg and breast both exposed.

Theseus's voice caught in his throat. He stumbled forwards, his bronze manacles clattering upon his wrists, making him seem even clumsier than he felt before this airy spirit. His men, on the voyage over, they had claimed Minos had two daughters, born in the years after the coming of the Minotaur.

If this was one of those princesses, she could not be so much older than him, and yet her eyes glinted with a timeless intellect. They were deep, he thought, when she glided to stand before him, her chest heaving as if she had been dancing here for hours. Indeed, a thin sheen of sweat glistened upon her brow and dribbled down her neck.

Part of him wanted to trace the water's path with his finger, but he could scarce tear his gaze from the consuming blue in the princess's gaze. He could drown in the depths of that sea, he knew.

"You must be Prince Theseus of Athenai," the woman—*goddess*—said, her voice as sublime as her motions. "The boy who boasts he will come here to slay my brother."

"Brother ..." Theseus managed to rasp.

From the shadows beyond a column, someone snickered. "Hera's rigid arse, this one's thick, isn't he?" The voice belonged to a girl, perhaps a couple years younger than Theseus, who stepped onto the mosaic to peer at him. She looked a mirror of the other, with her black hair and stormy Tethid eyes. Were it not for the age difference, they could have passed for twins.

"Phaidra," the older sister chided without looking back at the girl. "So, Theseus. You come now to the threshold of the Labyrinth itself."

"It's here." He knew he sounded a fool, but he still found himself enraptured by the princess before him.

"It's beneath us," she said with a dainty tap of her bare foot upon the mosaic. "You see, Theseus, tradition bids those who come here to dance with me upon this sacred space. Our footsteps rouse my brother, and when the next night falls, he ensures death comes swifter. It is a relic, you see, of the old days when the Men of Atlantis, before it was even Atlantis, held worship to Gaia and made her offerings." Now she did look to her sister and waved her hand at Theseus. "Phaidra, remove his fetters."

The girl sauntered over, gruff where her sister was graceful, though Theseus got the impression she too could have danced with preternatural lightness should it have suited her. She looked Theseus up and down before grabbing one bicep and squeezing. "Whilst he may have the brains of a drunk tortoise, he's got muscles fit to strangle you, Ariadne."

"He cannot well dance in chains."

The girl huffed but withdrew a ring of keys bound to her belt and set about unlocking the manacles that had already begun to chafe at Theseus's wrists. "Yes, well, maybe she's, in fact, hoping you'll do some squeezing of her." It was more a grumble than a statement.

And yet ... Theseus found himself again staring into her sister's indigo eyes. "Marry me ... Ariadne." He'd made no conscious choice to propose any such arrangement. Indeed, Athenai and Knosós remained enemies, and such a union could not hold. But ... but ... Was it a self-destructive madness that had taken him, to come here intent to slay a monster and instead find himself seeking to marry the creature's sister?

Phaidra slapped her palm to her forehead before shaking her head and backing away. *She* clearly believed him mad.

Ariadne quirked a sad smile. "Were I to marry, I would choose a husband with a chance to live long enough to actually reach the wedding." And yet something in those deep eyes bespoke another answer, and he could not surrender his hope. Had she done something to him? Had she enchanted him with some supernatural gift of her Nymph blood?

The woman took his hand and pulled him to the mosaic's heart. He spared a brief glance down, enough to see that, in this depiction, an open space lay at the heart of the maze. The den of the Minotaur?

"Phaidra," Ariadne commanded.

Her sister disappeared back behind the columns. A moment later, a grinding sound filled the landing, as of great gears of stone and creaking wood lurching into motion. Then those sounds were drowned out by the thrumming of music, haunting and mournful, somehow spilling through the hall without source.

Ariadne had not released Theseus's hand and now placed it upon her exposed left hip. Theseus could not stop himself from tightening his grip, digging his fingers into her bare flesh with his insatiable hunger for her, as if he might consume her through the palm of his hand. Ariadne's lips parted, ever so slightly, and she began to sway, drawing him into the rhythm of the music.

Time unfolded in dreamlike waves, and he was caught in its current. He could not have said how long had passed. Not to save his own life.

Though Ariadne stood, in fact, a hair taller than Theseus, she laid her head upon his shoulder. Her voice, when it reached his ear, was but a whisper, so faint he might have mistaken it for a part of this waking dream. "Poor, mad Daedalus built this Labyrinth, you see, at the command of my father."

"Who?" Theseus still thought himself dreaming now. The gentle tracing of Ariadne's finger upon the lines of his abdomen jerked him, suddenly and unequivocally, back to alertness.

"An artificer of unparalleled genius whom my father once employed. Or perhaps employed is the wrong word, for Minos made a slave of Daedalus and refused to let him leave, especially once he had crafted this Labyrinth. Some claim Daedalus was an Oracle. He told me, once, a man would come to me, love me, and slay my brother in the hopes of claiming me, as well. He told me I too would love this man, despite myself, and for him betray my father.

"Do you think that a strange prophecy, Athenian?"

Theseus remembered himself enough to hold her at arms' length and glanced about the landing. Sitting beneath one of the columns, he saw Phaidra, watching them, though probably too far off to hear their conversation. Of his captors, he found no sign. "I think it more than passing odd, yes."

Ariadne smiled, but a sadness had crept into her face now. "Who gave birth to the Minotaur?"

"Pasiphaë, daughter of the Sun God, Helios."

"And where is the daughter of the god?" Ariadne's face held a sadness too deep to fathom.

Theseus shrugged. Other than her shame of having birthed a monster, he'd heard little else of Pasiphaë.

"It broke her, that horror, down to the pith of her soul, and she lay abed, speaking to no one, eating only if forced to it. You might have thought her useless to all the World. Oh, but Father had yet one use of her. He still needed a legitimate heir, you see, and not lightly would he cast aside Helios's daughter and take another wife. Assuming he even could do so—there is a rumour he cannot lie with other women without destroying them. How fortunate for him that Mother's mind needed not be present for her to conceive."

The callous obscenity of what she implied landed like a blow, forcing Theseus to break away from Ariadne. He stumbled a step backwards and gaped. His mouth worked but refused to form words. His mind could parse what she'd said. He could understand the cruel, cold logic by which Minos had operated. But abhorrence left him speechless.

"I'm told," Ariadne said, "that when my mother—or I suppose my mother's body, really—birthed me, he took me to a window and appeared to consider tossing me into the sea. A girl, after all, cannot be an heir. Obviously, he restrained himself. So he tried again." Her gaze swept over to Phaidra, who rose, her fists closed at her side, though it did not stop her whole body from trembling. She *did* hear what Ariadne told him now.

"Well, still not the desired result." Ariadne's voice quivered but did not quite break. "I imagine ..." She paused and swallowed. "If there was some part of my mother still inside the shell of her mortal form, I imagine she must have tried to will herself to death. I was too young to recall what response Father had to receiving another girl child, though I'm told he took a slave girl to his chamber and that, in the morn, they carried what remained of her out in a satchel."

"Ariadne ..." Theseus reached for her, wanting to offer comfort, though his own voice sounded more pained moan than reassurance.

She slapped his hand away. "I am not finished, Athenian. Because, of course, neither was King Minos. He would have an heir out of his Pasiphaë, if it killed her. And it did. She ... blessedly ... did not survive birthing my youngest brother, Deukalion. And at last Father had his heir. But King Minos does not waste that which comes to him, so I, his firstborn—aside from my brother below—was named Mistress of the Labyrinth." Now she edged close enough she could place a hand upon his breast. "I dance with his sacrifices in offering to Gaia and the Minotaur. You see, he named the bull after himself, though I took to calling him Asterion, once, hoping some humanity lurked within his breast. But it does not, and with each offering of Man-flesh, Asterion grows larger and more monstrous. The Labyrinth is vast, but I wonder if one day not even its maze will be enough to contain my brother.

"So, yes, dear Theseus. I have long pondered Daedalus's words, his claim that I should betray my father and help bring about the death of my brother. Mayhap he was an Oracle. Or perhaps he simply had the intellect necessary to predict the inevitable." Now her fingers clutched at his shoulder, as tight upon it as his had been upon her hip. "Today I must lock you in the cells beyond those columns. Tomorrow night, Minos and his court will come to see you thrown behind the iron doors that seal the Labyrinth."

"They took my sword."

Ariadne nodded as if she knew all he would say. "That, and other tools you'll need, I will see secreted away just inside the Labyrinth. I am its Mistress, after all." Another swallow. Theseus wondered how difficult all of this must have proved for her. How long she must have dwelt with these sorrows and the burden Daedalus had placed upon her. "Release my brother from his maddened rage and, in so doing, punish Minos for his wretchedness. Then, we shall see about Daedalus's prophecies of love." With that, she pushed away from him.

Before Theseus could form a coherent thought, Phaidra took his wrist and led him to a cell behind the columns. The younger girl twisted a gear upon the wall and an iron portcullis rose, opening the way to a dim room that stank of human waste and the damp of the underground. Instinct demanded he refuse to enter so foul a place, but Theseus forced himself to step inside. "What happened to Daedalus?"

Phaidra frowned, clearly pained by the subject. "He escaped not long before you arrived. He tried to take his son with him, but ... Ikarus died in the process." Had Phaidra known him well? Raw grief upon her visage made plain she had. A playmate? A friend? Something more to her? "Father spread a rumour that Daedalus had built wings and flown from his tower. It rankled his pride to think a man might simply have outsmarted him. Now, he offers fortunes in drachmae to any who can tell him where fled his precious artificer." Phaidra sniffed. "Rest, if you can, Theseus."

She once more twisted the gear. The grinding of the iron grate, as it settled into place, felt like a weight crushing him. Its final screech drove home the utter reality of his situation.

It had never been a dream. He had walked, willingly, into a nightmare.

☙

NIGHT FELL, and as Ariadne had warned, Minos's sneering warriors arrived outside Theseus's cell. The malice in them left him shaken and stupefied. It simmered in their shadowed eyes. It seeped from their very pores. He could not help but wonder what terrible wrong they imagined themselves avenging against him. The death of the king's nephew, an event that had transpired before Theseus—or many of these men—was even born?

No. Men might convince themselves their vitriol stemmed from just cause, but the hatred itself soon became the fuel for its own fires. It was the self-sustaining malevolence of a pack having whipped themselves into a frenzy, their reasons but a thin veneer to disguise a more primal need: to unleash petty revenge for all the inequities of their lives upon a target, *any* target from which they believed themselves impervious to retribution in kind.

They grabbed him roughly by his biceps and dragged him from his cell, though he'd have willingly walked. They shoved and mocked, transforming in his mind from individual Men to a mass of limbs and gibbering faces, like the profane tales of the Hekatónkheir that had warred against the gods during the Titanomachy.

Ariadne was there, between the columns, half in the shadows, her face hidden beneath the folds of her himation, though he desperately wished to look into those ocean-deep Tethid eyes once more. He needed a friend. He needed a look, a single glance of compassion to carry with him into the darkness. But the princess, silent as a ghost, pointed to a doorway beyond the rim of torchlight.

Executioners who enjoyed their work far too much, the mob of Minos's men heaved him forwards, their faces blurring in his mind to cackling monstrosities, sick and inhuman. Maybe Minos was there. Theseus found, given the maddened pounding of his pulse, he could scarce focus upon any one aspect of the chamber, save for that beckoning doorway. A relief within the pediment above the frame depicted a bull with hands feasting upon the flesh of a man, tearing muscles away with its teeth. Though the man had no lower half remaining, from the frantic look upon his face, he remained, in inexplicable awfulness, somehow still alive and aware of his wretched ending.

Beneath the macabre display, the door itself was comprised of massive stone blocks, inset away from the wall, and divided by a seam down the middle. The blocks were engraved with a multicursal pattern similar to the floor mosaic, though Theseus could not say if it was a different design or the very same. From the corner of his eye, he saw Ariadne drift past his captors and insert something into a hole in the wall. The stones within the doorway shuddered, trembling as though even they, immutable though they were, feared the creature beyond their threshold.

The grinding that followed had him clenching his jaw. The rumbling seemed to pass through the core of him, a promise of the rending of his flesh that must soon follow. For a bitter, craven instant, Theseus considered begging for mercy. What utter madness had led him here? What a fool he had been to volunteer for this fate!

If he had thought, for a moment, Minos might have spared him, he might have broken then. But that was what they wanted of him, he knew. They were a crowd of bullies, Minos chief among them, and a bully loves naught more than to see their victims weeping before them, thus affirming their own importance. So, Theseus locked his jaw and held silent.

The seam broke apart, the two sides drawn away from one another by unseen mechanisms, stone grinding upon stone. Through the curtain of dust that fell, reflecting the faint light from the torches, he beheld within a darkness so complete it might have seeped from Tartarus itself. The groaning of the doors echoed into halls where light was so foreign as to seem but a memory of a dream.

Then the roar came.

A bellow that shook the stones, setting Gaia herself trembling with horror that something so foul might lurk within her depths.

Theseus's resolve fractured like ostraka hurled from a rooftop onto cobbles below. He opened his mouth to protest—surely no Man could do this to another person. No one, no matter how stricken with malice, could be so bereft of empathy as to condemn another to a death of such consuming dread. His unspoken words were lost when another shove sent him stumbling into the black.

His knees banged upon the cold, unworked stone of the ground beyond.

Even as he turned, considered hurling himself out of that Stygian darkness and back into the balm of torchlight, those doors began to groan once more. Closing.

He could still make it. Could cast himself upon the spears that were being levelled in his direction to prevent his escape. He could refuse this obscene sacrifice.

Sheer will clenched his fists. Though he could not make out the faces of his foes and they surely could see even less of him in this dark, he stared defiance at them.

Even unto the last, when that final, all important sliver of light winked out, leaving him in utter blackness.

29

KIRKE

3 Bronze Age

"I slew Tethys's drakon," Kadmus said, "and in the decades since, my family and my kin have faced unending hardship until I cannot help but think some curse must have lain within the foul creature's blood." The old king rubbed his weathered face, much changed from how Kirke had seen him in Tyros, the day prior. "Take the child, Kirke, just take it. I … I cannot continue. My grandson, Pentheus, he is a man of ambition, though young, and I shall hand the kingdom to him. Trouble arises in Illyris, and I think I shall seek one last adventure there. The babe Dionysus is not safe here."

No, that much was certain. If Hera learnt of Zeus's bastard, she might come for him, and who knew if even Zeus would tolerate the child after what he'd done to Semele. And that was assuming Pentheus or anyone else of this bloodline would want the child here as a potential rival. Yeah, little Dionysus would not live long in Thebes—nor perhaps anywhere in Elládos—but Kirke could not well raise the child as her own, either.

Harmonia had seen Kirke well provisioned, granting her a hundred drachmae, a fine peplos, and an exquisite amaranthine himation of Nusantaran silk, embroidered with gold trim. Her satchel laden with supplies and the babe tucked in one arm, she was just leaving the palace when the prince Polydorus stopped her, pressing a scroll into her hand. The prince was Semele's little brother, not yet twelve, and he had wept for his sister with the same fervour as had his parents.

"My sister Ino married the king of the Minyans, Athamas, half a day south." The Minyans ruled the plains and wilds in central Elládos. None of their settlements had the power of the great poleis, but collectively they posed a force to be reckoned with, as well she knew. "Perhaps she can help you more than us. We are ... broken here. Crushed beneath the sandal of Fate."

A sentiment Kirke knew all too well. She tucked the scroll into her satchel. "I'll seek out Ino."

Though she remembered her brother's tale of the woman and what she'd had done to the children of Nephele. *Another* of Zeus's victims.

In truth, Kirke could not have fled Thebes soon enough. The very air had grown so thick with melancholy that the dolour seemed to seep into the water and the wine, draining both of colour and flavour.

The child cried when Kirke walked, and she had no milk, nor aught else to offer save dribbles of wine from her wineskin. This she poured onto her finger and let Dionysus suck it until he fell into a blissful—perhaps drunken—sleep. The Minyan capital was a hill fort known as Orchomenus, lying on the road between Thebes and Korinth, and Kirke reached it midafternoon.

While most places greeted Titan guests with obsequiousness, the guards here eyed her with suspicion, at least until she offered each a tetradrachma. Coinage made everything flow, she found, in most any age.

And, indeed, a few more drachmae earned her an audience with Queen Ino, who agreed to walk with her along the colonnade that rimmed the agora, her guards trailing some distance back. The queen had given her little brother's scroll a perfunctory look before returning it.

"Taking in the child would expose Orchomenus to Zeus's or Hera's ire, too," Ino mused, strolling with her hands behind her back. How like Harmonia she looked. The woman had more of her mother in her than her father, of that Kirke was certain.

"Yeah, well maybe it'll make up for convincing Athamas to sacrifice his twins over that drought."

Ino stumbled to a stop, mouth open a hair as she cocked her head at Kirke, staring. Oh. Oh, well wasn't that a steaming pile of Cyclops shit? Aeëtes had told the tale so vividly of how Ino had tried to rid herself of Nephele's children to ensure pre-eminence of her own, and Kirke had thought of naught else on the walk here. But like a fool, she'd been choked upon the crime she hadn't bothered to ask if it had even happened yet.

And from the malignant grin now spreading across Ino's face, she had just given the woman the idea. Oh, that was nice, wasn't it? Kirke always wanted to be responsible for attempted kinslaying. It was one thing missing from her list of accolades. Yeah ... fuck.

Kirke's mind whirred over what to say to dissuade Ino—and dare she do so? If Ino didn't try to kill Nephele's twins, Phrixus would never come to Kolchis and marry Khalkiope, Kirke's niece who adored her husband, and by Nyx's pitch-black arsehole was all this going to drive Kirke mad.

Before she came up with aught, Ino shrugged as if no treason had passed between them. "I'll think on what to do with my nephew. In the meantime, I can at least arrange a wet nurse to see him well fed."

"Yeah, he likes wine, too," Kirke added, drawing an askance look from Ino.

Probably shouldn't have mentioned *that*, either.

A SURREAL SENSE of the expanse of Fate had settled upon Kirke as she watched Athamas, befuddled by Ino's words, call the priest of Zeus down, ready to smash in the head of Phrixus. Aeëtes, in telling the story, had left out the part where the flying golden ram had dropped down on the priest, kicking his head in and sending everyone else, save Phrixus and Helle, scampering away in fear of the wrath of gods.

Too, Aeëtes had neglected to mention—or perhaps Phrixus had not known it to tell—that not a fortnight later, Athamas had hounded Ino out of his palace, screaming at her in the night, calling her a witch and blaming her for the madness that took him in betraying his own. As if the fact Ino had suggested it abrogated his blame for attempted kinslaying.

As if Kirke's words had not led to this.

Either way, dress torn and lip bloody, Ino stumbled from the palace in the middle of the night, and Kirke watched, following without a word, Dionysus in her arms, as though all of this had become some hypnogogic trance. The Moirai played them like puppets.

Go, little Phrixus, fly away and marry Kirke's niece in Kolchis. Tell them how an evil spirit had come upon your stepmother to give her such vile thoughts.

Left speechless, Kirke slipped her free arm around Ino's waist and helped the woman away from the palace that had been her home. Would Ino ever return here? Perhaps. Kirke did not know enough about how this story would play out, in truth. Perhaps none of it mattered.

Only, she had promised Kadmus to see Dionysus raised, and that, at least, she would achieve.

A few obols to a wealthy merchant got them a room in his home for the night, and the man's wife promised hot food in the morn.

"What have I done?" Ino moaned, shaking her head while sitting on the straw-laden floor of the chamber the merchant had given them. "My children ... What if I cannot ever see them again?"

Kirke rocked the infant in her arms. "There is a child who needs you now. A nephew whose life is like to prove as difficult as those who have fled. And, yeah, I know it's hard, but you're the only one who can save your nephew." Kirke handed Dionysus off to Ino, who took the babe with more tenderness than she'd expected, as though the child might replace the two she'd lost. "Can you take him somewhere beyond the reach of the Olympians?"

A while Ino held silent before at last nodding. "My sister Autonoë, her husband holds some lands in far Nysa, in Kumari Kandam. I could ... Olympus would not come for us there. No one would come so far."

Kirke nodded. It would be far enough, that seemed certain. "Swear to raise him as your own. Swear to see him safe."

"I swear."

Saving only a tetradrachma for her own use, Kirke gave Ino the remainder of the coins she'd gotten from Harmonia. "Hyperion watch over you and the babe."

IN THE MORN, Kirke and Ino left for Korinth. There, she helped the princess book passage on a ship bound for Ugart, having to trust Ino to make her own way to Nysa from there. The journey was far, but the other Nymph had money enough if she took care.

When the ship was away, Kirke found an alley in Korinth and dug the Box out from her satchel. How much more of this madness could she take? She needed to be home, and Aiaíā had become a distant dream now, a precious prison she longed for compared to the tumult of her journey through time.

The last adjustment she had made to the Box had sent her fifty years forwards in time. So, maybe if she tuned it just right, she could manage another six hundred and fifty and then—

The top popped open and the World shifted again.

"WHO ARE YOU?" a woman demanded behind her. The speaker, a young girl really, had lain on the floor, studying some scroll, hair tied up in a tight bun. No one Kirke recognised. "When did you get in here?"

"I, uh ... Well, yeah, I was visiting. I mean visiting because I came here before and I wanted to visit again and I, uh ... Do you know where Themis is?"

The woman pointed off into the green, where sure enough, the dark-haired Titan was among the pankration students, unclad as the others, body glistening in oil. And her immediate student was the raven-haired Heliad, Pandora, her too wearing naught save a linen tied around her nethers. Themis hurled her to the ground with comical ease, then stood, hands on hips, staring down at her pupil, while Kirke approached.

❧

DRIZZLING RAIN SPLASHED HER FACE, drawing her from the daze the Box induced. This place Kirke recognised mere moments after shaking off the disorientation produced by the Box. The more she used the device, the easier it seemed to become, a thought that both comforted and terrified for its implication this might now have become her life.

Though different and lacking the village houses among which she had once lived, this place would become Marsa, of that she had little doubt. Against the rain, she drew her himation over her head like a cloak, wondering at seeing the place so empty.

On the lower slope of Ogygia's single mountain, a short distance from where Kalypso's home would one day stand, lay a simple cottage. A modest dwelling offering her little save perhaps a hot meal and shelter from the incessant wetness of the day.

The damp had turned the surrounding ground to a slosh of mud that sucked at her sandals as she climbed. Ahead, upon the small portico a couple sat, the woman cradling a flame-haired babe in her arms, lost in conversation with the man.

That was Prometheus ... and Pandora?

Shock settled upon Kirke and she dropped into a crouch, though she could not have said why she felt the need to hide from either of them. Once, on visiting her island, Prometheus had admitted to being Mother's own father, making him grandfather to Kirke and Athene.

Since then, Kirke had not had much chance to converse with him on the subject, nor to demand why he had never taken more interest in her life.

Perhaps he would do so now, though. Perhaps now, in the greatest depths of her desperation, he would at last choose to become the kin she needed. Because Kirke had no idea what she would do elsewise. The whole of her existence had come untethered, her conceptions of life loose and turbulent, much as she flitted through time.

Drawing the amaranthine himation tighter about her shoulders, she stood, approaching the cottage. Prometheus saw her first and said something to Pandora, who rose with the babe and set out for a stroll, heedless of the rain, though the woman cast a surreptitious glance at Kirke. For her part, however, Kirke found her gaze rather settling upon the babe in her arms, that auburn hair. Prometheus's child ...

Was it possible? Gaia shifted beneath Kirke's feet. Or perhaps that was just the squelching mud because she could not accept this madness.

Saying naught, Prometheus beckoned her, guiding her not into the warmth of the cottage but up the mountain slope, perhaps intuiting the need for privacy or to conceal Kirke from Pandora. Her grandfather's hand fell upon her shoulder, a bulwark of strength keeping her on her feet, and not just against the weather and rain-slicked escarpment they climbed.

When they reached a rock outcropping that jutted off the mountain, Prometheus settled down, feet dangling off the edge without apparent care for a drop of a several dozen feet. Shuddering, Kirke slumped down next to him, though she folded her legs against her chest instead of letting them hang.

"That babe will be my mother." She wasn't even sure if it was a question anymore.

"I saw your coming in the flames, though I do not even know your name."

"Funny, I wasn't certain you knew it in my time, either." She tightened her arms around her legs, refusing to meet his sapphire gaze, though she knew he tried to catch her eyes.

From the slight tightening of his muscles, perhaps her words had struck him. Either way, he fell silent a moment.

Pushing him away now, when he neither knew her nor owed her aught, would avail Kirke little. Even as much as she wanted *someone* to blame for the uncontrolled spiral of her life. "Um ... I need to say something and I don't quite know how, so maybe the best way is just to say it because if I don't I think I might erupt from the pressure. Yeah." The words spilt out of her with such haste he might well not follow, but she could not slow them. "So, I got this Box which sent me careening through time and I met Pandora in different times and now I think she's my grandmother and I found out a while ago—a long time from now, really—that you're my grandfather, even though you've been too much of a duck's puckered arsehole to tell me that for most of my life. And I'm not sure if this Pandora here is before or after the one I just saw, for her I mean, so I have no idea if I can ask her aught, but I'm asking you because I think you always know more than you let on. Yeah. And, uh, if you could be bothered to tell me how to work the thing so I can get home, it would even maybe make up for you ignoring me for several thousand years. Ahem."

For a time, he stared at her until she had no choice but to look up and fall into the depths of those sparkling blue eyes of his. "You still have not told me your name."

"It's Kirke."

A slow nod, and he held out his hand. Reluctantly she took it, which caused him to quirk a smile. "The Box, Kirke."

"Oh. Right." She jerked her hand away and retrieved the damn thing from her satchel, pressing it at Prometheus. "Yeah, fix this thing."

"One has to appreciate the irony in being repeatedly asked to fix something one has not yet created."

"Yeah, one has to help one ... other ... get home if one doesn't want a heel connecting with one's stones." Kirke suddenly realised she had threatened one of the most powerful Titans outside of the Olympians, but her grandfather seemed more amused than offended.

For a time, he fiddled with the device and Kirke watched in

silence, trying—and perhaps failing—to understand the implications of the settings he made.

"How do you know what to set where?" she asked when she could contain herself no longer.

"A combination of remembered pyromantic insights of this moment and of having studied Pandora's version of this Box. Yours seems to have had some adjustments made, which I might actually be able to implement in *hers* now." Pandora's *version*? Was it the same Box? Where there two of these damn things? There was not enough wine in the whole of history for this sort of thing. "I think this will get you where you need to go, Kirke, but I cannot say for certain. I, too, am still discovering the extent of this thing."

With a glower, she snatched the Box when he proffered it. "Don't think this absolves you from having ignored me for my whole life. What in the depths of the Underworld possessed you to hide our connection from your own grandchild?"

"If I had to guess, I would say this conversation," Prometheus said, face creased in a bare hint of pain.

His words were a slap that left her sputtering a moment. "I, um … Yeah, I'm pretty sure the proper answer to that, and I'd have to check to be sure, maybe do a bit of research, but I'm pretty certain the thing to say is 'fuck you, Grandfather.'"

"Kirke …"

With a rude gesture, she popped the top to the Box.

30

HERAKLES

726 Bronze Age

From Athenai, Herakles had sailed across the Strait of Korinth, too eager to be away from the Argo and her captain. The voyage to Kolchis had allowed Herakles to complete two of his labours. He ought to have revelled at the thought he'd brought the shades of his children that much closer to peace. Whilst stealing Hippolyta's girdle hardly benefited Mankind, clearing the Axeinos Sea of the harpies would make Gaia a safer place.

Yet Herakles found his skin felt caked in a sheen of filth he could not scrub clean. Medea's murder of her brother, her kinslaying, it had summoned the shades of his boys, their eyes flashing with disgust. The act had polluted the whole crew of the Argo, and Herakles could not say he felt wholly cleansed of it by whatever prayers Medea's sorceress aunt had offered. Indeed, witchcraft seemed to wreak chaos, the ill far outweighing its possible good.

Iolaus had sailed with him, though his nephew had sensed his mood and given him space to wrestle with his dark musings. Perhaps the murder of Absyrtus and Herakles's brushes with the Art were not all that troubled him.

He could not explain his actions in Ilium. It was as if he had become another person. No, not so much a person as ... an enraged army. A man might control himself. But an army, blood up with the awful thrill of violence, that became a force in and of itself, beyond reason. Though a good general could direct an army, no one could ever really *control* one. Armies were mobs, and mobs were driven by atavistic instincts, reverting from Men to packs of beasts with blades in their hands.

Such thoughts weighed heavy upon his mind as he plodded the beaten path through the rocky hills between Korinth and Mykenai. Within every shrub, every cluster of thistles, he could have sworn lurked the shadows of judging eyes, watching his progress. Since that day in Ilium, an unspeakable fear had begun kindling in his breast. Upon the sea, he had pushed down his incipient terrors, forcing his traitorous thoughts ever back onto the omnipresent dangers he must protect his crewmates from.

But now, returned to Elládos, those fears crept upon him, demanding shapes he could no longer deny them. Was the impossible violence that had overcome him and driven him to sack a city the same paroxysm that had led to the murder of his own children? It had felt like something in the depths of his soul had begun clawing its way to wakefulness. And naught Herakles had seen—not the maws of drakons nor the weapons of Gigantes nor even the atramentous depths of Tartarus—offered greater horror than the dread of that force within himself coming to life.

With a frustrated growl, Herakles kicked a rock, sending it skittering along the path. The action sent blessed pain shooting through his ankle. A reminder he was still a Man. That he was not this ... cruel, calamitous entity stirring within his breast. He was more than a force of uninhibited destruction.

Iolaus cast a wary glance his way. "I believe the stone is entirely slain, Uncle."

Herakles drew up short and fitted the younger man with a

heavy look. "What if ..." Maybe it was better not to burden Iolaus with his doubts. Maybe, but part of him yearned for someone to share these weights with. "What if one day you happened upon a water so still it offered a perfect reflection. And yet, when you looked into the pool, you saw you were not the man you thought yourself to be."

Iolaus thought that over a while before answering. "I guess I'd say it's not about who you thought yourself, but who you wish yourself to be."

Were it only so easy.

Beset by these burdens, he parted from Iolaus at the gates of Mykenai and came at last back to the throne of Eurystheus, in what had once been their common ancestor Perseus's great megaron. Maybe it was such dark musings that drove him to it. When he came before Eurystheus's throne, he hurled the girdle at the king's feet. "A prize stolen from the queen of the Amazons."

His cousin could not have missed the contempt dripping from Herakles's voice. Certainly, the king frowned at Herakles's action. And yet, unless Herakles missed his guess, Eurystheus saw naught amiss in the thought of stealing the treasures of another for his own daughter. Admete was cut from her father's cloth, without doubt, and the princess motioned for a slave to snatch up the girdle and bring it to her. If the princess had the least shame over demanding her father send Herakles to foreign lands as a thief, she did not show it. Rather, with her mouth widened into an impressed "O," she turned the belt over in her hands, admiring its lustre.

"The birds of the Axeinos are slain," Herakles added. "Trade across the sea may resume." Though he doubted Kolchis would hold much welcome for any Elládosi in the foreseeable future.

"Well, well," Eurystheus said. Herakles almost wished the king would have risen to the provocation he'd offered. And perhaps his cousin knew that, for he held his composure, plastering a mirthless smile upon his face.

He drummed his fingers upon the armrest of his throne, his wicked smirk only deepening. "I imagine you must be weary from your voyage. You have my leave to rest yourself some days before undertaking the next of my labours for you."

Herakles almost sighed. Half his labours for his belligerent cousin were now complete. Had he brought any semblance of peace to his boys? Had he salved any of the pain of his own soul? He was no longer certain any of this did anyone any good. But if he faltered, he condemned himself and his boys to eternal suffering. "I believe you already have somewhat in mind."

To which the king offered a cocky shrug. "Perhaps you tire of slaying monsters, cousin. I thought, then, maybe it is better to offer you a simple task, one to the benefit of my friend, the king of Athenai. You know of King Aegeus, I take it."

Theseus's father. The young man had spoken, oft enough, of his intent to present himself to the king and claim his birthright. Since he'd left Theseus in Athenai, by now, the young man must have done so. "I've not met him in person."

"Yes, well, Athenai is well known for its fine horses, and none finer than the collection of the king. Aegeus's royal stables are so vast, it is said you could walk among the horses from dawn until dusk and not lay eyes on every last steed."

Herakles folded his arms over his chest. Did his cousin intend to send him to steal horses now? Was this, in fact, Athene's point in assigning him labours in service to Eurystheus? That she knew his cousin would degrade and shame him, and Herakles must be forced to bridle his temper and submit himself to the will of another, no matter how it chafed his pride?

"I visited these stables whilst you were away, cousin, and I can confirm they are truly vast. Also"—his eyes gleamed with malice—"that they reek worse than Hades's own chamber pot."

"What has any of this to do with me?" Herakles demanded.

"I think you ought to help Aegeus out by clearing the dung from those stables."

For a moment, Herakles stood there, staring at Eurystheus. Maybe Athene had wanted to test whether he could control his temper. He could see why she might think an outburst would result from this sort of treatment. But sometimes, when confronted with the truly preposterous demands of those in power, disbelief smothered indignation. Herakles could not even summon his wrath at such an inane order. "You want me to muck out another man's stables."

Maybe he *did* feel the first stirrings of a dangerous ire inside his breast. With that growing darkness, he wondered if, should he kill King Eurystheus upon his very throne, his sons would ever forgive him.

"Well, that doesn't quite sound challenging enough for one of your labours, does it?" Eurystheus rubbed his chin, his manner making plain he had rehearsed this absurd performance. "Let's make it more interesting, then, cousin. You are to clean the whole of his stables in a single day before Hyperion's last rays dip beneath the horizon."

In the shadows behind the throne, Kreontiades watched him, his little eyes so intent to see whether his father would humble himself on his behalf. To risk life and limb was, sometimes, perhaps easier than to tear down the fragile edifices of one's own pride.

But a man who had slain his children had no place left for dignity.

"It will be done." What else could he have said?

DIVERTING a river down from the mountains, Herakles had washed out Aegeus's stables, then stopped in to call upon Theseus. His friend had taken well enough to palace life and received him with open arms and feasting Herakles found himself unable to enjoy. However vile his cousin was, however insipid the tasks Eurystheus set before him, Herakles had to admit he was almost *eager* to resume them.

Because when he'd lowered himself to muck out Aegeus's stables, Deikoon and Kreontiades and Therimachus had stood by and watched. And though he could not have said for certain, Herakles fancied he'd seen Deikoon nod in approval.

Thus, he felt not the least regretful, the next spring, when Eurystheus sent him to steal cattle from Helios's fabled island of Thrinakia. He had neither feared nor demurred, even when Helios's bastard daughters sent the three-headed Gígas, Geryon, to thwart him. Some few years ago, he learnt, that godsdamned thief Autolykus had raided cattle from the island already, and thus had the sun sisters bargained with Geryon to guard the cattle against further thieves.

Misshapen, with extra arms and too many gangly legs, the Gígas relied on its awful appearance and prodigious strength rather than skill or the least cunning. Extra legs upon a humanoid torso did not, as it turned out, enable faster running. Thus, whilst Geryon had tried to close the distance between them with his uneven gait, stumbling over the rock-strewn hills, Herakles had launched arrow after arrow into the Gígas until, at last, his foe fell.

Grateful that Helios's daughters did not come themselves—he was not certain he could have brought himself to shoot women—Herakles had claimed the cattle which now shuffled about his ship, filling the air with their incessant mooing. The sea breeze cut down the reek of their dung but failed to stifle it entirely.

He'd have a long sail back to Elládos. He'd need to thread his passage between sea monsters and whirlpools. He might even have to moor somewhere for the winter and continue when the weather turned clear.

But such things mattered little.

Because now, he had begun making real progress toward the appeasing of his sons. He began to have hope that peace might come to their souls at last. Thus, with the wind ruffling his locks and the sun upon his face, for the first time in years, the hint of a smile began to tug at the corners of his lips.

Pandora had been right. Maybe there was hope.

31

HEKATE

45 Bronze Age

*Y*ears flowed by like an unfurling procession of dreams. There were times, lost in the haze of drink and the pleasures of flesh, when Hekate could no longer distinguish between waking and oneiromantic wanderings. Ever, revelation teased, dancing upon the fringes, almost close enough to caress it with her fingertips, if she could but delve a little deeper.

God's blessed Bacchic wine opened the doors of their souls to the Truth.

Some nights, they spoke directly of this elusive Ontos, the breadth of Dionysus's wisdom serving as undeniable proof of his connection to an Elder God. For Dionysus was, himself, the true God. This she knew within her quivering soul.

Gathered around a flickering campfire, the living God and his followers would brush over the secrets of the Otherworld. Each of the women had, in varying degrees, the Sight. The great gift manifested differently among them. A fisherman's daughter, Akoitea could hear the voices of ghosts. The Nysan, Aanya, beheld pyromantic visions. Nikkal, a Phoenikian woman, could push her mind into the body of a hawk, seeing through its eyes. The Heliad Nymph, Aura, could feel whenever any presence drifted close from the far side of the Veil.

And Hekate ... managed more than any of them.

Tonight—if now still had meaning—a brume of burning poppies filled up the cave in which they reclined. All women, the God's Maenads, for he drew in men only for orgies and, when the women had their fill, most oft tore the spent males to pieces. Their livers and hearts they ate raw, leaving Hekate to wonder how much she must consume before becoming a Gígas.

They were naked, of course, their clothes discarded at the cave's hidden entrance, deep within the hills of Phrygia. God, in his infinite wisdom, commanded all should be bared for the mysteries they shared each night. His voice now reverberated along the walls as if uttered by a dozen throats at once, all coaxing souls free of bodies, offering the insight necessary for spiritwalking.

Some of the women merely collapsed into delirium, intoxicated on the poppy but unable to shed their mortal shells. Four others, though, joined Hekate and Dionysus in projecting across the Veil. Awareness lurched back in through the opiate fog, and Hekate realised her self-image here wore her favourite khiton. The others bore local garb from their own native lands.

The God, though, remained unclad. Or rather robed in enwrapping vines from which streamed fraying moss. The antlered skull mask Dionysus oft wore had, in this state, become his head in truth, his fevered intellect glinting virescent within the otherwise empty sockets.

Their master raised coarse hands upward, beckoning.

And they followed. Always they would follow.

❧

DOWN SECRET WAYS THEY PLODDED, pushing through the tenebrous expanses of the Spectral Realm, Hekate the first behind Dionysus.

This Realm cast the jungle in ultramarine hues. It twisted trunks into bent panoplies of arthritic pain. The streams lost substance. No moonlight poked through the sporadic breaks in the canopy. Though she saw animal and land spirits on the fringes, none dared approach her God as he led them further into the heart of the jungle.

Aura cast an apprehensive look to Hekate, and she nodded to the Heliad in reassurance.

They passed beneath an arch formed of warped tree branches, then doubled back, making their way through another which Hekate could have sworn was not there before. A third arch seemed to form across an empty streambed, and when they had passed through it, the Spectral Realm gave way to the deeper, swirling Dark of the Roil.

Obsidian edifices rose up around them as if in mockery of the trees that had stood but a heartbeat ago. A forest of the deepest darkness. Perhaps they only brushed against the Roil, though, for she thought it but moments before they found themselves in a twilight wood. Here, the moss-draped trees towered like mountains, some so thick around she could not even guess at their circumference. Gazing up at one, craning her neck, she beheld an endless canopy high above. Though she could make out naught, she could not shake the sensation that something watched from the boughs. Something alien, predatory.

It took an effort of will to tear her gaze from the roof of branches and leaves and take in her more immediate surroundings. Great roots rose from the ground, arching like bridges wide enough numerous wagons could have passed along them side by side. Boulders and rocks—these too coated in moss and sprouting mushrooms—broke up the forest floor ever so often. In places, she could see where plant growth had rent rocks asunder, leaving broken shards cast to either side.

"Behold the grandeur of the Gloomwood," Dionysus intoned.

Following the God, they wound their way through the colossal forest. The sheer size of the trees forced them to take long, circuitous routes. And yet, no matter how much time passed, twilight did not dim. In fact, if aught, it *almost* seemed to lighten a hair, as if they marched against the ordinary flow of time.

Dionysus offered no explanation and none of the women, Hekate included, dared breach this extraordinary moment with questions. For, with his guidance, they had moved beyond the Roil and entered the Otherworld. No spirit Hekate had questioned gave clear answers about their native Realm. Some indicated there were many, separate worlds, while others led her to believe the Spirit Realm was divided more by continents, almost like the Earth. Then again, spirits lied, especially to sorcerers.

This Gloomwood, she mused as they walked, seemed much akin to the Cedar Forest mentioned in Ninevehan legend. Perhaps one and the same?

Leaves rustling overhead drew her eyes. Her heart clenched as she caught sight of what looked like a boa—one many dozen feet long. But the snake ignored them, perhaps held back by the power of God, and they pushed onward.

In time, they came to a swift river that had carved a passage through the wood, some fifty feet wide. More arcing roots formed precarious bridges over churning rapids. Blessedly, Dionysus did not ask them to climb such mossy routes but rather followed the course of the river downstream. Another hour, maybe, and they came to a valley. Amid burgeoning palm trees stood a wooden enclave of tightly clustered buildings with steep, pitched roofs that reminded Hekate of palaces in Nusantara. Some structures stood free, whilst others jutted out of massive trees. Covered bridges joined balconies with the tree-houses, creating a maze that must allow the inhabitants to wander between homes with ease.

The river bisected the village, joined by a stream issuing from falls she could now see flowing off the mountain on the far side. As they drew nigh, the sense of being watched redoubled until she felt certain something awaited their arrival with ancient patience and Otherworldly hunger.

But she trusted her God.

Onward Dionysus led the Maenads, into the streets of beaten-down dirt. Up close Hekate realised the structures here had no joins, as if all cut from a single enormous tree. Or perhaps the inhabitants had somehow *grown* their village. She saw them then, peering down at her around pillars supporting the covered bridges, crouched atop roofs, or perched in palm trees: dryads.

In a Man, flesh the colour of fading willow leaves would have looked sickly, but on these beings, it made them seem extensions of the wood. Their eyes, with vertical, lizard-like pupils and starburst irises, seemed to see all the depth of her in an instant. Hekate felt naked once more, and indeed, her clothes had vanished. And still, those reptilian eyes delved deeper, scraping her core until she gasped for horror that any should see her base nature exposed.

The other Maenads had recoiled as well, their clothes too having vanished. Nikkal and Aanya had fallen to their knees, claimed by lachrymal convulsions for which Hekate had no pity to spare.

A dozen dryads clambered down walls, headfirst, clinging to the sides without apparent effort, only to remain on all fours when they reached the ground. Skittering, they closed in around Dionysus, most female though Hekate saw a handful of males, too.

Drumbeats resounded through the village, spilling out of the largest house like a pounding heart. Her pulse was in her head. A lightness in her chest. A euphoric tingle rushed through her, had her stepping forwards to meet a male and female dryad who approached. They rose up, took her hand, and guided her toward stairs leading into that central house.

Her senses blurred. She was within the house, staring up at a shadow play unfolding on the vaulted ceiling. A story, a memory, a dream contained within the beating drum. The female dryad caressed her hips, while the male fondled her breasts. Her body writhed in time with the music, gaze locked upon the hinted antiquity playing out overhead.

An intimation of two races, first together, then breaking apart. A war ... an eternal war. Individuals sundered even within the disparate races, schism upon schism, until the pieces of the old were cast too far apart to ever rejoin.

With desperate, seeking fingers she reached toward the ceiling. But the prurient currents had her, dragged her beneath its heaving waves.

LYING amid a mound of sweat-slicked flesh, languorous, Hekate peered up at the ceiling. But the drums had ceased, and with them went whatever secrets she might have apprehended. A sense of loss surged inside her, so deep she had to clench her fist to keep from crying out.

She had to know these things.

She had to know *all* things.

Answers, every question in the cosmos was here, if she could but sort it into a semblance of order. To draw so close and be denied was like having a blade jerked from a wound. A fresh agony that left her bloody and beleaguered.

Unable to stand it, she squirmed out from beneath the tangle of limbs atop her and slid onto the floor. Casting about, she found Dionysus. The God squatted on his haunches, knees up by the skull mask that had become his head. Twilight streaming in through the window wove bands of light and shadow across his figure, though his eyes still gleamed green in their sockets, watching her.

A groan beside her drew her eye, and the Nysan Aanya wriggled as a dryad kissed her. To Hekate's eyes, it seemed the dryad tried to shove its tongue down Aanya's throat, deeper and deeper. Not just the tongue, in fact, but the whole of the dryad's head had begun to flow into the woman's mouth. Then, all at once, Aanya and the dryad flowed into one another like merging streams.

As Hekate turned she saw the same unfolding with Nikkal, who melded with another female dryad.

"The weak have their uses," Dionysus said, voice echoing off the wood.

Before Hekate could think on it, a vicelike grip seized her ankles and yanked her prone. Another female dryad crawled over her legs to mount her, leering down at Hekate with those lizard eyes that stole voice and thought and will, leaving only fear and an unbidden, rising lust. They would take her, too. Her mind screamed at her to fight back, but the fiery irises and slitted pupils had become her World, and her body refused her.

They had taken Aanya and Nikkal, taken their souls. The dryads could use those souls to reach the women's bodies and claim them for themselves. Every sorceress's greatest fear, and Dionysus had given those two over to such. And Hekate, too, must share their fate.

"She has one of us inside," the dryad purred.

Already inside ... Tithorea. They sensed the spirit bound inside Hekate.

With delicious, awful slowness, the dryad prised apart Hekate's lips. She needed to shut her mouth, deny the kiss, but she could not move. Creeping dread, like being stalked in utter darkness. Like a dream where she could neither run nor speak to escape an approaching threat. How many times had her dreams left her impotent and moaning in terror she could not voice? And now she lived it.

The dryad leant closer, so close her nose touched Hekate's, her sappy breath stirring Hekate's hair. But she did not kiss her. Instead, the hand that had forced open her mouth worked its way deeper. Down, past Hekate's tongue, into her throat, her elbow banging upon Hekate's teeth. Gagging convulsions seized her.

She couldn't breathe! She was going to suffocate!

Crawling intrusions tore through her insides, fingers digging like worms.

Though breathless, her body refused to die. The agony stretched on, the dryad content to dig around inside Hekate without hurry. Then the spirit's fingers closed around something, a vein, a pipe, a wire—something wrapt around Hekate's heart. The sudden tug threatened to rip her heart out of place.

Stabbing pain shot through her core and down her left arm.

Please, let her just die ... But then, worse torments would come for her.

She needed to weep and scream and beat someone all at the same time.

Another yank, and Hekate's heart stopped beating. Pain. An ocean of pain, swallowing all other senses.

A tug, and the cord unspooled, torn free of her heart. The dryad began to withdraw her arm. Hekate felt it, dying as she was, as the cord thickened, scouring her throat with its coarse surface. The dryad pulled a vine out from inside Hekate and tossed it aside.

The house began to dim. Then Dionysus's hand was on her chest, pushing in a rhythm that sent shocks jolting through her. A sudden, painful beat of her heart forced her back to life.

As vision returned, she saw the discarded vine warped and writhed, thickening and growing until it became another dryad. One that rolled over, turning a loathing, reptilian gaze upon Hekate.

Tithorea?

Hekate coughed, spitting out mouthful after mouthful of blood from her gouged throat. She could not speak. But if the other dryad had freed Tithorea from her control ... Tithorea waited just long enough for the fear to dawn.

Then she snatched up Hekate's ankle and yanked her out from beneath Dionysus's grasp. Hekate managed to cast a pleading glance at her God, but he had resumed crouching on his haunches and only cocked his skull-head to the side at her.

Tithorea wrapt Hekate's big toe in her fingers.

Wait, Hekate wanted to beg but only managed to sputter on more blood. Surely the dryad she had so long enslaved knew what she meant, for the look that spread upon her face was one of such malevolent glee it could have chilled the blood of even the most hardened of killers. A sudden jerk, and Tithorea broke her toe, drawing forth a screaming wail of spraying blood.

Tithorea grabbed the next toe.

One by one, the dryad snapped each of Hekate's toes. She prayed for unconsciousness, but, of course, a disembodied soul could not find such easy escape. Ten broken toes, and then Tithorea straddled her, wriggling her hips and licking her lips.

"You bound me for thousands of years," the dryad purred. "Now, I will take your body and wreak such havoc with it. I will use you in ways that make you wish you could tear out your own eyes, sorceress. Behold the price of mortal hubris in thinking to master immortals to your will."

Spirits lied all too oft. But in the creature's face, Hekate could read the absolute truth of her intent. Panic had her thrashing in vain hopes of dislodging Tithorea. Titan Potency gave her enough strength that Tithorea had to seize her wrists with both hands to retain her position.

The ravaging of Hekate's insides had left her weak, though, and she could not hold out long ...

The mirth in those eyes told her Tithorea knew it, too.

"Stop," Dionysus commanded. "This one is my strongest Maenad. She is mine to hold in thrall. Mine forever."

Tithorea turned a withering glare at God, but only for a moment. Whatever she beheld in the depths of those virescent eyes, the dryad scampered away on all fours an instant later, fleeing out the door.

Hekate collapsed, desperate to weep. All she managed was a dribble of blood down her cheek.

Upon re-entering her body, Hekate found her chest caked in dried blood. Her insides ached almost as if her physical form had suffered the same torments as her soul. Dionysus had guided her and the others back the way they had come, and, despite her wretched state, Hekate had made a point of memorising the route. She could not imagine a desire to return to the Gloomwood, but all knowledge was valuable.

The other Maenads plied her with Bacchic wine to soothe the pains. Aura massaged her swollen throat. Questions bombarded Hekate about what she had seen, but she found her gaze drawn inexorably back to the Lord.

"Now you have witnessed a great mystery," Dionysus said as he settled once more before the fire within the cave.

The greatest of mysteries, for never, in all Hekate's studies and wanderings, had she before beheld the Otherworld with her own eyes. Truly, her Lord was glorious.

"The wonders of the Gloomwood," God continued, "are the purest expression of nature, the very abode of the Elder God, Pan. Only the worthiest among you might be fit to ever stand in his presence."

An overwhelming urge to prostrate herself seized her, seized all the Maenads. Before she knew it, Hekate had pressed her face to the floor, certain the others had done the same.

"We have already made an offering to him," Dionysus said, voice thrumming through the ground, deep as Gaia herself. "Bear witness."

When Hekate looked, Aanya and Nikkal were among them, lingering at the cave's threshold. Their postures, the slow way they craned their necks, it bespoke something ... reptilian. Dryad-possessed, those two Maenads met her gaze a moment, then slunk away into the forest.

"I make this offering," Dionysus said, drawing every eye back toward his glory, "to myself. For a piece of the Elder God lies within this breast." He thumped his chest, the sound like a massive leather drum. "I am he who was dead and had risen anew. Young, old, and timeless, born between life and death. Who better, then, to serve the cycle of nature?" Their Lord's shadow grew, its antlers streaming about the cave, melding into the dark beyond the firelight.

A dawning apprehension teased at Hekate. Knowledge she ought to have grasped, though the majesty of the incarnate God before her swallowed all else.

"I have beheld the turning of the Wheels. I have stalked the Stygian depths of the Underworld. I, son of the dead and scion of nature."

Son of the dead ...

"I have borne many names." To Hekate it seemed his virescent gaze now fell only upon her, piercing through to her core. "Speak one, abject sorceress, and behold the Ontos."

"Zagreus," Hekate rasped, the knowledge at once rising within her and bursting forth without the least regard for her will. Zeus and Persephone's ghost son, reborn as a living God.

The bone mask obscuring his face *smiled*. "Come drink of my honey ... and taste eternity."

Akoitea beat Hekate to it, her mouth around the Lord's phallus in an instant. The Maenads all gathered for their turn.

Because they were his, Hekate knew. *She* was his until the end of time.

❧

THE MAENADS WENT BEFORE DIONYSUS, heralds to his glory sweeping through Delphi, Argos, and Korinth. Bacchic wine flowed in endless streams, and where they walked, men and women and Titans danced naked in the streets. The thin veneer of civilisation—the profane illusion against nature—cracked in their wake. For life was glorious and the sum of it came to drinking, feasting, and fucking. All the edifices of Man were but hubris from those self-deluded into believing themselves above beasts.

Hekate watched as aristoi were brought low by their own primal urges. She laughed in jubilation as false lords ate their own horses raw. As their queens welcomed entire guard battalions into their beds. As their sons bludgeoned to death those who slighted them, marking their territories across poleis with urine and faeces.

Maenad numbers swelled with an influx of fresh women drawn from every village, town, and polis. Some knew they had the Sight, some remained but latent talents. On occasion, they drew in those too weak for Dionysus to awaken, and the Lord ate their hearts, as was fitting and right, for God *must* have his due.

❧

THEY CAME TO THEBES, mighty and self-important upon the cliffs, flanked by twin rivers. Here, Hekate had grown into womanhood under the loathsome tutelage of Tethys and her brood. Tethys had fled far from the Elládosi world now, though, and even Demeter who had ruled since the Titanomachy was now gone.

While their God communed in the woodlands, Hekate had led the Maenads into Thebes the night prior. Her women had filtered into the streets, spreading their illustrious Bacchic wine. It was a wine the God called up by his will alone, filling their amphorae each night in proof of his divinity.

This afternoon, a throng had gathered in the agora, drawn in by the glory of Dionysus—though he had not yet come himself—seeking more of the precious draught.

Hekate smiled, watching the imminent decline of civilisation, the shedding of all pretences. Men and women copulated in the alleys. She saw a number of same-gendered couples who, blessedly, had cast aside inhibitions to follow their truest desires. Others grouped in small orgies, their moans forming a chorus of pleasure rising in Thebes.

A manifestation of Truth.

Beside a great fountain in the agora, Hekate watched the collapse of delusions. Soon, God would come, and then these revels would seem but prelude to the euphoric carnage that would follow.

As she turned, looking toward the acropolis, she saw a cluster of warriors, all formed up around a king. A mortal—or demigod, rather, as a descendant of Harmonia—king. This man, this grandson of Kadmus, he marched down his cobbled streets, escorted by a force who somehow believed they might stand against the Lord. That they might deny the force of Ananke.

King Pentheus saw them, his people come in the hundreds for a mere sip of the sacred draught of Dionysus. Delicious frustration fair dripped off the mortal king, its reek seeping from his pores like sweat. "What madness claims you all?" the impotent king bellowed as he reached the agora. "You Thebans, who have never retreated from a battle, will surrender your wills to *women*? Will you allow this soft boy and his concubines to steal your polis from you? You think this pretender a *god*? This Dionysus is no Olympian, he is the son of my aunt! My mother's sister, Semele, fled in *shame* to preserve the life of the squalling brat you now worship." The king looked to his guards, seemingly oblivious to looks of consternation even upon their faces. "Find my cousin and bring him to me in chains."

Dionysus had made plain that no Maenad was to harm Pentheus, but even so, Hekate found herself primed to draw upon Khione's power. That any should speak with such disdain of God offended her to the pith. In her mind's eye, she imagined the Maenads mobbing the warriors, beating in their skulls with their own helmets. She saw herself freezing the blasphemous tongue out of Pentheus's mouth.

It was, however, a long-bearded man with a cloth tied around his eyes who interposed himself before the king. "Be you warned, King," the blind man stated. "Your cousin holds within more than his flesh might attest."

Pentheus waved away the blind man. "Your prophecies did little enough to aid my aunt when he was born, Tiresias. I've even less need of your aid in this matter than she had."

An Oracle? Oh, but there was something beyond even the grace granted to most seers within this Tiresias. Hekate could feel it, in the man. God would wish to see this one, she was certain. She embraced the Sight and peered through the Veil, studying the seer's aura. There was something odd about it, something she could not quite identify. As the energy within was, at once, both male and female, or some unique mix thereof. To her shock, the seer turned his—or her?— attentions upon Hekate after she had studied that aura for only a moment.

Blinking away the Sight, Hekate slipped away into the crowd. When Dionysus came, the God himself would attend to his cousin. For Pentheus's claims did indeed hold some misguided truth. The God had shared his heritage with his inner circle. His words, between the crackle of flame and the hooting of owls, had told how Zeus had come to his mother in the night, his identity concealed. Had lain with her. How the King of Olympus murdered Semele himself when rumour of his indiscretion threatened to reach Hera. How one of Semele's other sisters, Ino, had taken the babe to far Kumari Kandam decades back, to be raised in Nysa.

The warriors, of course, did not find the God, who no doubt bided his time until nightfall. A commotion drew Hekate back to the agora, however. Within, she saw Akoitea dragged before the king, arms held by two warriors, blood dribbling down her chin. The men had blackened one of her eyes and ugly purple bruises had formed along one cheek.

"Who is this?" Pentheus demanded. "Where is Dionysus?"

"We couldn't find him," a warrior said. "We grabbed one of his women to make her tell us where to find him." A slight hesitation. "She's not talking. Might take a bit more time, my king."

Would Dionysus disapprove if Hekate stormed up to those men this moment and beat them to death with Titan strength? Perhaps, and Hekate could not risk God's displeasure. Akoitea ... she meant naught compared to glory of the Lord.

Pentheus cupped the woman's chin in his hand. "They think to torture you. I won't let that happen, though." He shook his head. "No, no. You see, if you don't talk, I'll have you run through this instant, as warning to any of your kind who think they can do here what they did in Korinth. So ..." He released her face and took a single step back. "Tell me your name."

The Maenad didn't tremble, at least not more than the quivers of pain Hekate would have expected. "Akoitea, a fisherman's daughter. I am no one to one such as you." From the way her lip curled, Hekate expected the woman to spit in Pentheus's face." Instead, she continued. "When my father died, I was left with naught save the skills he had shown me with boats and nets. But I learnt more, got my own small ship, recruited a five-man crew, and set out for trading."

"You?" Pentheus sneered. "A woman, captaining a ship?"

Akoitea ignored the jibe as she ignored the blood dripping from her chin. "One night we moored on a little island off the coast of Kumari Kandam, a place so small no one has ever heard of it. Tired of fish, we went ashore to hunt for game. In the morn, I returned to my ship to find my crewmen dragging a boy with them, one addled with wine." The woman smirked, causing Pentheus to fume, curling a hand into a fist as if he thought to beat her impudence out of her. "Strange, the weavings of the Moirai, no? I looked in his face, in his eyes, and saw an aspect so much more than a Man. I told my men such, and they laughed in my face, insisting they could ransom him, or, if he was no one, sell him as a slave. My hold upon them was less strong than I might have wished, I'm afraid."

"You truly think that bastard divine, don't you?" Pentheus paced, some unseen war in his head over how to handle the woman. He had, to Hekate's ears, said he would kill her if she did not speak. Now she spoke, but naught of what Pentheus wished of her.

"In mockery, the crew asked him where to go. 'Naxos,' the youth told them. 'Ananke promises me a prize shall one day await me there.' I shortened sail to steer in that direction, but one of them shoved me aside, heading us instead for Knosós. 'This is not the course I asked for,' the youth soon said, so placid in his complaint the men laughed at him. 'Better slave markets in Knosós,' our new helmsman mocked, 'especially for pretty boys like you.' The youth looked to me, then sat upon the deck, eyes closed. Perhaps they thought him resigned to his fate.

"That was when vines burst from the oars, entangling the mast and sails, bringing us to a dead stop. Phantasms of tigers and lions prowled the ship, and the men, they went mad with the weight of their transgression. They tore at their own eyes, their throats, their tongues. I watched in horror, wondering, when the same sickness would claim me. But when the last of my crew had cast themselves into the sea, the youth—now a towering Titan—he looked to me, and God claimed me as his own."

Pentheus threw up his hands. "Enough of this blather, girl. Tell me where to find my cousin, or my men will drag you to cells beneath the palace and rend you limb from limb."

Akoitea chortled at his threat, glad to give her life for God. As any Maenad would be. Yes, it was only right, Hekate decided, that some should be sacrificed to prove the depths of their loyalty.

As the warriors hauled the woman away, Hekate slunk back into the shadows. Soon, the God would come, and he would know his own.

❦

CALL IT JUSTICE, call it vengeance; either way, Hekate had made sure the king's mother, Agave, daughter of Kadmus and Harmonia, drank the sacred Bacchic wine. The delicious irony of watching the demigod woman writhe beneath the heaving orgy was *almost* as enticing as participating herself. Almost.

It was Aura who drew her into the midst of that glorious melding of forms.

The now-abandoned Temple of Demeter rang with the throes of passion. The aroma of lust saturated the evening air, though the smell of smoke wafted in. Some of the Maenads had set fire to parts of the acropolis, Hekate assumed, once she managed to disentangle herself from the mass of bodies for a breath of air.

Riots and looting no doubt unfolded in the lower city, the masses rising up against the inequities foisted upon them by the aristoi. If Mankind was but beasts, then the artifices by which some set themselves above others were but contrivances. Only personal strength and cunning ought to hold weight, and now, the oppressors must learn whether they *alone* were truly stronger and more cunning than those they lorded over. If, when there were a hundred slaves, servants, and peasants for every fat merchant, they were quite so fit to rule as they deemed themselves.

The king's guard burst into the temple, shouting obscenities at the loving scene before them. Profane, they dared call the ultimate expression of nature. As if their own self-righteous delusions were not the greater profanity.

Hekate did not resist when they arrested her and the others. She made no comment as they dragged them all, even the queen, down to cells and bound them in bronze manacles. She did not break the chains, though Titan Potency would have allowed her to do so.

She did not do aught.
For God was coming.
His will would soon be known.

WHETHER PENTHEUS'S threat had been an idle one or his men had been too preoccupied hunting for other Maenads to carry out the brutal execution he had promised Akoitea, that woman, too, shared their cell. The only light came from the distant wobbling of a torch filtering through a panel in the door, making it hard for Hekate to make out Akoitea's features. Her wheezing breath made plain the bruising of her face, though.

The temptation to break her chains and go to check on her fellow Maenad had waxed and waned through the untracked hours spent down here. She knew what she was meant to do. It was right to await the arrival of God. To bide her time and prepare for his coming. Still, vestiges of empathy not yet scoured from her by her sorcery worked at her like an itch in her mind. A ceaseless need to do *something* besides just sitting here.

Aura dabbed at Akoitea's face with the hem of her khiton.

The God would not have approved if they did more, Hekate knew. She must control herself to let his will be worked. Dionysus would have a plan, one beyond her ken, beyond the understanding of any mere Titan.

A tingling along her skin drew up goosebumps, warning of something pulsing through the Ether of the Spectral Realm. Even as Hekate blinked her eyes to peer through the Veil, her manacles—all their manacles—verdigrised, then began to flake away, crumbling to dust. Psychic aftershocks of whatever miracle God had wrought sent ripples through the Etheric air.

The next instant, the same happened to the lock upon their cell door.

Hekate arose, as did Agave, the queen mother, then Aura, then all twenty of the Maenads held here. It was time.

God beckoned.

THE MAENADS FLOWED through the palace like a retributive wave, sweeping over the last of the unprepared guards in a shrieking mob. Nails gouged cheeks and eyes and throats. Teeth tore off men's lips or noses. Hurled oil lamps turned screaming blasphemers into blazing effigies. Hekate watched as one of the flaming warriors dashed down the hall, his wild flailing setting aflame tapestries and, on his collapse, a long carpet.

In the courtyard, the Maenads gathered around Pentheus and his last remaining pair of guards. Others they had passed who had partaken of the Bacchic wine, choosing life and Truth over the wrath of the God. Fallen King Pentheus backed away from Hekate's throng of slavering women until his heel bumped against the fountain.

The guards brandished hoplons and xiphe, but from the looks upon their faces, they knew they were doomed.

Then *he* came. His strides, though silent, seemed to cast momentous echoes along Hekate's skull. His presence filled her nostrils with the aroma of euphoria and righteousness. His glory sent vines sprouting from the ground, encircling columns in creeping spirals, even as lurid, hissing flowers burst amid the greenery.

Dionysus swept into the courtyard. A whirlwind of power. A barely contained storm of glory. The God lifted his arms out to his sides and the fountain burped. Bacchic wine replaced the flowing water, its heady scent saturating the courtyard.

One of the guards wavered before dropping his sword and shield. The man turned and dunked his head into the fountain, drinking so deep Hekate thought he might well drown himself. A worthy death, if so; one pleasing to God.

Pentheus gaped, not at Dionysus but beyond the God to Agave. "Not you, Mother. Let it not be you!"

A simple twist of one of the God's hands broke the dam that held back the Maenads. In a torrent they surged forth, bodies burying the guard who managed naught but an abortive scream. Hekate was on Pentheus then, clawing, biting, rending, smashing. Skull banged upon the fountain's marble rim, limbs bent backwards. Her fingers—empowered by Potency—hooked a cheek and ripped it out.

Blood flowed in the wine, an incarnadine muddle of divine elixir.

"This gift I give you," the God intoned. "The beginning of the end of the great illusion. Behold the breaking of chains, the once-meek freed from the oppression of their so-called betters. Affluent lords shall tremble before the mere shadow of our retribution." Dionysus's voice reverberated through the whole of the palace, seeming to cry out from the acropolis for all of burning Thebes to hear. "Even as the kings of Men perish for their hubris, so too shall we tear down the self-proclaimed gods of Olympus! Mighty Zeus, blight upon all womankind, shall soon know the pain he has inflicted. The true God commands it!"

32

THESEUS

728 Bronze Age

When darkness grows deeper than any mere absence of light, the hearts of even the bravest of Men must begin to falter. Or so Theseus told himself as he sat on his arse, waiting for his eyes to adjust whilst knowing, in truth, one could never adapt to such sepulchral tunnels.

It stank of shit and stale air and utter dread.

His pulse kept hammering in his ears, some incessant gong he imagined the Minotaur might follow back to him and rend him limb from limb. The thought did little to help him still his frantic breaths or pounding heart.

Puerile instinct rose in him, tried to convince him that, if he could not see, neither could he be seen. As if darkness might protect him from one of its own vile denizens.

Hades, he ought to have pissed before they brought him in here.

"Get up," he whispered to himself. Gods, but he wished Herakles was here now. Or Pirithous, his dearest friend. Someone to walk alongside him and hold his hand in the dark. What would the Lapith have said then? "Move your arse, Theseus," Theseus muttered, almost hearing it in Pirithous's voice.

In the oppressive gloom, he could almost have sworn he felt his friend's hands beneath his arms. Offering him a hint of strength. Enough to get him moving once more. Choking on his terror—and still feeling apt to spill his bladder any moment—Theseus crawled back in the direction of the door.

Ariadne had sworn to see him with the tools he'd need to survive this night. If the princess wanted him to find them in the dark, she would have needed to place them somewhere close to the entryway. But not in a place where chance might have allowed her father's men to spot them whilst they cast him to his doom.

The floor was uneven, he realised as he crawled. Formed neither of natural nor properly cut stone. As if cyclopean blocks formed the Labyrinth, but the builder, in madness or sick genius, had laid them offset from one another. It left corners jutting up in sharp angles upon which he might shatter a knee and depressions where he could catch and break an ankle.

But there was no sign of aught left for him by the Knosian princess. Theseus gagged, panting. It had to be here. She'd said it would be here. It was here somewhere. His palms slapped cold stones and rough-hewn edges, his desperation adding a maddened frenzy, until he knew he flailed about in the dark.

"Where is it, where is it, where is it? Pirithous, help me ..." He couldn't breathe. Though he could still see not a damn thing, could not hear aught save his own wild panting, he *felt* the walls closing in, the irregular, cruelly shaped tunnel constricting about him.

She'd betrayed him. The inchoate thought had danced about his mind for a time already, he realised. Now, in his despair, he had no choice but to acknowledge its existence, bitter draught as it was. Ariadne had toyed with him. The false chance Minos's daughter had dangled before him was but one more aspect of the torment. Those plummeting from the precarious cliff of hope must crash all the harder when they landed upon the rocks of despair.

Was any thread of her tale a true one? Did she so loathe her father as she had claimed, or was the whole of it but a bard's spinning designed to pluck the strings of his heart?

"But if she spoke in earnest," Pirithous's voice whispered in his ear, "then she might have hidden what you seek in one of the depressions created by the irregular cyclopean blocks."

More vain, damning hope, and this time Theseus deluded himself. He imagined himself rising to his knees and pissing in any random direction, heedless that it might well dribble back down upon him. What difference would such make now?

And yet ... and yet he found himself not quite willing to give in to despair. He clutched onto even false, useless hope, and once more began poking his hands into the groves, feeling along the blocks, seeking hollows where Ariadne might have given him a chance.

"Please ..."

His fingers brushed something soft and smooth. Leather. Leather meant something not native to the stone Labyrinth. His hand closed around a strap, yanked it toward himself. A satchel, and within poked out the hilt of a sword.

His heart surged, and he choked once more, this time upon a sob of relief. She had kept her word. Ariadne had saved him.

At least, assuming he could, in fact, slay whatever abominable monster her brother had become. Theseus rooted around in the bag. Cold metal studs upon leather bands. He ran his thumbs over the fabric. Bracers? Perhaps she could not have brought his full panoply but had hoped the bracers might offer some protection.

As he tried to withdraw them, something else tumbled from the bag and landed upon the stone with a soft thud. Theseus patted around until he found it. A wooden haft. He lifted it. It stank of whale oil. A torch. She'd given him a torch.

Which meant within the bag must also be flint and steel. Careful not to spill aught else from the satchel, he felt around until his fingers identified what he sought. A few strikes of the flint, and sparks flew, catching upon the oil-sodden rag wrapt around the torch's end.

The flame that sprang up stung his eyes for a moment, harsh after the total darkness. Theseus blinked until blurred shapes resolved themselves into the scope of his prison.

He gasped. This was a place wrought by a mind deranged. As he had suspected before, great blocks of stone—mismatched marble and limestone and granite—formed a rounded tunnel, corners poking inward like inverted spurs of some dragon's scaly hide. The ceiling, such as it was, perhaps twenty feet above him, retreated into the shadows too deep for him to make out much of aught up there. The walls, though, were streaked and stained with brown splatters. Some of the stains flaked like dried blood, whilst other marks could have been shit, though how that wound up ten feet in the air in some cases, Theseus could not speculate.

There were bones.

Broken femurs stuck from crevices between cyclopean blocks as if set as impaling spears. Skulls rested in alcoves, piled atop one another. Many were small enough they'd have fit in the palm of his hand. Children's skulls …

Theseus retched, his stomach convulsing though empty. His abdominal muscles rejected the sight before him even as much as his mind had.

Far too many skulls here to be the sacrifices sent by Athenai in the past decades either. Dozens of skulls and … and … And Theseus knew what the powder upon the stones was. Shivering, he raised his palm to the torchlight. A white dust caked his fingers.

Ground-up bone.

Unbidden, an imagine flashed into his mind. A child's skeleton torn from her body. Her hand pulverised to now coat his own.

In horror, Theseus dropped the torch and rubbed his palms upon his tunic. He had to get it off. Had to get it all off. Oh, gods, fucking *gods*, what in Hades's dark domain was this place? Had Daedalus, rather than build the Labyrinth, dug instead some tunnel to the twisted recesses of the Underworld?

Tears blurred his vision.

Blinking, he snatched up the torch once more.

The Minotaur must die. Only that remained certain.

As if it had heard his very thought, another bellow set the dust spilling from the ceiling and the bones dancing along the floor. Gaia trembled in anticipation.

Pushing down his shudders, Theseus held the torch over Ariadne's satchel. Its flickering light fell over a second torch, in case this one should burn out. And if that one should fail ... It was better not to think of such things, he supposed. Beneath that lay a silken ribbon, a thread no doubt woven in some eastern land of which he knew not even the name.

Theseus wound a strand of it around his fingers, raising it to his face to inspect it. It was dyed in Tyrian purple. Was this some token of the princess's favour? No, but the thread filled the better part of the satchel, hundreds of feet long. Why would she want him to have ...?

A thought arose. He looked to the door. The one and only means of egress in a maze that tale claimed stretched so vast a man could wander it until thirst brought him to his knees—if the monster did not get him first. Should he succeed in besting the Minotaur, to exit the maze, he would need to retrace his steps.

And Ariadne had ensured he could do so.

Theseus scrambled to the door. This side, like the reverse, featured a gable with a bull relief. One detailed enough to have horns that jutted beyond the pediment's rim. Theseus twined the thread about both horns, wrapt it twice more to be certain, and gave a tug. It held firm.

A harder yank.

And still the thread kept him rooted to the exit of this accursed place.

So, then. Sword at his hip, torch in one hand, and slowly unspooling thread in the other, Theseus ventured deeper into the darkness.

❧

TORCHLIGHT WOULD ALREADY NO DOUBT ANNOUNCE his presence to the beast, Theseus knew, but still he strove to keep his footfalls soft as he wandered the maze of the Labyrinth. If he had even the smallest chance of catching the creature unawares, he'd take it. Sporadic bellows shook the tunnels, but he could not gauge whether they drew closer or farther. Indeed, were it not for the thread he unravelled as he plodded—careful not to allow it to snag on any of the oddly angled stone blocks—he might have thought these halls shifted as he wandered them. He felt fair certain he'd passed under tunnels he had earlier come through; the only explanation he could see for how he had made so many twists without crossing his own path once more.

And again, he found himself musing that Daedalus had been tinged with a sickness of the mind, to create this maze. The place defied mortal geometries, tunnels rising and falling at odd angles that had him climbing or hopping down. The blocks kept their impossible angles, as if some giant had grabbed a hall and wrung it like a rag until corners poked out at all sides. Sometimes, he came to cavernous openings, and he could see, in the dwindling light of his torch, hints of his thread in paths above or below, though he had no recollection of passing over such vaults before.

His mind rejected half of what he saw, even as the absolute dread kept trying to close in around him, crawling closer and closer, fear itself skittering upon a thousand spidery legs, ready to sink its fangs into his heart. No mere human madness could have engendered the Labyrinth or its occupant, of that he was certain. No, whatever had touched this place with its foulness, it had come from somehow beyond even the expanse of Gaia. Something born from the engulfing darkness of Nyx herself, and Earth cringed at its presence.

Or, maybe, that was exactly what had wrought the twisting of these tunnels. Whatever was in the Minotaur, it was something so dire Gaia curled herself back into a foetal ball to shun the horror.

"You indulge your own fears," Theseus mumbled, forcing his mind to stillness.

He had come here to slay a monster that truly, beyond doubt, needed slaying. More skulls and bones and white powder had decorated every step of his passage.

Theseus climbed atop another massive limestone cube. The path up ahead rose, and it would take a great deal of effort to reach the summit. He could double back and choose another branch of the path at the fork he'd seen not long ago. Perhaps there was an easier way to—

Another bellow erupted, and this one *was* closer. So close, noxious air blew past him.

His breath catching, Theseus hurled the torch out below himself and off to the side, dropped his thread, and scrambled away until his back pushed up against a granite block.

The next moment, snorting and snuffling filled the tunnel. The creature reeked of rotten meat and putrid dung. Theseus dared not breathe, much less move. And yet, he must see it. He must do what he had come here for. Slowly, he twisted his neck around until he could peer into the dark depths above.

His torchlight scarce reached into the opening to the higher tunnel. Yet he could see the glint of luminous red eyes, peering down into the passage whence he'd come. Searching for its prey. More snuffling. It leant forwards enough to expose horns larger than Theseus's entire body. The creature must have stood three times the height of a Man, if not more. It would have towered over the greatest Titans he knew of. Would have seized Olympians and broken them upon its horns, he half suspected.

Thank Zeus he'd stopped to piss down a hole before now. Even so, he wanted to whimper. He wanted to flee, though it would only chase him down.

The Minotaur huffed and turned about, stalking back along the upper tunnel. At his passing, the sound of metal grating along something echoed through the Labyrinth.

Theseus allowed himself a pained exhalation. A moment to let the panic rise in its surging tide, rather than deny it and risk drowning beneath it.

Far below, his torch was sputtering out.

He looked to his xiphos, strapped to his hip. Suddenly such a tiny thing. It would be like trying to kill a bull with a sewing needle.

"No more sacrificed children," he whispered to Pirithous. It helped to think the Lapith here, now, buoying his spirits. "It or me." A deep breath. "It ... or me."

Well, then let it be the monster who fell. After retrieving the thread, Theseus lit his second torch and resumed his climb. The Minotaur had to die.

At last, he crested the rise, but rather than stand, he lay prone, peering over the side. After this much effort to reach the upper tunnel, the floor fell away ahead of him, down into an open chamber. This one was broken by pillars of the cyclopean blocks, not vertical, but rather criss-crossing the hall like netting. The floor, too, was uneven, rising and falling like frozen waves. Other passages led from this chamber: some high, some low, but all seeming to converge here.

Because this was the very heart of the Labyrinth. The lair of the Minotaur.

And indeed, the hulking creature stalked about from one tunnel to the next, snuffling, seeking its prey. After spending its whole life in the dark, perhaps those eyes didn't even work. But it would smell and hear him soon enough. Theseus bound the thread to a spot where it would be visible from below, then crawled farther forwards, to get a better look.

Despite the torchlight spilling from his position, the Minotaur did not glance in his direction. It stomped around on cloven hooves, shaking its massive head. Now he could see it had skulls dangling from those horns as trophies. Which meant, for all its savagery, some modicum of—twisted—intellect lurked within the beast. Then he caught sight of its arms and Theseus stiffened upon seeing what had made the metal-grating sound earlier.

Clutched in massive paws with nails so long they might be called claws, the Minotaur carried a rose-gold metal ball, as wide around as a Man was tall. Chains sprouted from the ball, enwrapt it, and ran up to the Minotaur's left arm. The chain was looped round and round the flesh to make it more manageable, but past it, threads of the fetter burrowed *inside* the Minotaur's arm. They wound through its flesh, in and out, only to twist back into a hoop.

Bile scorched his throat once more, this time at the cruelty of what had been done to this creature. When it was smaller, perhaps the weight of the ball had kept it trapt here in the Labyrinth's heart, unable to wander beyond the length of those chains. Now the Minotaur could heft the apparatus and walk about with it, but it still could not tear it from its flesh without ripping its own arm off.

Minos was given a child of monstrous shape. And, through his own monstrosity, had ensured it grew into the monster he saw it as. Cruelty fed with cruelty would compound until it became an end, complete unto itself. The cycle of violence, of base rancour, it lay writ plain before Theseus.

Writ so raw he longed to stalk from here. For he *pitied* the creature, much though he loathed what it had done to all these children. All these victims. Still, part of his soul screamed to see so wretched a creature.

But then death may have been a mercy, twisted as this being had become? Was he to leave it, to continue its macabre feasting upon the flesh of Man? Or to release it, as if it might cast aside its hunger for that flesh? No, the only peace he could offer the Minotaur was the peace of death. And, doing so would be almost as much a service to this creature as it would to the innumerable parents who would not need grieve children fed to its hunger.

Or so he told himself.

Theseus tossed the torch down into the hall, and it clattered along the stones. *That* drew the Minotaur's attention, and the beast snorted and bellowed, charging in the torch's direction. A leap sent it hurtling through the air, dozens of feet, before it crashed down with an impact that splintered rocks.

And yet, it still had not seen him.

Theseus eased free his sword and plodded, silent as a ghost, from stone to stone, descending into the chamber.

The beast sniffed. It turned toward him.

Well, fuck.

Another furious charge had the Minotaur racing in his direction. Theseus leapt from atop a stone block and dove into a roll the instant before the beast pulverised his former perch. It had swung that metal ball like a weapon, shattering granite with little effort.

Panting, Theseus came up in a crouch, sword point out before him, for all the good it would mostlike prove. Again, the beast charged, all crashing hooves and snarls and great sweeps of that orb. Theseus flung himself to the side and swiped with his xiphos.

The blade bit into the Minotaur's leg, but no doubt served more to annoy than hobble. The Minotaur huffed and bellowed. Incensed that a mortal would dare even try to strike it.

It might have felt better to learn Theseus wanted to run screaming through the tunnels.

The creature turned about, stomping one hoof and looking around the cavernous hall as though it could not quite make out its prey. Theseus held stock still. After a moment, the monster fixated upon the torch, opposite where Theseus stood. Perhaps it could make out the flickering flame, but if he held still and breathed as little possible, perhaps ...

The Minotaur charged the torch, churning a rivet through the stone floor in its passage. The crash of its hooves splintered stone. A great sweep of the rose-gold ball sent the torch hurtling through the air, a flickering star of light over an ocean of darkness. Debris rained over the torch until it all but winked out.

"Oh, Hades's big dead balls," Theseus moaned.

And the Minotaur heard him. With a jerk, it unspooled the chain from its arm. The heavy weight dropped to the floor, cracking it. What did it intend to—

The Minotaur wrapt the chain around its hand. And then it lunged. And Theseus, realising what was about to happen, hurled himself forwards. The beast heaved the chain up in an arc over its head, the orb coming down like a falling meteor.

A deafening impact resounded as the seemingly indestructible improvised weapon obliterated the floor. Shards of rock exploded like missiles propelled in all directions. Theseus had but time to half rise before the Minotaur yanked back at the chain and swung once more.

This time, gasping, he rolled under the scything fetter. The ball smacked into the wall, blew through it, and kept going as if naught could impede its fated arc. The chamber trembled, stones the size of horses plummeting from above and crashing into the floor. Some exploded into fresh projectiles, filling the air with a hail of razorblades.

Theseus scrambled, frantic, dodging another wild charge of the beast. It didn't seem to know where he was. It didn't seem to fucking care anymore. It smashed that chain weapon left and right, attacking the noise of its own previous impacts, sending stones flying in every direction.

Evading one attack, Theseus leapt from where he'd stood upon a stone, kicked off another block that shifted as he hit. Still, he managed the height to swipe his blade across the Minotaur's snout. A black-clawed hand swiped at him, tore his tunic, and he hit the ground hard. Couldn't catch his breath. Had to roll to the side as a hoof tried to stomp him.

His blade slipped from fingers numbed by impact.

A back somersault carried him between the Minotaur's legs and behind the beast. The absurd manoeuvre had the creature stomping and huffing for all it was worth. So enraged, its own wrath stirred up so much noise it would never hear him.

Breathless, Theseus managed his feet and raced—or staggered, really—toward one of those lopsided columns bisecting the chamber. His lungs would explode. His legs seemed sluggish now, useless as pudding. Vision was dimming. With a hand upon his knee, he gasped, desperate for more air.

He'd drawn blood. He supposed that was probably more than most had managed against the monster. It still didn't mean he'd die happy about all this.

He wasn't ready to die at all. But if he had to, he was sure as Ares's arse taking this abomination down to the Underworld with him.

Theseus edged to the far side of the column so its angle worked for him and started climbing, one cyclopean block to the next. Doing so at all was challenging. Managing it without gasping for breath was impossible. And yet, he'd gotten maybe twenty feet off the ground, and still it had not looked to him.

He supposed it was about time to make good on the bravado. Clinging on for dear life, Theseus wormed his way back around the column. The Minotaur had finished stomping about. It succeeded in collapsing half the tunnel Theseus had come in from. Could he even reach it to follow his thread now?

Not like he was ever going to get the chance. But he needed the Minotaur's attention now.

"Done with that tantrum? I hear Hades ... has a spot warm for you. In his hearth fire, you walking hunk of beef ..."

Maybe it understood him. Maybe it just followed his voice, caught up in its maddened paroxysms as it was. Either way, the Minotaur charged. It swiped with that ball and chain. Theseus had known it would hurt, leaping off the column to fall twenty feet. It would hurt less than getting pulped by the ball. The chain snared the column, wrapt around it twice, and then the ball crashed into where Theseus had vacated.

Despite dropping into a crouch, as predicted, the impact felt like a horse had kicked out both his knees. Theseus fell over sideways, clutching his kneecaps and moaning. It gave him a perfect view as the Minotaur bellowed. The creature gripped its chain with both hands and heaved.

Huh.

The column groaned. Dust poured from the mortars in a chain of cataracts all the way from floor to ceiling far above.

Another bellow and another tremendous yank.

Pain forgotten, Theseus scrambled away, frantic and shrieking, as the column cracked. Blocks—some large enough to be a poor man's house—fell from above in an avalanche of destruction. The column crashed down upon the Minotaur. Half the ceiling followed, tons upon tons of raining stone and dirt in a crushing wave.

Other columns strained under their increased load and the shifting of the whole ceiling. Fractures split along blocks all around him.

In a wild dash, Theseus stumbled toward the closest tunnel. It was not the one he'd entered from. It was not the one with that precious thread that might help him wind his way free.

And that hardly mattered now.

Gaia's bellowing roared a hundred times greater than even the Minotaur's awful cries had ever managed. Crashing, choking earth pitched into the Labyrinth's heart as Theseus hurled himself clear.

He'd lost his father's sword, he realised as darkness settled in around him once more. He'd lost his sword. And worse, having lost the thread, he'd now lost *himself*.

WANDERING, in darkness. Fingers tracing the uneven walls. Did the maze have the same shape It had when he'd first entered? He was lucky not to have brought the whole Palace of Elektra down upon his head with his stunt. Sometimes, as he made his abortive progress—or not progress really, he supposed, since he paced at random—he wondered what those above thought had happened. Did they ever imagine their precious monster might lay entombed within Gaia's unabating embrace?

He wasn't certain why he kept pushing on. The darkness had closed in around him, the Moirai alone knew whether it would suffocate him before the stale air did. He'd never find his way from the maze, so why torture his bruised and exhausted body by trying?

Whatever else happened, he'd saved Athenai. That abomination would haunt no more parents with the merciless fear their child would be the one chosen by the lots. That spectre of dread would fly now from their hearts, and they might be free to offer their young full love, without guarding their hearts.

His fingers brushed against something soft. Silken. A thread.

Almost, he could not believe it. His mind rejected the hope. His heart surged over it. But he gripped the thread, and it was real.

The last, final thread of his hope. Maybe there was a chance to wend free from this maze.

Maybe, in the end, someone might escape the Labyrinth.

HE FOLLOWED THE THREAD, hope lending him the strength to push down the uncounted aches that otherwise would have reduced him to a foetal ball. Hand over hand, he followed it, refusing to acknowledge so much as the fear that the shifting and collapsing of the Labyrinth might have caught that thread and blocked his passage.

But now light glinted in the distance, and he was making the best attempt at a dash he could manage in his state, over the uneven ground.

Silhouetted against the doorway, Ariadne stood, beckoning him closer. "Run, Theseus!" she cried. "Phaidra has locked the outer doors, but we must flee."

Of course. Of course, they would know something unexpected had unfolded beneath the palace. The Mistress of the Labyrinth took a single unsteady step into its dark halls. And then another, and then she was running to him, caught his elbows. He could not make out her face, not with the light directly behind her. But on seeing him, she sucked air between her teeth. Must have been bad. He must have looked a terrible fright, indeed.

"There's another exit from this chamber," she said, ushering him outward. "A way out, into the cliffs below the acropolis. Daedalus connected the Labyrinth's entrance to old tunnels, places he said once home to Earth spirits, now departed."

None of that made much sense to Theseus, but then he was dizzy, half-blind from torchlight as she guided him back to the dance hall— the mosaic was cracked here, he saw—and bleeding from too many places to count.

In a daze, he let her lead him to what seemed a solid wall. But Ariadne inserted a key into an unseen hole and twisted. Another seam appeared in the wall, and the two sides began to groan as they withdrew in mirror of the Labyrinth's entrance.

"They'll break through soon," Phaidra called, racing around the columns to join them, bearing a torch.

"No one knows about this passage," Ariadne assured her as she shoved Theseus inside. He collapsed against the wall of a tunnel. Another tunnel. He had rather hoped to have seen the last of tunnels for a while. A few decades, at least.

Inside, Ariadne inserted her key into some other hole and twisted. And just like that, Theseus was again closed up inside the earth. He almost wept.

IT PASSED IN A BLUR, their frantic rush toward the harbour, and Theseus remembered little of it. Ariadne must have had the right of it, and no one could have imagined where they'd fled or how, for Minos's men gave no chase. At least not in the time it took to get himself aboard, and for his men to make sail.

After that ... he vaguely remembered collapsing on a bunk. Maybe someone had carried him there. Next he knew, he awoke upon a bedroll, soft and warm enough the comfort of it *almost* won out over his sudden need to know where he was and how he'd come there. He lay within a wide tent with one flap pinned back, such that he could see the crackle of a low fire just outside. It was still night. His entire body felt one giant bruise—or perhaps a mound of bruises piled one atop another. He must have groaned, because someone beside his bedroll shifted, at his side at once.

Ariadne mopped his brow with a damp cloth. The gentle brush of her thumb over his cheek offered a soothing balm over his worn soul, and sleep rose up to grasp at him once more.

A WOODED path opened before Theseus, narrow and broken by protruding roots. The only path forwards, for to either side was a maze of trees and undergrowth and hanging vines. The sense of creatures slithering amidst

the brush overpowered. A vague reek of putrescence wafted in on the wind as it rustled the leaves overhead.

Theseus could not have said why he walked this path. He knew, somewhere behind him, an open field lay, warmed by untrammelled sunlight. He could not look back. Something compelled his steps, and with each plodding pace forwards, a gloaming drew closer. It was not that dusk settled upon him. Rather, that he himself entered into such a liminal space.

Innominate dread coiled around his spine. It yanked him forwards, no matter how much his soul screamed at him to turn away. To flee. The wood closed in upon him, every bit as oppressive as the Labyrinth had been.

He wanted to call out, to cry for aid from any other living soul, but he dare not attract other notice in this place. Lilac bands of light pierced the increasingly dense canopy, speckling the path in alternating patches of light and spreading shadow.

His heart had begun to crawl up into his throat.

Ahead, a towering oak rose, drenched in lichen and draped with thick vines and creepers. So tall was the tree, its boughs vanished into the dark mesh of growth above. But Theseus had the sense of branches bending back toward him like grasping fingers. The stench of rot escaped from rents in the bark.

Something shifted beneath that broken bark, the tree throbbing as though massive worms writhed just under its surface. As he watched with growing horror, Theseus became certain the vines, too, were moving, as if slowly strangling the oak. He fell back a step.

What he had imagined rents and spots of decay had taken on a more sinister aspect. In the midst of the trunk lay an image his mind begged to reject. A face. Not a human face, but something more caprine, with curling horns and onyx eyes.

A face in the wood.

Skittering, slithering, whispering. All around him.

The face looked at him. It looked into him. He was but a nameless mote of dust before the enormity of that intellect. Tendrils of its grasping awareness bored into his consciousness. In a single instant, the pith of his soul was weighed and apprehended. With awful insight, he knew then that Men lived their entire lives blessedly beneath the notice of such cosmic minds.

It noticed him now.

It knew him. His every thought and fear and secret shame was torn from him and brought burbling to the surface, all at once. It became the sum of him. No longer a Man, no longer aught more than this moil of squalid emptiness.

He was on his knees. It saw him, the face in the wood. It saw all of him there ever had been. All there ever could have been.

And on seeing him, it sneered, the face limned with malice beyond mortal ken.

He wept. He pissed himself. He hid his eyes.

But it compelled him to look once more. No longer was it a rent oak but a shattered one, the trunk splayed like open fingers, forming a throne. Upon this throne sat a being that towered above him, six, seven times his height at least. Its form was Man-like only in the most profane sense. Shaggy legs over cloven hooves. A bloated, dangling phallus. Bulging arms covered in wolf fur. Fingers ending in scythe-like claws. A muscled torso marred with obscene blue spirals that shifted as he looked upon them.

But it was that head that stole the breath from him. It swallowed even the memory of joy and left only the bottomless void of unutterable panic.

Pinpricks of virescent gleam inside eyes black as wells of liquid obsidian. Curling horns in profane amalgamation of goat and stag. A canine maw from which slavered viscous fluids that seemed, themselves, alive. A mane, tangled with leaves and twigs and bones.

The face in the wood had awakened. And he saw it was meaningless even to name such an entity as ancient. For it came from beyond petty conceptions of time. It held eternity within the fell light of its eyes.

Even the Minotaur would have proved a speck beneath the mammoth will of this entity.

The being upturned its palm, curling fingers forming a cage of claws. Within this cage, an apparition took shape. A shifting of leaves upon a swirling breeze became a dancing girl, sleek and joyous. She looked for him. Waited for him.

A name came to him then, though he had not one even for himself. Ariadne.

SURRENDER YOUR FALTERING CLAIM UPON MY BRIDE.

The voice writhed up from every squirming root, every grasping branch in the dusk-shrouded wood. It echoed inside his skull until he could have sworn it would shatter him and leave the last vestiges of his sanity oozing from the cracks.

And still, he mouthed her name. Tried to hold on to it, as if keeping her upon his lips would spare her from whatever depraved violations this abomination intended for her. As if he could shelter anyone from such a thing.

The other clawed hand reached for him.

He stood in Athenai, looking about twilight-darkened streets. Men and women and children, his people, they turned to him, looks of stricken horror upon their faces. His father strode in their midst, face sallow, arms imploring to him. Calling out, though his name had been cleft from him and thus his father's cries were more inarticulate moan than coherent plea.

Before he could close the space between them, roots burst out from the cobbles, churning the streets in sudden violence. Vines slithered about the Colonnades, crushing columns, and sending hunks of marble tumbling amid the shrieking populace.

Those roots continued to crawl. They snared his father's feet and punched through the man's heels. They burrowed through flesh. The name-less man could but watch in horror as his father shrieked, lumpy worms crawling up his legs, over his abdomen. Skin ripped apart and branches ejected themselves from the seams.

All through Athenai, the populace shared the fate of his father. Their bodies were stolen from them, turned into a wood now burgeoning amid the shattered heart of the city. And yet, the stricken and agonised people lived. Vestiges of their consciousness lingered in their transmuted forms.

Putrescence filled the streets.

In the boughs of these new-formed trees, creatures crawled. Beings humanoid in shape, but something between lizard and plant themselves in aspect. They lunged at one another, and upon the half-corpses of the citi-zenry, they broke into obscene, furious copulation.

LEAVE ... MY BRIDE ...

One of those trees had grown higher than the others, monstrous, warped as if in pain. Decaying rents opened along its trunk. Mucous eyes looked into his shrivelled soul.

A face was in the wood.

⬥

"I don't understand," Phaidra protested upon the deck of Theseus's ship as it threaded the pre-dawn waters, sailing from Naxos. "Where in Hades's dark domain is my godsdamned sister? Why is she not here?"

Theseus did not want to look back at Naxos. Doing so evoked a nameless dread, like worms wriggling through his gut and consuming him from the inside out. He did not want to see again the wretched island where visions of such horror had unfolded. He did not want to ever so much as think of that place again.

And yet, of its own accord, his neck craned around, and he found himself staring at the rapidly dwindling silhouette of that rocky island. Already, he could scarce make out details. All that was left was a chiaroscuro, an impression of an island against the deep lavender of the sky and the darker blue of the unlit waves.

And yet, he saw. In his mind, he saw Ariadne awakening from the other bedroll in the tent. Moving to check on Theseus and finding him gone. He could feel her shock, carried across the waters between them. Disbelief giving way to indignation. Even that must soon dwindle to fear.

Theseus had abandoned her.

A god had claimed her, what was he to do?

Theseus had betrayed her.

Surely this deity who named her his wife could give her a future … And Theseus could not thwart the will of a god. He could not do aught …

He was a craven who had dreamt of valour.

From the way Phaidra gripped the balustrade, perhaps the girl thought to leap the side and swim back to her abandoned sister. It was too far, already, and even if Theseus had thought to let her join Ariadne, it would have meant Phaidra's death.

He grabbed her wrist, holding her in place. Was it further cowardice, refusing to let her die for Ariadne? Die as he ought to have done? Or did he merely hope to spare himself culpability for her death as well?

He wanted to weep. He'd have bled, have *killed*, for the chance to release the welling pressure inside his heart. But tears refused to offer him even such minor salves. Grief warred with guilt for the chance to see which of them would suffocate him first. Or maybe all such emotions must forever become a choking miasma, their toxins feeding upon one another and conspiring to poison a soul. Already, he knew, this would be a wound that would never heal for him; this venom could never be leeched from the depths it would reach.

"Ariadne is gone," he rasped.

"We have to go back for her!" Phaidra protested, trying to jerk her hand free.

Theseus tightened his grip upon her wrist. "Men cannot thwart the will of gods." Or Ananke. Fate had made him dance upon invisible puppet strings, pulling one thread after the next, in mummery of heroism.

Such were the words he would tell himself when shame and regret kept him awake, shivering in the cold of night. But Theseus was no hero, and now he knew he never would be.

33

ARTEMIS

728 Bronze Age

She sat beside a campfire, clad now in tattered remnants of torn fabric, inhaling fumes from smoke tinged purple by whatever strange drugs Dionysus had cast into them. God sat across from her. Other Maenads were there, in the periphery. But Artemis was the first and greatest of his new disciples, and thus the place of honour had gone to her.

Beside the fire, the sanguine cocoon, moist and glistening, creaked with the shifting of the metamorphosing child within. The erubescent flesh reeked of blood and pain and new life, tickling her ursine senses.

It was so hard to focus now. A cup of wine was in her hand, and reflexively, she downed another sip. The sacred brew soothed her disquieted mind.

"What has Aura to do with such things?" The question crept up upon her, for she'd not thought of her old friend in years. More than nigh seven centuries since the Nymph had killed herself. A long, long time Artemis had grieved. Uncounted nights she had lain awake, staring at the stars, wondering if she might have said something, done something, that could have spared Aura whatever secret pain she'd harboured. Could she, with one more embrace, have *saved* that life? Could she, with the right probing question, have uncovered the hidden agonies within Aura she had not even known the girl suffered?

"The spark of Man—and Titans are, in the end, but Men—is a fragment of Light, spun out by the Wheel of Life." Dionysus's voice no longer boomed from the forest but whispered to her in quiet intimacy of which all the other Maenads must no doubt writhe in jealousy. "Man lives and dies and lives again in endless circles, in accordance with the will of Ananke. With Ambrosia, Titans profane the cycle of life and death."

The haze of the smoke clouded her mind. She shook her head, but it sent afterimages of the hilltop skittering across her vision. "I don't understand."

"Aura was one of my first Maenads." Perhaps it was the drug's play upon her mind, but Artemis could not parse the pathway between his answers. "I lapped at the glory of her flesh and the spark of Light lingering within it. Born in her as it had been born before, with frightful puissance. As it is now born once more, and soon for me to reclaim."

Maenad ... He'd made her a Maenad. He'd raped her. And when the Bacchic wine had, for reasons Artemis did not understand, released Aura, she could not live with the shame of what Dionysus had made her. And she'd taken her own life, seven centuries prior.

An ember of rage burnt through the drug-induced fog. It seared away even the wondrous rapture of the Bacchic wine on which she had remained so drunken for what must be months. Or longer, perhaps. She wanted to move. To leap across the fire and throttle the Titan who had stolen her cousin from her. Who was, even now, stealing Atalanta and Artemis *herself*.

But her limbs refused her. She had sworn herself, in her desperation to save Orion. She had sworn her soul to this ... incarnation of an Elder God. And it was no oath she could break, no matter how much she might wish it. His power was wrapt around her core, and he denied her choice. Denied her will. He stole from her the right of herself, of her body and mind alike, as surely as Zeus had.

Worse, even.

For much of the time God, in his infinite glory, did not permit her even the indulgence of hating him for his arrogance or oppression. There was only the irresistible demand to love.

She must love God, or feel her soul flayed to bits.

She must love God, for God demanded it.

A too-wide smile crept upon Dionysus's mask, bone creasing in fearful intimation of real emotion, making plain he saw the depths of her despair. He quirked a finger, and her body responded, spreading itself for his entry. As if to punish her for such a blasphemous train of thoughts, he used her without allowing her the retreat into drunken pleasure his presence oft induced.

And when he had finished, he rose, and the cocoon ruptured. Fingers, small and yet profanely too large for the babe that should have been, burst through fleshy seams. Sticky webs of fibre clung to those digits as the girl—now wearing a form old enough to belong to a six-year-old though not six weeks had passed—clawed its way free.

At the same time, Atalanta approached, a newborn babe in her arms.

"Take my child," Dionysus commanded. "Take my Deianeira to her mother's husband and bid him raise her as his own, for love of me." Now the God looked more directly at Atalanta. "And be rid of your own brat however it best suits you, girl. We leave soon for Phlegra and have little time for the squealing of piglets."

Artemis opened her mouth to protest. To bid her daughter save her son from this. But even that defiance was denied to her. So she lay on her back, powerless.

Wishing she could weep.

And understanding why, given a single moment of freedom, even one like blessed, innocent Aura would have taken her own life.

THE VEIL STRAINED beneath the weight of such debauchery as Dionysus engendered. They came to Phlegra and he called to him all the wild things of the woodlands. Snakes and wolves and bears followed in his wake. At night, dryads would claw their way sap-stained from the trunks of trees. Dionysus would select some of the Maenads and send them to lie with the dryads, and they would count themselves blessed by God and granted pleasures of beyond the ken of Mankind.

Perhaps there was truth in those suppositions. Artemis had her doubts. For the God would select those weaker in will and Pneuma, or who faltered in their faith. And though few of the other Maenads seemed to notice it, Artemis noted that most of those sent to the dryads did not return.

And the World ached with God's unending need. Dionysus would take a dozen women a night to lie with him, and some of them would grow thick with child. Until Artemis counted it a blessing he had not once more called upon whatever profane forces he'd used to sacrifice Althaea and bring about his daughter's unearthly growth spurt.

Then came the centaurs, and she knew why Dionysus had sought for Phlegra. For there the beasts congregated, in the wild forests and untamed mountain slopes. They came with cravings ravenous for all manner of unseemly pleasures, and to them, too, Dionysus would give up those of little use to him. The centaurs would carry off women and use them over and over until their screams died. Once, Artemis had found a Maenad's body, broken beyond recognition, though she'd known her, and would grieve her, if God permitted it.

Too, so many of the centaurs had developed a taste for Man-flesh, and they were gone mad with cravings for it until no other meat would suffice. Like Gigantes, they twisted themselves, grown ever more monstrous by their appetites. They spoke of it—though

Artemis had not the least desire to engage the bestial creatures in conversation—in gut-churning low voices, as if gnawing upon the marrow within the bones of Man offered nigh as much pleasure as their sexual releases. They ate the males Dionysus offered up, and any children the Maenads bore God now demanded be offered in sacrifice to the Man-eating horses.

The Maenads spread far and wide, bringing their message of liberation to the people of Phlegra. They told the women to cast off the shackles of patriarchy and join the God in his endless celebration of the dance of life. Such light would kindle in their eyes, such hope that, after ages of her gender existing to serve the needs of men, that Artemis felt herself *almost* believing in the message that spilt unwilling from her lips.

Some of the kings of Phlegra bent their knee to Dionysus, renouncing their loyalty to Zeus's son Ares. Artemis shuddered to think how the self-proclaimed God of War would react to defiance. Ares was given to psychotic fits, his sadism heightened to such erratic mania he would, perhaps, *delight* in the excuse to punish the Phlegrans. King Pelias of Iolkos swore allegiance to Dionysus, and in exchange, the God promised Pelias he would not need surrender his throne to his upstart nephew, despite the younger man's better claim.

Idly, Artemis wondered if Dionysus had the least intention of keeping his promise to aid Pelias, should this young Jason return for his crown. She rather doubted it.

Others, like Lykurgus of Edoni, mayhap in fear of Ares's wrath and lacking knowledge of the awful splendour of Dionysus, refused the God. Artemis was there, one night, beneath the full moon, beside her master, when one of the Maenad Nymphs came to him. Thetis, her name was, a daughter of Poseidon, though not one Artemis had known well before she joined the Maenads.

"King Lykurgus has thrown a dozen of our sisters into his dungeons," Thetis said. The Nymph had the stormy blue eyes of her Tethid heritage, and they flashed with indignation born from her frenzied faith in God.

Artemis wanted to speak out. The Maenads, those Dionysus

seemed inclined to keep rather than serve up to dryads or centaurs, had grown in number. She could not have said how many they were, but pushing two hundred women, at least. In her mind's eye, she saw revelation. She saw tree after tree dotting the hills of Phlegra, and from each, the body of a woman dangling from a self-woven noose, legs waving limply in uncaring breezes.

But Dionysus fair tittered with excitement, exulting in the chance to wreak vengeance upon Lykurgus for daring to doubt his majesty. And Artemis, ever compelled to stand by his side, had no choice but to accompany him when he came to the king's court. Like a plague, his voice billowed through Phlegran halls, infecting those within with depravity.

Children bit their parents. Not the bites of play or anger, but of masticating *hunger*, ripping flesh away to devour. Wives abandoned their husbands to couple with strangers in the halls. Servants set fire to the chambers of their masters.

The king, cleft of all his wits, mistook his son for ivy growing upon his chamber walls. With his family sword, he hewed away his heir's limbs and nose and face. Such was the price for doubting God.

"How can you expect Men never given proof before their own eyes to know your divinity?" Artemis asked as Dionysus forced her to watch Lykurgus maim and murder his beloved child. Arms trembling at her sides, she longed to interfere. But her question was the only defiance she found herself able to muster.

God spoke of freedom. He spoke of unshackling the will and giving true choice to all. But such freedom was pretence and extended only to actions taken in accordance with *his* will.

And yet, her moments of lucidity grew longer. She had regained her perceptions of time, such that she thought she could judge that perhaps two years had passed since God had drawn her into his Maenads.

Dionysus scoffed as though her doubts were the most insipid thing he had ever heard. "Now all Phlegra will have proof."

He did not permit her to point out the patent absurdity of his logic. He did not permit to do aught save watch. And when the boy was dead, like poison lanced from a wound, he withdrew his touch from the king's mind and allowed the full scope of the crime to crash upon the king. And Lykurgus broke, leaving behind not a man, but a slobbering wreck cradling the body of his only child, heedless of the tears and snot streaming down his face and bubbling upon his lips.

Artemis strained against the divine will that fettered her. So desperate to move, to strike out against God beside her. A single finger managed to rise in accusation. To drift toward a knife she would never reach.

Dionysus gave no acknowledgment of the bitter war that waged inside of Artemis. "Now drag the king out into the agora and feed him to the centaurs."

She fought. She strove against that cyclopean will until blood vessels burst inside her nose and the taste of iron filled her mouth. Until she was certain her teeth had begun to crack from straining her jaw.

She fought.

And she lost.

And she dragged screaming, broken Lykurgus out into the agora. And she fed him to the centaurs.

ARIADNE DANCED, *and it was the joy of her life. It was the screen behind which she concealed agonies of her life from herself. In the rush of blood and whirl of skirts, she pretended she did not dwell in perpetual despair.*

But every dance needed to end. And always, gnawing horror crept back upon her.

"WHY AM I SEEING THIS WOMAN?" Artemis asked when the vision infiltrated her thoughts once again. The halls of what had once been Lykurgus's megaron in Edoni flowed with rivers of Bacchic wine—as needful as Ambrosia now—and it sometimes induced hallucinations of this Ariadne. There was a haunting familiarity to her, of one known well and yet completely forgotten.

Sometimes, too, she saw her memories of Aura, so real it was more like living them once more. Waking left behind the hollow of the knowledge that such memories could never compound, for the heart of them was gone forever. It was the taint that forever seeped into recollections of those who were gone and turned even the happiest of such memories bittersweet.

Though she hated herself for imbibing it, Artemis sat upon the lip of a fountain and scooped another handful of the blessed draught into her mouth. She imagined holding her own head under in mimicry of the same initiation into the faith she had given Atalanta. She imagined it, only instead of someone pulling her up, she pictured remaining below until her mind and heart grew still. She wondered if she would have the strength to do so.

Was it not better to die than to live enslaved to the will of a capricious deity?

Dionysus, ever present, stepped from walls overgrown with ivy. Roots had broken through the marmoreal floors, leaving a field of sharp debris the God navigated without needing to look down. Grapevines choked the halls and tangled through every doorway. The wild had begun to reclaim this polis. Artemis ought to have thrilled at the resurgence of nature. Would have appreciated it, had it sprouted from another source.

Lions prowled these halls, and bears laired in emptied larders below the palace. Packs of wolves stalked the streets at night. Even these predators were minor threats compared to the dangers of the centaurs and dryads who preyed upon those on the fringes of Dionysus's cult.

"Why do you think?" He loomed over her, a colossal shadow. Though she knew better, she could not help but feel the antlers of his mask ought to have scraped the ceiling.

Revelation tingled upon the edges of her senses. Then the dam burst—did he feed it to her, or did she reach this place on her own?— and she knew. For he had told her already, of the Wheel of Life. "Ariadne *is* Aura. As is she more than that, a greater soul born again and again in mortal form."

Power. There was power in her, even if the girl knew not how to wield it. Dionysus sought to control it.

"I will have her as my bride."

A pang of accursed, bitter jealousy tugged within Artemis's breast. Shameful, hateful, and undeniable, it lurked within her. Loathe him though she might, part of her longed for such a title for herself. The Bride of God.

Still, Artemis found herself gaping to hear Dionysus speak thus. She had thought him beyond all conceptions of mortal bonds, most of all contrivances such as marriage. The God bucked all mores 'til now and yet sought to tether himself to this Ariadne.

"A faltering mortal sought to lay claim to what is my due," Dionysus said, unaware or uncaring of the turmoil inside Artemis. "Thus, I have reached into his wretched mind and ensured he realises the error of his intent. And you, champion, must sail to Naxos and retrieve my bride for me."

"No." She had not known the strength lay within her to refuse him any command. But if Ariadne *was* Aura, born again centuries after her death, then Artemis would not fail her cousin again. Whatever she had lost in her last life, she would have set right in this one.

"Defiance?" Behind his bone mask, she could not see his expression. No, but she felt it, grim and yet rising to her challenge. His chuckle, if such was what it was, sounded like wind whistling through brittle tree branches.

With a momentous effort of will, Artemis's hand drifted to the knife on her belt. For God, she had slain a great many unbelievers with this blade. Had sacrificed even more of the faithful, in his offerings to the Underworld. Now, if she could but force herself to draw it, she might strike down God as well. A grunt of frustration escaped her. The knife whispered in its sheath, edging a hairsbreadth free.

Other Maenads had gathered, summoned by God's unspoken command, watching her with their condemning eyes.

"You begin to apprehend the import of the Wheel," Dionysus said, voice pitched for her ears alone. "You see that we, all of us, are born again and again in service to its turning. You, I take for my champion, for I know the warrior's relentless heart that lurks within your breast. You, who in days gone slew invincible Raktavija himself. You, whom others thought before now unbreakable, I bent to my needs." Dionysus cast a lazy glance around himself, taking in the gathered Maenads.

Atalanta was among them, her eyes judging Artemis for daring to even think of thwarting the will of God.

"On your knees, warrior," God commanded.

Without thought, Artemis slipped from the fountain's edge and knelt before Dionysus. Her own body betrayed her once more. Artemis could have screamed in fury at such impotence forced upon her. "Then who are you?" she managed through gritted teeth.

A pair of lions circled her. With a silent command, she knew Dionysus could send the beasts pouncing upon her. He could have them rip her entrails from her body whilst she remained helpless on her knees. He could, if it suited him, make her *thank* him for her own murder.

Dionysus cocked his head. And yet, despite her impertinence, she had the sense he was *pleased*. Had he, perhaps, hoped for the chance to draw her toward the truth? "If you would have the answer, ask then, why would I so loathe Zeus?"

Her mind worked in slow circles, striving for it. He wanted to bring down Olympus, yes, but he especially loathed the king. And who would not despise Kronos's wretched son? The man had more rapes and murders on his ledger than anyone she'd ever heard of. "You're one of his bastards ..."

Dionysus stooped so that his shadow engulfed the whole of her. "In the wake of the Gigantomachy, Zeus took by force his own demigod granddaughter, Semele. He killed my mother before she birthed me back into the Mortal Realm."

"Zeus raped and murdered your mother." If he would have let her rise from her knees, she might have almost pitied him. How many women shared the same fate of Semele? The list stretched back through the ages of Zeus's reign.

Dionysus snickered. "Ah, but before that, I was *already* his blighted spawn. I remained trapt in the Underworld, never quite alive. At least until I had arranged a vessel for my soul to be reborn into."

And he'd come back with something else inside himself. A piece of the Elder God of the Wood, Pan.

"You see it," Dionysus said. And now, once again, his voice came not from his mortal shell but from that deep, unknowable, horrible space behind the world of Man. "You know whence I come for my terrible vengeance. And to that end, I will have my bride." Still, he had not risen. "You complained to me that Men could not be expected to believe without proof. So I will give others proof. I will show them the price of defiance, even if it lurks within the shadows of their own minds. Make not the mistake of thinking your thoughts are your own."

Without rising, Dionysus looked then to the lions. Artemis felt the end closing around her. The noose Aura had woven would do for her, as well. And at last, she would have respite, even if it meant her death before the condemning eyes of her adopted daughter.

And then the pair of lions pounced, not on Artemis, but upon Atalanta. The first of them bowled her over. She managed scarcely a shriek before their claws ripped away the flesh of her throat. Slavering maws tore her limbs apart whilst the Maenads watched.

On her knees, Artemis screamed defiance. She threw all there was inside of herself into her attempt to rise and drive that knife into Dionysus's belly. But already, her will was faltering. She could not compete with his engulfing strength.

When Atalanta was no more than a bloody mess of gristle strewn across roots and broken marble, at last Dionysus permitted Artemis to collapse onto her hands and knees and weep. Sobs wracked her, and she beat an impotent fist upon the ground. Potency infused her blows and she pulverised stone, the only outlet for her obscene grief.

"Go, Champion," God said. "Go to Naxos and bring me my bride."

He leant even closer until his lips brushed her ear. "And I trust we need not have this conversation ever again."

No. No, she knew his implacable grip upon her soul. She would serve, from now, until he deigned to at long last let death release her. Artemis was his creature.

34

PANDORA

Gloaming Era

When Pandora's vision cleared from the time distortion, she found herself in what seemed another world. In place of the etiolated ruin in which she had sheltered, she found a creeping metropolis. Ornate spires stretched toward the purpling twilight firmament, stark against a looming moon that sometimes peeked out from behind angry black clouds. Flying buttresses connected sprawling structures intent to claim the sky itself as their domain. Pointed arches framed massive doorways in the greater buildings, whilst smaller apartments crouched in the expansive shadows of their cousins.

Evenly spaced gaslamps flickered above cobbled streets. As she emerged from an alley, she saw men and women cast furtive looks around before scurrying about their business. The men and women were both clad in intricately embroidered shirts, oft topped with strange vests. Their fashion seemed absurd, but then, they would no doubt think the same about her Amazonian furs and cloak.

Woozy and awed, Pandora steadied herself against the stone abutment of a nearby building. What alien wonder she had stumbled upon. What perversity of time, that such soaring heights should represent the forgotten past, remembered only as the accursed Time of Nyx.

As she caught her breath, a brume began to waft in, slithering snakelike over streets and around alleys. While far from the oppressive wall of mist that had choked the frozen world of the future, still, something about the vapours set her nerves tingling.

She had not come here to dawdle upon the threshold of an alley or to ogle the architecture, strange and terrible though it was. The locals would notice her out-of-place garb, but she could never avoid that.

Still somewhat wobbly, she made slow progress down the street, clinging to the sides. As she watched, a covered cart of some sort clattered over the cobbles, drawn by a large horse. Lamps hung from both sides of the vehicle, and the driver whipped his animal as though unsatisfied with her progress. The man's gaze roamed over Pandora and lingered a moment, though he did not stall his hurried journey and soon moved out of sight.

Judging her location, mapping it to the ruins she had wandered in the past, proved challenging but not impossible. In her mind's eye, she pictured the great structures collapsing in on themselves, shattered by the quake that had swallowed the heart of Vulgeth. Using this, she thought the library she'd visited before must lie down the next alley.

She started that way but faltered, looking up at the sky. She must have wandered this place for an hour, and the twilight had not yet given way to full night. How long could the sun hang thus, caught on the edge of sleep? It gave the city an eerie sense of sitting somehow outside of time, a thought that had that pinching feeling in her chest returning.

Pushing on, she reached the building she thought had housed the library in the past. Twin spires rose from its sides, both ornamented with jutting spokes fit to impale the sky. With a pointed arch, double doors banded with dark metal rose up, twelve feet tall at least. While she might have thrown the doors wide and marched within, she doubted the occupants would much approve of a stranger barging in and demanding to see their library. Instead, she circled the building until she found an angled shutter barring access to the space below the behemoth structure.

Casting a look around to make sure no one observed, Pandora poured what little Pneuma she could spare into Potency, grabbed the handles, and yanked upon the doors. Metal squealed in protest, but it was the wood that splintered first, snapping open to expose a pitch-black vault below.

Burning Pneuma to ignite her hand would drain her even more, but she saw no other choice. With a snap of her fingers, she set a small fire in her palm, a flickering candle that more emphasised the dark than combatted it. Wooden stairs descended into the cellar. Pandora had taken a half dozen steps down them when a wave of vertigo rushed over her, leaving her flailing. She reached for a wall to steady herself on, found none, and pitched over sideways, crashing onto the cold stone of the floor below.

Her flame puffed out.

For a time, she lay there, groaning and exhausted. Slowly, as her eyes adjusted, she realised total darkness had not seized this place. Hints of moonlight filtered down through the opening whence she had come, adumbrating the cellar in silver accents. Enough she could make out an oil lamp upon a table.

Pandora groaned. However that abomination had drained her Pneuma, it was not returning with half the speed she'd hoped. To begin to reclaim her strength, she'd need a hearty meal and a good night's sleep. She couldn't have either unless she managed to make a friend among the skittish locals, and what little she'd heard of their speech told her she had no common language with them.

First, she would check the library. Then she would see about finding something to eat.

⚜

THOUGH WEARINESS DRAGGED at her limbs and set her eyes to burning, Pandora splayed yet another tome on the floor. She'd found an ink well and a quill and set to scribbling notes in her attempts to translate the language. Here, she found so many of the same books she'd seen in the future, as yet still whole, unravaged by the passing of ages.

"Falias ..." As best she could guess, the term referenced a place, but what it meant and why it appeared in so many of the ancient records, she could not determine.

Beside her sputtering oil lamp, she sprawled onto her stomach, making notes on spare sheets of something resembling papyrus, though cut more precisely. Maybe Falias was another name for Vulgeth? Pandora tapped a finger against her lip before drawing a line between the two names.

Her stomach grumbled, but she wasn't willing to give over her search as yet. All the answers had to be here if she could but figure out where to look. With a stretch, she climbed to her feet, steadied herself on the table, then made her way back to the numerous shelves of tomes. She traced her fingers over the spines before grabbing one at random.

What had precipitated the fall of this place? Had Gaia herself opened to swallow Vulgeth, or had some other catastrophe caused the earthquake?

She flipped through the book she had chosen, knowing well enough it wouldn't hold *those* answers. No tome written before the city's collapse could explain those events, though the mystery niggled at her, a puzzle that demanded solving. She opened the tome, holding it in one hand while thumbing through the pages with the other. So close if she could but find a key to translate ...

The main door into the building creaked upon its hinges, and a tall man came striding down the stairs bearing a lantern that cast a play of shadows upon his features. He wore a long black coat, held together not by clasps but by small discs in the fabric. On his head was a ridiculous hat. This he removed as he reached the base of the stairs, and Pandora gasped.

Though his skin had grown a shade fairer, his hair now more blond than platinum, and his beard was trimmed, before her stood Kronos. The truth of him lurked in the shape of his face and the depths of his pale blue eyes, and, though she could not understand the change in him, neither could she deny whom she looked at.

He spoke, voice deep, words guttural and unrecognisable, thick with harsh consonants.

"Kronos ..." she breathed. She had found him.

Where did it begin, you perhaps wonder? In Vulgeth, we might have said, huddled in dark vaults and ruminating over the vagaries of our fragile, immortal existences, so precariously perched upon the edge of the Abyss.

The Ouranid—the man who would become an Ouranid—cocked his head at her a moment before stalking closer. "The Mirrors said you would come."

He could speak her language! How in all of Gaia could he speak a language before it existed? Pandora stammered, uncertain where to even begin. His presence here had shifted her every conception of this Era. And what did it mean of her own world? Had Kronos *recognised* her on meeting her during the Titanomachy?

On the stairs behind him, other figures lurked, some bearing long-bladed swords.

Kronos reached her, tossed aside his hat, and snatched the book from her hand. "Farkos's third *Treatise of Man*," he said after turning it over to glance at the spine. He let the book tumble to the ground beside him, not offering it another look. "You have walked the halls of time, have you not? Give it to me, girl. Give me the means to spite Fate. Give it to us."

The Box ... Oh, Gaia. Her mouth hung open.

I know who you are! I know what you are! Give me the Box and you may live.

On Ogygia, after Pyrrha's birth, Kronos had come for her then. Because he knew her now. And only many centuries later, during the Titanomachy, would he seek to make an ally of her.

In her moment of hesitation, Kronos lunged, his speed inhuman. Pandora tried to twist aside, but his fingers wrapt around her wrist, strong as marble. Strong as the mountains, and she had not the Pneuma left to fight him.

A contemptuous look upon his face, he tossed her aside, sending her careening into the shelves. The impact hazed her vision and had her dropping to her knees. His thugs closed in around her now, descending the stairs in a throng, half a dozen of them.

Desperate, Pandora reached toward the flame within Kronos's lantern. The last of her Pneuma, the last she could expend and still breathe, she poured into the fire. It burst from its housing, exploding glass lacerating the Titan and those nigh to him. Flaming oil sprayed over the shelves and books strewn among the floor, coated Kronos and another man, both of whom erupted into screams.

Unable to gain her feet, Pandora scrambled on all fours toward the cellar entrance, desperate to escape from the rapidly expanding inferno. She reached the stairs, but anywhere was better than here.

A hand closed around her ankle.

Pandora withdrew the Box and twisted the gears to pop the top.

A sudden tug yanked her along the floor, Kronos's hand slapping the Box from her. Wrath now limned his features, turned all the more sinister as he ignored the flames spreading up his coat. He shouted something to his men, and two of them closed in, grabbing her arms.

One snapped a manacle around her wrist, and the last of Pandora's strength trickled out like a fountain closed from an aqueduct. Panicked, she looked at what had bound her. Rosy-gold metal.

Orichalcum chains, just like those that had bound Prometheus.

A man's fist collided with her temple. The dark swooped in upon her, pulling her into its hungering embrace.

EPILOGUE

*A*fter Chandi and Naresh had gone through the Time Chamber, Kala had vanished, in further pursuit of Veles, Amirani had to imagine. Perhaps they too had fled through time. Either way, Vulgeth was aflame, and Amirani had no more time to waste. He needed to find Kersnik and Vorsanos before the Eschaton completed itself.

The Forgotten were unleashing—

The ground undulated and Amirani's stomach lurched.

No.

The whole of the World shuddered, convulsing with pain. Spires above him cracked and splintered, blanketing the city in a rain of stone that shattered the cobbled streets. Great chunks of falling rocks crashed with the roar of an avalanche, and ahead of him, a tumbling gargoyle splattered a werewolf to a pulp. Exploding blood from the corpse drenched Amirani. His boot slipped, and he fell to one knee.

As he rose, a cathedral ahead imploded as if some great force had sucked it down a funnel. Chunks of the road jutted upward, ripping open fissures that swallowed whole neighbourhoods. Men and women and children vanished into the rift.

Then the real madness began.

Every shadow across the dark city pulsed, throbbing before receding. The city ruptured into a million disparate pieces. From every crevice exploded forth caliginous tendrils of night glinting with perverse starlight. The sky above spiderwebbed with cracks, and pieces of the firmament began to fall away like dust. More tendrils of night wormed their way downward, grasping at their earthbound kind with prurient need.

Amirani gasped in boundless horror at seeing another Elder God revealed in all its awful glory.

The amorphous strands of Naamah throbbed, and the broken sky lurched closer. Incipient mouths and vulvas and phalluses rose and faded among the tendrils, which themselves divided again and again, racing through the streets in salacious need.

Waves of sexual energy bombarded Amirani, like a gong inside the whole of him, demanding he claim someone—anyone—to sate his momentous lust. Groaning, he stumbled through the rent streets, barely avoiding the thrashing tendrils of the Archon. In prurient frenzy, she would suck out the souls of those the tendrils claimed, gorging herself in the most depraved Eschaton yet.

And he must reach the Destroyer before all the World fell to this and faltered. This must be ended, at any cost. Vulgeth had become a nexus tethering the Mortal Realm to the Nightspan, and if the bond was not broken, Mankind would be subsumed into the darkness, devoured by Naamah, Nyx, Ratri, or whatever she—*it*—wished to be known as.

Desperate, he broke into a run, darting around the debris of a city collapsing in on itself, dashing around the flailing tendrils connecting land to sky. A shadow passed overhead, then dropped down before him in a crouch like a golden comet. A woman, clad head to toe in aureate plates, with sapphire eyes glinting from beneath the helm.

Eyes like his own ...

Amirani faltered. "You serve the Fates?"

"I should have known you would betray once again," she spat at him, rising from her crouch, wings outstretched behind her. "Perfidy runs deep through your soul, Matarśivan. You have aided the Gnostic fools in their imprudent quest, and worse, you act as ally to the Destroyer."

What? It took an effort not to gape at her. "The Fates sanctioned the creation of the Destroyer and the Eschaton Cycle!"

"Not this one, who ravages through time, beholden to none and so keen to upend Fate."

Kala? Was Kala the one who—

The golden angel launched herself at him like a shooting star, forcing Amirani to dive aside. He came up in a roll, but already her foot flew at his face. He blocked the blow on crossed arms, but it carried such force as to drive him skidding down the street.

Sending Prana coursing through his meridians, he increased his reflexes and lightened himself. A vicious beat of her wings had her hurtling toward him once more. This time, he dodged aside, vaulted the side of another broken cathedral, and leapt to the remnants of a fallen tower, dashing upward along its surface.

Naamah's sweeping tentacles bombarded the building, not so much in accordance with his attacker as in a random orgy of destruction. With his gravity lightened, Amirani leapt ten feet into the air to clear the tendril. The angel crashed into the wall an instant later, sending them both spilling into the broken shell of what had once been a bell tower.

He landed in another roll, coming up even as she recovered.

The great bell itself lay wedged between two halves of the floor and a gaping abyss of snapping maws of starlight. The angel lunged again. Amirani evaded and her plated fist smacked into the bell with a tremendous clang, folding the metal inward and sending the whole of it pitching into the masticating jaws below. It vanished into the consuming Dark.

Amirani's own uppercut caught the angel under the chin and sent her staggering backwards. He moved to close and she defended herself in a stance he hadn't seen since the collapse of Ayodhya. Perfect form, perfect counters to his every probing attack.

She had called him Matarśivan.

Another *Watcher*.

Amirani feinted, then, rather than going for a crushing blow, snared the top of her helm and yanked it off. The woman beneath snarled at him, her aspect as it ever had been, save for eyes become as vibrant blue as his own. For she must have been an agent of the Fates somewhat akin to what he had become, if not their avatar of history.

"Vinata," he rasped.

"I am Nemesis!" she spat at him. Her rage was palpable. This was not a mission from the Fates, he suspected, but one of vindication. His revelation of the painful Ontos was a personal betrayal to Vinata. Forced to confront the lies of faith, some chose rather to dig in their heels and, rather than permit doubt, redouble their convictions. Even in the face of evidence to the contrary. Especially in the face of such evidence.

"How can you serve the *monstrosity* laid plain before us?" He spread a hand to encompass the void that had swallowed the bell and was even now widening, probing for them with grasping tendrils of darkness. "Can you yet deny the Ontos? The Archons are abominations!"

"I serve the Order! Beholding the grandeur of their true form, you somehow forget they are the reason we—or this world—ever existed! The World demands we bow to Fate, and Fate is ruled by the Archons. You have betrayed the Elder Gods!"

Amirani backed away from her in abject horror at her words. To see the Truth and derive from it yet another Lie. The sheer capacity for self-delusion beggared the imagination. It left him hollowed, mouth agape in aphonic objection. How did one even respond to a person drawn so deep into a deception they would deny their own eyes?

One did not. Such a person, though he had once loved her as a sister, was beyond all hope.

"And I thought the Gnostic Cabal blind," he said. Rather than give her another chance to attack, he hopped over the dark chasm and then, Prana flooding his system, leapt high through the tower's broken roof above.

Not waiting for her to follow, he rushed forwards, dodging more caliginous tendrils that thrashed in the street. He leapt over debris, racing up to an inferno raging inside the shattered cathedral. Predictably, the angel slammed back down into the street ahead of him.

Through Surtr, Amirani reached into the flames and called them to him. The fires burst through the husk of the building, sending it collapsing into ruin as they arced toward him in flaming parabolas. He felt the spirit within tightening its claws around his heart, but he needed to make his point with this Nemesis, and make it fast, for the Eschaton had arrived. He would not allow the Destroyer to face it alone. Not if Amirani could help it.

Roaring, he slapped his hands together, unleashing successive waves of fire that shot over the angel. She leapt into the sky, relying on the strength of her wings to carry her over the conflagration. Not fast enough. The blaze must have scorched her feathers, for she fell, screaming, onto the street, and landed in a smouldering heap.

She lay moaning, twisting in a mockery of her former glory.

Amirani knelt beside her. Vicious burns had ravaged her face and any other flesh left exposed by her armour. Incandescent embers still glinted off her wings, which flapped in agony.

She would live, mostlike. And perhaps he ought to finish her now, for she had tried to kill him and clearly intended to interfere with ... whatever Kala was doing.

But how could Amirani do so? How could he slay a woman he had known from the dawn of time? How could he allow her to be ended, when those of them who remained would be, for better or worse, forever tied to one another? It was like severing a part of himself. He could no more take her life than amputate his own arm.

Inside his mind, Surtr cackled in perversity, willing him to immolate the broken angel.

Instead, Amirani laid a hand upon Vinata and fed a trickle of

Prana into her body. Not enough to allow her to rise and assault him, but maybe enough to help her live and escape this place.

This Era was ended, and soon, the uriași would rise as the Titans. This he had foreseen. They would take Vorsanos as their leader, though time would change his name. The Titans would call their liberator Ouranos. At least until, not wanting to answer questions about this time, he took the name Kronos.

As if it had been the fallen Watcher to save Man from Nyx.

But then, history never got things quite right.

AUTHOR'S NOTE:

When Theseus arrived in Crete, Ariadne, the daughter of Minos, fell in love with him and promised to assist him if he would agree to take her away to Athens and have her as his wife. When Theseus agreed on oath to do so, she asked Daidalos to reveal how it was possible to escape from the Labyrinth.

—Apollodorus. The Library of Greek Mythology (Oxford World's Classics)

Theseus's most well-known story comes in his tale of surviving the Labyrinth, slaying the Minotaur, and absconding with the princess Ariadne who made his exploits possible. What happens after gets a bit less attention. In some versions, Artemis murders Ariadne (for ... reasons ...), but in most cases, Theseus abandons Ariadne on Naxos.

Maybe he had a reason. Often, the tale goes that Dionysus laid claim to Ariadne. But did Theseus abandon his betrothed who gave up everything for him because of this, or did Dionysus merely sweep in and claim the woman left behind? Different versions of the myth disagree.

This runs in parallel and opposition to the tale of Jason and Medea, where in all versions, Medea gives up everything for Jason (sensing a pattern here?) and he later casts her aside. Medea then, in grief or rage at his betrayal, murders their children and runs away to make mischief elsewhere. But history is written by the victor, and in this patriarchal society, almost certainly by men. What if Jason's claims of her crimes are just after-the-fact justifications for decisions he made?

When first re-reading the original myths for this series, I quickly realized Medea's point of view seemed far more compelling than Jason's. In fact, Jason's actions so often seemed selfish or cringeworthy, I entirely cut him as a point-of-view character out of my outlines.

Rather than make both these heroes straight-up awful people, I opted to give Theseus a bit less culpability than Jason. He abandons Ariadne not because he wants to, but because he is too weak to stand up against the cosmic horror of Dionysus. I hope the contrast of the two tales provided some entertainment and gave a little pause for thought.

If you've enjoyed this book, I encourage you to join the Skalds' Tribe newsletter and get access to exclusive insider information and your FREE copy of *The Moments of Kadmus*. **I generally send every week or every other; I promise not to mail more often than that.** No spam, no selling your email address to marauding warlords, none of that.

Join me here to grab a free novella and stay connected with me: https://www.mattlarkinbooks.com/skalds/

Thank you for reading,

Matt

PS Pandora's journey continues in *The Face of Hekate* ...
https://books2read.com/faceofhekate

Join the Skalds' Tribe newsletter and get access to exclusive insider information and a selection of free books to kickstart your Matt Larkin library.

https://www.mattlarkinbooks.com/skalds/

ALSO BY MATT LARKIN

Tapestry of Fate

The Gifts of Pandora

The Valor of Perseus

The Inferno of Prometheus

The Madness of Herakles

The Threads of Theseus

Heirs of Mana

Tides of Mana

Flames of Mana

Queens of Mana

Gods of the Ragnarok Era

The Apples of Idunn

The Mists of Niflheim

The Shores of Vanaheim

The High Seat of Asgard

The Well of Mimir

The Radiance of Alfheim

The Shadows of Svartalfheim

The Gates of Hel

The Fires of Muspelheim

For my Juhi and Kiran.

Special thanks to my family and my team that helps bring these projects to life: Sarah, Regina, Felix, Shawn, Tawny, and Francesca.